Winds of Change

Also by Gilbert Morris

THE AMERICAN CENTURY SERIES

1. *A Bright Tomorrow*
2. *Hope Takes Flight*
3. *One Shining Moment*
4. *A Season of Dreams*

THE HOUSE OF WINSLOW SERIES

1. *The Honorable Imposter*
2. *The Captive Bride*
3. *The Indentured Heart*
4. *The Gentle Rebel*
5. *The Saintly Buccaneer*
6. *The Holy Warrior*
7. *The Reluctant Bridegroom*
8. *The Last Confederate*
9. *The Dixie Widow*
10. *The Wounded Yankee*
11. *The Union Belle*
12. *The Final Adversary*
13. *The Crossed Sabres*
14. *The Valiant Gunman*
15. *The Gallant Outlaw*
16. *The Jeweled Spur*
17. *The Yukon Queen*
18. *The Rough Rider*
19. *The Iron Lady*
20. *The Silver Star*
21. *The Shadow Portrait*
22. *The White Hunter*
23. *The Flying Cavalier*
24. *The Glorious Prodigal*
25. *The Amazon Quest*
26. *The Golden Angel*
27. *The Heavenly Fugitive*
28. *The Fiery Ring*
29. *The Pilgrim Song*
30. *The Beloved Enemy*
31. *The Shining Badge*
32. *The Royal Handmaid*
33. *The Silent Harp*
34. *The Virtuous Woman*
35. *The Gypsy Moon*

★ NUMBER FIVE IN THE AMERICAN CENTURY SERIES ★

Winds of Change

GILBERT MORRIS

Revell
Grand Rapids, Michigan

© 1997 by Gilbert Morris

Published by Fleming H. Revell
a division of Baker Publishing Group
P.O. Box 6287, Grand Rapids, MI 49516-6287

New trade paperback edition published 2007

Previously published in 1997 as *A Time of War*

Printed in the United States of America

Library of Congress Cataloging-in-Publication Data
Morris, Gilbert.
    [Time of war]
    Winds of change / Gilbert Morris. New trade pbk. ed.
        p.   cm. — (The American century series ; no. 5)
    Originally published: A time of war. Grand Rapids, Mich. : Fleming H. Revell, c1977.
    ISBN 10: 0-8007-3205-7 (pbk.)
    ISBN 978-0-8007-3205-9 (pbk.)
    1. Stuart family—Fiction. 2. World War, 1939–1945—Fiction. I. Title.
PS3563.O8742T54   2007
813'.54—dc22   2007011217

Scripture is taken from the King James Version of the Bible.

To Lillian Finley—faithful friend
From Johnnie

CONTENTS

PART FOUR   Enemy Territory

THE STUART FAMILY

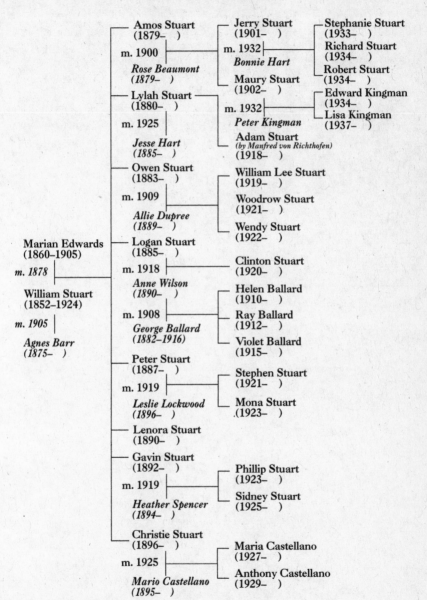

Marian Edwards
(1860–1905)

m. 1878

William Stuart
(1852–1924)

m. 1905

*Agnes Barr
(1875–)*

Amos Stuart
(1879–)

m. 1900

*Rose Beaumont
(1879–)*

Lylah Stuart
(1880–)

m. 1925

*Jesse Hart
(1885–)*

Owen Stuart
(1883–)

m. 1909

*Allie Dupree
(1889–)*

Logan Stuart
(1885–)

m. 1918

*Anne Wilson
(1890–)*

m. 1908

*George Ballard
(1882–1916)*

Peter Stuart
(1887–)

m. 1919

*Leslie Lockwood
(1896–)*

Lenora Stuart
(1890–)

Gavin Stuart
(1892–)

m. 1919

*Heather Spencer
(1894–)*

Christie Stuart
(1896–)

m. 1925

*Mario Castellano
(1895–)*

Jerry Stuart
(1901–)

m. 1932

Bonnie Hart

Maury Stuart
(1902–)

m. 1932

Peter Kingman

Adam Stuart
(by Manfred von Richthofen)
(1918–)

William Lee Stuart
(1919–)

Woodrow Stuart
(1921–)

Wendy Stuart
(1922–)

Clinton Stuart
(1920–)

Helen Ballard
(1910–)

Ray Ballard
(1912–)

Violet Ballard
(1915–)

Stephen Stuart
(1921–)

Mona Stuart
(1923–)

Phillip Stuart
(1923–)

Sidney Stuart
(1925–)

Maria Castellano
(1927–)

Anthony Castellano
(1929–)

Stephanie Stuart
(1933–)

Richard Stuart
(1934–)

Robert Stuart
(1934–)

Edward Kingman
(1934–)

Lisa Kingman
(1937–)

Part One

Before the Deluge

PROLOGUE

A mericans measure time in many ways. One of these methods seems to be counting off history by decades, giving these periods names that indicate their nature—for example, "The Roaring Twenties."

The thirties in American history will be remembered as the time of the Great Depression. It was a time Americans went hungry, yet it was also a period when the country grew together as a nation, neighbors learning to help neighbors. There was a solidarity of the people of the republic during this period.

This decade ended sharply, almost abruptly. It could, in one sense, be said to have ended on December 15, 1939, and one could find a symbol of the old giving way to the new in Atlanta, Georgia, on the evening of that particular date.

Limousines lined up in front of the Atlanta Grand Theater, which was decorated to resemble Twelve Oaks, the plantation where Scarlett O'Hara dallied with her beaus.

At six o'clock the theater was roped off to keep the stars from being crushed by the happy mob. Clark Gable put in his appearance at eight-forty, and a few women fainted at the sight. Rebel yells in the street greeted this premiere of *Gone with the Wind*, and when the three-and-a-half-hour spectacle was over, Margaret Mitchell, the author of the best-selling novel, gave a speech. In quavering tones she said, "It has been a great thing for Georgia and the South to see the Confederates come back." *Gone with the Wind*, in one sense, closed the

13

door on hard times. America saw the rich opulence of Tara and the antebellum South as it was enthroned in glittering Technicolor as a farewell to the gritty black-and-white hardships of the 1930s.

Something called Tara Mania burst on the American scene. Everyone had read the book, and now everyone saw the movie. Scarlett O'Hara and Rhett Butler were discussed as if they were real people. The book won the 1937 Pulitzer Prize and was translated into twenty-seven languages. Across America people were naming their newborns Rhett, Ashley, and Melanie.

But if *Gone with the Wind* brought down the curtain on the 1930s—another sort of wind was sweeping over Europe, stirred and fanned by the voice of Adolf Hitler. Many Americans tried to ignore the dark shadow that Hitler cast over Europe, and *Gone with the Wind* was influential in bringing people out of their homes to a theater to immerse themselves in a past that seemed relatively safe. Americans looked ahead with a hope colored with apprehension, wondering what sort of America would emerge.

There was in the air the knowledge that a trial by fire was hovering over the world. America was about to be thrown into a crucible—and while Rhett and Scarlett could act out their fantasies on the screen, Americans from Maine to Florida, from Oregon to Virginia, knew that this decade would be unlike any other.

The fifth decade in the twentieth century would be a time of war.

1

A SLIGHT CASE OF ASSAULT

A high-pitched, keening scream split the night air startling the pedestrians who were strolling down the canyon between two rows of towering buildings. Dwellers of Los Angeles were not unaccustomed to such sounds, and most of them merely gave a glance to the black car with Los Angeles Police Department emblazoned on the side as it careened around a corner, tires squealing.

Los Angeles, California, had become in some sense the dreamland of America, but as one wag put it, "Everything *loose* rolls right to Los Angeles." The invasion of the city by teeming hosts of hopeful actors and actresses had begun in the twenties, and now others were drawn to the movie capital of the world. What had been a sleepy small town in which jaywalking had been one of the most serious offenses handled by police had begun to feel the pressures of a new urbanization sprawl. Hollywood had not yet become what S. J. Perelman would call it—"A dreary industrial town controlled by hoodlums of enormous wealth, the ethical sense of a pack of jackals, and taste so degraded that it befouled everything it touched"—but it was on the way. The morals of the Midwest seemed to evaporate when transplanted to this small area of Southern California.

Inside the squad car, a huge officer grabbed at the seat to avoid the door handle and to keep from falling into the driver's lap. "Hey, Irving," he said, "what's the rush? There ain't nothing on fire!" The speaker was an enormous man

15

well known as Jumbo Yates. He had played tackle for the Green Bay Packers during his younger years, and now his bulk spilled over in every direction.

The driver, a small, trim officer named Irving Marks, did not even glance at his partner. "It gives me a bellyache," he cut the words off sharply, "having to baby-sit a bunch of drunks—especially rich drunks!"

Jumbo Yates glanced out at the towering hotel on the right, ahead of them. "Well, if they're in the Sky Room, they're rich all right—don't usually get a squeal for a spot like this."

Marks brought the patrol car to a screeching halt directly in front of the Lawrence Hotel, blocking off all traffic. He grinned at his partner saying, "Let 'em drive around if they want to get in. Come on, Jumbo."

As the two officers climbed out of the car, the doorman, a tall, distinguished looking man with a worried look began, "Officer, couldn't you park your car—"

Jumbo simply brushed him out of the way with one massive arm, saying, "Take it easy, Pal; we'll be back with John D. Rockefeller under arrest. Don't let nobody touch that car, you get me?"

Entering the massive lobby of the Lawrence, the two officers made their way to the elevators. Marks jabbed the button with his thumb and, when the door opened, stepped in quickly, snapping his fingers impatiently. "Come on, Jumbo, we ain't got all day!" As soon as Yates was inside, he punched the button marked Sky Room and the elevator shot rapidly upward.

Jumbo Yates was a rather placid man, dangerous when angry, but ordinarily good natured enough. He also had a streak of cynical realism that caused him to say, "Hey, Irving, let's be a little bit careful around here. What do you say?"

"What do you mean *careful?*" Marks's dark eyes came to rest on Jumbo and he shook his head, a sour expression on his lips. "These people are just like anybody else!"

"Yeah, just like anybody else—except they're rich. That means they got pull down at city hall. Just watch it, OK?"

The elevator came to a smooth halt and the door opened, but Marks did not bother to answer his partner. They stepped out into what appeared to be a reception room, and their ears were immediately assaulted by the crescendo from a swing band in the Sky Room. Marks, not even glancing at the guests in tuxedos and evening gowns, forged his way across the room. Jumbo Yates followed, like a huge ship guided by a small tug. He knew that Irving Marks had ambition, that he intended to go straight to the top of the Los Angeles Police Department structure. Since Marks had no influence, the only way he could do that was to make an impressive record. It had led him to do such strange things as charging into a dark alley to face an unseen gunman. Jumbo had halted on the outside that night and had listened as gunshots rattled the night air. He had seen Marks come out dragging the victim, a wanted murderer, by the collar. This was *not* the kind of thing that Jumbo himself was interested in! Now as he looked around with some apprehension, he found himself impressed by the Sky Room and by the denizens of its space.

Most of the Sky Room was roofed with glass so that the stars outside and the silver moon could be seen overhead. An enormous glass ball covered with tiny facets of silvered mirrors swung slowly and cast yellow, red, and green reflections over the room, giving it an unearthly appearance.

Glancing to one side, Jumbo took in the long table covered with food, noting rather hungrily the turkey, lobsters, fruits, and cheeses. Adjacent to it was another table lined with whiskey, wines, champagnes, and beer, all handed out by white-coated attendants. Jumbo's glance shifted to the dance floor, where strange things seemed to be happening.

"They didn't dance like this back when I was dancing!" Jumbo growled to Marks. "What is that stuff?"

Marks had hesitated for only one moment. His hooded, black eyes fell on a group parading in a circle, noting that their hands soon joined and a caller was telling them to go to the middle and "shine."

"I think that's called the Big Apple," he said. "Come on; there's the trouble over there!"

Some sort of argument or disruption was happening out where the doors of the Sky Room opened onto a balcony. Marks spotted a man, obviously an employee of the hotel, who was trying to quiet down a group of shouting people.

"That's the trouble, Jumbo; let's put the quietus on it!" Marks said, a grim light of enjoyment in his eyes. He pushed forward demanding, "What's the trouble here?"

"Oh, Officer, I'm glad you're here!" The speaker was a small, pale-faced man wearing a double-breasted gray suit. He was obviously not one of the paying crowd, for all the other men were wearing tuxes, the women evening dresses. "We're having a little difficulty—"

At that moment, a young woman, wearing a daringly low-cut silver-and-black evening dress, pushed forward and slapped the manager on the chest. She was obviously drunk, for her speech was slurred and her lipstick was grotesquely smeared across her lips. "Why, you dirty little shrimp—you called the cops!" she yelled loudly over the sound of the music and the raucous shoutings.

"Miss DeCamp, I'm so sorry—" the manager said, wringing his hands tensely, "but the other guests have complained—" With a shock, Officer Irving Marks recognized the young woman. He had seen her in a movie only the night before—not a leading role, but she certainly had caught his eye. Suddenly she began screaming and slapped the manager's face, a string of obscenities falling grotesquely from her smeared lips.

"Enough of that!" Marks stepped forward at once in front of the manager, who had turned pale and touched his cheek where the imprint of her hand stood out plainly. "You're going to have to hold it down, Miss!"

"Hold it down, nothing!" Jean DeCamp had enormous eyes, and they flared with anger. She turned and screamed, "Hey, look at this; the gendarmes are here, the cops! And look at 'em; they look like Laurel and Hardy!"

She turned again. "Are you Stanley, the stupid one?" she asked Marks. "You look stupid to me!"

"I'll have to put you under arrest if you don't calm down, Lady!" he said, his lips thin and his eyes glowing with anger.

Jumbo Yates took a step closer, for he had seen the crowd behind the young woman beginning to coalesce, forming a line. Most of them, he noted with a practiced eye, were dead drunk, and he fingered the night stick on his belt thoughtfully, giving it a tug to see that it was loose. His mild blue eyes grew hard as he thought, *I didn't expect no trouble out of these rich people—but I guess they're no different from the drunks down on Skid Row when it comes right down to it. A drunk is a drunk!*

The two officers had been lectured on how to handle trouble, and both of them had handled enough of it in the course of their duties. Los Angeles was, in some sense, a wilder place than the old Wild West towns of Cheyenne and Deadwood. There were at least as many people carrying guns, although they were not worn on their hips in plain sight. Both Marks and Yates had seen other officers die in the streets, and now as the crowd began yelling and screaming, they grew tense and their eyes more alert. Yates eyed the young woman thinking, *She's the one that could set it off!* He moved to Irving's left, light on his feet for such an enormous man, his eyes sweeping the crowd for possible troublemakers.

Yates muttered, "We better just get the dame, Irving, and that'll stop the rest of 'em from causing trouble!"

This was Marks's idea as well. His eyes shifted, and he met those of his partner, who nodded at him slightly and eyed the young woman. She gave Marks an excellent opportunity, for she decided to slap the manager again and tried to shove by him. Instantly Marks clamped his hand down on her wrist. "That's enough, Miss!"

Suddenly Jean DeCamp twisted, trying to get away, and when she couldn't, reached out and, with a swift, catlike motion, raked her sharp claws down the policeman's face. Taken off guard, Marks released his grip and shut his eyes, for the nails had come dangerously close to his eye. He felt the skin pull away, and anger suddenly raged through him. "All right—all right," he said grimly. "You're under arrest for assaulting an officer!" He reached behind his back and had his cuffs out at once. Before the young woman had moved he had clamped one wrist and was about to clamp the other one when suddenly something hard struck him across his chest. It drove him backwards, and he nearly fell to the floor.

"Take your hands off her!"

The speaker was a young man around twenty years old, wearing a tuxedo and looking trim and fit. He was drunk, of course, as they all were, and anger had drawn his wide mouth into a white line. He had a rather square face, a wide forehead, a strong nose, and ears that lay close to his head. His light blond hair was mussed, and his most outstanding feature was his eyes, light blue and cold as polar ice.

"What's your name?" Marks said as he stepped forward and stood with his feet apart, ready for trouble. He saw the broad shoulders and narrow waist of the young man, and something about him told Marks that he would not be an easy man to handle.

"Adam Stuart—what about it?"

"Mr. Stuart, I'm going to have to arrest this young lady. Unless you move aside, I'll have to arrest you, too!"

"You're not arresting anyone! We don't need you here; get out!"

Adam Stuart saw the officer as if he stood in the middle of a single light. He had learned to eliminate everything except what he wanted to see, and the other guests, the dancers, the band, the great ball overhead, all faded away until he could see only the narrow face of the officer who stood before him. He spoke in the careful tone of a drunk, pronouncing each syllable: "Get out and leave us alone! We're just having a little fun—and keep your hands off of her!"

Marks knew, at once, he could not pass this by. He stepped forward saying, "I'm taking you in, Miss." He reached out to touch the young woman, but, as he had expected, Stuart's face flushed and he pulled his shoulders together and his fist shot out. Irving was surprised that, even drunk, the man's reflexes were so quick. The blow caught Marks on the neck—the force of it driving him off balance. He was propelled backward against the manager, and before he had time to recover, Stuart pummeled him with blows that seemed to come from everywhere. They were strong, powerful blows and Irving Marks had time to think, *If he wasn't drunk he'd kill me!* As it was, he could not stop the onslaught. One blow caught him squarely in the mouth, and the room seemed to go around. He felt a blow catch him over the eye, and blood spurted out, blinding him. He knew that he was being whipped, and he fumbled for his night stick, but he was overwhelmed.

Jumbo Yates had been taken off guard by the assault of the fair-haired young man, but he leaped forward, in one motion pulling the night stick. Lifting it in the air he brought it down expertly on Stuart's head with just exactly the right amount of pressure. Yates was not a smart man, but he was an expert in such things. He knew that if he did not hit hard enough it would only inflame the man—but if he hit too hard, he would crush the skull. The stick tapped Adam Stuart on the head, making a slight *thunking* sound.

For Stuart the pain was nothing, but it seemed to drain his strength. He felt the stick as it struck his head, but followed through the blow he had started by sheer instinct. The lights around him exploded into an enormous orange shimmer of light. He tried to go on, wanting to kill the officer whose face was fading. The last he saw was the blood streaking down Marks's face, and the last desire he had was to hit him again!

"You are mistaken, Sir! You could not have proposed marriage to me in any form that I would have found acceptable!"

Lylah Stuart Hart watched critically as the diminutive woman wearing the simple white gown looked up into the eyes of the tall man who stood opposed to her.

As she watched the scene unfold, she was not aware of the lights to either side of her nor of the camera that whirred almost inaudibly to her right. She was more aware of the face of Allister St. John, for his reaction was to her more important than anything else. He was a tall man, extremely thin, with reddish hair and electric blue eyes—one of the best directors in Hollywood.

St. John did not move his head, for he had intense powers of concentration, but as Lylah watched him closely she remembered when she had first mentioned her pet project. They had been in her office and she had said, "We'll get Lady Mary Worley to play Miss Eliza Bennet, and we'll get Clyde Scott to play Mr. Darcy. It'll cost an arm and a leg, but it'll be the best filming of *Pride and Prejudice* that's ever been made—or ever will be!"

That had been a year earlier, and it had taken every bit of pressure and every dime, practically, that Monarch Studios could raise to pull the chemistry together, but looking at Scott's lean, hearty, aristocratic face as he spoke his lines she thought, *It's been the right thing to do!* A sense of satisfaction came to her, for the burden of running a motion picture studio during the thirties had been great indeed. Many studios had sprung up, and most of them had died stillborn. A few giants had emerged—Metro Goldwyn Mayer, Fox, Columbia. Monarch was not to be considered in their category in size and the number of pictures. Lylah and her husband, Jesse, had decided early to make few pictures—but those few would be quality.

Now, as she saw the scene from her favorite novel unfolding, a glow touched her, and she was satisfied with what she saw. A voice whispered in her ear, "Mrs. Hart—"

Lylah turned around to find her secretary, Charles Kent, standing beside her. The actors were still speaking so she held up her hand until St. John said, "Cut!" and announced, "That's a take!"

At once Lylah went over to the actors. She smiled at Lady

Mary Worley, who was not pretty in the Hollywood sense, but the character she played, Miss Elizabeth Bennet, was not all that beautiful either. "Very fine, Mary!" she said. "Just the way I pictured Eliza Bennet!" She took the Englishwoman's smile, then turned and looked up at Clyde, who at six-four was one of the tallest actors in Hollywood. "You did fine, Clyde, couldn't have been better!"

"Thank you, Lylah," Scott said. "It's easy working with Lady Mary."

St. John said, "It was all right," which was high praise coming from him. He was a driver. He slapped his hands together in an irritated fashion saying, "Well, let's get on—we can't stand around here all day!"

Lylah smiled at his mannerisms, then turned and walked away to where Kent was waiting. "What is it, Charles?" she asked.

"We'd better go to your office."

Somewhat surprised, Lylah nodded. "All right." She followed him off the set, across a narrow alley into the main offices of Monarch Studios. As soon as they turned down a hall, they entered her office, then passed by the secretary who looked up and said, "A call came from Isabel's agent, Mrs. Hart."

"I'll take it as soon as I'm through with Charles," Lylah replied. She entered the office, which was rather simple as such offices are. One entire side was covered with books, and there were easy chairs with lamps where one could sit and read. A massive desk, neatly organized by Kent, dominated the room, but Lylah did not sit down. She turned and said, "What is it?"

For one instant Charles Kent studied his employer before he spoke. Lylah Stuart Hart had been a beautiful woman all of her life. Now, at sixty she looked no more than forty-five. She had kept her figure, and her auburn hair still had its reddish glints without the help of her hairdresser. She was not tall, and her face was not beautiful in the classic sense, but she had a rich complexion. Whatever it is that makes men look at a woman—Lylah Stuart Hart still had it.

"It's Adam—he's in trouble."

"What's happened?" She felt a sudden stab of fear. "Has he been in an accident?"

"No, not exactly," Kent hesitated. "He's been arrested."

"Arrested, for what? Not drunken driving, I hope?"

"Worse than that, I'm afraid, Mrs. Hart. I just got a call from the Eighth Precinct. They're holding him—he's charged with assaulting a police officer."

Lylah stared into the round face of Kent, unable to speak for a moment. Quickly she tried to pull herself together, but she knew she could not keep the dismay that rose in her from showing on her face. "Have you told Jesse?"

"No, Mr. Hart evidently hasn't come back from the lawyer's office yet. He's probably on his way right now."

"What did they say exactly, Charles?"

"He was arrested at the Sky Room along with Jean De-Camp."

Kent noticed Lylah's lips tighten at his use of the young woman's name. He was aware that Lylah and Jesse disapproved of Adam's affair with her, but he was also aware that there was little that anyone could do to stop it. Kent had not been with Monarch more than a year, but he had learned that Adam Stuart was not following in the path that his mother and stepfather would have liked. Adam had become a playboy and had brought lines into Lylah's face that nothing else had been able to do. "They said that he's charged with public drunkenness, which is nothing—but striking an officer is. I think we'd better get Dennison down there right away."

"I'll go myself, as soon as Jesse gets here!"

"I still think we'd better call Mr. Dennison." P. D. Dennison was the chief lawyer for Monarch Studios and a personal friend of the Harts. "You're going to need a lawyer on this one, Mrs. Hart."

"You're right, Charles—try to get him, will you? Then I'll see if I can find Jesse."

As Kent left the room, Lylah turned and walked over to her desk. She sat down carefully in the leather-covered chair, leaned forward, and put her forehead in her hands. The silence in the room was broken only by the sibilant hissing of the Casablanca fan overhead. For a long time she struggled with the fear and apprehension that threatened to overwhelm her. "Oh, Adam, Adam," she finally murmured softly. An image of this son of hers that had lately brought her so much grief came before her eyes and with it the image of another man. The two were separate for a moment but were very alike, and then they seemed to merge into one.

The second image was one of Manfred von Richthofen, Adam's father. Lylah had been in Germany in 1918, had met von Richthofen, and had been swept into a secret, wildly passionate affair with the German ace. When he died, Lylah was carrying his child. The baby was born in France, but Lylah had never acknowledged his father to the public—although she and Jesse had found it wise to tell Adam.

Now, Lylah Hart thought of Manfred, the young man who had lived under a doomed star. Those days sometimes seemed long ago, but from time to time they came to her with a brilliant intensity. Lylah had loved the young German flier with a wild, unreasoning passion—but she had known for a long time that had he lived, they could never have been happy together.

Now she had Adam, the son of the famed Red Baron, and she saw nothing ahead for him but tragedy—for he was a young man without a star to steer by. Tears of frustration and fear came to her eyes, but quickly she found a handkerchief in her pocket and wiped them away. She sat there until the door opened, then looked up to see Jesse Hart enter. Lylah had fallen in love with him as she had never fallen in love with another man—not even Manfred. Hart was no more than five-ten and a trim 165 pounds. Now, at the age of fifty-five, his crisp brown hair was going gray, but his neat, short beard had never changed from the day she first saw him.

"Jesse, it's Adam—he's in trouble."

Hart came to stand before her as she stood up from the desk. He took her in his arms, holding her for a moment. He knew her well and understood that what was happening was tearing her to pieces. She was now a godly woman, this wife of his, and had much faith—but Adam's life over the past few years had been a severe test for both of them. "It's all right, Lylah," he said, "we'll just trust God. Now, what is it Adam's done?"

Sergeant Milton Cavanaugh did not like rich people on the whole. True enough, he did not know many of them, and those he did encounter were inevitably like these two who stood before him, in trouble of some sort. Cavanaugh was a pudgy, red-faced man with dark brown eyes and a shaggy mop of hair that continually fell over his forehead. He brushed it back now, saying with some sharpness, "Look, I'm sorry, Mr. Hart, but I don't make the law! The charge is assault of a police officer, and you're not going to get bail for that—not tonight! It's Friday night, and the judge ain't in his chambers."

"But isn't there some way we can get him out, Officer?" Lylah had allowed Jesse to speak to the officers when they had arrived at the precinct headquarters. She had noted that Sergeant Cavanaugh was tired and irritated, and although anxiety made her tense, she kept her voice quiet and said, "We'd do anything that's necessary, of course."

Cavanaugh hesitated for a moment. *These two are a little different—not like most swells.* He did not know either of them, but their dress and their bearing identified them as what he called the upper crust. Sighing, he leaned forward and put his hand on the desk, flat before him, spreading his short fingers out and studying them for a moment. The room was filled with the muttering of conversation, mostly by people waiting to get someone out of jail and by officers who came by laughing and joking, totally oblivious to the misery of those who waited. It had become their natural environment. Trouble to them was like water to a fish or air to mammals. It was just there, and one learned to ignore it.

"I'm sorry for your trouble, and if it was just drunkenness something could be done, but assaulting a police officer? Well, we just can't overlook that, I'm afraid."

"Can we at least see him?"

"I suppose that can be arranged. Not exactly what the rules say."

"We'd be very grateful, Officer!" Jesse said quickly. "We appreciate your consideration."

Accustomed to being bombarded by anger, sarcasm, and insults, Cavanaugh yielded. "Well, just for ten minutes, you understand?"

"Thank you very much," Hart said quickly. He took Lylah's arm and soon the two of them were directed down the hall, where they waited in a bleak, bare room containing only a table, three chairs, and some battered filing cabinets that had been unsuccessfully repainted an odious orange color. There was no window in the room and it stank of cigarette and cigar smoke—and the smell of fear was almost palpable.

The door opened, and when Adam entered, it was closed again by a burly officer. Lylah turned to say, "Are you all right, Adam?"

"Certainly!"

Adam Stuart had sobered considerably in his brief time in the jail cell. The cell was occupied by winos harvested off the streets of the ghettos of Los Angeles. One of them had thrown up, and the smell had almost sickened him. However, now he stood straight and looked his mother full in the eyes waiting for her to speak.

"I don't think we're going to be able to get you out right away," Lylah said.

"That's all right." Adam's words were short and clipped—there was a stubbornness in his back—and he held his head at a certain pitch that suddenly and terribly reminded Lylah of Manfred von Richthofen. *He's got that same kind of stubbornness that Manfred had!* The thought flashed through Lylah's mind, but she drove it away instantly. "P. D. will be down as soon as he can," Jesse said quickly, "but from what the sergeant said, I think we'll have to wait until the judge is available, and that will be Monday morning."

"Don't worry about me!"

Lylah moved forward and put her hand on her son's arm. She felt the strong muscles there grow tense beneath her touch, and although he did not withdraw physically, there was a wall there that saddened her. They had been so close when he was growing up, but after he had reached adolescence, a gulf had begun to form. He had gone his own way, and when he had become a man, the gulf had widened. Now he was almost a stranger to her. "We won't go to Arkansas, of course."

"Of course you'll go!" Adam said instantly. "No sense your staying here just because I'm in the clink!" His own words sounded harsh, and as Adam saw the effect of his words reflected in his mother's eyes, suddenly he was sorry. "Look," he forced a smile and put his arm around her, "Christmas reunion with the Stuarts means more to you than any other holiday. Of course you'll go." He turned to Jesse and said, "Dad, don't let her talk you out of it. It won't do any good for her to sit home grieving over the prodigal."

"I'll do what I can, Son." Jesse Hart had been a good father to this young man, and well did Adam know it. Actually Adam was bitterly ashamed of his conduct and hated himself for what had happened. Something, however, kept him from saying so directly. He had manufactured a veneer that covered his feelings quite successfully. Now he managed a smile and said, "Maybe I'll get out in time to fly down and catch the tail end of it for Christmas."

"Are you sure, Adam?" Lylah asked. "I don't mind staying here, and after you get out—"

"No, Mother." Adam shook his head firmly. "You go on down to the farm! I'll get there if I can. Have a good time."

They stood talking briefly, and then the officer entered and shrugged. "Time's up!"

Adam leaned over and kissed his mother, and she clung to him for a moment. He almost managed to say the words, "I'm sorry," but somehow could not bring himself to do it. Instead he laughed and said, "Ah, this won't be so bad. Give me some time for some meditation." He turned and slapped Jesse hard on the shoulder. "Take care of her, Dad. You two have a good time!"

After the guard led Adam away, Jesse said, "Come along; we'll talk to P. D. Perhaps there's some way to get him out anyway."

But that was not to be the case. P. D. Dennison arrived thirty minutes later and spoke to the sergeant. He then pulled Jesse and Lylah to one side, saying, "It's out of the sergeant's hands, so it'll have to be Monday morning. I can have him out then. You're going to your family reunion in Arkansas, aren't you?"

"We were—"

"Go on and go. I'll get him out and put him on a plane. He'll get there for part of Christmas anyway."

"All right, P. D." Jesse said firmly. "Thanks a lot."

When Jesse and Lylah were outside, Lylah looked up into the dark skies where clouds covered the stars and a thin moon showed only intermittently between the tattered remnants. She waited while Jesse brought the car, then got in and sat down silently. He drove the car away expertly, and neither of them spoke for several blocks. Finally, Jesse said, "I think we've got to go to Arkansas since everybody's expecting us. And Adam's right—it wouldn't do him any good for you to stay here."

"All right, Jesse."

She sat silently until they reached the house. They went inside and began to pack their things. Two hours later they were on the plane winging its way eastward. Looking down on Los Angeles as the plane soared higher, Lylah saw that the lights glittered as far as she could see, then the plane went through the cloud cover, and she lost sight of the city.

Turning to Jesse she asked almost plaintively, "Have we been too lenient on Adam, Jesse?"

"We've done the best we could." His hard hand took hers; he lifted it to his lips and kissed it. "He'll be all right. We've been praying for him for a long time now, haven't we? Well, God's got those prayers filed away somewhere. He won't let them fall to the ground!"

2

"Wendy Has a Man at Last!"

Thick drifts of snow lined the sides of the roads, and black-birds wheeled over the frozen brown earth that made up the Arkansas hills. The black automobile that bounced and skittered from side to side over the gravel road tossed the four people inside roughly.

"Blast this car!" Owen Stuart complained, hanging on to the enormous steering wheel of the '39 Packard with his left hand. His other hand was missing, replaced by a gleaming steel hook that he used to suddenly tap the dashboard impatiently. "As much as this thing cost, you'd think it'd be a lot better car!"

"How much did it cost, Dad?" two voices asked simultaneously. William and Woodrow Stuart exchanged grins in the backseat. They had heard this story before. Woody was the smaller of the two and, at the age of nineteen had an air of confidence about him. He was small like his mother, Allie, who sat in the front seat next to Owen, and he was towheaded, with dark blue eyes.

William, better known as Will, was a student at Vanderbilt studying premed. He had big shoulders and heavy bones like his father, and his chestnut hair had gleams of red in it. His eyes were dark blue like those of his brother. "Why, this thing must've cost at least five hundred dollars!" he said, winking this time at his mother, who turned to smile at him.

Owen snorted contemptuously. "This automobile cost exactly one thousand one hundred sixty-six dollars and ninety-two cents when I drove it out of the showroom!" he announced. "I wish I'd kept my Studebaker! These blasted Packards are not worth a dime!"

Allison Dupree Stuart, better known as Allie, at the age of fifty, still had honey-colored hair that she kept done up around her head in a fashionable manner. She had a square face and a determined chin but rather delicate, smooth features. "Will you stop cussing, Owen!" She turned her head and winked merrily at the young men. "You'll be a bad influence on our children!"

"Why, Allie, I'm not cussing; it's all right to say 'blasted'!" Owen insisted. He dodged a pothole successfully, but the back end fishtailed over the frozen road on a patch of ice. He muttered to himself, then when he got the car straightened said, "I hope Wendy and Alex find the farm all right."

"Wendy will find it." Allie nodded confidently. "I just hope they're not late. It was a long drive all the way from Nashville."

Owen glanced out at the hills, noting that the trees were stripped naked, and suddenly said, "Look, I must've shot a thousand squirrels in woods like those over there." He thought of the days when he had grown up on this rocky, Ozark farmland, and nostalgia came to him. His lips curled upward in a smile and as Allie watched she thought, *He's still handsome. He doesn't look fifty-seven, either.* She said aloud, "You know, for a preacher you're not a bad-looking man!"

Owen grinned, enjoying her teasing. He was, in fact, an evangelist and relatively well known over the United States. Most of his ministry in recent years had been tent meetings outside of large cities. He had lost his right hand in the Great War, and previous to that, he had been a prizefighter. He'd met Allie when he was taking on all comers in a carnival. The two of them had had a rocky time of it after they'd married, for preachers made little money—especially evangelists. Now he looked over at her and said, "You're not bad looking for a preacher's wife!"

Woody nudged Will with his elbow. "Will you two stop romancing, and let's get on with it!"

"I'm hungry," Allie said. "Can't we stop up there and get something to eat?"

"I guess so. We need to gas up anyway." Owen pulled the car in front of the gas pumps, which featured large glass enclosures at the top. "Look at the price of that gas—eighteen cents a gallon! Might as well make cars that run on pure gold!"

They all got out of the car and stretched their legs. It had been a long ride from Nashville where they made their home. Owen was gone much of the time with his meetings, and usually Allie went with him.

They all waited as a raw-boned, youthful attendant came out and grinned. "Fill 'er up?" he inquired.

"Yes, and check the oil." Owen watched as the young man serviced the big automobile, then pulled it around in front of the cafe, which bore the image of a large ill-drawn bumble bee. Beneath it in large handmade letters were the words, The Busy Bee Cafe. Sounds of music came forth, and Owen grumbled as they moved toward the front door. "They have one of those blasted jukeboxes! I wish they didn't—I like to eat in peace!"

They entered and were greeted by the raucous music. It was a long building with the gleaming jukebox at one end and a small floor space allowing two or three couples to dance. Close beside it sat a pinball machine where three young men in overalls gathered. One was shifting and punching at the machine while the others gave him encouragement in loud voices.

"Let's get as far away as we can from that mess!" Owen murmured. He led them down to the other end of the cafe. A door at the back led, evidently, to a kitchen. Along one wall were three booths, and there were four round tables with cane-bottom wood chairs scattered around them. Owen said, "Let's sit at a table; I hate those little dinky booths." He pulled out Allie's chair. They all sat down and were approached by a heavyset young woman with a discontented look on her face. She had brassy yellow hair in tight curls and wore too much lipstick. Her fingernails, Owen noticed as she handed them some flyspecked menus, were bitten off short, which accounted for the fact that they were not dirty. Her apron was stained with the remains of several encounters with the food, and she said, "What you gonna have?"

Allie glanced down the menu and said, "I want a hamburger with lots of pickles."

"You want onions?"

"No."

"They come with the hamburger; you can have 'em if you want 'em."

Allie smiled at the woman and said, "No, thank you, just a hamburger."

The others found nothing better, and all four settled for hamburgers and Cokes. After the waitress left, Owen glanced toward the pinball machine. "Those things are doing a lot of harm. I've been doing some research on it." He settled back and waited until the waitress had brought four bottled Cokes and set them in front of them. Owen looked up and asked, "Can we have some ice in glasses, please?"

"I guess so."

After the waitress left, Owen said, "I read about these things. It's kind of interesting. You'd never believe where they started." He launched into a discussion informing them that bagatelle had been a game mentioned in Dickens's novel *Pickwick Papers*. "They used a billiard cue to shoot balls into holes located in the middle of a table," he said. "Then later on, in America, there was a game called Log Cabin. It had pegs and holes in it and this article had a picture of President Lincoln playing Log Cabin, but it was a pretty sleazy outfit, I think."

Woody looked over at the three youths and said, "It's just a game, Pa."

"It's a waste of time, and I wish it had never been invented!" He was a man who liked to know about things, and he persistently informed his family. "A fellow named David Gottlieb made a game called Baffle Ball; had seven steel balls. He sold fifty thousand of those things, and now everywhere you go we got these pinball machines. It's as bad as that jukebox!"

"Why, Pa, you always liked music," Will grinned. The song that was playing was a hillbilly song about a pickup truck, whiskey, blood on the highway, and a mournful mother. "Why, that song's got a message! You ought to like it!"

Owen gave Will a disdainful look. "Like that kind of mess? I've heard cats fighting that sounded better than that fella!"

"I guess you looked up the history of jukeboxes, too!" Woody said, winking at his mother. "You sure are a fellow for studying things, Pa."

Owen had seen the wink but nevertheless said, "I remember when they started. Allie and I both do."

"That's right," Allie said. "They started out where you went to a parlor to hear recorded music." She leaned forward to put her chin on her hand. "Every box had listening tubes, and you had to hold them up to your ear. There wasn't any amplification, and the music then was a little better, mostly classical."

"Well, the stuff on that jukebox sure isn't classical!" Owen growled. He continued to pontificate against the evils of pinball machines and jukeboxes, adding, "You know what *juke* means?" When no one spoke up he said, "It comes from Africa. It means a house of prostitution, and that's what our young people are doing today, listening to immoral music off of a machine that's named after prostitutes!"

Finally the waitress brought the hamburgers, and they all ate heartily, ordering another round of Cokes. When Owen paid the bill, which came to two dollars and sixty cents, he left a quarter on the table for the young woman, saying, "I guess it won't hurt to overtip a little bit. She looks like she needs to buy some Lifebuoy soap, something with carbolic in it, to get that mess washed off her face."

They resumed their journey, and Owen became more cheerful as they came closer to his old home.

"It'll be good to see everybody again. I look forward all year to Christmas." As if they didn't know, he said, "My brothers and sisters and I have always said we're going to have this reunion no matter what else we miss. So far we've been able to do it."

"It may not be possible for a while, Pa. This war that's coming up, it may put a stop to a lot of things," said Will.

His words fell on the others, and there was silence for a while. Owen finally said heavily, "You're right about that. That fella Hitler is sure doing a lot of damage in this world."

"Isn't she darling?" Carol Davidson stooped down and cooed as she ran her hand over the silky hide of the calf that had come tottering up to stand beside her. She stuck her finger out, and the calf immediately began sucking at it. Looking up, Carol said, "Isn't she precious?"

Clint Stuart leaned against the corner of the barn. He was a tall, lanky young man of twenty, with tow-colored hair and hazel eyes. His hands were hard, and working under the sun in the fields had given him a deep tan. He had craggy features and a wry sense of humor.

"She looks delicious!" He waited for the complaint that he knew would come.

"Clint, what an awful thing to say!" Carol exclaimed.

"Well, that's what we're raising her for, to eat! I didn't notice you turning down any of those pork chops we had, and you loved that little pig they came from, remember? You called her Teeny when she was born."

"I don't like to think about such things!" Carol rose to her feet. She was a small woman, but very well formed. Her hair was black as hair could possibly be, and her eyes were deep blue. She was wearing a woolen black-and-red mackinaw that belonged to Clint, and her hands receded from view as she stood up. Glancing up at him, she said, "You do say awful things!"

Clint reached out and pulled her forward, holding her in his arms and looking down at her. He wore thin jeans and a blue wool shirt, despite the cold in the December air. Weather seemed to have no effect on him. He could put in a day's work under a 110-degree blistering sun, and while others were dropping from heat exhaustion, Clint could virtually ignore the temperature. Cold weather had no effect on him either, it seemed. His shirt was open at the collar, and he shoved the green John Deere cap back on his head. "You know," he said thoughtfully, holding her closely, enjoying the sensation of her young curves pressed against him, "I been thinking about starting a new business."

"A business?" Carol looked up at him. He was a handsome man to her, and she resisted the impulse to reach up and stroke his cheek. "What kind of business?"

"I'm thinking of starting a business called Edible Pets." Clint's face was totally solemn, and he nodded, "Yep, what I'll do is sell little cuddly things like rabbits, and kids can play with them. You know how kids like little rabbits. And then when the bunnies get big enough—why, the kids can eat 'em."

Carol burst out into laughter and began to beat his chest with her fist. "Let me go, you beast! That's the most horrible thing I've ever heard of in my whole life!"

"If I'm so horrible, why do you love me so much?" Clint suddenly leaned over and kissed her. She put her arms around his neck and pressed herself against him. There was a passion in this young woman that matched his own, Clint had found, and he savored the moment, the softness of her lips, the clean smell of her hair, and the light perfume she wore.

Carol pulled away and said breathlessly, "That's enough!"

"For you maybe!"

"For you, too! You're a selfish pig. I'm ashamed of you sometimes!"

"Because I love you?"

"No, I like that," Carol smiled. Then she said, "Listen, isn't that a car?"

Clint lifted his head for a moment listening, then nodded. "Family probably starting to arrive," he said. He paused a moment and then studied this woman before him. "I want to get married as much as you do, Carol," he said abruptly. "But I don't see how we can."

"Well, why can't we?" Carol had decided firmly that Clint Stuart was the man she wanted for a husband. They had had a slow courtship, for she had been popular with the more affluent neighbors in the community. She had had a serious suitor, the son of the local banker, and she was well aware that Clint had hung back knowing that he could not compete with the fancy automobile and the entertainment that Dale Turner could provide. Still, Carol had known her own heart. She saw in this tall, rugged man before her the man she loved and said, "I don't care what we have or where we live, Clint. It doesn't matter, if people love each other."

"I think it does!"

Carol stared at him, surprised. "You think money is that important?"

"Sometimes I think it means the difference between success and failure."

"Your parents didn't have any money, and they've had a good marriage."

"Lots of people don't, though. I expect lots of marriages break up over fights over money." Clint heard the car pull up and turned to walk to the house, still holding his arm around her. "Anyway," he said, "they started the draft last month. I expect I'll get drafted into the army. I'm the right age and I'm not married."

"Then let's get married and you won't get drafted!"

Clint looked down at her and grinned. She was impulsive, and he loved her more than he was ever able to say. "I don't think that's a good enough reason for getting married. Let me get myself established, Carol." He became serious. "I'm studying hard, and one of these days I'll find a way to become an engineer."

Clint Stuart was a farmer, for that was the life he had been born into. He still lived with his father, Logan, and his mother, Anne, on the farm that had been the Stuart farm for genera-

tions, but he did not really like the farm. He liked to build
things, and he liked to study. He had taken every study course
that he could find through the mail, and everyone in the community knew that if an engine or anything needed fixing,
Clint Stuart was the man to take it to.

"Just give me a couple of years, and then we'll be ready."

"Two years?" Carol shook her head. "We can't wait two
years!"

"There's the matter of your father. He needs you pretty
bad." Ralph Davidson, Carol's father, had been ill a great deal,
and it had been difficult for her. She'd lost her mother when
she was only six, and the relationship between father and
daughter had become very strong. Sometimes Clint thought
that it was *too* strong—for Carol relied on Ralph to make all
her decisions. When Davidson's heart attack had come, six
months earlier, Clint had seen Carol through it. Now as he
looked down at her, he thought, *She's still a little girl in so many
ways. And she leans too much on her dad*.

Carol heard the horn blow, and voices began to call out.
"We'll talk about it later, Clint—but if we love each other we
won't have to wait that long."

Clint moved around the house, following Carol, doubt
coming to him strongly. He had seen enough poverty in the
hills of the Ozarks, enough women worn down with one child
after another as their husbands tried to eke out a meager
existence from the rocky hillside farms, and he wanted none
of this. As he looked up and saw the black Packard pulled
up in front of the house and his uncle Owen and his cousins
piling out, he wondered if there was any way to become an
engineer without money.

Logan and Anne Stuart had come out of the house to greet
the visitors. Logan was fifty-five, and wore a pair of faded
overalls and a blue sweater over a worn cotton shirt. Anne was
a small woman, rather plain, and wore a simple cotton dress
and had put on a brown sweater to come out into the cold.

"You're late," Logan said, shaking Owen's hand hard and
clapping him on the shoulder. "We've kept the meal hot."

"We had hamburgers on the way, but I could eat again. You're looking good, Logan." Owen turned to Anne, greeted her, and Anne smiled saying, "Come inside; everything's on the table."

They went inside and, despite the protest of the visitors that they had eaten recently, soon were all sitting at the round oak table eating fried chicken, mashed potatoes, and canned green beans.

Logan leaned back in his chair and listened as the others talked. Before long, he asked, "What about Wendy? She didn't come with you?"

Owen hesitated only for an instant, but even so, it caught Logan's attention. "She's driving from Nashville," he said briefly.

"Alone? Why didn't she ride with you? Isn't that a long way?" Anne inquired.

Owen picked up his cup of coffee, swirled it around, then drank it. "Well, actually she's driving down with a friend of hers, a young man named Alex Grenville."

Clinton lifted his head, interest brightening his hazel eyes. "Is he a boyfriend?"

"You might say that," Owen nodded. He seemed preoccupied for a moment, picking up his fork and pushing his mashed potatoes around aimlessly. Looking up, he grinned and shrugged his broad shoulders. "Wendy has a man—at last!"

"Tell me about him," Carol said quickly. "When did she meet him? What does he look like?"

"Maybe you ought to hear Allie tell it," Owen suggested. He seemed disinclined to talk, which was unusual for him. He leaned back in his cane-bottomed chair and listened as Allie began to speak. "He's a musician," Allie said quietly. "Actually, he is a professor at the Nashville School of Music."

"A professor? Is he a pretty old guy?" Clinton inquired.

"Not at all. He's twenty-three, five years older than Wendy, but he was some sort of a musical prodigy. He not only teaches at the music school but conducts a symphony orchestra."

As Allie described Wendy's young man, there was an air of dissatisfaction about Owen, and although Logan said nothing at that time, later when the meal was over, he and Owen stepped out on the porch. The two talked quietly for a while, mostly about who was coming to the reunion. Finally, Logan asked, "What's the matter, Owen?"

"The matter with what?"

"You don't care for Wendy's young man, do you?"

Owen gave his brother a glance. He tried to smile and shrugged his shoulders. "I never could fool you very much, could I? Well, we've been wondering when Wendy would become interested in some young man. Most young women by the time they're eighteen have already made some headway in that direction. But she just never showed any interest—not until she met this fella."

"What's wrong with him, Owen?"

Owen shifted uncomfortably on the porch. He reached out and tapped the railing with his steel hook tentatively, then turned to face Logan. "He's got everything a man ought to have, Logan—except he doesn't know the Lord."

Logan blinked, then shook his head. "Wendy's always been such a fine Christian. I'm surprised she'd take up with a fella like that."

"I've talked to her about it. She says she can change him."

"Maybe she can."

"Maybe so—that's what Allie and I are praying about. You can pray with us." Owen looked out across the field. Over three hundred yards away, two does stepped out from a grove of pine trees. They stood immobile for a moment, then something startled them. They broke into that beautiful run, punctuated by graceful leaps, and Owen watched them until they disappeared into the thickets. "That's beautiful, isn't it? I've missed that in the cities." He was silent for a moment, then shook his head and said, "I hope we have a fine reunion. It'll be good to see everyone again."

Alex Grenville steered the car skillfully down the steep mountain road. He was proud of the car, a 1936 Cord with a "coffin" nose and crank-up headlights. He liked speed, and this one could put most cars far behind. He ran his hand over the steering wheel in an affectionate caress, then turned and asked, "How much farther, Wendy?"

"Only about ten miles."

Wendy Stuart was wearing a silver-gray dress that matched her gray eyes. She had on a green fingertip jacket, and the sunlight caught her auburn hair, bringing out the red gleams in it.

Alex glanced at her and smiled. "I don't know how a city slicker like me is going to make out in the country. I've never been around country folks before."

Reaching over, Wendy put her hand over Alex's where it rested on the wheel. "You'll do fine," she smiled. "They'll love you just like I do."

"Well, maybe not quite that much."

"Who wouldn't love you?" she teased.

"I can give you a long list." Alex laughed shortly. "Mostly graduate students that I just flunked in a music course."

The two chatted as the car rolled along past open fields as they came down into the valley. Alex looked around and said, "This is beautiful country. It reminds me a little of upper New York State." He suddenly pulled over with such an abrupt turn of the wheel that Wendy gasped. "What are you doing?" she cried.

"Just want to stop and talk a little bit." They had come to the lip of another small ridge where they could look down on the valley. He pointed the nose of the Cord over that view, then reached out and pulled her to him. She turned and met his embrace openly.

Alex Grenville was a demanding young man in every way. He had added a drive to his profession that had brought him to the attention nationally of those interested in classical music, especially symphonies. Everything he did was given his com-

plete and undivided attention. Now, as he kissed her, there
was the same insistence in his manner.

Wendy enjoyed his kiss. She enjoyed the strong feeling
of his arms around her, for truthfully she had begun to worry
whether she would ever find a man that would please her. She
had had several boyfriends through her high school years, but
none had drawn her serious attention. When she met Alex
Grenville she had been a student in his class. At first she had
disliked him, for he had driven his students with almost a fury.
Many had dropped out, but Wendy had grimly remained and
proven to be tough enough and talented enough to survive
his ruthless teaching methods.

Even as he was kissing her and she felt his hand run down
her back, she thought about how he had invited her out and
she had gone—not at all satisfied that she would ever like
such a man. Their courtship had been swift, and she had
been almost breathless with the haste with which he pres-
sured her. Now, she felt him begin to caress her in a way that
startled her. Pulling back, she murmured, "Don't–don't do
that, Alex."

Grenville shook his head. "You're such a Puritan, Wendy!
What's a little caress between friends?"

"I just don't like it, that's all."

"You like being kissed well enough."

"Yes, I guess I do. That's different though from what you
were doing just then."

Grenville moved his arm and then leaned back against the
door of the car studying her thoughtfully. He was a trim young
man, well built, of medium height. He had crisp brown hair
and alert brown eyes and English features. He had known
many women in his life; being attractive, he had naturally
drawn them. He had found they played games with him, and
he had joined in. Now, however, this young woman had captured him most of all by her dewy innocence. He smiled and
pulled a cigarette out and lit it with a gold lighter. He puffed
at the cigarette, letting the window down, and rested his arm

on the side of the door. "I don't know what we see in each other," he finally said. "You're an angel, and I'm a devil."

"That's not true!" Wendy said sharply. "You're no devil, and I'm certainly not an angel!"

"Look," Grenville said, "you and I love each other. Sooner or later we're going to get married. Why shouldn't we enjoy everything there is for young lovers?"

Wendy knew he did not like her to mention her religious convictions. Nevertheless, she said firmly, "We've talked about this before, Alex! After we're married, we'll have each other, but until we are I intend to stay just as I am!" She gave him a direct look and said pointedly, "I think that's what you liked about me in the first place, isn't it?"

Realizing that she had figured him out, Alex grinned ruefully. "You're too sharp for me, Wendy!" He tossed the cigarette out, rolled the window up, and said, "Come on; let's go down and let the family look me over. I feel like a prize hog going to the county fair."

Relieved that the moment was over, Wendy moved closer to him and held on to his arm. "They'll love you, I guarantee!"

They arrived at the farm ten minutes later and found that the yard was already swarming with relatives. "Good grief!" Alex said. "It looks like a town meeting! Are these all Stuarts?"

"Yes—now come on; let me show you off!" Wendy said eagerly. She was aware that some had wondered at her courtship, and she was pleased as she took Alex around and introduced him to Logan, Anne, and then to Clinton and to Carol Davidson.

"Come on," she said. "I especially want you to meet my cousin Mona. I warn you, she'll try to steal you."

She led the way to where a middle-aged couple was standing with two young people. "This is Peter Stuart, my uncle, and his wife, Leslie. I want you to meet Alex Grenville."

"I'm glad to meet you, Sir." Grenville shook Stuart's hand, and Peter Stuart, who was six-feet-four, looked down at him. "Don't call me *Sir*; I'm going to be a grandfather soon enough,

I suppose." He winked at Leslie, who, at the age of forty-four, still had clear ash-blonde hair and not a wrinkle. "She'll be the best-looking grandma in town!"

"And this is Stephen, and this is Mona."

Stephen Stuart, not nearly as tall as his father but with the same good looks, grinned as he shook hands with Grenville. "He doesn't even have a kid married yet, and he's already counting his grandchildren."

Mona Stuart, at seventeen, was so pretty that for one moment Alex blinked. She had pure-blonde hair, enormous green eyes, and the powder-blue blouse and skirt she wore covered by a dark royal-blue sweater revealed a stunning figure. "Hello, Alex!" she said, and gave him her hand. There was an aggressiveness in her that Alex recognized at once.

"I'm glad to know you, Stephen and Mona." He stood chatting, and after he was taken away by the men, Mona turned to Wendy. "Where did you find a dreamboat like him?" she whispered. She stared contemplatively at her cousin and said, "I thought you'd arrive dragging some stiff lawyer in a black suit. He's really something! Tell me all about him."

For the next twenty minutes the two young women talked excitedly. Wendy knew that Mona thought of nothing but young men. By the age of seventeen she had already been studying them for several years. Now, however, as her abundant young womanhood was so obvious in her figure and also in the glint of her green eyes, Wendy was happy that she had not brought an old man in a black suit. "Isn't he something, Mona?" she said.

Mona cocked her head to one side. "You better hang on to him, Honey—there'll be *plenty* standing in line for a man like that!"

"You've got enough men, Mona!" Wendy smiled. She really liked her cousin a great deal, but there was a serious note in her voice as she said, "You've got enough boyfriends of your own. Let me have this one."

Later that night Wendy and Mona shared a bed in the attic,

and they stayed up talking until very late. Wendy mostly listened as Mona excitedly told her about her latest conquest. "He's the quarterback at the University of Oklahoma, Denton Norman. You've heard of him, haven't you?"

"I'm afraid not."

"You haven't? Well, he's leading the conference in passing. Oh, and he's a dreamboat; he really is!"

Satisfied that Mona had no designs on Alex, Wendy lay back and listened as the young woman laid out her life. "I'm going to enter the Miss Oklahoma contest next year," she said. "I bet I win it, too!"

"And after that you can be Miss America!"

"Why not?" Mona laughed. "You know how when they name Miss America, she always cries? You just wait; I won't cry; I'll laugh and say to those losers, 'There, now we see who the real winner is!'"

"You wouldn't do that, Mona; you'd cry just like the rest of 'em."

Mona sighed and stretched like a cat, her supple young body arching outward. "I suppose so," she admitted. She was getting sleepy now and said, "I like Alex. I bet he's a handful, isn't he?"

"What makes you think that?"

"He's got that bedroom look in his eye. I've seen it often enough to recognize it, but I can tell he loves you, so you hold out for the wedding ring."

Wendy was somewhat disturbed at Mona's attitude toward what she considered a sacred thing. She heard the house stirring, for it was full of visitors and voices. Finally she drifted off to sleep, wondering what her family would make of her marrying someone who wasn't a Christian.

3

The Stuart Clan

Brother Harlan Crabtree came to stand behind the walnut pulpit and looked out over his congregation. A smile tugged at his lips as he said, "Some churches get run over with mice, but it looks like this morning Grace Church is run over with Stuarts!" He waited until the laughter died down, and then said, "Every year it is a joy to those of us who have known the Stuarts for years to welcome them back to our community. I grew up with the Stuart boys—Owen, Amos, Logan, Pete, Gavin. We've hunted the woods and fished the streams and lakes together. At one time or another I tried to court all the Stuart girls—Christie, Lenora, and Lylah—but all of them had better sense than to take up with the likes of me." Again mild laughter ran around the auditorium.

The bright sunlight came down through the stained glass windows on each side of the simple wooden structure, fanning out and touching the faces of the worshipers. The seats were made of pine and designed more for utility than for comfort. The walls were also pine, painted white, and only recently had the two large wood-burning stoves been replaced by gas furnaces. Today, despite the cold outside, the church inside was at least bearable.

"As usual, I've asked Reverend Owen Stuart to bring our message. Brother Stuart, come and speak what's on your heart."

Owen rose from the seat on the platform and came at once, a worn black Bible in his hand. He laid it on the pulpit, opened

46

it, and then looked out over the congregation. "I've preached in some pretty large churches and tents," he said quietly, "but it always gives me a special thrill to come back to this place where, as a boy, I sat on that bench right over there with my brothers and sisters, my father and mother. I thank God for those days, and I thank God that all of us are now members in the household of God."

As he went on speaking, Lylah was watching him carefully. She reached over and took Jesse's hand, leaned over and whispered, "I remember the day I left town to go to Bible college. Owen and Amos caught me smoking tailor-made cigarettes out behind the barn. Wasn't I a bird to go to Bible school?"

Owen was soon into his message, and no one listened more closely than Alex Grenville. He had been warmed and charmed by the welcome he had received into the family the day before but had been apprehensive about attending church. He himself was not a church member of any sort. He had come from a broken home and had been passed around to relatives who had little enough religion, and what little they had had not rubbed off on him. He had heard of Owen, of course, before he met Wendy, for Owen had some reputation nationally as an evangelist. This, however, was the first time he had ever heard him preach, and he could not help but think, *Well, he may be a preacher, but he looks tough enough to be almost anything.*

Owen began by reading a psalm. "What is man, that thou art mindful of him?" He read slowly, then he looked up after repeating this and said, "This morning we are thinking of the birth of Jesus, and ordinarily we speak of the manger, the miraculous birth, and we think of wise men coming with gifts. However, this morning I would like for us to think of three questions that every one of us in this church building and every man and woman and young person in the world ought to answer. They are very simple. One: Where did I come from? Two: Who am I? And three: Where am I going?"

He began to preach at once, and the words came from his

lips easily. He was filled with an earnestness, and Alex understood at once why he was such a popular preacher. He had expected a ranting sort of preacher and was surprised when Stuart quoted not only from the Bible, but from poetry and history, drawing all the thoughts together. He was pleased to understand quickly that Owen Stuart was a methodical preacher, and Alex liked methodical things. Music, too, is methodical, and the sermon was built and founded on certain basic truths that Owen stressed over and over again.

"Where did I come from?" Owen asked. "The religions of the world have no answer to that, none whatsoever. The modern society in which we live has declared that evolution answers the question, and what does evolution say? That we've come from some sort of primordial soup." Owen grinned then and waved his steel hook in the air. "But where did the soup come from? Nobody's ever been able to answer that. All the scientists and all the laboratories of the world have not been able to create one grain of sand!" He went on stressing that the world and most religions had no answer, and finally he said, "The Bible says that in the beginning God created the heavens and the earth. And the New Testament says, speaking of Jesus, 'All things were made by him; and without him was not any thing made that was made.' In Colossians we read that 'He is before all things, and by him all things consist.' That means," Owen said quietly, "the stars are in their places because he holds them there. The very universe itself is held together by the power of Jesus Christ."

He moved on soon to the next part of his sermon, which asked the question, Who am I? and here, too, he shrugged his shoulders eloquently. "And once again, the religions of the world have no answer as to the nature of man. The world—the liberals and the humanists of this world—tell us that since man is not of God he is nothing but a bit of protoplasm, no different from any other animal. But Scripture says that God made man in his own image. In the image of God, every one of us is like God—not that God has arms and legs—he's a spirit. But we're like him in that we are spiritual beings."

Alex Grenville had never heard preaching like this. The Scriptures seemed to flow easily, without effort, from Owen Stuart's lips, tying together his thoughts and keeping the audience's mind on the essential part of the message. Alex found himself being stirred by the sermon in a way that was unusual for him. Usually only music or art stirred him, or a beautiful woman, but this was different from anything he had expected.

Owen said, "And the last question is, Where am I going? The mystic religions of the East say that we're all headed toward something like a big bowl of hash. Everything loses its identity. I won't be Owen Stuart; you won't be who you are. We just sort of melt together. The worldly people say that we're just a bunch of cold carbohydrates headed for destruction, but Jesus said, 'I go to prepare a place for you, and if I go . . . I will come again.'" Owen stopped and said, "The only hope is in the Scripture and in Jesus Christ. He made us, he keeps us alive spiritually and physically, and he will come to get us to spend eternity with him. Now, let me tell you about this Jesus. . . ."

Grenville listened as Owen spoke of Jesus coming to earth, God in the flesh. He spoke eloquently of Jesus' perfect life, then how he moved among men and women showing love and compassion. And then Owen spoke of his death on the cross and said, "On Christmas we like to think of the manger, which is somehow glorious and wonderful, but that baby in that manger came for one reason: to be crucified for the sins of the world. Prophets said: 'With his stripes we are healed,' and there is no other healing in this world."

The church grew quiet as Owen concluded, and he said, "If there are those here who do not know Jesus as your Savior, I call upon you to do two things. One, repent of your sins. There's nothing else you can do with them. They're too strong for you. Repentance means turning. But you turn *from* one thing *to* something else, so it's not enough to repent. The second thing is to look to Jesus Christ in faith. Come to him, and he will save you as he saved me, as he saved others in this church, as he has saved millions."

The invitation was given, and two people walked to the front of the small church. Grenville felt the pressure of Wendy's eyes. He did not move but stood staring down at the songbook as the invitation hymn was sung and when the pastor announced that the two had given their lives to Christ.

It was with relief that Alex Grenville endured the benediction. He turned, at once, and stepped out into the aisle, waited for Wendy, and the two joined those who filed by to shake hands with the minister.

Then they stepped outside, and the cold sky overhead was illuminated by a pale sun. There was a snap in the air, and strips of snow that had fallen the previous night lined the yard that was now filled with pickups and cars of every description, mostly older models.

Wendy said, "We're going to the hotel now and have Sunday dinner. It's what we always do when we come home." She hesitated, then said, "Did you like the sermon, Alex?"

"Your father's a fine speaker." He shook his head and smiled. "He could have been a president, I think, or a governor at least."

"Daddy would never do that," Wendy said quietly.

"No, I don't suppose he would."

He made an effort, saying, "I've never been to a church exactly like that. On the other hand, I haven't been to many churches—but I'm glad I came."

Wendy felt relief, for she had been apprehensive about Alex's response. Now she gave him a warm smile and said, "Come along; we'll go to the hotel and beat the rush."

The restaurant at the Delight Hotel was dedicated to Stuarts that day. Every year Amos and his brothers paid the difference to Merle Baxter, the owner of the hotel, so that they could have it all to themselves. When the crowd had arrived from church and entered, they found that Mrs. Baxter had, as usual, decorated the restaurant by putting tables together in three long rows and had covered them with white tablecloths. She had even arranged for poinsettias to be brought in and had placed them up and down the tables.

"Let's all find a place," Owen said. "Then we'll have the blessing—and then we eat."

Alex found himself standing at a place with Wendy on his left and a woman seated in a wheelchair on his right. "This is my aunt Lenora Stuart. Aunt Lenora, this is Alex Grenville." Lenora Stuart was fifty years old and had a clear complexion, ash-blonde hair, and hazel eyes. She wore the uniform of a Salvation Army officer, and when Grenville took her hand he found it firm and hard. "I'm glad to know you, Alex."

"Thank you, Mrs. Stuart—or is it General Stuart?"

"Well, I'm not much on titles, but it's Miss, I guess, or just Lenora would be better." With clear eyes, she inspected the young man and apparently liked what she saw. "I guess you got a double dose of Stuarts this morning. I hope you don't feel overwhelmed."

"I've been made to feel very welcome. I have no family of my own—so this is quite a treat for me."

"Well, we've got enough family to go around, so don't worry about that," Lenora said wryly.

At that moment Owen said, "Nobody elected me anything, but let's ask a blessing and get on with the eating."

"Better let me ask it, Owen!" Amos Stuart was to Owen's right. The oldest of the Stuart boys, he was now sixty-one and somewhat overweight. He had light hair that was receding, dark blue eyes, an oval face, and very determined features. Of all the Stuarts he was perhaps the most famous, having won a Pulitzer Prize for reporting. He had a radio program that dealt with political issues and was the friend of presidents and congressmen. Now he grinned at Owen and said, "You preachers tend to be a little bit windy. I could always say a shorter blessing than you could."

"Go ahead, Amos," Owen grinned.

Amos bowed his head, and a silence fell on the room. "Lord," he said in a quiet voice that carried throughout the room, "we thank thee for this food, and we thank thee for this time that we have together. What a blessing it is to have love in a world that doesn't know much about that! Thank you in Jesus' name." He glanced up, nodded shortly, "Now, *that's* the way food should be blessed." He turned and called out, "Bring it on, Mrs. Baxter!"

Agnes Baxter came out at once bearing a large platter. She was followed by four young women and one young man who immediately began loading the table down. The air filled with talking and laughter, and Alex was introduced to foods that he had never tasted before. There was fried chicken, which seemed to be called for by law in the South, and pork chops. He was introduced to pork neck bones and buttermilk potatoes. Afterwards he had his choice of persimmon pudding or shoofly pie.

It was a happy time, for the Stuarts did not see each other as often as they would have liked. They called back and forth, bringing each other up to date on their families; Alex found himself intrigued by Jerry Stuart, who sat right across from him with his wife, Bonnie. Their three small children, the twins Richard and Robert, age six, and Stephanie, age four, were arranged on either side of their parents and behaved very well. Jerry Stuart was a handsome man with black hair, green eyes, and a very direct look. He wore the uniform of a captain in the United States Army Air Corps and kept those who could hear him entertained by tales of his experimental flights.

Owen stood up and said, "You got your dinner down, and now it's time for the speech." He ignored the false moans that went up over the room and said, "We're all making speeches tonight. We're going to hear it from every one of the Stuart brood, but we're going to begin with the youngest and wind up with the old man, Amos, here. Christie, let's hear what you've been doing."

Christie Stuart Castellano, the youngest of the children

of William and Marian Stuart, was an attractive woman of forty-four with blonde hair and dark blue eyes. She wore a well-tailored, pale apricot dress and stood rather shyly. Her husband, Mario Castellano, was beside her, a stocky man with dark hair and eyes, and their two children, Maria, thirteen, and Anthony, eleven, flanked them. "I'm not going to make a speech. Since my husband's a lawyer, I'll let him do all of that, but I want to say only that since God has given me a husband and two beautiful children, I thank him for it. I miss all of you and wish we lived in one town where we could see each other like this every day."

She flushed as Owen groaned, "We'd eat each other up in a week!"

"No, we wouldn't!" she said. She looked down fondly at her sister Lenora, then her eyes ran around the other members of the family and she said, "I'm glad to be a Stuart."

There was a round of applause, and then Owen said, "All right, Gavin, it's your turn."

Gavin Stuart, the youngest male in the family, was forty-eight. He had very dark hair and dark eyes and was married to Heather Spencer, an Englishwoman with fine bones in her face and mild blue eyes. His two children, Phillip and Sidney, were as different as night and day. Phillip, at seventeen, had blonde hair and blue eyes like his mother, but Sidney, fifteen, had dark hair and almost violet eyes and resembled her father greatly. Gavin was president of an airline now and had served in the Lafayette Escadrille in the Great War. He still had the look of eagles, and he spoke briefly, thanking the Lord for his family, wife, son, and daughter, and then sat down.

"All right, Lenora," Owen smiled down the table. "Let's hear it from you, but no sermons. I know you well enough to know you've got one in you."

Lenora Stuart had been injured as a young woman in a fall from a horse. At fifty, she still had some of the fresh beauty, but the severe cut of the uniform spoke of her life. She had gone to Chicago to serve in the Salvation Army and had risen in its ranks. As she spoke from her wheelchair her voice was clear, and she ended by saying, "I will never have children of my own, but it looks as though I'm going to be aunt to a host of them—for which I am very grateful." She looked up, around, and said, "And I, too, am grateful to be a Stuart."

Owen smiled at her, then said, "All right, Pete, your turn."

Pete Stuart had grown up the hard way. He looked like a man who worked every day, which he did. He owned a small oil company in Oklahoma, and his face was burned with the heat of thousands of days, and his hands were gnarled with hard work. He wore a casual jacket, and the necktie looked strange around his neck. He glanced down at his wife, Leslie, and said, "I can't think of a thing to say." He looked over at Stephen, his nineteen-year-old son and said, "Steve, maybe you ought to make this speech."

"Not me, Dad, this is your hour."

"Mona, what about you?"

"I'm a cheerleader. You go on, Dad," Mona said cheerfully.

"Well, you may have to lead a cheer," Pete said. He looked down at his hands, feeling very awkward. "I hate speech making, especially when I make 'em." He hesitated, then said, "You know, when we were grubbing around on the farm as kids, not knowing where the next bite was coming from, I never thought that we'd all survive." He looked over at Owen and at Amos, at the others, then said, "God has been good to us. I remember a line of Scripture; it says: 'The lines are fallen unto me in pleasant places; yea, I have a goodly heritage.'"

He sat down to hearty applause, and then Logan Stuart arose. He said briefly, "I'm the host, and I'm the only one that stayed on the farm. So, I claim that I don't have to make any speeches. I'll just listen, but I'm glad to see you all here. It's good to have Stuarts back in this place."

After Logan, Owen said, "My turn, but I had my say at church this morning. I'm glad to be a Stuart. I'm proud of every one of you." He looked across and said, "Lylah, you're the actress; now, let's have some dramatics."

Lylah flushed and rose to her feet. She was wearing a smartly cut suit, and her hair was carefully fixed, as it always was. She said, "I remember when I left this place to go to Bible school. I wish I'd had sense enough to stay there, but it didn't turn out that way. I guess I can think of a thousand things I wish I'd done differently." Then she laid her hand on Jesse's shoulder and said, "But the one thing I did right was to marry Jesse Hart. I wish," she said, "Adam could be here, and I hope he'll be with us tomorrow. But I thank God for bringing us all together in this place."

"All right, Amos, you're the old man—the eldest son," Owen said. "What have you got to say?"

Amos stood to his feet, looked at his wife, Rose, then over toward Jerry, his son, and at his daughter, Maury, who was flanked by Ted Kingman, her husband, and their children Edward, age six, and Lisa, who was three, and said, "I agree that God has done great things for the Stuarts. . . ." Amos spoke for some time, rather eloquently, of how God had kept them all, preserved them all. Finally, however, he said, "I suppose I look at the news more closely than most of you, since that's my business. I am concerned about the cloud that's over Europe. It's a dark cloud, and it's moving across the ocean. It will not be contained in Europe. Soon America will be under it. I pray to God that we will all be kept through the trials that are coming."

Amos looked around and then smiled. "We'll all be leaving here, some of us later on in the afternoon, but I'll be here, the Lord willing, next Christmas for the meeting of the clan." He paused briefly, then said, "I think it might be well if we prayed once again for God to watch over us all. I feel apprehensive about this decade, the forties. I think it's going to bring something that the world, perhaps, has never seen before. Without being a prophet of gloom, I join with many others who see this as a time when America will pass through a fiery crucible, and I want to ask God to bring those of our blood through it."

They all rose, bowed their heads, and Amos prayed briefly,

calling each member of the family by name, his brothers and sisters, their wives, the in-laws, the grandchildren. Finally, he stopped. Lifting his head, he smiled around at those of the Stuart blood and said, "God will continue to be with us."

The next day was Christmas. It was impossible to get everyone into the small living room of the old home place. They filled the house up from top to bottom, and after they had a breakfast prepared by many hands, the opening of the presents took place. They had long ago agreed not to buy anything expensive for these days, so it was a time of passing of small mementos. And after it was all over some stayed to clean up the debris while others went out.

Outside Wendy and Alex walked through the snow that had fallen the night before—only two inches—but it made the world into a wonderland. The bare trees that had been black and almost ugly were now glittering with a pristine whiteness, and tiny icicles gleamed like glittering diamonds. The two made their way down a pathway that led to a small pond. They spoke quietly, as all sounds seemed to be deadened. When they passed over a field unmarked by any sign of human habitation, Alex said quietly, "This is beautiful. I missed out on this growing up in the city."

"It is pretty, isn't it?" Wendy looked around and said, "Being in the country does something for me. Things are so busy and noisy in the city. It's good to get out and just listen to the quietness."

Alex glanced over at her, admiring the sheen of her auburn hair as it caught the glow of the morning sun. She had on a red stocking cap with a fuzzy ball on the end, and it dangled down her back, swaying when she walked. His present to her had been a soft, powder-blue sweater, and she wore it now. The garment outlined her trim form, and he said, "You look very pretty—but you always do."

Turning to him, Wendy smiled and took his hand. She wore mittens, and he wore the fur-lined gloves he had received from her. Squeezing his hand she said, "It's been good, hasn't it?"

"Yes, it has. I hope we can do this every year." It was the closest that Alex had ever come to mentioning a permanent relationship, and Wendy glanced at him quickly. If he had asked her to marry him, she knew she would have said yes. She knew, also, that her family did not approve since Alex was not a Christian. *But I could help him!* she thought, her eyes lingering on his face for a moment. *He's a good man deep down, and all he needs is someone to pray for him and show him the way.*

They moved on through the woods, stopping once when a large fox trotted out fifty feet ahead. It gave them a sharp look, then without concern, disappeared into the underbrush. "He's pretty bold, isn't he?" Alex said. They stopped when they got to the pond and took time to throw sticks and stones out to break the skim of ice that was holding up the fine, light carpet of dazzling white snow. Then he turned to her and said, "I guess we'll have to get back."

"I suppose so."

He took her in his arms and kissed her, and there was an insistence in his caress that both drew her and repelled her. She surrendered for a moment to the pressure of his lips, found her arms creeping around his neck. When he grew more insistent, she drew away whispering, "We'd better go back."

Alex gave her an odd look, and a wry grin touched his lips. "The last of the Puritans, that's what you are! Well, come along." They made their way back, and at noon, when they left the farm, waving at those who had come out to see them off, Wendy said, "Thank you for coming with me, Alex."

"No, it was good of you to have me." He drove silently for a while, and said, "We're very different. I've had no home life at all, and you have warmth and love and your people around you. That's made a difference in us."

"Yes, I know."

"I'm not sure," he said slowly, "that you know how much, Wendy. Your people are very religious; so are you—and I'm not."

Timidly Wendy touched his arm. "You will be. I just know you will."

He did not answer, but there was a slight frown on his face as he steered the Cord down the snow-covered road. He did not know how he felt. There was a youthfulness and a virtue and a goodness in this woman that part of him craved, and yet, he still knew that deep down she had values that he could not even understand, much less embrace. Still, he was a man who had had success with women, and turning to smile at her, he was secure in this knowledge.

"Adam called," Lylah said as she came out to stand on the porch beside Jesse, Gavin, Owen, and Amos. She added, "He can't come. The airport's closed down. They're having the beginnings of a bad storm in California. It'd be too dangerous to fly."

"Probably best," Jesse said quietly. He was disappointed but said no more. The five stood for some time watching the dogs as they treed a rabbit out at the beginning of the woods. Lylah said, "Do you remember when you came to the hospital the day Adam was born?"

Gavin said, "I've never forgotten it."

Amos turned to look at Lylah, "Yes, I remember it very well. The nurse, she was just a tiny bit of a thing, and she didn't know what to make of all of us." He put his arm around Lylah and grinned at her. "I didn't know much about babies then. He was so new that I tried to think of something nice to say, but all the time I was thinking, he looks like five pounds of hamburger."

Lylah's thoughts went back to that time, and she said, "I couldn't have made it without you all through the years—and Jesse. I remember what you said, Amos, when you picked Adam up for the first time."

"I don't remember that. What did I say?"

"You looked down into his little face and said, 'He has a goodly heritage, Lylah.'" Tears came to her eyes and she shook her head. "I've held onto that all this time. I believed it, sometimes when it didn't seem possible."

"What is it, Lylah? Is something wrong, I mean more than Adam's trouble with the law?"

"Yes, it's more than that. He's troubled about the war in Europe, especially about Germany."

"Because he knows his father was a German?" Owen asked gently.

"Yes, he hasn't said anything about it, but I know it bothers him. I see him reading the papers, and after he reads about Germany invading another country, he just sort of turns me off. He turns the world off, doesn't he, Jesse?"

"He's a very sensitive young man." Jesse nodded, his face utterly serious. "I wish I could've done more to help him."

Immediately Lylah said, "You've done all that any father could have done!"

They stood for a while, occupied with thoughts of Adam Stuart. They were a close-knit family, close in blood, close in emotions, and finally it was Owen who said, "God will bring him through, Lylah. He'll bring us all through this thing."

It was beginning to snow. Tiny flakes fluttered down through the air, glittering as they were swept along by a moaning wind that was rising in the east, driving them into swirls around the trees, and then into the darkest corners of the woods. They grew larger, some almost as large around as quarters, and finally the five turned and walked back inside the house.

4

TOO HIGH A PRICE

As the story has it, Nero fiddled while Rome burned. This incident may be part myth, but certainly America during the year of 1940 went about business as usual while the conflict in Europe escalated into what was obviously becoming a global war. The Soviets attacked Finland and crushed that courageous people after a tremendous struggle. Winston Churchill replaced Neville Chamberlain as prime minister in Britain and in his first speech said, "I have nothing to offer but blood, toil, tears, and sweat." Almost at that same time the German army invaded the Low Countries, demonstrating the effectiveness of the blitzkrieg, or "lightning war."

Pushed back by ruthless and successful German advances, British, French, and Belgian divisions were trapped at Dunkirk. All Germany had to do was advance—but for some reason never fully explained, Adolf Hitler ordered a halt to the assault. The British Royal Navy led a successful exodus of 340,000 Allied troops. While averting complete disaster, the Allies lost nearly 130,000 dead, wounded, or captured. In a speech to the House of Commons, Winston Churchill proclaimed that "Wars are not won by evacuation." And then in ringing tones he declared the intention of the government to carry out the battle against the Nazis: "We shall fight on the seas and oceans; we shall fight, with growing confidence and growing strength, in the air, we shall defend our island, whatever the cost may be, we shall fight on the beaches, we shall fight on the landing grounds, we shall fight in the fields and in the streets, we shall fight in the hills; we shall never surrender!"

Well might the British need this sort of resolution, for the Germans took Paris, forcing that country to sign a humiliating armistice. The Germans immediately began an aerial blitz over Britain in July, and Hermann Göring was astonished when Royal Air Force planes flew a bombing raid all the way to Berlin. The attack lasted three hours and caught Hitler totally by surprise. He had been assured that British bombers would never reach Berlin.

While the war raged in Europe, life went on in America. Americans went to see Henry Fonda starring in *The Grapes of Wrath*, the movie based on Steinbeck's novel about Okies pushing toward California in search of a better living. Oldsmobile came out with a car that had no shift, a *hydromatic*, as it was called. Walt Disney produced *Pinocchio*, which taught the evils of untruth. Wendell Willkie was nominated for president by the Republicans and threatened to give President Roosevelt a hard fight for the highest office in America.

The average price of a home for a middle-class family was $6,500 and was usually bought at 4.5 percent interest. Ads jumped off the pages of magazines such as *Saturday Evening Post* and *Life* assuring housewives that happy marriages depended on gleaming bathrooms, dust-free living rooms, and punctual evening meals. On the radio a catchy tune had millions of Americans singing, "I'm Chiquita Banana and I've come to say, bananas have to ripen in a certain way." It ended with a caution that bananas love a tropical climate, "So you should never put bananas in the refrigerator." The refrigerator they were likely to use was a Crosley Shelvador that sold for $99.50. And everyone was humming, "Pepsi Cola hits the spot, twelve full ounces, that's a lot."

So America turned its eyes away from Europe hoping that somehow the war would go away. Deep down in the hearts of most Americans, however, was the knowledge that what was happening in Germany and Poland and Austria and all over Europe was *not* going away.

Wendy Stuart woke slowly, coming out of a short but very deep sleep. The pale sunlight that slanted down from the high window in her room was filled with millions of dancing motes as it fanned out over the bed, which practically filled the small bedroom, and warmed the young woman's face. The heat of it caused her to stir, and she muttered something, then turned over and pushed her face into the pillow seeking to go back to sleep. However, the thoughts of the previous night's triumph came to her, and she rolled over, then sat up and blinked sleepily with a smile on her lips.

"It was my best concert!" she said aloud—then shook her head and ran her hand through her hair, laughing softly. "I must be going crazy—talking to myself."

Getting out of bed, she moved to the tiny bathroom where she quickly showered, washed her hair, then dried it, all the time thinking of the previous evening. She had sung with the symphony—her first full-scale concert. Alex had directed, of course, and the auditorium had been comfortably filled. She had sung excerpts from *Carmen*, and her voice had never been as strong and clear.

As she was putting the last touches on her hair, she leaned forward and studied herself in the mirror. Her eyes were slightly puffy from loss of sleep, for she had practiced long and hard for this concert, and she knew that she had reached some kind of a plateau. There had been influential people in that audience, and her career was about to take off—or at least so she felt.

She rose and put on a gray skirt and a frilly white silk blouse, then sat down at the telephone and dialed her mother's number.

"Mother? I've got to tell you about the concert. It was wonderful!"

At the other end of the line, Allie Stuart sat listening as

Wendy described the evening in detail. When she finally had a chance she exclaimed, "I wish I could've been there, Wendy. I know it must've been marvelous!"

"It was the best I ever sang, and Alex was outstanding with the symphony!"

"Did the two of you go out and celebrate?"

"Oh, yes—and we're going out again tonight! Alex said he has something to tell me, but it's a secret."

"You have no idea what it is?"

Actually, Wendy did have an idea. Alex had behaved peculiarly in the past week, hinting at times that big things were going to happen. He had been almost secretive, and Wendy had finally come to the conclusion that he had made up his mind to ask her to marry him. She hesitated for one moment, then said breathlessly, "Mother, I–I think he's going to pop the question tonight, as they say in romantic novels."

"Ask you to marry him?"

"Yes, I think so! Oh, he hasn't actually said anything about it—but he keeps hinting around that tonight he's got something big. And what can be bigger than getting married?"

Allie hesitated. She and Owen were disturbed over Wendy's choice. "I know you love him, Wendy," she said quietly, "and I wouldn't want to discourage you for anything—but have you talked with him about the things of the Lord?"

"Well, not really, but I will. After we get married, I'm going to insist on his going to church."

"If he won't go with you now, why do you think he'll go after you are married?" Allie asked. She then added, "Most men will do more for a woman before they marry than afterward."

"Oh, Mother, it'll work, you'll see! He loves me—I know he does, and I love him so much!"

Allie could not find it in her heart to press her point. She only said, "Your father and I will be praying for you. Getting married is such a big decision. Next to finding God, it's the biggest decision anyone ever makes on this earth, I think."

"Of course, Mother, I understand that, but deep down

Alex knows that he needs God. I just know he does. I haven't wanted to press him, but Dad's sermon at Christmas touched him, and he's mentioned it many times. It made such an impact on him that he still remembers the outline." She laughed, a trilling sound on the telephone, and said, "'Where did I come from? Who am I? and Where am I going?' Alex quotes that to me all the time—and he's read so much philosophy you wouldn't believe it. He's really thinking about religion."

This did not pacify Allie, but she could not think of a way to warn Wendy any more clearly. "Be very careful, Dear," she said, "and call me!"

"I will, Mother. Tell Dad I love him—and Will and Woody. Good-bye!"

Replacing the phone in the cradle, Wendy sat for a moment thinking of the conversation. *I know Mom and Dad are worried about me*, she thought. *But it'll be all right, they'll see.* She rose at once and put on her coat and went down to the studio at the school, where she practiced all morning and studied for the rest of the afternoon. All the time, however, she was thinking of the evening they would have together, she and Alex, and she dreamed of the moment when he would say simply, "I love you, Wendy, and I want you to marry me."

The best place to eat in Nashville was Jimmy Kelly's, and it was to this spot that Alex took Wendy for dinner that night. She had dressed carefully for the occasion, knowing that it would be a memorable night. She wore a light aqua dress made of silk, trimmed with silver, and the earrings of jade that Alex had given her matched perfectly. As they pulled up in front of the restaurant, she said nervously, "This looks expensive, Alex!"

Alex leaned over and kissed her on the cheek. "A night like this comes but once in a blue moon!" he grinned. "Now, let's go inside and let them see what we look like." He stepped out of the Cord, and at the same time a doorman opened the door for Wendy.

"Have you ever been here before?" Wendy asked as they moved inside.

"Yes, twice. It's an odd kind of place," he mused as the maitre d' came up to them. "You have to buy a good table!" He handed the waiter a bill and was rewarded by a smile. "Why, of course, Sir, right this way!"

He took them to a fine table right on the edge of the dance floor, not far away from the orchestra, and they sat down and studied the menu.

After ordering steaks, the specialty of the house, Alex turned to Wendy. "Someone ought to come by and ask for your autograph after your performance last night." He saw that his remark flustered her and shook his head. "You have no ego at all, do you, Wendy? I never saw a woman get so flustered by a simple compliment."

Wendy was pleased by his compliment far more than if he had said something about her appearance. She desperately wanted to succeed in her profession, for she knew that Alex was going up in the music world, and she wanted to go with him, side by side.

After they had eaten the meal, they danced for a while. The bandleader was a tall young man named Harry James. He played trumpet like no one Wendy had ever heard. "He's so good, isn't he?"

"Yes, he is. I expect he'll be going up in the music world."

They stayed for three hours dancing and talking, and during this time Alex drank most of the wine that he had ordered. Despite his urgings, Wendy steadfastly refused. She had never taken a drink, and he teased her by saying, "Don't you know that Prohibition is over? But you're a preacher's daughter and that makes a difference."

"I've seen so many lives get ruined by drinking. You remember that young French-horn player? What was his name— Larry Johnson, wasn't it? You said he had more talent than any young man you'd ever seen, but he didn't make it because he drank too much."

"Larry just didn't know how to handle it."

"I think I'd rather not even learn whether I can handle it or not. If I don't take the first one, I'll never have problems with the second one, will I?"

"That's one way of looking at it. Come on; let's dance again."

Finally, they left the restaurant and got into the Cord, which the doorman brought around. Alex drove away singing, "I'll Never Smile Again," which the band had played. He did not have much of a singing voice, but he did have perfect pitch, and when Wendy joined in with him, adding her rich contralto, he grinned and said, "It sounds better when you help! Come on; sit by me. I'm lonesome way over here."

Wendy moved over, and he put his hand on her knee, caressing it gently. She did not protest for the moment, but it made her very alert.

Finally he took her to her room and said, "I want to come in. I haven't told you the big secret yet."

"Well, I suppose it'll be all right, but it's very late. You can't stay long."

Alex didn't answer. He got out of the car, opened the door, and led her inside. They took the elevator to the second floor, got off, and she moved to the door of her room.

"Let me get that!" Alex took the key from her, opened the door, then stepped back. Wendy moved inside and turned the light on, glad that she had cleaned up the place. "Would you like some coffee?" she said.

"No, I don't want coffee; I want to talk."

"All right." A flush came to Wendy's face. There was an intensity in Alex that she had not seen before. "What is it, Alex?"

He removed his coat and hat, tossed them on a chair, then turned to her, his eyes gleaming with excitement. "Something I've got to tell you. I haven't been sure of it until today, but now it's certain."

"What is it, Alex? I've never seen you so excited!"

Reaching out, he took her by the arms and held her very tightly. He had strong hands and sometimes did not know his own strength. "It's the biggest thing that's ever happened to me, Wendy," he said, and shook his head almost in disbelief. He looked very handsome, trim, and fit, his eyes alight with whatever it was that was stirring him so. "I've been offered a wonderful position!"

"A position? You mean you're going to leave teaching?"

"Yes, a new symphony is being formed in New York, and I've been asked to take over."

"How wonderful!" Wendy exclaimed. She was very conscious of the pressure of his hands on her arms, and she said, "Come over here and sit down. Tell me all about it!"

"All right, but I'm so excited I don't know where to start." He began telling her how he had been approached some months ago on the possibility of leaving teaching to form and direct a new symphony. His hands moved excitedly, and from time to time he touched her as if to assure himself of her presence.

"And it's not just a symphony. It will be broadcast over radio nationwide once a week for an hour."

"Why, that's wonderful! You'll be famous, Alex!"

"I suppose I will, but here's the part that I've saved for the last." He smiled at her, his teeth even and white against the tan that he somehow maintained all year long. Suddenly he reached out and took her hands and squeezed them. "The symphony will have a soloist, and I've demanded the right to choose who it will be." He lifted her hands, kissed both of them, and said, "Guess who I'm going to have?"

"You don't mean—you don't mean *me*, do you? Why, you could have *anybody!*"

"I don't want anybody; I want you, Wendy Stuart." His eyes flashed as he said, "You don't know how much talent you have, Wendy. You've barely touched the surface. You could be the greatest singer this country's ever had, and I want us to be together. We can go right to the top! There's no limit!"

Wendy was thrilled over the news. She had not expected anything like this even though she was not unaware of her talent. She knew she had a good voice and had been wondering how she would be able to make a living. She had no desire for popular forms of entertainment such as movies, but this was *exactly* what she had always wanted.

Alex fell silent. He lowered his gaze and seemed to be thinking hard, but he looked up quickly and said, "Wendy, I want you to go with me. I want us to be together!"

Wendy gasped, and her eyes grew starry. "Oh, Alex, I'm so happy!" she said. He kissed her then, pulling her close, and for once she did not protest his demanding caresses. She pulled her head back and said, "You don't have to eat me alive!"

He laughed and said, "You're the loveliest thing I've ever seen! Now, we're going to be really one!"

"I don't want a really big wedding," Wendy said. "I've thought about it a lot, and some people seem to like that, but I don't really see the need of it. We can go home, and Dad can marry us in the living room. Would that be all right with you?" She looked up and saw that her words had some sort of strange effect on Alex. He stared at her for a long time, and the smile was gone from his face. "What's the matter," she said, "you don't like that idea?"

Alex dropped her hands and stood to his feet. There was a strain in his face, and he seemed to find difficulty in speaking. She stood up, and when she did he said in a strangely tense voice, "Wendy, I love you, but we can't be married. Not for a long time."

"Not be married?" Wendy said, blinking in confusion. "I thought you said—"

"I said we'd be together, but I got this opportunity because I didn't demand a lot of money. Someday I'll be able to demand more, but right now it's going to be tight for a few years. All the money is going to the orchestra and to the broadcast."

"But it doesn't take that much money!"

Alex hesitated. "I can't marry you. I'm just not a marrying

man, I guess." He put his arms around her, or tried to, but she stepped back and his eyes half narrowed. "We can't go on like this, the way we have been."

A silence fell across the room. Temptation, keen and strong, touched Wendy Stuart as it never had. She had never loved a man before, and as she looked at Alex, she thought, *I'm going to lose him if I don't agree.* Everything in her longed to say yes, but she finally whispered, "I can't live with you, Alex; it would be wrong."

This seemed to strike against Alex. He had half suspected it would be this way, but he had put all of his hopes in the new arrangement thinking, *If I can just get her the job as soloist, that will be enough.* He saw that she was pale, but her lips were drawn together tightly, and her back was as straight as a ramrod. "I suppose I've got my answer," he said slowly. "It'll have to be my way, Wendy."

She took a deep breath and said, "It's too high a price, Alex; I won't do it."

Silence fell over them. Pain seemed to come from deep down in Wendy's breast. She saw a shadow cross Alex's face. He stared at the floor for what seemed like a long time. The Seth Thomas clock made a steady cadence that seemed to grow louder in the silence. Alex looked up with one quick, final gesture and said quietly, "I guess that's it then. Goodbye, Wendy." He turned and picked up his hat and coat, slipped into them, and when he got to the door he opened it, stepped out, and did not look back.

The sound of the door closing seemed to trigger a final sorrow in Wendy, and she began to tremble. Turning, she fell blindly on the couch and drew herself into a fetal position. The raw sobs coming from her throat she could not stop, and the pain in her heart felt as if it would break it in two.

Pulling up in his '36 Ford pickup, Clint Stuart automatically registered the sound of the engine, noting that it was not running as smoothly as it should. *It needs a new set of valves pretty soon, I guess.* He got out and parked the truck in front of Shorty's Gas Station and Grocery Store. On a bench outside, two older men were sitting, their faces reddened by the cool breeze of September. They wore what was a uniform in their world, faded Toughnut overalls, cumbersome ankle-top shoes, and bill caps that they shoved back on their heads. One of the caps had the Coca Cola logo on it, and another read in faded letters, New York World's Fair 1939.

"Hello, Ed, Micah!" Clint greeted the pair. He stopped for a moment and grinned at them. "You still arguing about who shot the most possums this year?"

The taller of the two leaned back and said, "He ain't never gonna catch up with me, Clint!" Then he shifted and said, "You wanna come by and take a look at that Chevy of mine when you get a chance? Billy, down at the garage, said he couldn't do nothin' for it."

"Sure, I'll take a look." Clint moved on inside, and the taller of the two said, "That fella can fix anything that's got parts! Now, about them possums. . . ."

For the next few minutes Clint collected groceries and supplies from the shelves, and while Mel Stottlemeyer totaled them up on a small tablet, he listened as the sound of Jimmy Rogers spilled out of the wooden radio that sat on a shelf nailed to the wall.

I'm a thousand miles away from home
Waiting for a train. . . .

The melancholy of the song seemed to touch Clint, although he did not know why. Lately he had noticed a restlessness in his spirit that was unusual for him. He had always been reaching out to things, studying this and that, had taken every course he could on radios and had even invented a few simple things that never came to much, but still, the sound of the song seemed to touch a strain in him that rose and swelled. *Sometimes I wish I were a thousand miles away from home*, he thought. Then when Stottlemeyer said, "That'll be $4.38, Clint," he snapped out of his reverie, reached into his pocket, and fingered through the bills until he found four ones and made the rest out in change.

"You going to the ball game tonight?" Stottlemeyer asked.

"Don't guess so. I got some studying to do."

Stottlemeyer, a thin, wispy, middle-aged man, scratched his head in puzzlement. "You're *always* studying, Clint. Ain't you ever gonna learn enough so you can quit?"

"I hope not, Mel. See you later!"

Moving back outside the store, he put the groceries in the pickup seat, climbed in, started the engine, and pulled away. He drove down Elm Street to where Carol Davidson lived with her father, stopped the truck, then went up on the porch. He turned the brass knob that rang the bell, and when Ralph Davidson came to the door, he said, "Hello, Mr. Davidson, is Carol here?"

"Yes, she's helping me fix supper. Come on in, Clint."

Clint followed Davidson to the kitchen and was soon sitting down on a chair, eating odds and ends that were going into the evening meal. Davidson, listening quietly, peeled potatoes as Clint talked of his day. Ralph was only forty-five, but a heart attack several months earlier had almost killed him, and now he moved carefully and spoke in a faint voice. He'd lost his wife when Carol was only six, and Clint understood that Carol was very dependent on her father. *Be hard on Carol if Ralph dies*, he thought. *She still looks to him for everything.*

Carol came in, and her eyes lit up at the sight of Clint. She was a small woman of nineteen with rich black hair and large, beautifully shaped eyes. She had a full figure for such a petite girl, and she moved with grace. "You're early," she said, coming to stand beside him. She reached up and smoothed his hair, saying, "You need a haircut."

"Can't afford it."

"I'll cut it after supper."

"Al Brown charges $1.25. How much do you charge?"

"You can buy me a milkshake at Benton's after the movie. Now, you go play checkers with Dad while I finish getting supper."

"He's beat me too many times," Ralph said. "I'll go read the paper."

As soon as her father was out of the kitchen, Carol pulled Clint's head down and kissed him, saying, "There, I wanted to do that when I first came in! Daddy sort of puts a damper on things."

"Don't talk about your dad like that. I've got to learn to please him. If he's going to be my father-in-law, we've got to get along."

Carol laughed. She was wearing a white apron over a blue, print dress, and her hair was covered by a cloth that she had tied over it. "I just washed my hair and set it before you came. I must look awful."

"You look good to me!"

For a time, as she prepared the meal, he spoke idly of his day, and finally he said, "Carol, did you hear about Wendy? No, I don't guess you would have."

"Wendy, your cousin? What about her?"

Clinton picked up a slice of carrot, bit off an inch of it, and chewed it thoroughly. He shook his head. "Well, you know she was just about engaged to that fella we met last Christmas at the reunion. You remember him?"

"Yes, his name is Alex, isn't it?"

"Right, Alex Grenville. It's not very good news, and I got it sort of third hand. Pa got it from Uncle Owen, who got it from Wendy."

"Did they break up?"

"That's about it. It sounds like he dumped her. I think he wanted more of her before marriage than she was willing to give."

Carol was mixing biscuit dough. She stopped suddenly and turned to stare at him. "I'm sorry to hear it. She was so happy. She talked about nothing else but getting married. We had quite a talk after dinner that day, and she was so proud of him."

"Well, it's all over, and she did the right thing."

Carol looked down at her hands and forearms, which were covered with white flour. Picking up the dough, she began to knead it thoughtfully, not thinking of what she was doing. Almost automatically she rolled it and, picking up an empty can, began to cut out circles of dough. Finally, she seemed to come to a decision. "Clint, let's get married!"

"Why, we've talked about that before. We've got to wait until I'm better able to take care of you, Carol!"

"I don't *care* about that!" There was an urgency, a fervent note in Carol's voice. She wiped her hands on a dish towel, then came over and took his hand and held it. She pressed it to her cheek and turning her head to one side, she made a most fetching picture. "I don't want to have to beg you. I hate women who chase men—but I love you, Clint! I want to get married and have you all to myself and start a family."

They talked for some time, but when they left the house after supper, Clint was disturbed. Nothing had been settled, and as he started up the Ford and they drove to the Elite, his thoughts were on Carol's face. *I love her*, he thought. *What am I waiting for? But I hate not to be able to take care of her better than I can now. Maybe if I got an extra job. . . .*

The marquee of the Elite Theater proclaimed the name of the film in garish yellow lights. *Knute Rockne*, starring Pat O'Brien and Ronald Reagan. Clint stepped to the box office, put down his dollar, and got two tickets. "Come along," he said to Carol, "we're a little bit late." He led her inside the theater, and the young man who took tickets grinned and said, "Picture just started, Clint; you better hurry!"

Clint took Carol's arm, and they made their way out of the lobby and groped in the darkness until they found two seats. He allowed her to go in first, then sat beside her on the aisle.

For the next ninety minutes, they sat engrossed in the story of the great Notre Dame coach and his star football player, George Gipp. The movie revolved around an incident in the life of Gipp, who contracted a fatal disease. On his deathbed, he reached up and gasped, "Sometimes, Coach, when the team's not doing good, tell them to win one for the Gipper."

Then later in the film, at a critical moment when the team was losing, the iron, square-faced Pat O'Brien, portraying Rockne, put out this challenge to the team. The Fighting Irish did go out and win one for the Gipper.

Clint and Carol left the theater and made their way down to Benton's Ice Cream Parlor, where Clint had a chocolate sundae, which he consumed noisily, and Carol ate a strawberry sundae a little bit more delicately. They talked about the movie and finally left in the Ford pickup. When they got to her house, he shut the engine off, and she waited for him to get out, but he sat twisting the wheel nervously. "I've got something to tell you, Carol."

Noting the seriousness in his voice, Carol asked, "What is it?"

"I got my notice today—my draft notice."

For one moment, Carol could not understand what he meant. No men in their area had actually been drafted yet, although she understood that the numbers had been drawn back in October. "Oh, no!" she finally whispered wanly and took his arm. "You're not going into the army!"

"No choice about it," Clint shrugged. "I got to do it; it's the law!"

"When do you have to go?"

"In a month or five weeks, I guess."

The harvest moon was large and orange, and they watched it through the glass of the pickup. November had turned cold, and the cab cooled off quickly. Carol finally took a deep breath. "Clint, let's get married!"

Clint had known she would say this. He had his arguments ready and began at once. "It would be no life for you. I'll be going to basic training and I couldn't be with you then. Even after I'm out of that, if you did get to come to me, it would just be to some fleabag of a hotel. . . ."

But the more he spoke, the more Carol pleaded. Finally, she put her arms around him and drew his head down and kissed him. She was crying as she said, "I can't live without you, Clint! Please, let's get married! We'll have each other for whatever time there is. I don't care where we have to live as long as I have you!"

Clint had purposed to deny what he knew she would ask, but as he held her soft form in his arms and heard her pleas and tasted the salt of her tears as he kissed her cheek, he changed his mind. "All right," he whispered quietly. "I love you so much, Carol, and I shouldn't let you do this—but I'm just selfish, I guess."

"We're *not* selfish!" Carol kissed him again and clung to him fiercely. "We'll have each other, and nothing else matters. . . ."

From that moment on, things moved rapidly. No one seemed very surprised when Clint and Carol agreed to marry. They had a wedding in the small church with Reverend Crabtree performing the ceremony. They had a weeklong honeymoon at Petit Jean Mountain with nothing really there but a lodge. They went horseback riding and rode in a canoe. The nights were theirs, and both of them were almost able to forget what would happen soon.

When they returned from their honeymoon, they lived at her house. "I'd rather we had a place of our own," Clint said, "but I'll be gone soon, and you need to take care of your dad."

Carol moved to hold him and whispered, "I'll miss you so much, but I'll be here when you get back."

Clint held her close, stroked her hair, and said nothing. There was nothing to say, for the war in Europe had reached out with a mailed fist and struck his life, shattering it, breaking it, but not, he hoped, beyond repair. *This will be over one day*, he thought. *I'll serve my time, then I'll come back and Carol and I will have a family. We can have a real marriage then.* He turned to her and held her close, putting this idea firmly in his mind as she leaned against him.

5

MAN WITHOUT A STAR

As Adam Stuart paused in front of the UCLA administration building, a sense of something close to fear seized him. He was not afraid of many things, owing partly to the fact that he had been raised in affluence. As the son of the owners of Monarch Motion Pictures Studios, he had been accustomed to having not only what he required but, for the most part, anything he wanted. He had made his way through the public school system of Los Angeles without great difficulty, not that he studied hard, but this had not been necessary. He had a brilliance that carried him through with a minimum of studying. As a matter of fact, he had never taken a book home throughout all his years of high school.

As he looked at the rising edifice of concrete, steel, and reflective tiles, the blank windows that gave back the rays of the early morning sun seemed to have a malevolence about them. The moment he had opened his mailbox and read the note that stated unemotionally, "Report to the office of Dr. Zimmerman immediately," he knew that trouble was brewing. He had the impulse to turn and leave, pack his things, and get away from the campus, but some faint hope stirred in him, and he mounted the steps and entered the building, his chin held high.

A young woman sat at the outer desk, which contained absolutely nothing on its surface except a telephone with an intercom and a single book. The woman herself was rather plain and wore a dress that looked as if it had not come from an expensive shop. She had mousy brown hair and a prim mouth, but admiration was in her brown eyes as she looked at the trim form of the young man who stood before her. He was wearing a pair of gray flannel slacks and a royal blue sweater over a white shirt. The royal blue set off the electric, light blue eyes that he put on her, and her heart missed a beat as she said, "Yes, may I help you?"

"I have a notice to meet with Dr. Zimmerman. My name is Adam Stuart."

"Yes, I'll see if Dr. Zimmerman will see you." The young woman pressed a button and said, "Dr. Zimmerman, Adam Stuart is here to see you."

"Send him in!"

Adam gave the girl a smile, which caused her heart to turn over, more or less, then he moved toward the door to his left. His mind was racing as he tried to summon his arguments. Adam had been able to talk himself out of most of his problems, including many traffic tickets and various problems with the administration of his high school. Those he could not talk himself out of were usually solved by his mother or his father.

As soon as he entered, his eyes swept the room quickly, taking in the austerity of it all. Each side of the room was lined with bookshelves, and the books matched in color and size. It was almost as if they were imitation books chosen to match the decor of the office. Exactly in the center of the room, set back toward a large window that allowed the pale yellow sunlight to filter through, a metal desk with a glass top caught those reflections, spread them out, and blinded him for a moment. On each side of the room were two chairs that matched, and one chair of the same design, of brown leather, sat in front of the desk. There were two pictures on the wall. One was a painting of a strong-faced woman dressed in a costume that was obviously foreign and out of date. The other was a reproduction of the self-portrait of Rembrandt. It was a strange combination of art, and Adam wondered fleetingly why those two pictures adorned the walls. He turned his attention then to Dr. Zimmerman, who sat silently watching him.

Dr. Karl Zimmerman was a second-generation American who had been educated in Austria. He was a slight man, not tall, but of such an erect posture that there was something faintly military in his appearance. He had light blonde hair, and his blue eyes were as light as Adam Stuart's. He was close-shaven, and his fair hair was fixed firmly in place, not a hair out of position. He held his hands placed flat on the table, as if preparing to stand, but he did not.

"Mr. Stuart?"

"Yes, Dr. Zimmerman, I'm Adam Stuart."

"Sit down, Mr. Stuart."

Adam slipped into the seat in front of him. It was lower than the seat that Zimmerman sat in, which gave the dean the higher ground. Adam knew that Zimmerman had arranged it like this to give himself an advantage, and he vaguely resented this. Looking across at the dean, he remembered stories about how tough the man was, and what little hope he had brought with him seemed to evaporate as he stared into the icy blue eyes of the official.

He looks like a hanging judge, Adam thought. *And if what I've heard about him is true, I don't have any more chance than a snowball in a desert.*

The rumors about Zimmerman all portrayed him as a man who was fair enough but absolutely without mercy. He would look at the grades on the paper and close his mind to every human consideration. Little was known about his background, but his German heritage was known, and with the rise of Hitler this had given him the nickname Professor Hitler. Zimmerman, if he heard these rumors, never spoke of them, nor did he ever allow them to intimidate him.

"I have your records, Mr. Stuart." Zimmerman pulled a folder out of a file to his right, opened it, and stared at it for a moment. "It is a very poor record, I regret to say."

What am I supposed to say to that? Adam thought. But with

the dean staring right at his past, as it was reduced to ink on paper, he could only say, "Yes, Sir, that's right."

Zimmerman had expected more of a defense than this. He lifted his head slightly and studied the young man before him, taking in the fair hair, the light, icy blue eyes, and the determination. He was looking for a weakness, which was his custom. But in the features of Adam Stuart, he saw none.

"I have the results of your IQ tests. There's nothing wrong with your mind," Zimmerman said. "Therefore the fault has to lie with your character."

Once again there was a pause and Adam felt obliged to say, "I'm afraid you may be right, Doctor." He had decided to stay humble, at least while there was a chance that he might escape the wrath of the dean's office. "I haven't given my best efforts to my work, I'm afraid."

"And why is that, Mr. Stuart?"

"I–" Suddenly Adam found himself unable to formulate an answer. The cold eyes of Zimmerman bored into him, and he could not meet them despite his intentions. He dropped his own eyes and shifted nervously in the chair. *Why didn't I study more?* he demanded desperately of himself. He had come to college determined to do better than he had in high school, but he had found himself instantly diverted by several factors. His own good looks had drawn the beautiful young women of UCLA to him without effort on his part. His intelligence, he had assumed, would allow him to get by without study-ing—which had proved to be a fallacy. And in truth, emotion-ally he was so disturbed about the war in Europe that although he never spoke of it, he had not been able to put his mind on his studies. He had gone out for the track team, and the coach had been wildly excited, for he was an excellent runner, but poor grades had eliminated him from that outlet.

"Well, Mr. Stuart, I'm waiting for your explanation."

Desperately Adam shrugged and said, "I have no justifica-tion, Sir." He hesitated for only a moment and said, "I suppose some of us just have difficulty adjusting to college life."

"I see." The bleak, brief statement gave Adam no hope. Zimmerman stared at the young man and despite the hard expression on his face felt a moment's sympathy. In truth, he was not a man without compassion, but he had come up the hard way. He had grown up in a Germany that was suffering after the Great War. His father had died in that struggle, and Zimmerman had been the sole support of his mother as soon as he was old enough. He thought suddenly of his mother, and pain shot through him. She was still in Germany, but he had not heard from her. News of the SS taking Jews off the street and hustling them into concentration camps were filtering through to America. Zimmerman had tried desperately to reach her, all to no avail. He, himself, was the victim of prejudice among some of the faculty and the students. It was not popular to be a German these days. Still, the obvious waste of the young man's life before him seemed to him very wrong. He folded his hands, leaned back in the chair, and said, "Mr. Stuart, I am always at a loss to understand why young people fail to appreciate their advantages. Not everyone has them. I, myself, didn't."

The personal remark caught Adam's interest. "You had a hard time of it, Dr. Zimmerman?"

"I grew up in a world that showed no pity, and we had nothing. My father was killed in the Great War."

Adam almost responded by saying, "So was mine," but managed to fight the statement down. It gave him a strange feeling, this sudden kinship that had been revealed with Zimmerman. He glanced at the picture on the wall of the woman and asked, "Is that your mother, Dr. Zimmerman?"

"Yes." The dean hesitated for a moment and said, "I'm very concerned about her. She's in Germany, and this is not a very good time for Jews to be in Germany."

Adam had read the reports of the atrocities against Jews, and suddenly his own problems seemed very small. He sat there silently, and Zimmerman said heavily, "I'm afraid there's little I can do for you." He reached out and tapped the records before him and said, "If there were only one problem, we might find a way to keep you in school, but you have multiple problems."

"But Dr. Zimmerman—"

Zimmerman shook his head. "Your grades are terrible, that's one thing. Your attendance, that's enough to lead to your expulsion. You've already missed more classes this semester than would permit you a passing grade, and your disciplinary problems do not help."

"They weren't really serious offenses, Dr. Zimmerman."

"Perhaps not, but combined with the other factors, I have no option but to send you home."

The words came to Adam like the closing of an iron gate. Here at UCLA he had his freedom, and now he wished desperately that he had performed better. He hated the thought of failure, and he could see in his mind now his mother's face. She would not show much, for she was a trained actress, but he would know that she was hurt by this—and so would his stepfather be, who took great pride in him.

"Isn't there any way, Dr. Zimmerman, that I could make it up?"

Zimmerman hesitated, then shook his head. "Not for now. There's no justification at all, Mr. Stuart, for this kind of behavior. I usually don't make personal comments, but in your case, I might say that there's a special tragedy here. You have everything that a young man in this country would want to have. A fine family, money, prestige—you are intelligent, a fine athlete. There's no reason for your failure here—except in your own character."

Anger flared through Adam, but it was anger at himself rather than at Zimmerman. He stood to his feet and said, "That's it then? I have to leave?"

Zimmerman stood. He nodded his head sadly and said quietly, "If you would care to apply for readmission in a year, I would add my recommendation. You have a great deal in your favor, Mr. Stuart. I hate to see a young life wasted frivolously as you have wasted yours."

The words came clearly to Adam and his face turned crimson. He could not deny the dean's words, nor could he feel anger at the man. He said, "You're right; I've fouled up, Dr. Zimmerman."

Zimmerman had been expecting anger, resentment, and perhaps even worse. Adam Stuart had a reputation for attacking his professors fearlessly, if sometimes foolishly. This was his first encounter with the young man—though he knew him by reputation. He resisted the impulse to reverse his decision but grieved over the needless loss of this young man.

Adam nodded saying, "Good-bye, Dr. Zimmerman."

When the young man reached the door, Zimmerman said, "Try again next year, Stuart; I'd like to see you give it a better shot than you have this time."

Adam turned and studied the smaller man with interest. He had heard so much about the man's hard character and hard ways that he had not expected this. "Maybe I will, Sir—and thank you."

The door closed behind Adam, and Zimmerman stood still for a moment. He had much on his mind, and his own troubles were greater than people knew. Nevertheless, a wave of pity touched him, and he muttered under his breath, "What a loss! What a loss!" He turned and went back to his desk; as he sat down, his eyes went again to the picture on the wall.

Adam left the administration building almost blindly, not noticing the admiring look of the receptionist. He went at once to his room where he found his roommate, Jake Greenberg, lying on his bed. Looking up from the book he was reading, Greenberg asked, "You're cutting biology again?"

"I'm cutting *everything*."

Greenberg, a lanky young man of twenty, put the book down and stared at his friend. "What's that supposed to mean?"

"I've been kicked out." Adam grabbed a suitcase and threw

it on his bed. Opening it, he began throwing his clothing into
it. He looked up to see Greenberg's shocked expression. "It's
not the end of the world, Jake."

"Wait a minute—what's this all about?" The long, sensitive
face of Greenberg showed confusion, and he got to his feet at
once. "You mean you got a warning from Zimmerman?"

"I mean I got booted out. No appeal—just out." Adam
tossed his textbooks on the bed, glared at them, then shrugged,
and moved to get his things from the bathroom. He explained
his meeting with the dean and shook his head when Greenberg protested that there had to be a better way.

"Not this time, Jake. I ran my string out." Adam had finished
packing and paused to go to his roommate. "Sorry to run out
on you, Jake." Actually Greenberg had been his only friend
at UCLA, though he knew many people. The tall young man
had been one of the few he could actually talk to—about things
that really mattered. The two of them had spent endless hours
together, and now it was a distinct pain to leave Greenberg.

"Adam, you can't go like this," Jake protested and for some
time argued that there had to be a way. Finally he gave up,
saying sadly, "I won't have a soul to talk to after you're gone.
I'll probably get a jock with a thick neck for a roommate!"

Adam tried to smile as he put his hand out and grasped
Greenberg's. "I'll miss you, Jake. Let's keep in touch."

Greenberg suddenly reached out and embraced Adam,
something he'd never done before. He squeezed hard, then
stepped back, saying thickly, "Well, get out of here before I
begin blubbering!"

"So long, Jake."

Adam left the room, surprised at the emotion that had
charged the farewell. He'd not known until this moment
how fond he was of Jake Greenberg. *Going to miss that fellow*,
he thought as he left the dorm and got into his Buick. As he
pulled away, he glanced up and saw Greenberg standing at the
window watching him. Adam waved, but the figure remained
still, and Adam's last glimpse of him he never forgot.

He shoved the pedal to the floor, roaring off campus, breaking every traffic law on the books. As he pulled out onto the main highway heading out of the campus, he suddenly realized that he had few choices. Quickly he put together the possibilities in his mind.

First, he could go home—but somehow the thought of facing his parents with nothing but failure was repulsive to him. "I'll dig ditches before I'll do that," he spoke aloud, dodging around to avoid a slow-moving cement truck. He pulled back in the line of traffic and slowed down, trying desperately to think of something to redeem himself.

Not much I can do, he thought. *At least not that pays anything.* He listed his skills, which included driving a car almost with professional skill; he could fly a plane, having been given lessons for his high school graduation present; he could run the hundred-yard dash better than most and even did well in some of the medium-distance races, but nobody was paying for that.

He deliberately turned away from the route that led to his home and drove out to the ocean. He found a bay that was not crowded with houses and people, got out and walked down to the beach, sat down on the remains of a tree that had been washed in, and sought desperately for some remedy.

The gulls found him soon and circled around him, crying harshly. He admired their sleek bodies and how they maneuvered, almost motionless in the air, waiting for scraps that he did not have. He got up and began to walk, leaving footprints in the damp sand. The sea stretched out endlessly, making a hard knife edge against the horizon where it met the blue sky. It was cold, and a shiver took him as the breeze came in off the water. He took a deep breath, enjoying the tang of the salt air, then turned and walked back down the beach. For over an hour he paced up and down seeing little that was before him. Once he bent down and picked up a shell that had washed ashore, admired its perfection, then tossed it to the ground again.

Finally, he made his way back to the car. Sitting in it without starting the engine, he tried to think of a job he could do. Being brought up in a wealthy home had not put him in touch with many possibilities. He sighed and hardened himself to the idea of going home. "I guess I'll have to face the music," he said. He started the engine, and as he got back on the highway and headed home, he thought, *I'd better stop and get the oil changed. It must be time.* The instant that came to his mind, another thought joined to it.

Oil! The thought of oil brought to his mind his Uncle Pete Stuart in Oklahoma, who owned a small oil business. Adam had visited there once and seen the rigs and the men busily working on them, and it had interested him.

Uncle Pete would give me a job!

He had barely enough money to make it to Oklahoma, but without a moment's hesitation, his mind was made up. He stopped only long enough to buy a postcard and write to his parents.

> Mom and Dad,
> Bad news. I've been expelled. I guess it's too hard to face you with it. I'm going to Oklahoma to try to get a job with Uncle Pete. I'll write you when I get there.

He hesitated, added, "Sorry," and then signed his name. He dropped it in the box, feeling cowardly, for he knew he should go home and explain his failure or at least call.

He got into the Buick, headed out of the service station, and promised himself, *I'll call them as soon as I get to Uncle Pete's. It'll give me time to sort things out in my mind, and they'll have time to get adjusted, too.*

Shortly he was on Route 66 headed east. He knew he had to find himself a new life, and he gritted his teeth firmly saying, "I can make it; I won't lose this time!"

The only thing Adam liked about the oil business was his cousin Mona. She was a very exciting young woman, and she liked Adam very much.

Actually, he liked his Uncle Pete, too. Pete Stuart had given Adam a job the day Adam arrived in Oklahoma. Pete had also given him a warning: "This business isn't for everybody, Adam. I don't think it's for you, but you can give it a try."

Adam had taken his uncle's warning lightly, but he had soon discovered that nothing about the oil business pleased him. He had started out on the rigs and had hated every day of that, then he had been turned over to the office of his cousin Stephen, and he liked the business offices even less. Stephen, he felt privately, was a stick who thought nothing of money grubbing.

It had been a boring time for him, and now as he moved toward his uncle's office, he had the feeling that the news was not going to be good.

"I think I'm having déjà vu," he muttered under his breath. "It's like going to see Dr. Zimmerman again."

But when he went inside, Pete smiled at him and said, "Hello, Adam, how did it go today?"

Adam had put in a long, boring day going down columns of figures under Stephen's hand, and he smiled ruefully. "Don't ask Stephen about that. He'll tell you I've got a real thick head!"

Pete laughed and leaned back in his chair. He had worked hard all of his life, and it showed in his hands and in his neck, which was creased and burned by many a blistering Oklahoma sun.

"I know what you mean. I can't stand keeping books myself. I'd rather be out on a rig."

"Well, to tell the truth, I didn't do too well out there either, Uncle Pete," Adam said. "It was good of you to try me out, but I'm just not cut out for this kind of work."

Pete had brought Adam in to talk to him because he sensed Adam was dissatisfied. He had dreaded it, for he liked this nephew of his very much, but now that Adam had brought it out he was vastly relieved. "You know, Adam, a man has to like what he's doing or life's not worth much. Me, I always liked playing around with oil rigs and things, although I don't like the business side." He thought back over the years he had drilled dry holes and the long, hard battle to win a place for himself in the wolfish world of oil. He thought of Lylah, with whom he had spoken on the phone several times since Adam had come, and was sorry that it had not worked out. He said carefully, "You're welcome to stay as long as you want, Adam—but I suspect you don't like it enough to make a career out of it."

"You're right about that!" Adam slumped in a chair, and for a while the two men talked. Pete asked gently, "Is there anything you would like to do? I'll be glad to help you, Adam; anything I can do."

Adam flashed a smile, and it made him look younger and more pleasant. He didn't realize how much he was frowning these days, and he laughed suddenly saying, "The only thing I've done is have a good time with Mona!"

A worried look crossed Pete's face. "I'm worried about her, Adam."

Adam was truly surprised. "Why's that, Uncle Pete? Why, she's got everything."

"She's attractive enough, but there's more to life than that."

"She'll be Miss Oklahoma someday; wait and see if she's not."

"And you think that would make her happy?" Pete frowned. "I haven't read anything about these beauty queens setting any records for successful living. What do you think of her, Adam? You've spent a lot of time with her. Her mother and I just can't understand her."

Adam thought about the time he had spent with Mona and said, "I guess she's like most young women her age. They like a good time, and they talk about clothes and makeup too much, but she'll settle down."

Pete shook his head, his lips drawn tightly together. "I hope you're right," he said, "but far as I can tell, she has no more thoughts than a goose. But we'll hope you're right." He stood up then and came around to sit down on the desk and study his nephew. "Will you be going back to college next year?"

"I just don't know, Uncle Pete. I could, I guess. The dean would help me get in, I know."

"Well, if you can stand it, I think you oughta go back. At least you can tread water." A thought came to him and he said, "What about this draft thing? You may get drafted into the army."

It was an unpleasant thought and Adam shook his head. "I hope not! Can't think of anything much worse than that. I'd rather dig ditches!"

Pete wanted to ask if the fact that Adam had a German father had anything to do with his distaste for it, but he felt himself ill fitted to begin such a conversation. "Well, what will you do now? I take it you'll be leaving Stuart Oil Company."

"I'm wasting your time and mine, Uncle Pete." Adam stood up and said reluctantly, "I'll have to go home again and face the music." He laughed shortly saying, "I was such a coward I couldn't even face Mom and Dad, but I'll have to now."

"I think that would be good." Pete hesitated, then said, "I've got something for you." He moved back behind his desk, opened it, and pulled out a checkbook. As he scribbled a check he said, "This is your severance pay, and you know I never did give you a proper graduation present when you graduated from high school. I'm making it up with this. You'll have enough money to get back home and to tide you over for a little while." He tore off the check, moved back around the desk, and handed it to Adam. "Happy graduation, Nephew!" he said.

Adam glanced at the check, and his eyes opened wide. "Why, this is too much!"

Pete Stuart clapped his nephew on the shoulder, then gave him a quick, affectionate hug. "Not a bit! Let's go out tonight and celebrate, then you can get a good start in the morning."

"Thanks, Uncle Pete, this will help a lot."

Adam enjoyed the trip back to California. He drove rather slowly, and he made a couple of side trips just to see things that he had heard about, such as the Petrified Forest. But as he pulled into Los Angeles, he was still apprehensive about seeing his parents. Time had healed some of the humiliation, but he was a sensitive young man, and he knew that he had behaved badly. "I guess I might as well go get my spanking," he said and drove at once to his home.

He found, to his relief, that neither his mother nor father were there, and he quickly moved into his room. He told the maid, "When my parents come in, tell them I'll be back."

"Yes, Mr. Stuart, I'll tell them."

He left the house to get something to eat. On his way, however, he had a thought and stopped at a picture studio where an old girlfriend of his worked, a starlet named Tamara Lane. Adam had written her from Oklahoma, and she had told him to be sure and get in touch with her as soon as he got back.

Getting by the guard at the gates presented some problem. He had to wait until Tamara came to assure the guard that he was all right. Adam obtained a pass, and when the two were walking away, he studied her carefully. She was wearing a period-costume dress and was made up heavily. "Is that dress for the picture you're in?"

"Yes," Tamara said. She turned to him and smiled. "It's good to see you. I've missed you, Adam." She was a tall woman with red hair and strange-colored eyes, a blue-green combination. She had a wide, sensuous mouth and an air of freedom that Adam had always liked.

"Do you want to come in and watch us shoot a scene?"

"Sure, then when you get off, maybe we can go out. I've got to be back to see my folks pretty early, but at least we could have dinner."

"All right."

Tamara led him to one of the sound stages where, for the next two hours, he watched with interest the scene that was being shot. He was, of course, familiar with the making of movies, having grown up with it, and was most interested in how Tamara fit into the scheme. He discovered she had only a small part, but it was the biggest she had had so far.

The movie, she told him, was just the beginning and she was expecting it to be her stepping-stone to stardom.

Finally the director said, "All right, that's a take! We'll knock off for the day."

Tamara came at once and said, "I want you to meet the producer. He's one of the biggest in Hollywood."

Soon Adam was standing in front of a short man who was smoking a huge cigar. "Mr. Vane, this is Adam Stuart, Lylah Stuart's son."

"Is that right?" Vane puffed at his cigar, and his grip was hard on Adam. "You've got a great set of parents there. Nobody better than Lylah and Jesse in the business."

"I think so," Adam grinned. "I saw your last film, Mr. Vane. It should've won an Academy Award."

Vane grinned and puffed at the cigar. "There ain't no justice, is there? Well, maybe this one will do it." He cocked his eyebrows and studied Adam. "What do you do, Stuart?"

"I raise Cain and get kicked out of college—that's what I do!"

Vane laughed explosively and winked at Tamara. "I did some of that myself when I was a bit younger. What did you get kicked out for, Kid, running around after coeds?"

"It was a combination of things," Adam said. He liked the stocky director very much. "I didn't leave any stone unturned. The dean had a list of things that I did wrong."

"He's not as bad as he seems, Mr. Vane," Tamara said quickly.

Vane was looking at Adam with an odd expression. "So what's up now that you're out of school?"

"I don't know. I tried working in the oil fields for my uncle, but that didn't pan out. I guess I'm just the prodigal son."

Vane joggled the cigar up and down in his mouth. He took it out after puffing on it rapidly a few times and then said,

"You ever do any acting? With a show-business family like yours, I guess you have."

"Oh, yes, in high school, just amateur stuff." A thought came to him, and he was almost startled. "Why do you ask?"

Henry Vane was not a classicist. He took his actors where he found them. He asked, "What do you think, Tamara? Could he play the Robertson part?"

Tamara was surprised also. She turned and studied Adam and said, "Well, he's good-looking enough, and it's not a very demanding part, after all."

"Wait a minute," Adam protested. "I'm not a professional actor!"

"You get your first paycheck, you will be," Vane said. He studied the young man carefully. "It's just a small part, not too many lines, but it's an important one. We haven't cast it yet. This character doesn't come on until a little bit late in the movie. Tell you what; why don't you let us give you a little test. If you can cut it, I'd be glad to have you."

Adam Stuart was very quick in every way. At once he said, "I'll be glad to try. If I can do the job for you, I'd be very happy, Mr. Vane."

"OK, Tamara, take him over to casting. Tell them I said to run a test. You know what it has to be, OK, Sweetheart?"

"Sure, Mr. Vane."

Adam stared at the back of the burly producer and said, "I can't believe what's happening."

"Come on before he changes his mind." Tamara grabbed Adam's arm and pulled him away quickly.

After that everything was a blur. Adam did what he was told. He was given some lines to read, and he memorized them almost instantly. It was a love scene with Tamara, and after the embrace of the first take he said, "I get paid for this?"

"Not for this," Tamara laughed. "You're just testing, but you did well. I think it's in the bag!"

Adam said, "Thanks a lot, Tamara. It probably won't work out, but if it does I'd be happy."

"Come on; let's get something to eat. We can talk about your future as the new Valentino!"

Adam did not say anything to his parents about the test when he went home. He spent an enjoyable evening with them, but he knew that part of his enjoyment was the anticipation that he might have a job.

The next day he got a call from Henry Vane at Daystar Studios. "That you, Stuart?"

"Yes, Mr. Vane."

"Hey, I saw the test, and it was great! Come on to work. We'll talk about money when you get here."

For a moment Adam could not believe it, then a sense of tremendous relief washed over him. "I'll be there, Mr. Vane."

He hung up the phone and was at once conscious of the strain that he had been under. He had no idea whether he would be a good actor or not, but at least it gave him breathing room. Besides that, he had done it on his own, and his parents had not had a thing to do with it.

When he told Lylah, her eyes had gone wide with surprise and he had laughed. "I'll probably be the biggest dud that ever was, but I want to try it, Mom."

"If that's what you want," Lylah said, "then it's fine with me and will be with your father. But acting isn't always the best life in the world—you know that."

Adam hugged her. "You've done all right, Mom," he said. He held her closely, something he rarely did, then suddenly kissed her on the cheek. "I don't know how you put up with me. I wouldn't put up with me!"

Lylah was enjoying his embrace, and she reached up and brushed his hair back. "I want the best for you, Adam," she said simply. "I always did."

Adam kissed her again, and as she watched him leave the house Lylah prayed, "Oh, God, help him to find his way! . . ."

6

DAY OF INFAMY

U sually for Wendy Stuart December was a time of great joy and happiness, bringing pleasure more than the other months of the year. However, this December she had been oppressed by the steel-gray skies and the sharp winds that whipped over the land bringing a promise of a wolf-lean and bitter winter. Snow had come early to Nashville, falling first in soft flakes that delighted the children who engaged in miniature wars and the building of snowmen. Wendy, too, had enjoyed watching the flakes drift across the skies, fluttering down softly and gently, cloaking the earth with an overcoat of beauty. This first snowfall, however, had frozen, and after several days nothing but ice remained, dangerous and treacherous to those who navigated the streets of the city.

Her mother had tried to talk to her, knowing that the breakup with Alex had been traumatic for her daughter. "Why don't you try to think about going to college again?" Allie had urged her.

"Oh, Mother, I don't have the money for that. I'll just get a job. Sooner or later I'll find something," Wendy had said.

"Well, we'll have a good time at the reunion this year." As soon as she said it, Allie realized that this was, in a way, a bleak reminder of Alex Grenville. It had been there in Arkansas during the previous Christmas season that Wendy had been the happiest. Now that Alex was out of her life, it seemed that a darkness had fallen over her, and her natural cheerful spirit was subdued.

Sunday morning came. The family had piled into the family car, and Owen had driven them to church, where they had heard a good sermon. For the most part though, Wendy received little of it. She enjoyed the singing, her clear contralto rising above the less-talented voices of those about her, drawing the admiring glances of many. She did not do this to make a spectacle of herself but because she loved to sing the songs of the church. Deliberately, she had to throttle back to keep from overwhelming the congregation's effort, but still, it was this part of the service that pleased her the most. She especially loved "Amazing Grace" and when that song was sung she had to deliberately restrain herself from filling the auditorium with her powerful voice.

After the service, Owen took them out to eat at a restaurant close by, and soon Woody said, "Have you heard anything from Uncle Logan about Clint?"

"Just that he and Carol are doing fine. Clint will be going to the army soon." Woody swallowed a mammoth-size portion of mashed potatoes, then immediately began operating on his meat with all the enthusiasm of a surgeon. "She's a fine young woman, I think, but they're going to have a hard time. It isn't easy for someone in service to have a family life."

"That's right," Allie said, "but they love each other, and they'll get by." She reached over and put her hand on Owen's and smiled. "It reminds me of some of those knotty-pine motels we stayed in when we were first holding meetings, pulling a travel trailer behind us in that old Studebaker. Do you remember it?"

Owen smiled faintly. "Those weren't the worst days of my life. We had everything but money." He thought about the past and nodded, "As a matter of fact, those were very *good* days. Not every woman could've put up with that though." He squeezed her hand, then his thoughts went back to his nephew in Arkansas. "In a way I hate for Clint to go into the army. I know how badly he wanted to be an engineer. Now, it looks like he'll have to put that off for a while."

"What was the army like in the Great War, Dad? You don't talk much about it," Will said.

In this he was correct, for Owen did not speak a great deal about the war. He said briefly, "It was mud and discomfort and disease mostly." He allowed the old memories to wash over him, then shook his head faintly, his brow furrowed. "I think the discomfort and disease were worse than the action. Most of the time we sat around in trenches fighting rats and trench foot, bored to death. That was it," he added quietly. "Long months of boredom and then a few hours of absolute terror."

"Well, it won't be a trench war this time, I guess. The Germans proved that when they overran France," Woody offered. "I think it will be an air war mostly."

"You may be right. The Luftwaffe has won the battle for Germany so far. We'll need quite an air force when we come up against them. England's done a magnificent job winning the Battle of Britain. I don't see how they did it. It was a miracle! I remember what Churchill said," Allie remarked. "'Never have so many owed so much to so few.' Those pilots who defended the islands against the Luftwaffe did a magnificent job."

Wendy sat listening, not saying much. She was paler than usual, and as she looked at Woody and Will, apprehension came to her, for any young man in America in those days had the shadow of war hanging over him.

They left the restaurant and went home, where Owen and Allie retired at once to take a brief nap. Will and Woody listened to the radio, and Wendy went to her room. She was tired, but it was not a physical weariness. She had taken a job temporarily as a librarian until she could find something in her own field of singing. It was a pleasant enough job, but it did not challenge her, and she was a young woman who liked challenge.

Sitting down, she sighed and began answering letters, a task that she had put off for too long. One of them was from her Uncle Amos whom she did not see too often. She wrote to thank him for his efforts to find her a job and closed by saying that she would like to see him and hoped that they would see each other at Christmas.

After she finished the letters, she went downstairs and found her parents up. Her father was in his study, and her mother was fixing supper. As Wendy moved in to help her, she noticed her brothers outside throwing a football around and smiled at their antics. "They're just like a couple of little boys, aren't they?"

"I hope they always stay that way," Allie smiled.

The two women worked for a while, and finally Allie said, "I can do the rest of this. Why don't you go and listen to the symphony."

Quickly Wendy shot a glance at her mother, knowing that she referred to Alex's program, *The American Symphony*. It was one of the few references that her parents had made to Alex, and Wendy suspected her mother did it just to test the waters to see if she was able to hear the name without visible reaction. As a matter of fact, she was not, and her cheeks grew slightly rosy as she said, "All right, I think I will."

She went into the living room and turned on the large radio that sat against one wall. She tuned the needle over the orange dial until finally she got the New York station. She had come just in time, for a few minutes later, she heard the announcer say, "And now we bring you direct from New York, *The American Symphony*, conducted by Alex Grenville."

For the next twenty minutes Wendy sat listening to the music. She could not help but visualize Alex, in her mind's eye, directing the orchestra, face intense, baton moving with power and authority. Perhaps, as never before, she recognized what a tremendous musician he was, for the orchestra seemed, to her, better than almost any she had ever heard.

Finally, she heard Alex's voice: "And now we have as our soloist, Miss Ann Marie Thomason. Miss Thomason will sing selections from *Carmen*."

The sound of Alex's voice had a peculiar effect on Wendy.

For weeks now she had tried to put him out of her mind, but this had proved impossible. Over and over again, her last meeting with him had come to her until it was almost like watching a movie. She could see his face before her as clearly as if he were standing before her in the flesh, and she remembered her dreadful struggle not to give in to his propositions.

Wendy listened to the soloist and admired the clear tones of the singer. A thought came to her: *I could be that soloist. I could be singing on the radio*. Again, she was torn by the decision she had been forced to make and fought desperately to cease thinking such thoughts.

She was brought back to the program by an interruption. An announcer, his voice tense with excitement, suddenly said, "We interrupt this program to bring you a bulletin of national interest! A special announcement from the government has informed us that American bases at Pearl Harbor have been attacked by enemy aircraft. Stay tuned to this station for further announcements."

Immediately the music continued, and Wendy sat there dumbfounded. It sounded ominous, and all she could think of was, *Where in the world is Pearl Harbor?* She thought there must be some mistake and sat uneasily in her chair as the program continued, but five minutes later the program was interrupted again. "Once again, we bring you a special announcement. Enemy aircraft have bombed the Seventh Fleet at Pearl Harbor. The details are few, but it is clear that this is an act of armed aggression by the Empire of Japan! The president has called his cabinet into special session, and we expect an announcement to be made from the president's office very soon."

This time there was no mistake. At once Wendy rose and went to her father's study. Stepping inside she said, "Dad, something is wrong. It's just come over the radio."

Owen, who was sitting in an easy chair reading a thin book, looked up with surprise. "What is it, Wendy?"

"They interrupted the radio station to say that the Japanese have bombed Pearl Harbor. Where is Pearl Harbor, Dad?"

"It's a naval base in Hawaii. Most of our navy's there." Owen got to his feet at once, his face serious. "Are you sure about this, Wendy?"

"Yes, you'd better come and listen to the radio. I'll go call the boys in."

Soon the whole family was sitting around the radio. They listened closely, and at first there was nothing to hear. They found another New York station where the Philharmonic was playing Shostakovitch's Symphony no. 1. "This is a powerful station," Owen said, tension in his voice. "If there is any news, it should come over this one." Even as he spoke the announcement was made. It was much like the ones Wendy had heard and gave little additional information.

A sense of shock had fallen over the entire family. Wendy, who had more time to think of it, saw that they were all dumbfounded.

"Japan has been in Washington for peace talks," Owen said bitterly. "We see what they're worth!"

"It means war," Will said. "There's no way out of it now." His lips drew together in a tight line and he shook his head. "The navy will be out of it for a while anyway."

"What do you mean, Son?" Allie asked.

"Most of our naval power is tied up at Pearl Harbor. All of our battleships and carriers, I think." Will kept up with world events better than the others, and he quickly outlined the situation. "If the Japanese wanted to knock out American resistance, they did a good job of it. Without naval power, there's nothing to stop them from taking over the East, then they'll have all the rubber and oil they want."

"But how could they have bombed Pearl Harbor?" Owen demanded. "That's too far for planes to fly from Japan."

"Had to be a carrier attack," Will said. "No other way they could have done it."

They sat up late that night and spent some time calling the rest of the family. Everybody, of course, was aware of what was happening, and finally, in the small hours of the morning, Owen looked around at his sons and knew that this day had changed everything for him. It was the beginning of the struggle that he had known would come.

"I guess we better go to bed. It's going to be a hard time," he said finally. They all agreed, although few of them slept that night.

That day changed America. Some twenty-eight hundred American fighting men lost their lives at Pearl Harbor. The battleship *Arizona* went to the bottom with most of her crew. The *Oklahoma* was sunk, and six battleships were severely damaged. The American fleet no longer existed as a viable strike force in the Pacific. Half of the aircraft on the island of Hawaii were destroyed.

A young ensign named John Kennedy was at the Eagles-Redskins game. After the game, he heard admirals and generals being paged through the stadium sound system and as soon as the game was over he got the news report. Kennedy requested sea duty as soon as possible. A brigadier general at Fort Sam Houston received the news when he was awakened from a sound sleep. Dwight D. Eisenhower told Mamie he was going to headquarters and had no idea when he would be back. Some time after the attack, Winston Churchill made a phone call. "Mr. President, what's this about Japan?" Franklin Roosevelt said, "It's quite true. We're all in the same boat." Churchill replied, "This actually simplifies things. God be with you." The British prime minister went to bed and slept soundly. At Pearl Harbor a seaman and a rescue party boarded the *Oklahoma*, which had taken six torpedoes below the water line and was on the verge of capsizing. He said later, "I was terribly afraid. We were cutting through with acetylene torches. First we found six naked men waist deep in water. They didn't know how long they had been down there, and they were crying and moaning with pain. Some of them were very badly wounded. We could hear tapping all over the ship—SOS taps, no voices—just those eerie taps from all over. There was nothing we could do for most of them."

On December 8, Adam Stuart sat in Tamara Lane's apartment. He had done well in his role and had visions of a career as a movie actor. Tamara had been delighted to begin an affair. She had taken him into her life, much to the dismay of Adam's parents.

Now, the two of them listened as the clear, reassuring voice of Franklin D. Roosevelt filled the airwaves.

"Yesterday, December 7, 1941—a day which will live in infamy—the United States of America was suddenly and deliberately attacked by naval and air forces of the Empire of Japan. Very many American lives have been lost. Always will our whole nation remember the character of the onslaught against us. No matter how long it may take to overcome this premeditated invasion, the American people in their righteous might will win through to absolute victory. We will not only defend ourselves to the uttermost, but will make it very certain that this form of treachery shall never again endanger us. We will gain the inevitable triumph—so help us God. I ask that the Congress declare a state of war."

A heavy silence hung over the room, and Tamara stared at the young man whose eyes were half hooded. "What does it mean, Adam?" she said.

"It means that America is in the same shape as Europe."

"Will you have to go?"

Adam Stuart had listened to the president, and a heaviness now lay over him. He seemed not to have heard Tamara's question, but after a time he lifted his eyes and stared at her.

"We'll all have to go," he said. He left her apartment and went home, but only after he had gotten blind drunk. By the time he reached the house, all the lights were out except the one in the living room. He staggered in, almost falling, and then heard his mother's voice. "Adam, let me help you."

"Leave me alone, Mom—I'm drunk!" he muttered.

"I know, Adam. Come along."

But he stood before her, and looked deep into her eyes. "Mother," he said, and there was a break in his voice, such as she had never heard before. Looking very young and vulnerable, he asked her, "How can I fight my father's people?"

Lylah had no answer for that. She stood with her arms around him, and he began to sob. And finally she whispered, "Come, God will help us, Adam—but now you must go to bed. "

Part Two

BAPTISM IN FIRE

7

COMBAT ENGINEER

For months before the attack on Pearl Harbor, America had been living under the shadow of war and turning itself into what was called "the home front." For the first time in American history, men had been drafted in peacetime, and government posters had a martial tone showing workers, soldiers, and sailors working together. The stream of women entering the labor force rose, finally reaching a flood crest of eighteen million during the war. The war meant well-fed Americans had their menus curtailed by food rationing, and a people accustomed to going everywhere by car had to adjust to gasoline rationing.

Home-front people worked harder and longer, earned more money, and had less to spend it on than ever before in their lives, so they bought war bonds, paid off old debts, and had their teeth fixed. Rationing hit everyone. Shoes were rationed, so Americans walked on thin soles. Coffee, cigarettes, liquor, train seats—all were in short supply, and the most common sight in America, perhaps, was long lines of cars waiting for gasoline at the local gas stations. Tires became worth their weight in gold, almost, and the shortage of silk and nylon stockings brought leg makeup into popularity. A few acrobatic women joined those painting their legs with makeup by adding a seam, but for most this was an anatomical impossibility!

There were blackouts all over the country as a precaution against air raids, and scrap metal drives took place from cities

as small as Two Egg, Alabama, to New York City. Everyone
did something useful. People served on draft boards and rationing boards; some even flew private airplanes over coastal
waters in search of U-boats. Others stood watch as aircraft
spotters and air-raid wardens. Householders ran war-bond
drives, and many plowed up vacant lots and planted enough
"victory gardens" to produce some 40 percent of the fresh
vegetables needed. Americans gave thirteen million pints of
blood to be administered as plasma to the battle wounded,
but not everything in America was quite as attractive as these
sacrifices. There were ugly episodes of racial violence. In
Detroit, 34 men died as whites rioted against Negroes. In Los
Angeles, young Mexicans, usually attired in the zoot suits,
were persecuted by servicemen.

One of the blackest marks against America's war record
was the harsh treatment of Japanese Americans. This was the
most indefensible of all, because it resulted from government
policy. The treachery of Japan's attack at Pearl Harbor, the
savagery of the early fighting, and the fears that mounted
with each U.S. defeat—these combined to create panic in
military and civilian leaders. More than 110,000 people of
Japanese descent were taken from their homes on the West
Coast and locked up in bleak concentration camps. Many
stayed there for most of the war, but not a single act of sabo-
tage or espionage was ever proven against them. It was not
until late in 1944 that the internees were permitted to return
to their homes.

Few Americans had any illusions about what kind of a war
it would be. Franklin Roosevelt called it simply the "Survival
War." In advertisements, the immaculate soldier at the beginning of the war quickly gave way to the begrimed infantry-
man plodding through war-torn villages. War reporters such
as Ernie Pyle and Bill Malden showed their GIs unshaven,
weary, bitter, and profane. The country realized that the war
would not end quickly or be fought easily. To dislodge Hitler
from his control of the continent would be a painful, bloody

business, and the road to Tokyo would be paved with the bodies of American men.

And the tools for the job, how were they to be obtained? For all practical purposes, the American navy was smashed at Pearl Harbor. There would be no carrying the fight to the enemy by the seas. The army had been reduced to a peacetime size after the Great War and was having to be rebuilt from the ground up. The Air Corps had been starved for funds for two decades, and even as late as 1938 was practically nonexistent, according to General Hap Arnold, especially when compared with the large air fleets constructed by Germany, Italy, and Japan. A three-hundred-million-dollar shot in the arm, voted by Congress in 1939, enabled Arnold to begin building a modern air force. The cherubic-looking but hardheaded officer sped the development of heavily armed fighters such as the Lockheed P-38 and the Republic P-47, and he finally persuaded Boeing to begin designing heavy bombers that would carry the war across oceans and national boundaries. When all was done, the skies over Germany would be blackened by flights of thousands of American bombers—but this was all far in the future, and with the shadow of Pearl Harbor still hanging over the land like a gloomy cloud, America geared up its loins and went to war.

Clint Stuart had been bending over his suitcase packing his few belongings, but a melody from the radio, which was in the living room, caught his attention. Standing up, he listened as the song, "Remember Pearl Harbor," filtered through the farmhouse. The song had become an instant hit. As he listened, Clint was swept with conflicting emotions. The dread of the unknown, perhaps dismemberment or death lay before him, hidden and shrouded in the uncertain mist of the future. He did not fear death so much, but the idea of being maimed and blinded, a cripple to be cared for by others, was a terror to him. He had always been an independent, self-assured man who could not bear the thought of being helpless without apprehension. The song ended, and immediately he heard the sound of Jimmy Dorsey's smooth orchestra playing "Tangerine," with Bob Eberly and Helen O'Connell joining together for the duet. He had liked that song since he first heard it, and he remembered when he had been at a dance with Carol at the American Legion Hall. Almost, it seemed, he could smell her perfume as she had moved around the floor in his arms, her large eyes smiling up at him.

The hands of the clock on the chest beside his bed moved inexorably forward, and he hurriedly threw some underwear into the suitcase, tossed his shaving kit on top, and shut it with a sense of finality. Picking it up, he moved out of his room, but he stopped and gave one last look. All of his life he had lived in this one room. He smiled as he saw the balsa airplane models hanging by thin threads from the ceiling, thinking of the hundreds of hours he had put in on them. His eyes moved over to the gun racks where his first rifle, a single-shot .22, still brought back fond memories. Beneath the .22 lay his twelve-gauge shotgun and below that his .30-06 hunting rifle. Everything in it was familiar, and he realized poignantly that he might never look upon it again.

With a decisive motion, he turned, shut the door firmly, and moved down the hall. He met his parents, who embraced him, unable to say what they felt. They were not an emotional pair, but Clint knew that his leaving was tearing part of their lives away from them.

"I'll take you down to the depot, Son."

"You won't do that, Logan," Anne said quickly. She was a small, plain woman who loved this boy who was her only child by Logan Stuart. "He'll want to say his good-byes to Carol."

Logan ran his hand through his auburn hair, still fresh and crisp as it had been when he was a teenager. "I guess you're right. A fella's got to have some romance when he leaves to go to the army. Come on, Son."

"Good-bye, Ma," Clint said. He embraced the small woman,

feeling the fragility of her bones, and kissed her on the cheek. She clung to him for a moment, then released him. He turned and went out the door, and the two men got into the Studebaker pickup. It cranked slowly, and Logan shook his head. "Got to get a new battery. This thing's about worn out!"

"You better get it overhauled, Pa. I meant to do that before I left, but I didn't have time."

The two men said nothing about the war as they drove into town, although it was on their minds. When they reached the Davidson house, Logan pulled the truck up but left the engine running. "I won't get out, Son," he said. He wanted to reach over and embrace this young man, but Arkansas farmers were not known for their emotional excesses. It was Clint who reached over suddenly, put his arm around his father and squeezed him hard. "I hate to leave you with all the work, Pa," he said.

"Don't worry about that. You just–you just take care of yourself." The slightest hesitation in Logan Stuart's voice told the young man all he needed to know. His eyes suddenly were blinded with tears brought on by deep emotion. He loved this father he had spent his life with, and both of them knew that his return was not at all certain. "I'll write you when I get to the camp," he promised. Getting out, he shut the door and waved as the ancient Studebaker rattled off.

As he turned to go to the door, he felt a moment's apprehension. The radio was on, and he heard the strains of a popular song: "Don't sit under the apple tree with anyone else but me, till I come marching home." *Might be a long time until that happens*, he thought. Putting this aside, he strolled up to the door, and at once Carol met him. She had been crying, Clint saw at once, but she had been crying a great deal for the last few weeks. "I went out to the place and got a few things," he said. "Spent a little time with the folks."

"Is it time to go?" Carol whispered, and there was a poignant note in her voice.

"I guess so. I've already said good-bye to your dad."

"He's not doing well this morning. He's asleep anyway. I'm glad you said good-bye to him though."

They stood there for a moment, and finally Clint said, "Well, let's walk on down to the depot. The train won't be in for half an hour, but we can have that time at least."

Carol nodded and, stepping back inside, got a light sweater. She put it on, and as she slipped her arms through the sleeves thought, *I've got to stop crying. I can't send him off like this! I've got to stop crying.* Turning, she fixed a smile on her face, stepped outside, and took his arm. "Let's go down and have a Coke at the drugstore," he said.

"No, let's have two chocolate malts, the thickest that Danny can make!"

"All right, that sounds good."

They moved slowly along the street, Carol clinging to his right arm while he carried the suitcase loosely in his left. Almost with every step, although they talked about general things, Clint was saying good-bye in his mind to a life. They had not been married long, but he had learned that Carol was very dependent upon him. She had transferred her dependency from her father to him, he saw, and this troubled him. He knew that he would not be there for her, and he had gently tried to insist that she try to stand alone—but it seemed to be a difficult thing for her. She needed a strong person to keep her happy, and her father was no longer able to fill that place. Now Clint was leaving, and from time to time he looked down at her almost with alarm. She was, he saw, keeping herself smiling only by an act of will, and he well knew that as soon as he left, she would go home and spend hours in their room weeping. She had already done so, more than once, with just the thought of his departure, and now as they walked along, he tried desperately to prepare her for the shock.

"I'll be getting a leave after basic is over," he said, squeezing her hand. "I'll come home, and you can show me off in my uniform. Then later on, you can come and visit me wherever

I'll be stationed. Maybe get someone to stay with your dad for a while. At least we can have weekends."

"Yes, let's do that, Clint," Carol said, looking up at him. She kept her eyes fixed on his lean, tanned face and reached up to shove a lock of light hair under his John Deere cap. She laughed then with an effort, saying, "You're not going to wear that ratty old cap off to war, are you?"

"I guess if it's good enough to plow in, it's good enough to go to the army in. Anyway," he said, "I won't be wearing it long."

They talked quietly and finally arrived at Thompson's Drugstore where they went in and sat down at one of the small round tables. Seating himself in a chair with an iron back, Clint grinned and said to the young man standing beside him, "Let's have two of your thickest chocolate malts, Danny. Don't hold back on the ice cream!"

"Right, Clint!" The soda jerk moved away and soon was back, and Clint and Carol began working on the thick malts.

"Have to eat this with a spoon," Clint said. "When I was little I used to come in and buy one of these about twice a year. I'd always squeeze the straw to make it last longer." He grinned then, and his hazel eyes crinkled at the edges as they did when he laughed. "I better squeeze the straw a long time; might not get another one for a while."

Instantly Clint regretted his remark, for he saw tears form in Carol's eyes. At the same time, the jukebox started playing a song that had become popular, "When the lights go on again all over the world. . . ." It was a haunting, plaintive melody and did nothing to help Carol feel better. Clint began speaking cheerfully, talking about things that had nothing to do with the war.

Finally, they got up and left and moved down to the train station. They were barely on time, for he cocked his head and said, "I think I hear it coming."

Carol could not speak for the fullness that was in her throat. She had thrown herself into her marriage with all of the strength that she had. She was aware that she had a tendency to be too dependent, but she seemed unable to do much about it. Now, as the whistle of the approaching train sounded faintly, she threw her arms around him and buried her face in his chest. "Oh, Clint, I wish you didn't have to go!" she moaned.

Helplessly, Clint put his arms around her and held her tightly. The two stood thus until the train pulled in, and finally he had to unwind her arms and say, "I've got to go, but I'll write. God will take care of you. He'll take care of both of us."

Carol could not answer. She was weeping and hated herself for it. She had determined she would not let herself go to pieces on his last day, but there was no help for it. She took his kiss, then watched through blinding tears as he swung on board the train. The whistle sounded, the engine huffed and shuffed, loosing a blast of steam, and then the drivers began rolling, and the train pulled slowly out of the small station. Carol stood, as it gathered speed, with tears running down her cheeks unnoticed. She waited until it had disappeared from sight, then turned and walked blindly away.

Chet Hanson, the station agent, turned to his helper and said, "There goes another one off to war. Gonna be hard on Carol, her with a sick dad as her only family."

Bill Matson said, "Well, she's got Clint's folks. She can lean on them."

"It ain't the same thing. When a woman's man goes off and leaves her, she ain't gonna find no satisfaction in nobody's family. A woman needs a man. You'll find that out if you live long enough."

Although Clint had some apprehensions about basic training, there was an excitement in him as he found himself among hundreds of other young men from all over the country. He had been sent to Camp Robinson, just outside of North Little Rock, which was no great distance. The camp was under construction, and it took no more than a few days for Clint to settle down in the barracks that contained ten double-decked bunks per room and a clothing locker for each man.

The toilets were adequate, with open showers and numerous sinks for washing and shaving. Clint found the lack of privacy the hardest thing to bear, but he soon was too busy to think much about that.

One thing that pleased Clint became evident from the very first. The young men who came in from the farms endured basic much better than the city men. Long hours of hard work in the fields, early risings before dawn, tramping in the woods hunting for endless hours had produced in Clint and his fellows from the rural areas a toughness that stood them well. On the first hike, carrying a full pack, Clint was somewhat shocked to see some of the men falling out after no more than five miles. He himself found it pleasant and caught the eye of Sergeant Jones. "You're in good shape, Stuart!" Jones said approvingly. He looked around and saw the pale, sweating faces of some of the men and shook his head. "You're in better shape now than these weaklings will be when they get out of here!"

Jones's words proved to be true, and Clint actually enjoyed basic training. The food was plentiful, though somewhat strange to his taste, and he missed the good cooking of first his mother and then Carol.

He was careful to send Carol a letter at least twice a week, and in one he said:

Dear Carol,
    I was so glad to get your letter and the package of food. It went down well with me and my buddies. You are the greatest cook in the world (but don't tell Ma I said that!). I'm sorry to say it didn't last the day, but you can remember that you made some lonesome fellows very happy here for at least a while.
    The worst part of basic is over, and it wasn't bad. Not at all like I thought. Some of the men got weeded out, just not able to take the physical hardship. Harold Barton was sent home yesterday, and he actually cried, but he really wasn't able to take the hard physical exercise. I'll miss him, and feel sorry that he won't be going with the group.

Tomorrow I start taking aptitude tests. Don't know what that means really, but I guess it will settle my future with the army. The scuttlebutt around here is that if you do well enough, you could go on to officers' training school, but I doubt if I'll be doing that. My head's too hard for that, and I wouldn't like to be an officer anyhow. Maybe, though, I can work up to sergeant. The pay would be a little better so I could help you more at home.

The letter went on for some time and was filled with small details as Clint searched his brain for something to fill out the pages. Actually his days were very much the same. He did spend a large part of the letter telling her about the church services that he had found very satisfying at Camp Robinson. He ended by saying:

The chaplain here is a great preacher. I wish he'd go on wherever we go from here, but he has to stay and preach to the next bunch of recruits.

I must go now for we'll have a full day with taking tests. I always did hate tests in school, and these will be very important. I love you very much and will write again day after tomorrow. Keep your letters coming, and keep praying for me.

Your loving husband,
Clint

He signed the letter, slipped it in an envelope, addressed it, then licked the seal, and affixed a stamp. Making his way out of the barracks, he joined several of his buddies who were on their way to take the aptitude tests. One of them, from Mobile, Alabama, said, "Here's where us city boys get it over you, Clint. You've outmarched us, I'll admit, but now we get down to the book work, and we'll see who comes out first."

"Probably right, Mac," Clint grinned. "Who knows, I may be saluting you pretty soon!"

"Private Stuart?"

"Yes, Sir, Lieutenant!" Clint had entered the officer's office and saluted smartly. "Private Stuart reporting as requested, Sir!"

Lieutenant James Redd nodded at a chair, "Sit down, Stuart; be at ease."

"Yes, Sir."

Lieutenant Redd picked up an envelope lying on his desk, opened it, and stared at it for so long that Clint was afraid the lieutenant had forgotten that he was there. Finally he looked up and studied the private, saying, "You ever been to college, Stuart? Your record doesn't show anything about it."

"No, Sir, just high school."

"Amazing!"

Clint shifted uncomfortably in his chair. He could not, for one moment, imagine what had singled him out for Lieutenant Redd's personal attention. None of the other men, as far as he knew, had been called in for a personal interview. The results had been posted on the board, most of the men going on to combat infantry units, a few being sent to specialty schools. Clint had been disturbed to find that his name had not been posted. Several of his friends, including the one from Mobile, had teased him saying, "I guess you country boys just didn't do well enough even to get sent to infantry school. You'll probably be cleaning out the latrines—permanent latrine orderly, I reckon!"

Clint had laughed along with the men but had been puzzled. The sergeant had said, "Report to Lieutenant Redd, Stuart!" And now as Clint sat studying the officer, he had qualms. "Is something wrong, Lieutenant? Did I do so bad that you can't even find a place for me?"

Lieutenant Redd, a short, chubby man with a round face and mild blue eyes glanced up over the papers and shook his head. "Nothing like that, Private. As a matter of fact, just the opposite." The lieutenant's eyes went back to the papers, and he shook his head in wonder. "You made the highest scores in the mechanical part of the test of any of the new recruits. How come you know so much about engineering?"

"Engineering? I don't know anything about engineering!" Clint was astonished. He blinked with surprise and shrugged his shoulders. "I read a lot, and I always wanted to go to school to be an engineer. Always liked to fool with things, but that's it."

"Whatever you've been reading must've stuck in your head. Look at these scores. I'm not supposed to show them to you, but I don't suppose it matters." He reversed the papers, and Clint ran his eyes down the figures and listened as Redd explained them to him.

"Well, I'm glad I did so well, Lieutenant."

"You did better than well—you knocked the top off the test!"

"What does that mean, Sir? My name wasn't posted anywhere."

"I didn't know what to do with you." Lieutenant Redd grinned abruptly. He looked more like a cherubic angel than a soldier, and now there was an odd, humorous look in his face. "I've got a proposition for you." He leaned forward and folded his short, rather fat fingers together. There was a picture of a pinup girl on the wall to one side, and he glanced at it for some reason, stared at the long-legged bathing beauty, then sighed. "This hasn't come up since I've been here, but the Air Corps needs engineers, mechanics, things like that I guess to keep the planes flying. Would you be willing to transfer to that branch?"

"Why, I guess so. I've never flown in a plane, but I have a cousin who is a flier—a lieutenant in the Air Corps as a matter of fact."

"Well, let me put it like this. The safest job in the whole war will be working on airplanes. They keep those bases back far enough and protect them with fighter planes so you won't be slogging across Germany in the mud or fighting in the jungles against the Japs."

"I'm not too good to do any of that, Lieutenant."

"Well, seems to me the best job you could do for Uncle Sam is to keep 'em flying. It's all settled then? You're willing?"

"Yes, Sir, I am!"

"All right, I'll get the papers started, and you'll be leaving right away. You'll be shipped to Shepard Field down in Texas. That's all. Good luck to you!"

"Thank you, Lieutenant, I'll do the best I can!"

Only three days later, Clint got another surprise. He had arrived at Shepard Field and had undergone further testing. These tests had been more advanced, but he felt that he had done well. Finally, he was aware that men were being assigned, and although he had not had time to make any close friends, he said good-bye to a tall, young man named Paul, from Missouri. "Looks like you'll be all right, Paul," Clint said with a worried look, "but they haven't said anything to me yet."

"Don't worry, you'll find a place. Well, so long!"

For the rest of the day, Clint roamed around the base, watching the planes take off and land out on the airfield. He spent most of the evening writing a long letter to Carol and went to bed, uncertain and unhappy.

Early the next morning, he reported to headquarters again, where a small group of some fifteen men were being processed. A door opened, and a voice called out, "Stuart!"

"Here, Sir!"

"Go down to that door on the left."

"Yes, Sir." Clint made his way to the room, and when he stepped inside found himself facing another lieutenant, this one tall and lanky with a shock of black hair. "Private Stuart, Sir!" Clint said.

"I'm Lieutenant Ramsey. I've been looking over your papers, and you've done very well. I can't believe you haven't had more experience and some college."

"Wish I had, Sir. Some day I'd like to be an engineer."

"Well, you could be one now, if you want to—of a sort."

"An engineer, Sir?"

"Yes, I think you might qualify for aerial engineer."

"Aerial engineer—what's that, Lieutenant?"

"Basically it's a flying aircraft mechanic, who's also an aerial gunner."

"An aerial gunner? You mean I'll be flying on combat missions?"

"Yes, but you have to qualify for that. Are you interested?"

"Yes, Sir, it sounds great to me."

"All right, we'll check you out, and if you qualify as a gunner, it looks like your career in the Air Corps is all settled." Ramsey hesitated, "There's some danger in it, you know. It's not quite like working on an airplane back on a base. You sure about this?"

"Yes, Sir, I am!"

"Good man!" Ramsey shuffled through his papers, rose, and said, "Come along, we'll get you started."

For the rest of the day, Clint went through the tests, which included dry runs in a large room with a .50-caliber machine gun that was wired electronically to score hits. Then he was taken out to actually fire one.

"Well," his sergeant said, after Clint had fired the exact gun, "you must be a hunter."

"Yes, Sir, I am."

"I figured that. You can track pretty good with those fifties."

"You mean I passed?"

"Yep, you passed. Go ahead and take these papers back to the lieutenant."

Two days later, Clint had his papers stamped by Lieutenant Ramsey. "All right, you're qualified for flight engineer, gunner. Good luck, Stuart!"

"Thank you, Lieutenant!"

"You'll be leaving for England right away. You got any letter writing, I suggest you do it quick."

"You mean I won't get any leave?"

"No, sorry about that. They need crews right away. Things are getting pretty hot. Get that letter writing done."

Clint hopped around with all the energy he had for the next two days. The hardest thing, of course, was writing to Carol and saying that he would not be able to come home on leave. He tried the best he could to explain his position:

> I think, in a way, this is the hardest thing I've ever done, not getting to come home to see you, Sweetheart, but I've got to do it. This is what I do best, or so the tests show. I will miss a leave that I would have gotten otherwise, but I know you'll understand. I have no idea when I will get a leave, but I love you and nothing will change that.

Clint looked down at the paper and realized how futile the words would be as Carol read them. He was, in effect, pulling out what little support he had to offer, but he felt that this was something he had to do. He sealed the letter, then got up and went to mail it.

The next day he boarded a transport plane and was on his way to England.

General Ira Eaker had arrived in England on February 20, 1942. He had been ordered by Hap Arnold to prepare the way for the arrival of the Eighth Air Force in Britain. He had been given a very difficult task, for the assault against Germany was to be carried on by day for greater bombing accuracy, despite the fact that the German Luftwaffe's fierce antiaircraft fire and cannon-firing bombers had already forced Britain's Royal Air Force to give up daylight missions and bomb only by night. And Eaker was to accomplish this task fast, within a year if possible.

But when General Eaker reached England, he had no planes, no crews, no airfields, no repair shops, nothing. America was woefully short of everything that an air force needed. Eaker, however, went quietly to work. He was a courtly, soft-spoken officer with a law degree and a model of diplomacy. His first job was to construct enough airfields to accommodate a projected force of thirty-five hundred bombers and fighters, and Eaker estimated there would be no fewer than 127. Putting that many runways, control towers, barracks, and mess halls into a nation smaller than Alabama—and already crowded with airfields and buzzing with air traffic—presented problems enough in itself.

Construction of the initial fields took time, and it was during this early period that Clint Stuart arrived at Ridgewell Airdrome in England. Shortly after dusk, a vehicle pulled into the base, and Stuart and a few others piled out of the truck that had brought them from another landing field. Looking around, Clint's first impression was of prefabricated metal buildings thrown hastily on top of English mud. A major appeared, examined Clint's papers, and said briefly, "You are now assigned to the 381st Bombardment Group at Ridgewell Air Base."

"That's a relief!" a man standing next to Stuart said.

"Why is it a relief?" Clint asked.

"Because this isn't one of the high-loss groups we've been hearing about."

The major said, "I'm sending you to the 533d Squadron, under the command of Major Hendricks. They're low on crews. A driver will take you to the squadron headquarters. Good luck on your new assignment!"

"Major," the man standing next to Stuart asked, "what kind of losses have we been having?"

The major hesitated, then indicated a large chart on the wall crowded with names. "See that chart? That's a combat roster. We've been here sixty days, and so far we've lost a hundred and one percent of our combat personnel."

"Why, that's impossible!"

The major said briefly, "You'd know it anyway in two or three days. Our strength is down, and we're happy to have you with us."

Clint glanced at the other men, noting that the color had drained from their faces. He himself felt somewhat shaky. "A hundred and one percent! What chance does that leave a man?" He struggled with the figures and finally was led to station headquarters where he was greeted by the operations officer. "I'm Lieutenant Swifton—welcome to the 533d Squadron!"

From that moment on, things went faster than Clint would have imagined. He was taken to a field, practically shoved out of a truck, with no instructions except, "Find your crew, then find Lieutenant Stratton; he'll be your pilot. He'll fill you in."

Clint made his way through a milling bunch of enlisted men and officers and finally asked a corporal, "Can you tell me where I'll find Lieutenant Stratton?"

"Yeah, go down this line of planes; find one that says "Last Chance" on the nose. That'll be him."

"Thanks!"

Clint hurried down the line of B-17s until he came to the one with *Last Chance* painted in black letters on the nose. He was somewhat shocked to see that the name was framed within the outline of a coffin. Cautiously he approached two officers who were arguing loudly about something and waited until one of them turned. "Yes, what is it?"

"Clinton Stuart reporting for duty, Sir! I'm looking for Lieutenant Stratton."

The two men turned to examine him. The shorter of the two said, "I'm Lieutenant Stratton; are you the replacement engineer?"

"Yes, Sir!"

"You took long enough to get here!" Stratton was a short, stubby man with blonde hair and the red eyes of a drinker. "This is Lieutenant Simmons, copilot."

"Glad to have you here, Stuart!" Simmons said. He was a tall, lanky man with red hair and harried-looking blue eyes. "Get your gear on board; we're ready to take off!"

Clint blinked with astonishment, "But, Sir, I haven't been trained—"

"Get on the airplane, Stuart!" Lieutenant Stratton snapped. "You can learn as you go!"

"Yes, Sir!"

Clint scurried to where he saw a sergeant standing under the plane and said, "My name's Stuart; I'm the new engineer."

The sergeant pulled something out of his pocket. Looking closely, Clint saw that it was a Moon Pie. The sergeant took a bite out of it and studied the new recruit. "My name's Jim Wilson—everybody calls me Moon—on account of I like Moon Pies. I come from Florida, Pensacola. Where you from, Stuart?"

"Arkansas, the Ozarks." He studied the short, chunky man carefully and said, "I'd better tell somebody. I don't know anything. I've never even been up in a plane like this."

Moon Wilson grinned. "Good, you've come to the right place! You see the name of this plane?"

"The *Last Chance*."

"That's right! I think they throw everybody here that can't cut it into this plane. It's the last chance to make it. Come on. I hope you don't shoot our tail off!"

Clint followed the stocky bombardier, for that was his position on the crew, back to one of the hangars. "There, we'll get you geared up," Moon said, pulling out another Moon Pie and crunching it. He helped Clint get into the flying suit, which was heated, Clint was interested to see, complete with a wire and plug. When this was on, he wrapped a thick towel around his neck, directed so by Moon, and afterward slipped into a fleece-lined flight suit.

"You better put on some of these silk gloves," Wilson said. After Clint had pulled the white gloves on, he pulled over them a pair of leather ones, then Moon said, "Come on; you can carry some of this ammunition on."

Soon, draped with live ammunition, Clint helped load the airplane.

"This is the tail gunner, Asa Peabody," Moon said, nodding toward a tow-headed sergeant with blue eyes.

"Howdy!" Asa Peabody said. "You might as well hear where I'm from now, 'cause everybody thinks it's funny." He looked aggressively at Clint and said, "I'm from Bucksnort, Tennessee."

Clint grinned at him, "Well, we're both hillbillies then. I'm from so far back in the Ozarks you wouldn't believe it!"

Peabody found this amusing and grinned. Then his face turned rather fearful. "It will be a no good flight. I heard a dog howl this morning!"

Moon Wilson slapped his thigh with impatience. "You heard a dog howl, so we're not going to have a good flight! You're the most superstitious human being I ever heard of!"

But the tail gunner shook his head stubbornly. "You'll find out. I ain't never heard a dog howl that something bad didn't happen!"

"Come on, don't listen to him. Every time somebody spills salt, he wants to go back to the States. Thinks we're going to get shot down!" Moon said. He introduced Clint to the waist gunner, a tall, thin Italian named Manny Columbo, from New York, then moved down to a smaller man, very trim, who was standing over the entrance to the ball turret. "This is Beans Cunningham," he said. "He's a ladies' man. If you got a girl-friend, don't let him get close to her."

"Can't help it," Beans said. "They just naturally find me attractive!" He had brown hair and brown eyes. He stood looking down at the turret. "Guess you're too big to fit in here. Wish I was!"

Cisco Marischal, a former bullfighter, was the navigator and nose gunner. He looked like a dandy in his flight uniform.

The last member of the crew was another waist gunner and the radio operator, Red Frazier. He came from Seattle and had flaming red hair and a pale face. His nose had been badly broken at some point, and Moon Wilson said, "Watch out for Red; he's a fighter!"

"A boxer?" Clint asked with interest.

"Yep, I was a contender for the middleweight champion-ship before I got this job." Frazier shrugged. "When I get out of here, I'll be back at it."

Moon Wilson led Clint forward to his position in the aircraft, the upper turret. He said, "Did you ever shoot one of these things?"

"Just once."

Wilson laughed and slapped his hands together. "Well, don't shoot down any plane you see that has a star painted on the side. Look for a swastika."

"You think we'll get shot at today?"

"I hope not!"

The planes took off and made themselves into a formation. Clint had never felt so helpless. He tried his best to appear nonchalant, but the pilot quickly found out that the young gunner had never even been in a B-17, much less had active training.

"Just stay out of the way, Stuart!" Powell Stratton said. He looked over at the copilot and snarled, "Why do they send us these babies? We need good men!"

Albert Simmons shrugged. "We all had to learn sometime, Powell. He'll be all right."

The mission was strangely frightening and strangely exhilarating to Clint. They saw no enemy fighters that day, and only once did black flowers seem to explode close to the airplane from the antiaircraft guns below. They flew for three hours, and when the bombs were dropped the airplane suddenly surged upward, frightening Clint for a moment. He thought they had been hit. When he realized what had happened, he turned and made his way back down through the airplane, studying the men. *I've got to become a part of them,* he thought. *And I'm so stupid, I don't know the first thing about anything!*

Moon Wilson had come back from his position in the nose and saw that Clint was looking forlorn. "Here, have a Moon Pie," he offered, pulling one in rather poor condition from his flight-jacket pocket.

"Thanks, I don't think eating cookies is going to make me a good engineer or a gunner, either."

"Well, you've come to the right place," Wilson grinned. He seemed happy enough as they turned and headed back toward the home base. "Everybody is so incompetent here, you'll fit right in!"

It seemed a strange thing to Clint that Wilson could accept being in such a poor crew. He was to discover later that everybody on the aircraft felt pretty much the same way. As the new man, he had high hopes and aspirations, but from the two pilots through the rest of the crew, there was a lackadaisical spirit about them.

Beans Cunningham talked to him about it after they had landed and he was showing Clint to the barracks. "Don't worry about it; we're at the bottom of the list. Everybody knows that the *Last Chance* is just what the name means. Unless they kick us out of the air force, we'll keep on flying."

Asa Peabody, however, was close enough to hear. "No, we won't," he said. "We're going to get shot down on the next mission."

"What makes you think that, Asa?" Beans asked calmly. He was accustomed to the tow-headed tail gunner's gloomy predictions.

"Well, Lieutenant Stratton walked under a ladder after we landed. Now, everybody knows—even uneducated fellas like you—that walkin' under a ladder is bad luck."

Cunningham seemed depressed by the superstition of Asa Peabody. "Will you shut up!" he said. "I don't want to hear any more about your blasted predictions!"

After Beans left, Asa turned to Clint and said, "He's just ignorant. He ain't got no idea how dangerous it is to walk under a ladder."

Clint was rather amused. He had known many superstitious people back in the hills of the Ozarks and said with a grin, "Well, I know about ladders. I heard about a neighbor who walked under one, and a year later he got hit by a car and killed."

"Why, sure!" Asa Peabody said. "You see, that's how it works." A gloom settled over him and he shook his head. "Sure do wish that pilot hadn't walked under that ladder."

As Clint accompanied Cunningham into the barracks, he was thinking, *It looks like it's going to take a little getting used to being with a crew like this!*

8

"TELL ME ABOUT MY FATHER"

As the tall, slender man holding a dagger in his right hand advanced, Adam backed away slowly. His eyes narrowed as he gripped the knife in his own right hand, moving lightly on his feet. The slender man had a dark olive complexion, and a thin mustache spread over a mouth that twisted in a sneer. He, too, was light on his feet and very fast, and suddenly the blade shot forward, driving toward Adam's chest. With a lightning-like reaction, Adam parried the glittering blade of his opponent's knife, reached over, and grabbed the lapel of his coat. With a quick, twisting motion, he threw the man into the air over his shoulder. Instantly, as the man hit with a grunt and sprawled on the floor, Adam was at him. Straddling him, he grabbed the man's right wrist and put his knife to the man's throat saying, "Do I have to kill you, Juan—or will you behave?"

"Go on! Cut my throat; I don't care if I die!"

Adam held the knife in place for one moment. His lips were drawn thin, and his arm tensed before delivering the fatal blow. Suddenly a voice said, "Cut! That's it!"

Adam grinned down into the face of the man beneath his blade and said cheerfully, "Maybe I ought to cut your throat anyway! You've beaten me out of too much money at poker lately, Tony." Then he rose and put out a hand.

Tony Marello allowed himself to be hauled to his feet. He fingered his throat nervously and scowled. "That was a little bit too real, Adam! For a minute there I think you forgot we were just playing a scene."

A clutter of voices went up around the two men, and then Henry Vane came up, his fat body pulsing with life, and the eternal cigar trailing a cloud of blue smoke. Jamming the cigar in his mouth he slapped both men on the shoulders, having to reach up to do so, and exclaimed loudly, "That was the real article! You guys did great!"

Tony shook his head. "I'm glad that's the last fight scene. Adam, here, puts a little bit too much into these things." He turned when a young woman came to whisper to him and left as she held on to his waist.

Vane grinned at them. "Real romance going on there, but there always is with Tony." He puffed at the cigar rapidly, then squeezed his eyes together as he thought for a moment. "We ought to wrap this thing up day after tomorrow. It's been a good one, Adam. I told your folks so the other day. Not the quality kind of movie they make, but for a young fellow you made a good beginning."

Adam pulled a handkerchief out and wiped his brow. The brilliant lights overhead illuminating the set were still flooding the area with light. He found the words of the producer pleasant, indeed. The making of the movie had been fun for him. Although his part had not been large, it had called for considerable acrobatics, and when the director, Charles Smith, and Vane had discovered his ability in this line, they had added several more scenes.

"I've got to thank you again, Mr. Vane," Adam said, pushing the handkerchief back in his pocket. "I really needed work, and this has been fun. I'm still not much of an actor, though."

"Don't you believe it, Kid. You've got it in your blood. Lylah's kid couldn't be anything but a great actor. Come on; I'll buy you a drink."

The two men moved out of the set and made their way to Vane's office. Vane poured them each a drink and then held his glass up for a toast. "Here's to the next matinee idol of Tinsel Town," he grinned.

Adam tossed the drink back and nodded at the producer. "Well—maybe it won't amount to that, but I'd like to try it again."

"Would you? That's why I asked you to come up. I've got another picture coming up that won't be starting for a month, but I've got a part in it for you—a bigger one than you had in this one, and I'd like to talk to you about it."

Instantly Adam nodded. "Sure, Mr. Vane."

"You got an agent?"

"No, I don't."

"Well, maybe you ought to get one if you think you can't trust me. Even if you can trust me, I guess you need an agent."

"No, I don't think so, not right now. Tell me about the picture," Adam said eagerly.

The two men sat for some time, Vane smoking constantly and waving his hands through the air, cutting enthusiastic signs. He was this way, Henry Vane—whatever project he had was the greatest in the world, and he had a way of convincing his hearers that they should be in on it. Finally he said, "You think it over; talk to your folks. Wouldn't be surprised but what they'll try to sign you up for their own pictures."

"I don't know. They're pretty fussy about their actors. Maybe they'll let me move the scenery around or something."

"You're better than that, Adam. I think you got a real future in this business." Vane punctuated his words by jabbing the cigar toward Adam, then stuck it in his mouth and puffed on it. It glowed like a tiny, cherry-colored furnace at the tip, and when he removed it, he blew a perfect smoke ring. Finally he said more seriously, "Nobody knows what makes a star out here. You take some fellow who will be as handsome as a guy can get, with a perfect voice, and can remember his lines—but nobody will pay a nickel to see him act. Then somebody else comes wandering in, can't even talk plain or walk right, but people go crazy over him. That cowboy, John Wayne, can't act a lick—but he's gonna be big. When he's on the screen, you can't watch anybody else. Maybe you got it, Adam; maybe not. Guess we'll find out."

Adam left Vane's office feeling as if he were walking on the clouds. His part had been minor, and he had been caught up in his affair with Tamara, but nagging in his mind had been the question, *What'll I do after this is over?*

He was moving down the street when one of the assistant writers on the picture saw him. His name was Ned Bonar, and he planted himself in front of Adam saying, "Hey, why don't you come on down to the back set with me. It's our favorites, Laurel and Hardy. They're shooting today."

"You think we can go in?"

"An important movie star like you and a big-shot writer like me?" Bonar grinned broadly. He was a thin, short man, almost a gnome, but with enormous vanity. "Come on," he said. "If they give us any trouble, we'll get Vane to back us up."

The two men marched down to the set, which was just around the corner, and were halted momentarily by a hulking guard whose ears looked like battered pancakes. He scowled at them, but Bonar said, "Come on now, this is Adam Stuart, Mr. Vane's favorite nephew. You don't want to make Mr. Vane mad, do you?"

The guard hesitated momentarily, then shrugged. "OK, I guess you can go in."

"Come on, Adam," Bonar said quickly. The two men slipped inside and made their way to the set where the lights flooded the stage that was set up as a room.

"Looks like they're up to their usual stuff," Bonar whispered. "Look at that mess!"

Under the blazing lights, a very fat man, with a tiny mustache that looked like a black caterpillar under his nose, was attempting to paper the room. His helper was a smaller man, thin, with a sad-looking rubbery face, who was doing little in the way of positive paper hanging.

This, of course, was the famous team of Stan Laurel and Oliver Hardy, the ultimate comedy team of the early movies. Adam had always enjoyed them and had seen many times over every movie they had made. He had never met them, and he watched as the two demolished the room and each other with falling ladders, wallpaper paste splashed in the face, falls on slippery floors, and all the time the big man utterly disgusted and the smaller one seeming not to understand the problem. Adam found himself breaking up, and Bonar whispered, "Shut up; they'll make us leave!"

"I can't help it," Adam said. "Why is it they're so funny? They do the same thing over and over again."

"I guess if anybody knew the answer to that, there'd be another Laurel and Hardy team, but there's not—probably never will be."

"You think we can meet them after the scene?"

"Don't see why not!"

The two men waited until the scene was over, then Bonar led the way confidently. Going up to the big man he said, "Mr. Hardy, I hate to interrupt, but one of your greatest fans is here. This is Adam Stuart, the son of Lylah Stuart Hart over at Monarch Studio, so he may do you some good there."

Oliver Hardy was an enormous man. He had smallish eyes that twinkled pleasantly, and his mouth turned upward in a grin. He had wallpaper paste in his hair and all over his face, and he dabbed at his eyes and put out a hand awkwardly. "Pardon the paste," he said. "Glad to know you, young man."

"I've admired all your pictures," Adam said quickly. "Where do you get all your ideas?"

Hardy shook his head, and shrugged his beefy shoulders. "You'll have to talk to Stan about that. He's really the thinking member of the team. All I do is play golf."

Adam found that hard to believe, and when he turned to look at Stan Laurel, it was even more difficult. He was so accustomed to the goofy look on the actor's face that he could not believe that the younger and smaller of the two was the brains of the team. "I'm glad to know you, Mr. Laurel," he said. "I've seen every one of your pictures."

"Well, I hope you've seen the old ones," Stanley Laurel said. There was a discontented look on his face and he said, "This one's pretty much of a lemon."

"Oh, I'm sure it won't be. Why, I broke up just watching you do this one scene," Adam said. "You've given me so much pleasure, and so many others. I know you must be very happy about that."

Stan Laurel shrugged. "I wish we had never stopped making one-reelers," he said. "We're really vaudeville folks. These feature films, they don't fit us—but it's nice of you to say so."

The two left, and Bonar said, "You know, they're just regular fellows, aren't they? On the way down now, though; their glory days are over."

"I guess so, but they've certainly left something for the world," Adam remarked. "Most people die and don't leave anything except a marker in a cemetery. But a hundred years from now, when those fellows are in their graves, people will still be laughing at them trying to paper a room and making a mess out of it."

"Why do you think people like them so much?" Bonar inquired, scratching his head thoughtfully. "They can't act, and they play fools in all their movies."

"I don't know. Maybe it's because we see ourselves in them," Adam said thoughtfully. "Everything they set out to do, they've got a logical plan. Like papering that room—that was a simple thing, but when they got into it things began to go wrong, and by the time it was over, it was nothing but a mess. I guess," he said slowly, "that's the way most of us are."

Bonar gave the young man a quizzical look. "You're too young to be pessimistic and gloomy like that. You're young and good-looking, maybe a movie star, and you got your life before you. Now get on with it!"

Adam shrugged his shoulders. "Okay, Ned!" he said and grinned. "Thanks for the tour; I enjoyed it."

Adam left the set and moved outside to pick up his car from the studio parking lot. He began to think about Tamara. She was busy working on the completion of the picture. He was besotted by her in a way that he had never been by any of his other women friends. There was a raw sexuality in her that almost frightened him at times. He knew nothing in their relationship was permanent, and sooner or later it would be over. *She'll be with somebody else*, he thought, and waited to feel jealous but, strangely enough, did not. "I must be pretty much of a dope," he muttered.

There was still some daylight left, so he went to the country club and played tennis until dusk with the pro, Byron Kimbal. Adam had never actually beaten him, but he played with a cold, furious fashion that won him many points. When the sets were over and the two men had stopped to wipe their faces and get a drink, Kimbal gave him a strange look. "You play tennis like it's a war, Adam. It's supposed to be fun!"

"It's only fun when you win, Byron!"

"No, that's wrong. Some of my best times have been when I lost."

"I don't like to lose."

"Well, I guess none of us do, but that's part of the way things are. It would be pretty boring winning all the time." Byron was a smaller man than his companion. He was made of rawhide, with piano-wire muscles, and had the unbeliev-able, quick reactions of a fine tennis player. "I'd like to see you get more fun out of the game."

Adam grinned and took a swallow of ice water. "I had fun today. I beat you at least once. Wait until next time!"

"Well, if you keep working on that serve, you'll beat everybody," Byron Kimbal said. "Tomorrow?"

"Maybe, I'm not sure."

Adam left the club and drove to his parents' home. He had promised his mother he'd be there for supper and would spend the evening with them. When he got home, he found neither of his parents had arrived yet, so he threw himself on the bed and picked up a novel that he had been reading. It was a religious novel called *The Robe*, written by Lloyd Douglas. Adam had found it on his bed without a note but knew that his mother had put it there. He was aware that the book had been on the best-seller list but had ignored it for some time. One evening when he could not sleep he had begun reading it and had discovered that it was a fine novel. Lying with his head propped up on a pillow, he followed the adventures of Marcellus Gallio, the hero of the novel, who had been ordered to crucify Jesus. The story gripped Adam, and he followed the breakdown of the young tribune after carrying out his orders.

"That would be pretty rough, I guess," Adam murmured aloud, "crucifying Jesus Christ. Of course, he didn't know who he was at the time." Then he read on and was rather shocked at his response to the book. His parents had taken him to church from the time he was a child. Both of them were outstanding Christians, but Adam had never responded as they would have liked. He found the personality of Christ interesting as he had read in the Bible when he was much younger. But as he grew older, he had turned away from such things, to the despair of both Lylah and Jesse.

However, the book was interesting, and he lay reading until a knock came at his door. "Yes?" he called.

The door opened, and his mother stood smiling at him. "We're ready to eat. Are you hungry?"

"Like a wolf!"

The two went downstairs chatting and found Jesse already seated at the table. "Nothing to eat but food," Jesse said, smiling at Adam. "Sit down and tell us what it feels like to be a big-time movie star."

Adam laughed and said, "I've told enough lies in one day!"

"Acting isn't lying!" Lylah said instantly, defending her profession.

"Well, it better be, because I tried to kill a man today. If I wasn't pretending, he'd be dead!"

They sat down at the table, and Jesse interrupted the discussion on acting as a profession by asking the simple blessing, including special requests that God would guide Adam, which more or less embarrassed the young man. He was accustomed to it, however, and after the amen was said he began at once to speak about the possibility of a new film with a larger part. He was excited about it, and his eyes sparkled.

Lylah was thinking, *He looks so much like Manfred! Surely he's seen a picture of him. I wonder if he ever thinks of such things?* She never knew how to approach the matter of her affair with Manfred von Richthofen when speaking to her son. One part of her told her that it was a shameful incident, and in truth it was the great tragedy of her life. On the other hand, when she looked at this fine young specimen of manhood sitting across the table from her, she could not be sorry. Despite the wrong she had done, somehow good had come of it—and she knew that God would take that which was not right and produce a fine young man.

The meal was pleasant, and afterward they spent some time in the game room playing pool. Jesse was an expert. "I used to be a hustler before I went straight," he admitted. It was obvious he enjoyed the game very much. After a while, Lylah threw up her hands and said, "I'll leave this to you two. It's too difficult for me!"

The two men laughed and continued to play. It was pleasant under the soft lights, with the green table marked by the rolling balls, with the click as they struck one another, and with the soft remarks and exclamations of dismay that go with such things.

The game was interrupted once when Adam missed a difficult shot that would have won the game for him. Without thinking, he picked up the ball and slammed it against the wall. It hit the paneling with a sharp crack and then fell to the floor, rolling along the carpet.

Instantly Adam's face flushed. "Sorry, Dad, I didn't mean to do that!"

"I know how you feel. I wanted to do it quite a few times myself," Jesse said easily. As a matter of fact, this disturbed him more than he would allow to show on his calm face. He had seen this latent fury in Adam for years. Usually it lay concealed under the smooth exterior of a pleasant, handsome face—but from time to time when something went wrong, even when he was a child, Adam would suddenly explode, striking out at whatever was near. Carefully Jesse said, "Sometimes it's hard to remember that it's only a game."

Adam glanced up quickly. From Jesse, this was the equivalent of a sermon, for throughout Adam's life the older man had been very gentle and easy with his advice. Adam had learned to read his stepfather, however, and bit his lower lip. "I've got too much temper. I wish I were more like you."

"I think God made you like *you*." Jesse smiled. "If everybody were like me, it would be a mighty dull world."

It was a novel idea to Adam. He picked up his cue, stroked the smooth, polished wood gently as he considered it. "That's something to think about," he said finally, "if everybody were just like me." He grinned suddenly, which made him look much younger, almost like a teenager. "If everybody were just like me, that wouldn't be so hot. All of us would be wanting to win, and only one can."

"You've always had a strong instinct to win at games and anything else. That's not all bad," Jesse remarked. He moved over, placed the cue in position, and with a smooth, easy stroke made his shot. Moving over for the next one, he said, "I think that desire to excel is in you for a good reason. I don't know what it is yet, but all you need to do is control it. Lots of fellows don't have it, and they give up when the going gets tough. But you never do. You remember that fight you had with Charlie Denston? He was beating you half to death, but you never quit."

Adam winced at the thought of the fight. The other boy had

been almost a third again as large as he was, and it had been a brutal loss. "I wanted to kill Charlie. I got over it, of course!" he said quickly. "It seems like it comes and goes."

"You're doing well, Adam. I'm proud of you."

"Not too well." Adam watched as Jesse ran another shot, then said, "All I managed to do is get kicked out of school and do a little acting."

Jesse did not argue but began talking about the new part in the new movie. The two men got along well. Finally when they said good night, Jesse went to his study, and Adam went back to his room and read more of *The Robe*.

He was almost ready to go to bed when his mother knocked, and at his word she entered.

Adam looked up with a smile, but at the look on his mother's face, came off the bed. "What's wrong?" he said.

Lylah had a piece of paper in her hand. "This just came. Mary didn't know it was for you, so she opened it and gave it to me."

"What is it?" Adam was aware that his mother's large eyes were affixed on him and that there was a sadness in them he could not explain. "What is it, Mom?"

Without a word, Lylah handed Adam a telegram. He opened it and looked at it for a moment. The words seemed to jump off the paper at him:

This morning Jake was reported killed in action. I knew you'd want to know. He treasured your friendship greatly, Adam. I know you will grieve with us.

It was signed Marian Greenberg.

Shock ran along Adam's nerves, and his hand trembled.

"It can't be," he whispered. "Not Jake!"

Lylah moved forward and put her arms around Adam. She saw that the letter had torn into him as few things had. He had a stoical way of hiding his emotions, but now the raw pain that suddenly leaped into his eyes was impossible to miss.

His lips twisted, and he blinked furiously, trying to hide the tears that came there.

"I'm so sorry, Adam! He was such a fine young man and such a good friend to you." Lylah hoped that Adam would allow his grief to show—that he would weep—but she saw instead that his lips grew into a white line. He dashed the back of his hand across his eyes and grunted, "I've got to get out!"

"Adam!" Lylah called after him. She moved toward the door, but he went down the stairs two at a time. By the time she was halfway down, she heard the front door slam.

Jesse came out of his study saying, "What's wrong, Lylah?"

"Bad news. Jake Greenberg's been killed in action."

Jesse stared at her, then shook his head. "What a shame! Adam didn't take it well."

"I think Jake was the best friend he ever had—maybe the only *real* friend. He never did get close to many people, but he loved Jake."

"Where did he go?"

"I don't know. He can't handle it. I hope he doesn't—" She broke off, and looked at him knowing that he had read her thoughts. Finally she said aloud, "I hope he doesn't do something foolish."

Jesse came over and put his arm around her. He said nothing for a while. They had reached that stage, so rarely attained in a marriage, where each knew what the other was thinking. And even more than that, each knew what the other was feeling. Jesse knew the grief that lay in Lylah's heart for this son of hers, for he shared it. Adam was like his own son after all these years, and the two stood mutely sharing the pain that rose within each of them.

Lylah heard the door close and moved out of the study. She was wearing a light robe over her gown, and she glanced at the clock, noting that it was after three. *He'll hate it that I've stayed up and waited for him*, she thought. *But I've got to talk to him*. Moving into the hallway, she saw Adam, and he turned instantly and faced her. "You shouldn't have stayed up!" he grunted.

"I wanted to talk to you." She saw, at once, that he had been drinking but gave a prayer of thanks that he had not wrecked the car and hurt himself. "Please, Adam, don't run away from me!"

"There's no point talking about it; he's dead!" The words were short and bitter, and Adam stood with his shoulders hunched together, his fists clenched.

"Just for a while, come into the study."

"All right, but it won't do any good."

Adam followed his mother inside. She pulled him down to the overstuffed sofa, and when she began to talk, he stared down at the floor. He did not really hear what she said, because his mind was numbed by the liquor that he had drunk and even more by the pain that he knew would not go away, even after the alcohol had lost its power. As she talked on, he thought about the good times he had had with Jake Greenberg. They had been different in many ways, but somehow the chemistry had been right. Now, all he could think of was Jake's bloody body lying somewhere in the jungles of the Solomon Islands. He could not bear to think of it and started to rise, then a thought came to him. He turned to his mother, and a strange expression crossed his face. "I don't know how to handle this, Mom," he said finally. "I never had anything like it."

"None of us knows how to handle it. We just have to endure, but God will help us through it."

"I don't know God—you know that!"

"But he knows you!"

Adam thought about this, then leaned back. His head swam when he put it back on the couch, and he felt nauseated from having drunk so much. He was conscious of his mother holding his hand, saying nothing, and for a long time, it seemed, he lay unable to move or speak.

Lylah kept her eyes fixed on his profile, thinking as she always did, how much he looked like his father. She said nothing, but she held his hand, which was strong and thick with muscle. Finally he lifted his head and straightened up.

She was shocked when he said, "Mom, tell me about my father."

Lylah had not expected this. It had been difficult enough to tell Adam the truth about his biological father. After she told him, he had never asked questions, which had surprised her. For years she had expected him to want to know more about how he had come to be conceived, but he had never asked. Now, however, the tragedy had stirred something deep within him, and questions were beginning to rise to the surface.

"Why do you want to know, Son?"

"A man ought to know about his father."

Lylah made a quick decision. She could put him off, but there was something demanding in his eyes, and there was a vulnerability in his lips and in his entire expression that told her she must not.

"I was visiting in Germany just before the war," she said slowly, "and I met your father through a friend of the von Richthofen family. . . ."

Adam sat listening as his mother spoke softly, pausing from time to time. He did not miss a syllable as she related how she had met the young German aristocrat and had no idea that they would ever fall in love. Then she related that, somehow, despite everything to the contrary, she had begun to love the young flier, and he had loved her. He listened as she spoke almost desperately of how she had fought against the attraction, then finally she said with tears in her eyes, "There's no excuse for what we did. It was very wrong. I've asked God to forgive me for it, and he has." The tears ran down her cheeks, and she suddenly wiped them away and said in a strange voice, "But I have you, Adam, and I'm grateful to God for that. I'm sorry that your life has been so complicated by something that you had no part in, but I want to tell you about your father. He was a fine man."

"He was a German fighting against Americans."

The bleakness of Adam's tone shocked Lylah. "Yes," she said, startled, and not quite certain of herself. "I knew that too, but love sometimes overrides nationalities and even wars. Can you forgive me and him?"

"I've thought about it for years. Jesse's been such a good father; that's taken the strain off of it, but now things are different."

"How are things different?"

"This war." Adam's voice was somewhat thick from the effect of the alcohol, but she saw that he was deeply moved and had trouble saying what he was feeling. "Hitler has brought it all back again, and now they've killed Jake, the Germans have!"

"He was killed in the Pacific."

"Doesn't matter; Hitler started it all. If it hadn't been for him, the Japs would never have attacked Pearl Harbor." The words were bitter, clipped short, and carved almost in stone. There was a coldness, indeed, in Adam's eyes now. Sorrow and grief were solidifying within him, and when he thought of his friend it was almost instantly turned to the enemy.

"I don't want you filled with hate, Adam."

"How can I help it; they killed Jake, didn't they? Do you expect me to love them for it?"

Lylah knew this was no time for a sermon. She sat for a long time beside Adam and saw how futile it was. She had never seen this hardness in him before, and she knew as she sat looking into the cold blue eyes of her son that the death of Jake Greenberg had triggered something in him that had been long dormant.

Adam got up quickly and said, "Good night, Mother."

"What are you going to do, Adam?"

"I don't know." He turned and left and went to his room. He saw *The Robe* lying on the bed and picked it up at once. He thought about what he had read—how the tribune had learned to forgive the enemies of Christ and to forgive himself. He stared at it for a moment, then finally said bitterly, "That's in a book— things don't happen that way in life!" He flung the book aside and threw himself on the bed, burying his face in the pillow.

9

A DECISION FOR ADAM STUART

For the sixth time, Carol read Clint's letter, savoring every word of it. She was sitting under the apple tree in the backyard where she had been peeling potatoes to boil for supper but had pulled the worn sheet of paper out of her apron pocket. Overhead the blossoms of the apple tree were white and fragile and beautiful, but she had no eyes for them. A bluebird flew across the yard making a brilliant dot of color against the green grass. It reached the birdhouse of cedar that Clint had made and disappeared inside. A faint cheeping sound emerged from the birdhouse, but Carol did not hear any of it. She was reading the words that she almost had memorized, but it gave her hope to go over them again.

The screen door slammed, and she looked up quickly. Seeing her father, she slipped the letter into her pocket, but Davidson had noted it. "Reading that letter again?" he smiled, taking a seat beside her. "You must have it memorized by now."

Carol laughed self-consciously. "I suppose I do, Dad. I wish I could get a letter every day."

"Takes a little longer than that to get a letter here from England." Davidson's face was worn and lined, and there was a weariness in his voice. He had lost weight and did not have good color. The colorful Hawaiian shirt that he wore drooped over his thin shoulders, and there was an emaciated look about his face that frightened Carol. He leaned his head

139

back, closed his eyes, and said, "It smells good in the spring. May was always my favorite month."

"Mine, too; the garden's going to be good this year."

"I don't think I'll be able to do a lot with it. You better get Jimmy Archer to come over and help."

Glancing at her father quickly, Carol felt a start of fear. The garden had been his pride and joy before his illness. He had put in long hours at his job, then had come home and seemed to find relaxation by pottering around with onions and carrots and okra. Now, however, he had lost interest, and she tried to think of something encouraging to say. In truth there was little, for he had gone down quickly in the past few weeks. She had had a secret meeting with Dr. Cotter, who had warned her that her father could go at any moment.

"What's in the paper?" Carol said, hoping to gain his interest.

Davidson opened the page and began to share the news with her. Sick as he was, it was the one thing he seemed to take an interest in. "Well, there's good news and bad."

"Let's have the bad first," Carol said, making a face. It seemed the war was never going to go well for America and her allies. "What's happened, Dad?"

"Bataan's fallen. The Japanese took thirty-six thousand prisoners there and are moving forward. They bombed Ceylon and sank a British carrier there. The British can't afford to lose any of those. There're too few of them." He read on for a while and said, "But here's the good news." He looked up and his eyes were somewhat brighter. "There's been a bombing raid on Tokyo."

"Tokyo!" Carol exclaimed. "How could they do that?"

"A general named Doolittle launched some light bombers, B-25s, off of the aircraft carrier *Hornet*. The carrier got to within six hundred miles of the coast of Japan, the paper says. The planes flew so low over Japan that Doolittle said they could see a ball game being played."

"That's wonderful!"

"Well, it won't mean much as far as winning a war, but it's good news—and we don't get much of that over here."

"Are we going to win the war, Dad?"

"Of course we will! It's just going to take time."

The two sat there until Carol finished the potatoes, then she said, "I didn't tell you, but Harry Bledsoe called me again."

"He still wants you to go to work for him?"

"Yes, and he offered more money."

"You don't need to go to work, Daughter. We can get by."

"I know, Dad," Carol said, "but I get so nervous around here. The housework doesn't take long, and I'd really like to do something. Would you mind if I did work at least part-time?"

"Not if you want to, Honey. What kind of job would it be, building parts in the factory?" Harry Bledsoe had a small parts factory just outside of Fort Smith. He had, however, another office and spent considerable time away.

"He says he wants me to do some of the book work. Some of it I could do at home, and some of it I might have to drive over to Fort Smith to do."

"It might be a break for you, Carol," Davidson nodded. He seemed exhausted by this simple conversation and finally rose, his hands trembling. "I think I'll go take a nap."

"All right, Dad. You sleep awhile. I think I'll call Mr. Bledsoe and tell him that I'll take the job."

Moving inside, she finished the preparations on a pie for dessert, stuck it in the oven, then went to the telephone. When someone answered, "Bledsoe Incorporated," she said, "May I speak with Mr. Bledsoe?"

"Hi, this is Carol isn't it? This is Harry."

"Oh, I didn't recognize your voice, Mr. Bledsoe."

"I hope you've changed your mind about taking the job. I really need someone, Carol."

"Well, yes, I have, as a matter of fact. But only on a part-time basis. When would you want me to go to work?"

"How about like right now?"

"Right now!" Carol was startled. "But—"

"Well, maybe not exactly right now. Could you come in in the morning? We could go over the books, and I think we can get you all straightened out pretty quick."

"All right, Mr. Bledsoe, I'll see you in the morning. Would nine o'clock be all right?"

"Great! See you then, Carol!"

The next morning, Carol dressed carefully and drove the ancient Hudson, which her father had kept in such good condition, to the factory. She found Harry Bledsoe waiting for her, and he greeted her effusively saying, "Well, good to see you! Come right in!"

Bledsoe was a man of forty, with brown hair and active, energetic brown eyes. He was ambitious and had built his business up by hard work, putting in eighteen-hour days. He had been married, but his wife had divorced him the previous year. No one was exactly certain why, but it was reputed that Bledsoe had been unfaithful to her. He took Carol's arm and said, "Come in, come in! How about something to drink—coffee, orange juice?"

"Orange juice would be fine." Carol was ushered into the office, which was cluttered, and took the glass of juice that Bledsoe handed her. He poured himself a cup of coffee and waved the cup around as he spoke. "I've been so busy, I need to be twins, Carol," he said. "Shuffling back and forth between Fort Smith, and I'm thinking of opening up another office in Oklahoma City. Big opportunity there."

"I didn't know your business was moving so fast."

"Well, this hasn't got out yet," Bledsoe said, "but I've gotten a government contract. We'll be making parts for military vehicles now. Going to have to expand, and that's why I need help."

"I never worked as a bookkeeper."

"You'll do fine. You had it in high school, didn't you? And you worked for Mr. Simms down at the furniture store, kept his books?"

"I'll do the best I can."

"Fine, fine! Well, are you ready to start?"

"I guess so."

Bledsoe gave her a careful look and shook his head. "You sure dress up this office." He admired the light green dress that she wore and commented, "I like the way your hair is fixed."

"Why, thank you, Mr. Bledsoe."

"Hey, it takes too long to say 'Mr. Bledsoe.' Harry will be fine, except when we got important government people here, then we'll be formal. OK?"

"Well, all right, Harry, if that's the way you'd like it."

"Sure, a small business like this, we're going to be working real close."

For the next two weeks, Carol found herself more and more interested in the business. She also found herself working more and more hours, until she was basically a full-time employee. It took her mind off her fears for Clint and also her apprehensions about her father. She could not deceive herself that he was better and constantly thought of what would happen if he died. She knew she should be with him more, but she couldn't face his declining health.

It was on the second Thursday on the job that they had worked late, until after seven. Everyone had gone, and Bledsoe was dictating a letter to her. He looked up at the clock with surprise and interrupted himself. "Hey, it's seven o'clock!" Grinning, he said, "Why didn't you say something? I didn't mean to make a slave out of you!"

"I don't mind, Harry."

"Well, I do. Come on; let's close up." He locked the doors, and as they stepped outside he said, "What about something to eat? I guess Harrison's is still open; we can get a burger."

"Oh, I really shouldn't!"

But Bledsoe insisted. "Come on, I'm not going to bite you! We'll go in my car. I'll bring you back to yours after we get a bite."

Harrison's was a small cafe that often stayed open late. The evening special sounded good, so instead of hamburgers, they

had steaks. The jukebox was on, and Frank Sinatra was singing, "All or Nothing at All." "I like that guy. He's got a good
voice," Bledsoe said. "Who's your favorite singer?"

"I suppose Tony Martin."

"Yeah, he's good, too." They discussed popular songs and
compared their tastes, and finally Bledsoe leaned across the
table and said, "You got good taste in music, and you're doing
a great job. I really appreciate all you've done."

"Why, it's been fun." Carol was somewhat nervous being
in the cafe with a divorced man. Small-town morality was
firmly fixed, and she knew that tongues would be wagging.
Finally, after they'd finished their steaks, she said, "I guess
I'd better get home. Dad will be waiting for me."

"All right." Bledsoe paid the bill, and the two got into his
car. When they got to the factory, Carol started to get out, but
he took her arm and said, "Look, I get lonesome sometimes,
Carol. There wouldn't be anything wrong with us taking in
a movie, something like that."

"Why, I can't do that, Harry, I'm married!"

"So you're married." Bledsoe's hand went around her
shoulder, and he shook her gently. He was an attractive man,
and now said persuasively, "I'm just talking about a movie,
maybe go to a concert, something like that. I'm gonna have
to ask you to go to Fort Smith sooner or later, to help with
the book work there."

"I couldn't do that. It wouldn't be right!"

Bledsoe smiled. "You're probably right," he said. "But I
get so lonesome sometimes. I miss my wife."

It was the first time that Bledsoe had mentioned his wife,
and Carol asked tentatively, "What happened, if you want
to tell me?"

"Well, nobody's really asked me. If you don't mind listening, I'd like to talk about it a little bit."

Carol listened as Bledsoe spoke for over half an hour. She felt
sorry for him, for, according to his story, he had done nothing to
deserve what his wife had handed him. "The truth is," he said

finally, shrugging his shoulders, "she was in love with another guy. That never came out, but that's the way it was."

"That's too bad. I'm so sorry." She was aware that Bledsoe's hand was on her shoulder, but there seemed no harm in it. Nevertheless, she said, "I've got to go. Thanks for the supper."

"Good night, Carol." Bledsoe moved his arm, but he patted her gently on the back saying, "It was a lucky day for me when you came to work at my place."

Carol made her way home, and when her father asked her why she was late, she hesitated. "Oh, I had extra work to do." For one moment she had considered telling him she had gone out with Harry Bledsoe and that they had talked for a time, then for some reason she decided against it. "I'm going in to write Clint a letter," she said. When she wrote the letter, however, she did not mention her job with Harry Bledsoe, nor the fact that she had gone out with him. It gave her a twinge of conscience to keep anything from Clint, but she didn't want to worry him. "I won't do it again," she said. "It was just that Harry is so lonely."

Wendy Stuart made her way through the noonday crowds and finally found a place to sit at the lunch counter. She ordered a chicken sandwich and milk, and when it came, she began to eat, conscious of the hubbub around her. The city, always crowded, now seemed to be bursting out of its seams. The war had done that to every place, she supposed. People who were once at home were now out working at jobs that they had never once thought of. She remembered the letter she had received from Mona and pulled it out of her purse. Unfolding it, she chewed thoughtfully on the sandwich and reread Mona's letter.

Dear Wendy,
   I'm sorry I was so late answering your last letter, but things have been happening so fast. I broke up with Charles—but then I don't think I even mentioned that I was going with

him. Anyway, he's a big man on campus here at the university.
The big thing right now is the Miss Oklahoma contest. It's
the most exciting thing I've ever been involved in, Wendy.
I've just got to win! I've got a friend who was entered last
year, and she said you have to do things like putting Vaseline
on over your lipstick so that you can smile all the time. Isn't
that funny?

Wendy's brow wrinkled as she felt a stab of worry. *Doesn't
she ever think of anything serious?* she thought. Folding the letter,
she put it back in her purse, wondering what it would be like
to have your life taken up with dances and proms and Miss
Oklahoma contests. Her own life had steadied to a routine.
She still had not obtained a job singing, but there was at least
one good prospect. She worked at the library part-time now
and spent the rest of the time either practicing or helping
with the USO. She had become very popular there and had
performed many, many times. The servicemen were so hungry for entertainment that she had laughingly told her father,
"They'd applaud if Andy Devine stood up and sang!"

Finishing her sandwich, she slipped off the stool and left
the drugstore. As she was passing through the door, she heard
her name called and turned to find Alex coming out of the
building. "Wendy!" he said. There was a welcome smile on
his face. He was wearing a pair of light blue trousers, a white
shirt open at the throat, and his face was tanned.

"Alex, I didn't expect to see you here!"

"I just got back in town. I've been down in Miami doing
a series of concerts there." Alex examined Wendy carefully
and said, "You look beautiful."

"Well, I'm not tan like you are."

"We can't stand here; come along. Where are you going?"

"I'm going to work."

"Where are you working now?"

"Oh, just a part-time job at the library."

"Aren't you singing at all?"

"Just at the USO; I may have a chance at a job though."

"Come on; I'll take you there—or is your car here?"

"No, I was going to ride the bus."

"Well, no need of that!" Alex put his hand possessively on Wendy's arm, which sent a thrill through the young woman.

He led her to the parking lot, and she smiled, "You still have the same car. I thought you might be driving a Cadillac by now!"

"No, they don't make 'em like this one anymore." Alex patted the old Cord affectionately, then opened the door. When Wendy got in, he shut the door, then walked around and got behind the wheel. As they drove toward the library, she listened as he spoke enthusiastically about the success of the symphony.

"I hear the program every week. It's magnificent, Alex; I'm so proud of you."

Alex turned to look at Wendy. "Nice of you to say that. Some young women wouldn't have been so generous."

"Why do you say that?"

"Well, after all, we broke up, and when couples break up there's usually some animosity there."

"I wouldn't feel like that. I'm proud of what you're doing."

Alex said nothing for a time. In fact he was struck by Wendy's fresh beauty, and warm memories were flooding back. He had felt something for her he never felt for any other young woman, and when he dropped her off at the library he asked, "What time do you get off?"

"Five o'clock."

"You're going out with me tonight, no argument! If you don't agree, I'll kidnap you. Then I'll be arrested and probably electrocuted. You don't want to be responsible for that, do you?"

Wendy had missed his teasing ways and said, "All right, I suppose I'll have to agree."

The day went slowly at the library, for she was thinking mostly of Alex. His appearance had brought memories back to her and sadness of a kind. However, when she went outside to meet him, she let none of this show.

"We're going back to Jimmy Kelly's. Remember the time we ate there?"

"Yes, but it still costs a lot."

"Doesn't matter. I've got it, and we're going to spend it!"

The dinner was fine, and after they had eaten and had left the restaurant, Alex said, "Want to take a drive around the lake?"

"All right."

The moon was out and Wendy enjoyed listening as Alex talked about the world of music. He was totally involved in the symphony, and finally as they came to park by a grove of trees, he looked up and said, "These are probably the only trees left in the whole city."

"The lake's pretty—look at that moon," Wendy said.

"Do you ever think about us, Wendy?" Alex asked after they had talked for a time. He turned to face her and admired the way the silver light of the moon touched her cheek, outlining her smooth features. She had beautiful eyes, and now she turned to him, her lips curved upward, and he thought he had never seen anything prettier.

"Yes, I think about it a lot."

A silence fell on them for a moment, and then finally Alex said slowly, "I've missed you more than I thought I'd ever miss anyone, Wendy."

Wendy could hardly speak as Alex took her hand and kissed it. "You shouldn't do that, Alex," she whispered.

Alex stared at her and shook his head. "You know, I don't know how to say this, but I still love you." When she did not answer, he released her hand, and then reached over and pulled her closer. He kissed her, and the pressure of his lips and the touch of his hands stirred her. She found herself responding, and her hand went up behind his head, and she pulled him even closer. And for Alex there was a sweetness in the kiss that he had never found with any other woman—an innocence and a lack of deception that drew him. Her body was firm against him, and he felt hungers rise in him and drew her closer. She pulled away, pushing at his chest, and he said huskily, "You haven't changed."

"I guess not. I don't suppose I ever will."

"Look, Wendy, the world is blowing up. We've got to take what happens as we can when it comes. I'm not a soldier, not risking my life every day, but life goes by pretty quick."

"So we have to take whatever fun we can? I don't believe that, Alex. There's more to life than that. After all, look at all the people you've known that have had affairs. After they're over, what's left? Nothing but bitterness, usually."

"It's not like that with us."

"It might be, but we'll never find out."

Alex Grenville put his hands on the steering wheel and bowed his head. There was a stubbornness in this woman beneath her fragile exterior and her gentle manners. He had the feeling that, if she needed to, she could shoot a man down and then treat the wound. He looked at her and shook his head. "I can't have you, and you're the only one I want." When she did not answer, he started the car and said morosely, "Why is it that we don't get the things we want in this life?" He turned the Cord around and headed back to the library. When he let her out she said, "Good-bye, Alex." And he felt as if he was losing something precious, yet he could not do more than say, "Good-bye, Wendy."

"I've decided to join the Air Corps."

Lylah and Jesse Hart had been paying attention to their meal, and Adam's abrupt announcement swiveled their glances, and they stared at him with disbelief.

Adam had expected such a response. For weeks now he had been walking around saying little, and when Henry Vane had shoved the contract for the new movie under his nose, he had not been able to sign it. Vane had been incredulous, but he had not been able to persuade the young man.

"The Air Corps!" Lylah exclaimed. "When did you decide this, Adam?"

"I can't say just when." Adam shrugged. He pushed the bit of asparagus around with his fork for a moment, then looked up and said, "I know it comes as a shock, but I guess you really know why I'm doing it."

Jesse looked at the young man carefully. "It's Jake Greenberg, isn't it, Adam?"

"Yes, I can't get him out of my mind."

"I'm not sure that's a good reason for joining the Air Corps or any of the services," Lylah said quietly. Fear had come to her, for she knew that the loss of this son of hers would ruin her life. "Why don't you wait a while?"

"It's too late; I've already enlisted."

Adam looked at the two and tried to explain. "I can only talk to you. Not many people know who my father was, but somehow I feel responsible for Jake's death."

"Well, that doesn't make sense, Adam. Your father was German, but that was in another war."

"I know it doesn't make any sense, but I've been going almost crazy," Adam said. He tossed the fork down and looked at them, then said, "I can't really explain it; I just got to do it!"

"How did you get in the Air Corps?"

"Well, since I can already fly, I think that made a difference. I had some college, although my scores are rotten, but they gave me a whole battery of tests, and I guess I must've done pretty well." He went on to tell them about how he had wanted to get it all done before he told them. "Maybe I was afraid I'd back out, I don't know. Anyway, I'll be leaving to go to flight school in a week."

Lylah could think of nothing to say, and she merely listened with a growing fear as Adam spoke about his plans. Finally, she said, "If you've got to do it, we'll pray that God will protect you, Adam."

Adam stared at her, "Thanks, Mom. I'll need all the prayers I can get."

10

MEN AT WAR

Never had there been any doubt in Will Stuart's mind about what branch of the service he would fight his war in. Somehow the United States Marine Corps had been real to him from early boyhood. He had read the history of the Corps and everything he could find about the heroes that made up that branch, and when the first news of Pearl Harbor had come over the radio, the words had leaped into his mind, *I'll be a marine.*

Now as he sat jammed in the passenger car of the Erie commuter train that passed over the Hudson River to downtown New York, he thought of that moment and wondered if he had been wise. The master gunnery sergeant who escorted the group of prospective marines to Parris Island was a slender man of middle age wearing marine dress blues. Now, standing up as the train began to slow, he grinned and said, "When you get to Parris Island, you'll find things different. You won't like it, you'll think it's stupid, you'll think those officers and noncoms are the cruelest, rottenest bunch of men you ever ran into!" He paused, looked around almost fiercely, and shook his head. "I'm gonna tell you one thing. If you want to save yourselves headaches, you do everything they tell you and you keep your big mouths shut!"

Will had listened along with the others, and as the marine left the car he said, "Thanks, Sarge!"

Sergeant Benton glared at Will with mock ferocity. "It's OK if you call me 'Sarge,' but from now on, don't address anybody, even a lowly PFC without saying 'Sir'!"

Will thought about that as they arrived at the station. Other marine recruits were arriving from all over the east. His unit was the last to arrive, aboard an ancient wooden train that puffed, smelling of coal, waiting to take them to the coast of South Carolina. As the train rattled on over uneven sleepers, all the men talked about the Corps. "What do you think it'll be like at Parris Island?" "Hey, you think the Japs are as tough as the newspapers say they are?"

By the time they got to Parris Island and formed into a motley rank in front of a red brick mess hall, they were all tense. Will walked along with a group in clumsy civilian fashion. In the mess hall they were fed bologna and lima beans—cold lima beans. Afterwards they were addressed by Sergeant Wilcox, a southerner with a fine contempt for northerners. He was about six-feet-four, weighed 230 pounds, and had a voice that could make your hair hurt. It pulsed with power as he counted out the cadence as they marched. It whipped at the men, stiffening their slouching civilian backs. They marched to the quartermaster's and were ordered to strip naked. Will stood before the quartermaster thinking, *Somehow, when a man hasn't got any clothes on, he's defenseless. Your clothes are kind of like your character.* Later he recognized that everything of the past was ripped from them by the Marine Corps. It was part of the plan to make marines out of civilians.

When Will emerged, he had a monstrous pile of gear: rain cap, gloves, socks, shoes, underwear, shirts, belts, pants, coats. And he had a number, 351000 USMCR. He had the feeling of being stripped of his personality, and looking around, he noted that everyone looked alike.

The haircut came next, and as they marched to the barber shop the cry, "You'll be sorry!" was heard. Sitting down in the chair, Will received the quickest haircut he had ever had. Four or five strokes with the electric clippers, and he was as bald as an egg.

He was taken to the second floor of a wooden barracks, and

for the next few weeks there were no privileges, except the privilege of marching.

March to the mess hall, march to the sick bay, march to draw rifles, slimy with Cosmoline, march, march, march. Feet slapping cement, treading the packed earth, always grinding to a halt with rifle butts clashing. "To the rear march! . . . Forward march! . . . Right shoulder arms!"

For the next few weeks nothing but discipline—no one at Parris Island seemed to care for anything except discipline. He heard no talk of the war, no fiery lectures about killing Japs. The drill instructors loved to beat into the raw civilians that had been handed to them the instant obedience to commands. Sergeant Wilcox, the drill instructor, delighted in throwing any discomfort he could upon his squad. He marched them toward the ocean on one cold morning, his chanted cadence never faltering. Right toward the ocean they went, and when the leader stopped, the sergeant went into a rage. "Who do you think you are? You're nothing but a bunch of stupid boots! Who told you to halt? I give the orders here, and nobody halts until I tell 'em to!"

The next day the platoon marched resolutely into the water, and he screamed, "Come back here, you idiots! Get your stupid behinds out of that ocean!" He would turn and address the universe, "Who's got the most stupid platoon on the whole island? That's right, me! I've got it!"

Will had enjoyed privacy most of his life and a semblance of good manners but found that both had ceased to exist. Most of the men had ideas of what passed for good table manners, but the meals were more like feeding time at the zoo. Will discovered that he was losing his sensitivity. Part of this was the ruthless denial of the slightest privacy. Everything was done in the open—rising, waking, letter writing, receiving mail. There was *no* privacy. Food in packages from home was appropriated by the drill instructor, and he would give a fine account of how good the cakes or homemade candy were. This caused rage among some of the recruits, which only delighted the drill instructors. In the morning the cold coastal weather brought shivers, and Sergeant Wilcox delighted in tormenting the northerners. "Hey, Yankee, I thought it was cold up north! Thought you was used to it! Look at them big Yank's lips chatter!"

A problem for Will was the continual cursing and blasphemy and obscenity that took place. It was like part of the air that he breathed. In time, he learned to shut his mind to it, but the air was filled with cursing, especially on the rifle range.

It was on the rifle range, however, that after being taken apart, they started being put together as marines. Most of the southerners knew how to shoot, and even a surprising number of big city boys. It seemed that those from Georgia and Kentucky were the best. There was a certain number of mistakes, shooting at the wrong target, shooting under the bull's eye, but Will wound up with an expert rifleman's badge. It had brought five dollars a month extra pay, a considerable sum to one earning twenty-one dollars a month.

Finally it was over, and as they departed, the newly minted marines passed a bunch of incoming recruits, still in civilian clothes.

"They look terrible, don't they, Sergeant Wilcox?" Will said.

Wilcox looked at Will angrily. "They look about like you did when you got here!"

"Ah, come on now, Sir. We haven't done bad, have we?"

Wilcox struggled with himself and then finally allowed a slight grin. "Time you smell a little powder, you might make a marine," he admitted grudgingly.

Will sat talking with the others as they waited for the supply trucks that would take them to the next stage of their training, the really rough part, they were told. As the fervor of activity went on around him, he thought how he had been made into something that he was not. He had learned part of the mystique of the marines. He spoke despairingly of soldiers as "dog faces," and sailors as "swab jockeys." He called West Point that "boys' school on the Hudson." He still could not accept as gospel truth unverified accounts of army or navy officers resigning their commissions to sign up as marine privates—but he was a marine.

At New River, where the First Marine Division was being formed, there were no dress blues, no women, no dance bands, nothing to make a man happy. As their sergeant warned them, "It's dull and depressing, gun drills and nomenclature. Know your weapon, know it intimately." Every hour there was a ten-minute break, and the major gave them the same talk every day. "There'll be no thinking!" he would shout. "No enlisted man is permitted to think! The moment you think, you're weakening the outfit!"

No one, however, was allowed to forget he was a marine. It came out in the forest green of the uniform, in the hour-long spit polishing of the dark brown shoes. It was in the jaunty angle of the campaign hats worn by the gunnery sergeants. Everything, every day, every hour, whether bayonet practice, the rifle range, or simply marching, was all marines. H Company was like a clan, or a tribe, and Will found himself in something like a family group. They all sank their differences into a common dislike for officers and for discipline, and later they would trade these off for the twin enemies in the Pacific: the jungle and the Jap.

As Will stood on the deck of the troop carrier, he saw fires flickering on the shores of Guadalcanal Island. In a drizzle in June of 1942, his ship had passed under the Golden Gate Bridge. Today, with battle imminent, he wished he were somewhere else.

"First Platoon over the side, down those cargo nets!"

The ship swayed in a gentle swell, and Will's rifle muzzle knocked his helmet forward over his eyes as he scrambled the nets. He held on tightly, but three feet above the rolling Higgins boats, the cargo nets came to an end. If a man missed, he could sink and drown, but there was no choice. Will shoved off and hit the boat, sprawling on the floor of it, and was immediately half crushed as two other marines landed on top of him.

The boat was soon filled, and Will poked his head up despite warnings from the sergeant. His ears were strained for the sound of battle, and his body tensed for the leap over the side. The boat finally struck the shore, came to a halt, and he scrambled out with the others.

"Hey, there ain't nobody here!" Bill Taylor said.

Along with the others Will expelled a sigh of relief. The marines wandered around Red Beach, and for ten minutes they had something like bliss and unspeakable relief at finding their landing unopposed—but even as they stepped from the white glare of the beach into the sheltering shade of the coconut groves, somewhere came a yammer of antiaircraft guns. The Japs had come, the war was on, and it would never be the same.

For two days they crossed rivers and recrossed them and climbed hills. They reached the Tenneru River and looked over the miles and miles of coconut groves. Then they reached a spot called Grassy Knoll. Exhausted almost to the state of unconsciousness, they waited for the enemy to come, as intelligence told them it would.

The night came on, and Will, along with the others, was cold and afraid. All night long he listened to the sounds that came from the jungle—the sound of moving things that seemed to creep closer. The darkness closed in, the trees dripped, the jungles whispered—but no one came. All the next day they waited for the enemy. The terrain of Guadalcanal seemed to be composed of mud, and their feet were continually churning on these undulating paths. But they saw no enemy. That night, however, Will awoke with a start. "Hey!" he yelled. "What's on fire?"

The squad came awake at once and grabbed their rifles.

"Those things are flares!" Sergeant Maddox said. He had come to stand beside the squad.

"Why are they firing flares? Are they coming after us?"

"No," Maddox said, "they're out over the ocean. They come from Japanese sea planes."

The flares hung over the whirls, swaying gently on their parachutes.

Soon they heard the sound of cannonading, and the earth seemed to tremble.

"What's going on, Sarge?"

"I reckon it's the navy." He hesitated, then said, "I sure hope they rip them Japs!"

"Ah, they will!" A young marine with a pale face said. "They can't whip us!"

They *did* whip us. The Japanese hammered out one of their greatest naval victories that night. It was called the Battle of Savo Island, which the marines learned to call the Battle of the Four Sitting Ducks. Three American cruisers and one Australian cruiser were sunk that night, and as the marines huddled in the slimy jungle, they did not understand what it meant.

Finally, dawn came and Sergeant Maddox led the men down to the beach.

"Hey, where are the ships?"

Will looked out with a sinking feeling.

The navy was gone, not a ship in sight.

"Uh, oh," Sergeant Samuels groaned, "that tears it!"

"What does it mean, Sarge?" Will asked.

Sergeant Samuels was a veteran of forty, his face lined with experience. "It means we're stuck on this island. The Japs got control of the ocean; they can bring in all the supplies and the men they want to to get us."

Will Stuart was tired and exhausted, but he knew what that meant. He wanted to ask the sergeant, "Do you think we'll make it?" but knew it was a foolish question. He moved back to the squad and thought about his family and the slender chances he had of ever seeing them again. He wondered about his brother, Woody, who was fighting in a tank corps in Africa, and wondered if he would ever see him again.

Slowly he pulled his helmet off, looked toward the jungles where the hidden enemy lay in wait, and muttered softly, "Take care of yourself, Woody. One of us has to last through this war."

11

NEW PILOT

Hey—look out, there!"

Clint Stuart, who had been sweeping the debris around the bunk and had leaned the broom up against the bed in order to get the dustpan, looked around at Asa Peabody, who had come off his bunk in a wild leap. Peabody's eyes were staring, and his face was pale.

"What's the matter, Asa?" Clint asked, startled, thinking that a bombing raid was coming, at the very least.

"Don't you see what you did? Look at that!" Peabody pointed at the broom that was leaning against Clint's bunk. Peabody's hand trembled and he said, "I thought you had better sense, Clint, than to lean a broom up against a bed!"

"Lean a broom against a bed? What are you talking about, Asa?"

"It's plumb bad luck to lean a broom against a bed! When you do that, the evil spirits in the broom will cast an evil spirit on the bed. Now, when you lay down in it, Clint, you're going to soak that bad luck in like crazy!"

Clint heaved a slight sigh, a mixture of disgust and relief, but allowed no irritation to show in his voice. He had become accustomed to Peabody's rampantly superstitious nature, and now he simply reached over, picked up the broom, and said, "I guess I forgot!"

"I guess you did! Now, if I was you, I'd carry that bunk out of here and get me a new one."

"Well, we don't have time for that, Asa, but I won't ever do it again."

Manny Columbo, the waist gunner of the crew, was lying on his bunk across the aisle. He stared up at the curving ceiling of the Quonset hut and took a long drag on his cigarette. "That's the stupidest, dumbest thing I ever heard! Like leaning a broom against a bed has anything to do with anything."

He sat up abruptly, and then swayed slightly, clutching his head and shutting his eyes. "Wow!" he said. "That must've been some night I had last night! I was so drunk I don't remember the last half of it." It was Columbo's habit to break whatever rules existed, and he managed to find new and rather innovative ways to do it. He had been gone practically all night, and Clint could not figure out how he managed to get in and avoid the MPs or, for that matter, how he managed to get out of the camp into the small town ten miles away. "You better pull yourself together, Manny. I think we've got a mission this morning."

Columbo groaned, stood up, and suddenly sneezed explosively. His eyes began to water, and he cursed fluently as he dug into his hip pocket for a handkerchief.

Asa Peabody stared at him and shook his head. "Well, if I was you, I wouldn't go on that mission."

"I wouldn't if I didn't have to, you jerk! Why this mission in particular?"

"Because you just sneezed, and it's Friday!"

Columbo stared at the smaller form of the tail gunner, examining him as if he were some sort of strange specimen. "Are there any more like you at home, Peabody? What in the world does sneezing on Friday have to do with flying this mission?"

"They don't teach you city fellas nothin', do they, in New York? Everybody knows about sneezing." He began to recite what sounded like verse:

Sneeze on Monday, sneeze for danger,
Sneeze on Tuesday, kiss a stranger.

Sneeze on Wednesday, receive a letter,
Sneeze on Thursday, receive something better.
Sneeze on Friday, sneeze for sorrow,
Sneeze on Saturday, see your lover tomorrow.
Sneeze on Sunday, your safety seek,
or the Devil will have you, the rest of the week.

Peabody looked around triumphantly and said, "See, it's Friday, and you sneezed. That probably means that if you go on a mission, you'll get killed."

Columbo reached over, picked up a book he had been reading, and threw it at Peabody, who dodged it. The leafs fluttered wildly, and the book struck the wall. Columbo turned abruptly and headed for the bathroom.

"I don't think Manny thinks much of your superstitions, Asa."

Cisco Marischal, the navigator and nose gunner, was already up and dressed. Clint could only imagine what he could be in civilian clothes, for he looked like a dandy in his flight uniform. He turned and positioned himself before a small mirror on the side of the hut and carefully smoothed his hair. "Now, me, I believe in luck. A bullfighter's got to have the luck or he's not going to make it."

Clint was rather fascinated by the Mexican. "Were you really a bullfighter, Cisco, or are you makin' all that up?"

Without answering, but with an air of disgust, Marischal reached into a small box under his bunk, pulled out what appeared to be a leather-bound book, and opened it up. "You see that there? You can't read Spanish, but this is from a Madrid newspaper. It says right here, 'Cisco Marischal is one of the brightest stars in the firmament of Spanish bullfighting. This young man will rise high in his profession. Yesterday afternoon he was awarded the ears of his bull, and we predict that he will make quite a collection of these. Viva, Cisco Marischal!'"

Peabody was staring at Marischal with fascination. "They gave you the ears for killing that bull?"

"Yes, certainly!"

"Well, you can't eat them, can you?" Peabody thought for a moment and said, "Well, back home we eat pig lips, so I guess over there you fellas can *eat* the ears if you want to."

"You stupid idiot, you don't eat the ears! They're a trophy, a triumph! When you kill a bull well, they give you the ears. If you do it especially well, sometimes the tail, too."

"Well, shoot," Asa grunted, "who wants a bunch of old bulls' ears and tails? I think you're crazy to get in there with one of those wild bulls anyway!"

Clint grinned. "I wouldn't want to do it myself."

But Marischal simply stared at them. "It isn't as dangerous as making a raid over Germany," he said. "I'd rather go against a bull anytime than against those Focke-Wulfs or Messerschmitts."

Asa shook his head with apprehension. "I did a little Brahma bull riding in the rodeo, back before I got some sense kicked into me. Those things are bad enough, but bullfighting, I just don't think I'd have the nerve for a thing like that."

"What did you kill 'em with, Cisco?"

"A sword, of course."

Peabody winked at Clint. "It's a good thing you didn't have a .50-caliber machine gun to do it with. You'd have missed the bull and killed half the spectators in the stadium!" Cisco flushed, for his bad marksmanship was legendary. He had the lowest scores of any gunner in the Eighth Air Force, as far as could be told. His method was simply to aim in the general direction of whatever came by way of an enemy and open fire and hope, by dumb luck, to get a bullet or two into the enemy aircraft.

Asa, on the other hand, was the best gunner on the *Last Chance*. He did have a bad habit of shooting at friendly aircraft and could not seem to memorize the silhouettes of the German planes.

At that instant, the door burst open and the operations officer stuck his head in. "Hey, you guys! You're flying a mission leaving at 0400 hours—chow's ready now. Come on; out of the sack!"

Clint made his way with the rest of the crew into the chow hall where they had fresh eggs for breakfast. As he looked around he saw that despite the fact that they had been in combat, there was no sign of a letup in tension. He had learned that the crew of the *Last Chance* did not work smoothly together. *It's no wonder*, he thought as he bit down on the toast over which he had smeared orange marmalade; *they've thrown the worst actors in the whole squadron into this airplane*. Somehow this took away his appetite, and he began to feel a little nauseated. They had flown three missions but had really seen no action, for they had been over targets not covered by enemy fighters. He had the feeling that this day would be different.

They moved outside, and trucks ferried them into operations. In the dark, they all assumed ghostly shapes. They talked, if at all, in subdued whispers. Mostly they were silent, for it was a black, gloomy predawn, and Clint felt that the spirits of all of them were in harmony with the cheerless atmosphere.

They listened with growing concern as the officer giving the briefing said, "Today we're heading for Kiel in northern Germany. There are several hundred fighters in the area, and you can expect a hot reception. Be ready for attacks halfway across the North Sea!"

Clint listened as the officer instructed them on weather and other elements of the mission. When they filed out and got into the airplane, he noticed that Lieutenant Stratton, the pilot, was more irritable than usual. As flight engineer, Clint had made it his business to cover before the mission as many of the problems as possible that can arise with a huge aircraft like a B-17. However, even as he entered the cockpit to give a report, Stratton began screaming, "Stuart!"

"Yes, Sir?"

"Why haven't you been through this flight check? Look at those needles on those gauges!" He ranted and raved while the copilot, Simmons, sat quietly beside him. Simmons himself was a calm man, very steady. The problem was, as the other members of the crew had soon found out, he was calm—but a terrible pilot. Whatever goes into a man that makes him able to handle a four-engine bomber, Al Simmons simply did not have it. His chief value to the crew was his ability to calm down the pilot, and this was a considerable achievement.

Doing his best to help Simmons calm down Powell Stratton, Clint finally was rewarded as the plane took off. The formation was better than he expected, for Stratton was not a good formation flier. Soon, Clint had done his checkdown, but when he got back to the cockpit, he heard Stratton say, "Number four, what's wrong with it?"

"Can't tell," Simmons replied, shaking his head. "Probably is the fuel pump, or the magnetos failed; won't do us any good today!"

"All right, feather number four!" The propeller slowed down and ceased to spin. "We're ten minutes from the enemy coast, heads up, everybody!" Simmons said over the intercom.

There was nothing to do but turn back, and Simmons began grumbling, "What good does this do? All for nothing, no credit. It won't help us get our twenty-five missions out of the way!"

Twenty-five was the magic number, for that was the point at which combat crews would be sent back to the States, relieved from active duty. The Eighth Air Force was so new that no one had even begun to get close to that number and certainly not on the *Last Chance*.

The airplane wheeled as Stratton threw it into a sharp turn and almost threw Clint against the bulkhead. He caught himself and had turned to go when suddenly a tremendous shattering noise came to him. Wheeling, he saw that the windshield in front of the pilot had shattered. Alarm ran through him as the airplane suddenly lurched forward and went into a dive. At the same time, he heard over his earphones the words, "Fighters, fighters! Get that Focke-Wulf!" Red Frazier was screaming.

Clint had no time to think about the fighters, for the plane was headed down. He moved forward and saw that the pilot was dead. He had taken a full burst of bullets in his chest and was slumped forward.

"You all right, Lieutenant?"

Simmons was struggling with the control column.

"They got me in the leg," he said, "but I can make it. Get to your gun, Stuart!"

Instantly Clint moved to the turret and at once saw another FW coming in, head-on. Firing the twin .50-caliber machine gun, he watched as the bullets reached out in a sweeping arc. He saw the arc connect with the Focke-Wulf, and it broke off its attack immediately. As they passed by, he heard the waist gunner's guns clattering, and then when he turned the turret to get another shot, he saw the tracers from Asa's guns meet. The Focke-Wulf exploded in a huge orange burst, and Clint yelled, "You got him, Asa, you got him!"

"Watch out for the other one!" Beans Cunningham yelled from the ball turret. "He's coming back for another shot! You see him, Asa?"

"I got him!"

Clint could not see the action, for it took place under the B-17. He did see the Focke-Wulf as it sped by, off the port side, and saw that it was trailing smoke. He got a shot at it and missed but saw the enemy aircraft fade away. "I think that's all," he said, sweeping the skies. "But keep a lookout!"

They saw no more enemy aircraft, and Clint moved forward to the cockpit where he found Al Simmons struggling with the yoke—his face pale.

"I better try to stop the bleeding in that leg. You've got to get us home, Lieutenant Simmons."

Clint found a first-aid kit and managed to patch up the wound. It was in the lower part of the leg and had bled copiously. He got the bleeding stopped, then straightened up to study Simmons's face. "Can you get us home and make the landing?"

"Got to," Simmons said. Forcing a grin, he added, "I got two boys and a wife to get home to."

"You can do it. God will help you."

Simmons gave Clint an odd look. "You believe that, don't you, Stuart?"

"Yes, Sir, I sure do!"

"Well, you better pray all you know how—because I'm feeling pretty woozy."

Indeed, Clint did pray. He did not know what the others were doing, but he knew that if the pilot lost consciousness, they would all have to bail out, and he had no relish for that. He glanced over to where the lifeless body of Lieutenant Powell Stratton was slumped to one side and regret came to him. As far as he knew, Stratton was a man without God, and now he had gone out to meet the God he did not believe in. He turned back and got some water and wiped Simmons's face with it, then gave him a drink. "I think I see the coastline," he said shortly.

"I see it," Simmons said. "We'll set down at the first strip we get to."

None of the others knew the extent of the damage or that the first pilot was dead or that Simmons was wounded. If they had, there might have been considerable anxiety. As it was, Simmons did an adequate job. As weak as he was, he bounced the plane twice into the air, then brought it to a halt with a screech of brakes. Leaning back, he closed his eyes. "I guess your God heard your prayer, Clint," he said. "I'm glad you were here."

"I'm glad I was, too." He looked over again at the pilot and shook his head. "I'm sorry about Lieutenant Stratton."

"He wasn't a friendly man, but I hate to see anybody get it like that. Could've been me."

They all helped Al Simmons out, and he looked down at his bloody leg and said, "I think it's broken. It looks like you guys will get another pilot and another copilot."

As the injured man was wheeled away to an ambulance, Moon Wilson, the bombardier, came to stand beside Clint.

The short, chunky man reached into his pocket, pulled out a Moon Pie, and took an enormous bite out of it. He seemed to be relatively resigned to being on a bad-luck ship. He himself had dropped bombs on the wrong town, reputedly destroying a hospital, and had a guilt complex about this. Now he stared at the pilot and said, "Well, that takes care of those two. Now there's seven more of us that's left in this blasted airplane."

"We'll make it, Moon."

"Make it? Not a chance!"

"We'll have to help each other," Clint said, "and we'll get a good pilot and a copilot, too."

"We'll get the worst they got! It'll be two guys that couldn't drive a bus, much less a B-17. Watch what I tell you; we'll get the worst!"

The crew of the *Last Chance* sat out the next two missions while waiting for a first and a second pilot. Eaker sent forty-one Fortresses of the Ninety-second and Ninety-seventh for Avion Potez, an aircraft factory in northern France that the Germans were using for a repair depot for their planes. This force came under furious attack as soon as it reached the French coast. Slashing through the Spitfire cover, the German fighters, mostly FW 190s of a crack fighter group, shot down two Fortresses.

After this raid, however, the wet English autumn weather slowed the missions down, and crews settled in on the hastily constructed fields.

During this period, Clint did his best to instill a good spirit in the rest of the crew. As far as he could tell, he was the only Christian among the men and soon had become accustomed to being called "Preacher Stuart." "I won't fuss about that," he said once with a grin as Red Frazier applied the name to him. "We've got some good preachers in my family, my uncle for one."

"I've got no use for sissy preachers!" Red sniffed. He shuffled slightly and shot his fist out in an expert maneuver.

"I'd like to get some of those preachers in the ring and see how they'd do."

"My uncle would have done pretty well. He was a fighter before he went into the army in the First War."

"A fighter? You mean a boxer?"

"That's right! He did pretty good, too, but the war put an end to that. He lost his hand—but he won the Congressional Medal of Honor doing it."

A reluctant admiration came to the eyes of Frazier. He grinned slightly, exposing a missing tooth. He was a little bit punchy from his fights and a good gunner, although his expertise with a radio was not of the best quality. "Well, I never met a preacher like that, but you can save your preachin' for yourself, Clint."

Clint did, indeed, save his preaching. He went to the services in a small church off the base, since there had been no chaplain assigned as yet. None of the crew would go with him, but he found ways to manifest his faith quietly. He knew that the *Last Chance* had a bad reputation in the group, and he determined to change that. Thinking about it as they waited for a new pilot, he was praying one day and asked, "Lord, send somebody that can put some life into this crew. I need to make it through this war, and so do the rest of these fellas. We need a good pilot and a good second pilot, so I'm asking you to put your hand on whoever it is that can pull us through."

The prayer had satisfied him. He had learned to cast his burdens on the Lord and to leave them there. In a war he could not see any other way. Even the brief combat he had seen had taught him that if a man thought about danger all the time, he would soon lose his mind—as some already had.

One consolation was the letters and the packages that he received from home. Packages came from all members of the family. His Aunt Rose never failed to send him cakes and cookies, which he shared with the rest of the crew, and Lenora wrote faithfully, also sending him small gifts and spiritual books that he deeply enjoyed. He heard from Wendy on a rather regular basis, who kept him informed as to the rest of the Stuarts in service, especially her brothers, Woody in the tank corps, and Will in the marines.

Most of all, he looked forward to the letters from Carol. At his request, she had bought a camera and sent him snapshots with almost every letter—not only of herself, but of the home place and of his parents and his siblings—even of his dog, Jupiter.

Carol's letters were not long, for she was better at speaking than at writing. The one he opened on October 7 was typically short and began with an apology:

> Dear Clint,
> I cannot write a long letter today, for I am late for work. I wish I didn't have to go. I wish that you were here so that I could stay home and take care of the house and you. But for now, this is the way it has to be.
>   Mr. Bledsoe has been very nice to me. He gave me a raise last week, and I didn't expect it. He's very kind—but sometimes I wish that he wouldn't be quite so attentive to me. I will write you again tomorrow when I have more time. I love you very much.

Clint studied the letter and wondered at the reference to Harry Bledsoe. *I wonder what kind of a man Bledsoe is.* This led to another thought, that some women had not been faithful to their husbands. One sergeant, the belly gunner in another aircraft of his group, had gotten what they called a "Dear John" letter only two weeks ago. He had married a young woman just before leaving the States, and in the letter she said that she had found someone else and was divorcing him.

That's foolishness, Clint thought with disgust. *I've got no right to be thinking that way of Carol. She's true as steel.* Forcing the idea from his mind, he sat down and wrote her a letter, putting as many encouraging things as he could in it. He sealed it up, and had started out of the barracks when he heard his name being called. "Hey, Clint—" Looking up he saw Moon Wilson

walking rapidly down the line of Quonset huts, his face alive
with excitement. "Did you hear about the new pilot?"

"No, have we been assigned a couple?"

"Well, one anyhow. Don't know anything about him, but
a buddy of mine in headquarters said that he'd come in."

"That's good; I hope he's a good man," Clint said.

"He won't be," Moon said philosophically. As his custom
was, he reached into his pocket and unwrapped a Moon Pie.
The source of these delicacies was a mystery to everyone.
They were not for sale in England, only in the States, as far as
Clint knew. He himself thought they tasted like candle wax,
with the same sort of texture, but he had grown accustomed
to Wilson's addiction to them. "Whoever we get will be a
dud; you can bet on that."

"No, I don't believe that, Moon. I've been asking the Lord
to give us a good pilot—somebody that can help us, that we
can support."

"Well, trouble with that is God doesn't make these as-
signments. Bomber Command makes them, and they got
our name in black up there somewhere. Every time a dud
comes along, somebody says, 'Well, here's another one for
the *Last Chance*.'"

Clint shook his head and slapped Moon on the shoulder.
"We'll be all right. Let's go tell the rest of the guys. We may
be flying sooner than we think."

All day long the crew waited anxiously to meet their new
pilot. They talked about him endlessly. Cisco Marischal said,
"I wonder if he's any good at formation flying?"

"He'd better be!" Manny Columbo nodded. He was cleaning his fingernails with a long switchblade knife he carried in his
hip pocket. It was a wicked-looking affair, and he waved with
it, gesturing emotionally. "You know what happens to B-17s
that are flown by guys who don't know what they're doing."

"That's right, those Germans can spot a new crew on their
first circle around the formation," Cunningham said. The ball-

turret gunner was barely large enough to make the air force height limit. He was considered a ladies' man, at least by his own admission, and had interrupted one tale of a romantic liaison with an English lass in order to join the conversation. "They'll tear into our rear ends on the first pass, 'cause they can always spot the easiest sports to knock down."

A silence fell over the group, and Clint said, "I wonder how they can tell which ones are the green crews and the new pilots?"

"That's easy," Moon asserted. He was sitting on his bunk, leaning back, and looked with disgust at the rest of the crew. "Green pilots can't stay in tight formation. They throttle jock back and forth—might as well flash a neon sign, Come and Shoot Me Down."

They were still shooting the breeze when Lieutenant Schmidt stuck his head in the door and said, "All right, your new pilot's here! He'll be here in a few minutes, so try to get your act together!" He looked at them with disgust and said, "It would take a miracle to get you guys to fly a raid without messing up."

"I love the confidence they got in us," Asa Peabody grinned. He kept his eyes on the door, as did the rest of them, and when it opened and an officer stepped in, they all came to attention.

The officer who entered had his cap pulled down over his eyes so that Clint could not see his face for a moment. They all saluted, and Clint studied the man as he pushed his hat back, and then a shock of recognition came to him. Without volition, he spoke, "Adam!"

Indeed, it was Adam Stuart who had stepped inside the Quonset hut! His eyes met Clint's, and he thought it strange for cousins to meet under such circumstances.

Clint said, "I'm sorry, Sir—I was just so surprised to see you."

Adam had stiffened with surprise but recovered quickly.

"I'm Lieutenant Adam Stuart, and I'm glad to see I've got a relative here. How are you, Clint?"

"Just fine, Sir. I'm pretty surprised to see you, though."

"Why don't you introduce me to the rest of the crew, Sergeant Stuart?"

"Yes, Sir, of course!" Clint went around the small group giving the names and combat stations of the rest of the crew. He was aware that several of them were giving him strange glances, and he was a little flustered. He finished the introductions and said, "We're very glad to have you, Lieutenant Stuart."

Adam looked at the men, who were staring at him with raw curiosity. He well knew what they were thinking. *They're all wondering if I can cut it,* he thought. *Their lives will be in my hands, and they don't look any too happy with what they see.* Aloud he said, "I've just arrived in England, so I don't have the combat experience that you men have. How many missions have you flown?"

"Three, Sir!" Clint said quickly.

"Well, as soon as we get a second pilot, I expect we'll be taking off. In the meanwhile, I think we can take a flight right now to get acquainted with each other."

"You mean right now, Lieutenant? This very minute?" Moon Wilson asked with surprise.

"Why not?" Adam said sharply. He had already known that the crew would have more experience than he himself. This would be a detriment, but he had purposed to throw himself into the work with everything he had. "Let's talk frankly. I'll be frank with you, and you can be frank with me. Do you have any questions you want to ask me, first of all?"

"Yes, Sir, I have one question," Moon Wilson said. "How much formation flying time have you had?"

"Thirty hours." Adam saw dismay wash across the faces of the men. "I know it takes seventy hours of high-altitude formation experience to be a fair pilot, but you'll have to take what I've got." There was almost anger in his voice, and he

said, "You can check me out, and I'll check you out. From what
I hear, the *Last Chance* is just what it sounds like. You've got a
bad reputation in the group. I even heard about it coming over.
The transport pilots talked about how sorry this crew is."

Clint said quickly, "Sir, I'd like to suggest that we just
begin from scratch. I'm sure you'll be a fine pilot. It's just
that the men are nervous about tight formations."

There were good reasons for the nervousness of the crew,
for a tight formation was essential to standing off German
fighter attacks. A bomber could not concentrate much fire
power against a fighter except on tail attacks. The Germans
knew that, so they hit mainly with a frontal charge. A single
Fortress could only bring to bear three guns in a head-on
attack—the nose gun and the two top turret guns. The navigator could only fire if the attack were approaching at an angle
to the nose. The tighter the formation, the more fire it could
bring to bear against the enemy. Therefore, a tight formation was the ultimate defensive tactic of a bomber force sent
beyond the range of fighter escorts.

Adam Stuart stood with his back straight. His light blue
eyes were cold, it seemed, and there was a harshness in his
voice as he said, "I joined the Air Corps for one reason, to
kill Germans, and I will do my job! If any man doesn't do his
job, he gets the worst I can give him. If I don't do my job, I
invite you to do the same for me!" He spoke coldly and for
some time, then finally said, "We'll fly in one hour. Sergeant
Stuart, check the airplane out."

Turning on his heel, Adam left, and a silence fell over the
room—but only for a moment—then they all began talking.
Marischal stared at Clint saying, "That's your cousin? Can't
say much for him!"

Peabody snorted. "It's bad luck, that's what it is! We're
not going to make it with him!"

"Wait a minute, you guys. Give him a chance, will you?
He may be the best formation flyer in the whole Eighth Air
Force," Clint protested.

"I'll have to see that!" Manny Columbo said. His eyes narrowed, and he opened his switchblade knife and clicked it shut again, then slammed it into his pocket. "Well, let's go see if he can fly an airplane!"

Three hours later, the crew was piling out of the aircraft. Columbo glanced around to be sure that the pilot was out of hearing, then said reluctantly, "Well, I'll give him this; he seems to be a pretty fair pilot."

"Pretty fair!" Clint exclaimed. "He's the best you ever saw, Manny, and you know it."

"We'll see how he does when we get over Germany. Lots of guys are good when there's nobody shootin' at 'em," Cisco said. "Lots of bullfighters are pretty good until they get in the ring, then they take one look at those horns, and boom, they're gone." His eyes were filled with doubt, and his mouth twisted as he said, "We'll see what Lieutenant Adam Stuart's like when the flak hits and the Focke-Wulfs start coming in!"

Adam flew every day with his crew but had gotten to know none of them personally. He kept to himself and was strict and businesslike in all of his affairs. Clint wanted to say, "Loosen up, Adam, you don't have to be so tough," but felt it was out of place.

Adam's first mission came on October 9. General Eaker had been waiting for his first one-hundred-bomber strike and had chosen locomotive shops at Lille in northern France.

The mission suffered ill fortune right from the start. Various mechanical problems forced nineteen Fortresses to abort and return to England. Ten out of twenty-four Liberators also turned back. The remaining seventy-nine bombers pressed on and were met by an estimated force of sixty FW 190s that screamed down through the Allied fighters' screen to attack the Forts and Liberators. As they approached the target, Adam said to the new copilot, a tall Texan named Tom Smith, "Keep your eye out for fighters, Smith, and pass that word along!"

Smith was a nervous individual and began at once chat-

tering over the loudspeaker, "Watch out for fighters!" And
almost at once Peabody yelled, "You see them coming at ten
o'clock high? Watch 'em; here they come! Shoot 'em down,
knock 'em down!"

Instantly, Adam broke in, "Peabody, I told you a hundred
times not to shoot when they can't hit us. That fighter is rolling away from us. Stop wasting your ammunition. We'll be
out before we get to the target! Don't shoot 'til you can hit
'em, then don't waste a single round!"

Over and over again, Adam kept telling the gunners to
save their ammunition. He insisted that when a fighter quit
firing the gunners were to forget about him and concentrate
on the next ones.

Adam searched the sky and saw a Fortress over on the
starboard side of his aircraft get hit and catch fire. Flames
streamed beyond the tail, and down it went.

"Nobody got out," Smith said, his voice shaking.

"Don't think about it!" Adam snapped. "We'll get in and
get this thing over with!"

The enemy planes began to come in furiously. Clint was
thrown all over the airplane, and his ammunition flew out of
the ammo cans and got fouled up. Once the *Last Chance* almost
collided with a fighter. Clint saw one ship catch five fighters
and it went down. "Poor guys," he said aloud, and turned to
see that Red Frazier was pale. "I wish I was out of this," Frazier
said. "It's worse than any fight I ever had in the ring."

The plane set down at Ridgewell Airdrome, and the weary,
beaten crew got out. Adam sat in the aircraft after the others
had departed and analyzed what his feelings were. He had
been able to meet the danger of combat coldly. It seemed as
though something had taken over, driven out the fear, and
he wondered if this were common. He decided that it was
not, for he had seen enough fear in his copilot to know that
he could expect little help from him. He got up and made
his way out of the airplane and went to interrogation. The
interrogation was long and detailed. He discovered that the

Eighth Bomber Command had taken a frightful, shocking loss—sixty B-17s shot down, twenty-seven of the Fortresses damaged too severely to be repaired.

After Adam sat through it all, then left with the rest of the crew, Smith approached, saying, "Come on, let's go have a drink, Stuart. I need one."

"You go ahead," Adam said, and he turned and walked away. Clint was standing nearby and did not comment, but later on he said to Lieutenant Smith, "You did a good job, Lieutenant; we're going to have a good aircraft here."

Smith was staring down at the ground. "I was scared out of my wits," he murmured. He looked up and shook his head. "Adam Stuart's a relative of yours?"

"Yes, Sir, a cousin."

"Well, he wasn't scared. He flew right into that bomb run like—like he was driving on a Sunday afternoon in the middle of town! That man's not human!"

"Yes, Sir, he's human," Clint replied slowly. "He's just afraid to show it."

In the days that followed through October, Clint tried desperately to get close to Adam but could find no way to do it. Adam kept to himself, was strictly business, and replied coldly. Even when Clint mentioned family matters, Adam turned him away. Naturally there was a great gap between an officer and an enlisted man. Still, Clint knew that some officers in the other aircraft were much warmer with their crews. He could not justify the cold, machinelike behavior of Adam for the rest of the crew and soon had to give up trying. The instant he began to defend Adam, the crew was down his throat.

Cisco Marischal had been castigated by Adam for his poor navigation on the raids and had learned to hate the pilot. "I don't care if he is your kinfolk," he said. "I'd trade him off for a man with a little human feeling in him! He's just like a machine, and that's what's going to get us killed. Maybe he's not afraid, but some of the rest of us are!"

Strangely enough, this was the feeling that Clint had. Courage was one thing, but Adam's behavior was something else. The pilot flew mechanically, almost perfectly, but he never wavered, never took evasive maneuvers, and above all, he never encouraged his crew in any way. It troubled Clint deeply, and he spoke of it in a letter to Carol.

> I wish that Adam would loosen up. It's as though he has put some kind of a stopper in any kind of emotion he's got. He never smiles, he seems angry, and the rest of the crew hate him. They think he's a dangerous man to fly with, and as much as I hate to admit it, I think they're right. He could be a great pilot, perhaps the greatest, if he would just bend a little bit, but he won't do that, it seems. So, just keep praying for us, Sweetheart.

In return to this letter, he received one from Carol in which she said,

> I wish you had another pilot. It sounds like Adam isn't the man you would have chosen. I am so afraid for you, and I feel so alone. Dad had a bad spell last week. He's in the hospital now, and the doctors don't give me any encouragement. Oh, I'm so afraid and wish you were here. If it weren't for the encouragement that Harry Bledsoe gives me, I don't know how I'd make it.

It was one week after this that he got another letter from Carol, containing only a few lines, which said,

> Dad died last night. I can't write about it right now; I have to see to the funeral arrangements. Harry has been good enough to help me, and your parents also. I'll write later, but right now my heart is broken.

Clint was terribly disturbed by this, for he knew how much Carol depended on her father. "I ought to be there to help her," he muttered, "but there's no way." He did not share his

burden with anyone, for a bit of frustrating news had come
to the group. The British-American High Command had instructed General Eaker to concentrate on submarine pens in
French ports. These pens were roofed with twelve-foot-thick
reinforcing concrete, and everyone knew that it would be the
most thankless and dangerous of all the objectives assigned
to the Eighth in its first operational year.

On October 21, Adam came in and took one look at his
crew. "All right, we're going to Lorient. Escort will be pro-
vided only part of the way. It's out of fighter range. I want
every man to be in top shape." He glanced at Manny Columbo
and said, "Columbo, you stay sober, or I'll see you in the
guardhouse. The rest of you, mind yourselves!"

"That was quite a pep talk, wasn't it? Makes a fella feel real
good," Asa Peabody said after Adam left. "This ain't gonna
be no good day for a raid."

"There's never a good day for a raid!" Red Frazier
complained.

"It's gonna be worse," Peabody grunted. "I killed a spider
this morning. Should've captured it and put it outside. It's
bad luck to kill spiders!"

"That's enough talk about luck," Clint said sharply. "Let's
go over our drill as well as we can and trust in God, and we'll
be all right."

But the raid did not go all right. Heavy clouds covered
the Atlantic, and only fifteen Forts of the most experienced
group made it through. Fortunately, the Lorient flight crews
were caught napping, and the B-17s dropped thirty one-ton
bombs on the submarine pens. Before the Forts could get
away, however, the thirty-six FW 190s of a crack Luftwaffe
unit came swarming after them.

Adam kept his place in the formation and directed the fire
of his guns. He had discovered that he had the best eyesight
of anyone on the aircraft, but he could only see ahead and
forward. His voice crackled constantly to Asa Peabody, the tail
gunner, and to Beans Cunningham down in the ball turret.

Finally the formation came together, and Adam glanced up to see something white floating by. It was a parachute with no one in it. Pieces of wings, tails, and fuselages littered the sky. Where there had been several aircraft the moment before, now there was nothing but empty space and falling debris. Adam caught a brief glimpse of one ship going down. The fuselage had torn off flush with the trailing edge of the wing, all four engines were still running, and the ship was revolving rapidly—the way a rectangular piece of paper will do when released in the air. *All fifty men*, Adam thought, shocked out of his steady frame of mind for a moment, *fifty men in a few seconds*. He gritted his teeth and glanced over at Tom Smith, the copilot, and saw that the Texan was pale as paper and his hands were trembling. "Smith, you see any more fighters?"

"No, nothing above us. Must've been an explosion."

"Pilot to navigator, did you see what happened?"

"No, I didn't see a thing until it was over."

"Pilot to ball, what's happening down there? How many planes were lost?"

"Air's all full of pieces and parts of planes. I see three chutes."

Adam thought, *Five ships and only three chutes*. He did some mathematics. *Five times nine, forty-five men, and only three left alive*.

Adam felt the bullets raking the *Last Chance*, seemingly from every angle. He felt a tug at his neck and knew that a bullet had touched his collar, but he paid no attention to it. When they finally reached the coast, they had been shot at by many Messerschmitts.

The battered group landed, and when Adam got out, Clint came over to say, "You did a good job, Sir. You're a great flier."

Adam looked at Clint. He suddenly had a desire for some warmth to break the moment and said briefly, "I can't get over seeing those men, nearly forty-five of them, five crews, all dead."

Clint dropped his head and studied the ground; then he looked up and his eyes met Adam's. "It was a terrible thing, but I'm glad God brought us back."

Adam considered this and shook his head. "I don't think God had anything to do with it. It's just like dice; sometimes you win, sometimes you lose."

He turned and walked away. Clint stared after him, and then murmured, "Adam, you can't live like that—not without faith in something. From the look I see in your eyes right now, you don't have faith in anything!"

12

FALL FROM GRACE

The year of 1942 had been, perhaps, the most traumatic the United States of America had ever suffered. They had come into the war unprepared and had learned how to fight. At the Battle of Midway, in June, the navy had badly beaten the Japanese navy, the biggest naval victory of the war. In Europe, General Dwight D. Eisenhower assumed command of the United States forces. At Guadalcanal, a tough marine force held off the Japanese, and in early November Allied forces landed in North Africa, where the British routed Field Marshal Rommel's Afrika Korps.

And on the home front, Captain Eddie Rickenbacker, the most renowned ace of World War I, had been lost at sea. He was, however, discovered with a few survivors, drifting in a raft after three weeks of surviving on army rations and one raw seagull.

America's search for a war song had not been completed, and on November 5, the man that gave World War I a song, George M. Cohan, died. Cohan, born on the fourth of July, gave America the great song, "Over There," to which the men in the ranks marched to war in 1918.

In the jungles of Guadalcanal, Will Stuart survived. The Japanese kept coming at them, battering at the lines every night and being thrown back, but every night Will knew that they would come again. Nighttime had become a terrible rhythm, like the breathing of a child frightened by sounds in the dark.

As dark closed in, Will crouched, holding his breath, looking around, peering through the darkness, waiting for the fanatical Japanese to come with their insane cries.

"You think they're going to come at us again tonight, Sarge?" Private Willie Deason crouched beside Will in the foxhole. He was only seventeen years old, had run away from home, and lied about his age to join the marines. Now, Willie wished he were back at home in Kentucky. Will understood. *And I wish I were home, too—so do all of us.* Aloud he said, "They'll come, and we'll throw 'em back. You'll be OK, Willie."

All day long it had rained, and now Will and Willie, drenched and shivering, shaken by fever, looked out into the darkness, straining their eyes. Fever raged in most of the men, and Will knew that half of the squad would be in a hospital if they were home in the States. He counted the odds, knowing that though the division had thrown the Japs back time after time, the crisis was yet to come. He sensed in the atmosphere the hostile presence, the great Japanese task force moving down from the north, and knew that if they succeeded, the marines would all go down. Suddenly a vast crash of thunder rent the air, and at first Will thought it was more rain—then abruptly he realized this was not coming out of God's heaven but was man-made thunder.

"Those are naval guns, Willie," he said. "Come on!" They made their way through the jungle, groping, and saw out on the sea what looked like a fireworks display.

"It looks like a volcano," Willie whispered. "Is them our ships?"

"They're our ships, Willie!" Will said, and heaved a sigh of relief. "They've come!" he said. "Now we're gonna see something!"

All night long the great battle raged. The sea was a sheet of polished obsidian on which the warships seemed to have been dropped and immobilized. The island trembled to the sounds of the mighty guns, pinpoints of light appeared, then grew and illuminated until the whole world was lit up, and the marines who watched in awe were bathed with a pale and yellow light. When morning came, Will knew for certain that the tide had turned on Guadalcanal.

"Look!" Will said, eyes turned to the sky. "Airplanes, and they're ours!"

It was electrifying. The noise of the airplanes brought every marine out of his hole, cheering. Will drew a sigh of relief, for he felt as a doomed man from whose ankles great iron bands had been struck. A great weight lifted from his shoulders. "They're runnin', Willie," he said. "We've got 'em whipped!" He took a breath of air, and though it was fetid and rotten with jungle rot, it was sweet, for he knew that Guadalcanal had been saved. The Japanese had been turned back, and things would be different for the marines from this point on.

The news of the lifting of the siege at Guadalcanal came as a breath of fresh air to the home front. Wendy had heard of it when she heard her father yelling downstairs. Thinking an accident had occurred, she pulled on a robe and ran down to find Owen Stuart in his bathrobe dancing around waving his steel hook in the air.

"What is it, Dad—what's happened?"

Owen, with tears running down his face, reached out and grabbed Wendy and swung her in a wide circle, leaving her gasping. Putting her down, he said with a voice that was unsteady and filled with passion, "It's over! Guadalcanal has been relieved!"

"Oh, Dad, what does it mean?"

"It means that we've taken the first step to winning the war, or maybe the second step. When the Japanese were whipped at Midway, that gave us a chance. Now, we'll see some real victories!"

At that moment, Allie came in, her eyes wide. "What is it? What's happening?" When they told her, she began to cry and said, "God be thanked! God be thanked!"

The three of them were too excited to eat, but finally Allie insisted and pulled them into the kitchen where they had bacon and eggs and toast.

As they were eating, Wendy said, "I got a letter from Mona yesterday. I've been meaning to talk to you about it."

"What is it? What's she doing now?" Owen said, chewing on a huge bite of toast, thickly layered with blackberry jam. "She's a good-looking filly."

"Don't call your niece a filly!" Allie said sharply.

"Sorry, Allie." Owen shrugged, but could not conceal a grin. "Well, she's pretty enough to be Miss Oklahoma. I guess the next thing she'll be doing is trying for Miss America."

"I think she will, Dad," Wendy said, "but something else has come up. She's got an opportunity to go on a USO tour to the Pacific."

Interest quickened in Owen's face. He leaned forward and studied Wendy carefully. "Is that right? You know that might not be a bad thing. She might even get to do her dancing before Will out there. Although I doubt if Guadalcanal's got a theater."

"She's going, all right—that is, if I go with her."

Both Owen and Allie looked surprised. "Go with her?" Allie said with some confusion. "Why, I thought only professional entertainers went on those tours."

"That's pretty much the case, but Mona says that she can get me a place with the group." She leaned forward, put her hand on her chin, and said quietly, "I don't think Uncle Pete will let her go unless I go with her. She didn't actually say that, but she said I'd be getting a call from him at any time. I'm pretty sure he'll want me to go look after her."

"Well, I will have to say that young woman needs some looking after," Owen said. "She's a good girl at heart, but she thinks about nothing but fun and boys and parties and dances."

Allie was studying her daughter carefully. "Would you want to go, Wendy?"

When the offer had come, Wendy had not been sure. She

had thought it over carefully and had prayed about it much of the previous night. She slowly nodded. "You know, I think I really would. I haven't been able to do anything much for the war effort. Working in a library isn't going to win the war." She laughed briefly and said, "Of course, singing light opera for the men won't win it either—but if I could help in this way, I think I would."

"Well, do it then!" Owen said explosively. He banged the table with his steel hook, then said, "It'll be an experience you'll never forget, and those guys over there, they really need all the encouragement we can give them."

Wendy was pensive, somewhat uncertain, but with her father's encouragement, she grew more and more positive. Later that day she called Mona and said, "All right, Mona, I'm going."

"Look out South Pacific, here we come! The best singer and the best dancer in the whole U.S. of A.!" Mona was excited and at once began making plans.

When Wendy finally hung up, she looked at herself in the mirror that hung on the wall and said wryly, "Well, I bet I'll be a star in the jungles. Not much competition there."

Carol looked at Harry Bledsoe with some surprise. He had called her into his private office and talked excitedly about a new adventure that he was about to launch into. By this time, Carol knew Bledsoe well enough to understand that anything new excited him. She smiled understandingly, listening until he finally said, "I've got to go to Chicago to get this thing off the ground, Carol, and I can't do all of it alone. You'll have to go with me."

Carol stared at Bledsoe blankly, thinking for a moment that she had misunderstood him. "Why, I couldn't do that, Harry!"

"But you've got to, Carol! I just can't handle it all alone. I'll be out talking to prospective clients, and I've got to have someone to do all the book work while I'm gone during the day." Bledsoe was wearing a new brown suit and had just gotten back from the barber shop. His cheeks gleamed with the fresh shave, and his brown eyes were excited. He had been sitting on his desk looking down at Carol. Now, suddenly he came over and took her hands and lifted her up. "I know it's not exactly according to the rules of order, but this is a war we're in, Carol. We've got to get these parts made. If we don't keep 'em rolling, the guys over there won't have a chance."

It was a statement that Bledsoe made often, and Carol knew there was a certain truth in it. The parts business had grown under government contracts, and now many of the Jeeps that were rolling off the assembly lines were fitted with the parts that came from the Bledsoe factory. Still, she was confused and said with a worried tone, "But it wouldn't look right, us going off together on a trip."

"Why, it happens all the time. It's just business, Carol."

"I know, Harry, but think what it would look like."

Bledsoe shook his head saying persuasively, "It'll only be for three days. You'll have your own room. We'll be on a public plane, and we'll be in meetings together part of the time. There's nothing wrong with it." He shrugged, saying, "I know I may have been a little fresh with you at times. You're so pretty, no man can help that, but this time I really need you. At least think about it, will you, Carol?"

"All right," Carol said reluctantly, "I'll think about it, but I don't see how it could be."

That had been on Thursday. Two days later Carol knew that she had to give Harry an answer. Somehow she dreaded staying alone in the little town that had been her life, and now with her father dead and with Clint so far away, the only activity in her life was her work. She dreaded sitting alone, night after night, listening to the radio, reading books. Life had closed in on her, and her nerves were frayed.

She was sitting in the office trying to make up her mind when the phone rang, and she picked it up. "Bledsoe Industries," she said. "May I help you?"

"Carol?"

"Yes, this is Carol; who's this?"

"It's Wendy, Carol. I'm just getting ready for a trip, and I wanted to see how you were before I left."

Carol was pleased, for Wendy had kept in close touch with her, especially since Clint had left. She knew that her cousin genuinely cared, and a moment of envy came to her as she said after they had talked for a while, "What kind of a trip are you making? Where are you going?"

"It's so exciting, Carol! Mona and I are going on a USO tour. We'll be going to the South Pacific to entertain the soldiers and the marines and the sailors there."

Carol listened with a pang as Wendy spoke with enthusiasm of the tour. Finally, she said, "I wish I could sing or dance. All I do is keep books for this parts company."

"Are you getting out some, Carol?" Wendy asked with concern. She was well aware of the loneliness of the young woman and wished that they lived closer.

"No, there's nothing at all in this little town. I've seen every movie and read every book in the library, I think. I spend a lot of time writing letters to Clint, but there's really nothing to say to him."

The two women talked for a while, and finally Carol said almost in desperation, "I do have a chance to make a trip myself, Wendy."

"Where? What kind of a trip?"

"Mr. Bledsoe, the owner of the company, is opening up a new branch in Chicago. He wants me to go with him and help with the correspondence and the business things there."

There was a moment's silence on the other end, and immediately Carol understood that Wendy disapproved. "It would just be a business trip, Wendy," she said quickly. "It happens all the time. Men have to take their secretaries with them." She was very defensive and grew almost angry at herself and changed the subject at once. "I hope you have a wonderful time on your trip."

Wendy was disturbed, and after she hung up the phone,

she sat in the chair wondering if there was anything she could do. *That's a mistake, going off with her employer. No matter what the circumstances, she doesn't need to do it.* Slowly she rose and, for the rest of the day, from time to time would offer up a prayer for Carol. She knew that Carol Stuart was playing with dynamite to even consider such a thing.

Clint pulled the wrinkled envelope out of the pocket of his flight suit, and extracted the letter. He glanced out the window at the clouds floating by but did not really expect to see fighter planes. They were headed for a city deep in the heart of Germany, and he knew that soon enough the air would be filled with enemy fighters. At the briefing that morning, Cisco Marischal had asked him, "How do you think the operations officer feels when he reads out our names, the ones of us who are going, and he knows some of us won't make it back?"

"Someone has to do it, Cisco."

Cisco thought it over and said, "Which would you rather do, take the risk yourself or have to choose which men may die?"

Clint had answered instantly, "I'd rather go myself. I think I'd feel responsible for those who didn't get back."

As the B-17 kept close formation, Clint read through the letter again. Something about it troubled him, although he could not say what. Most of it was just the usual news—what movies Carol had seen lately, reports of a visit to his father and mother. Much of it was filled with news of her job. The paragraph that troubled him was:

It's been so boring here. I know that sounds awful to say, but it's because you're not here that I'm bored, Clint. One thing has come up that will maybe be a break in the routine. The company is opening up a new operation in Chicago. It's going to be a very big operation, Mr. Bledsoe says, and he wants me to help set it up. I'm not sure I can handle it, but at least it will be a challenge.

Clint read the rest of the letter, then folded it up and put it back in his pocket.

"Chicago," he muttered. "How could she help set up an operation in Chicago while she's living in the Ozarks?" The thought troubled him, partly because he still had some sort of a foolish guilt complex. He knew that he could not be with her, but from the tone of her letters he knew that the death of her father had prostrated her. She had leaned on her father greatly all of her life, and now he was gone. "And I'm gone, too," Clint whispered as he got up and started to check the airplane. "I wish I could be with her."

He made his check, and soon he heard over the intercom, "This is the pilot; enemy coast in five minutes!"

Later he heard Adam Stuart's voice again, saying, "Pilot to crew, keep alert!"

Clint waited, then said, "Engineer to crew, oxygen check!"

"Tail OK!"

"Ball, rajah!"

"Radio, oxygen OK!"

"Turret OK!"

"Cockpit OK!"

Suddenly the voice of Smith, the copilot, broke in, "Fighters coming in—eleven o'clock low!"

Boom! The airplane rocked, throwing Clint off balance. His head struck the bulkhead, and he was thankful for the helmet.

Pulling himself up, he heard the voice of Beans Cunningham, "I'm wounded!"

"I'll see to it!" Clint said, and made his way to the ball turret. When he looked inside he said, "You OK, Beans?"

"Yeah." Cunningham held up his foot and was saying, "I think just a fragment of it got me. I think I can handle it."

Clint slapped him on the shoulder. "You better; you're the only one small enough to fit in that thing."

"I can handle it, Clint." Cunningham suddenly looked out

and said, "Uh-oh, there they come! Bandits, three of them. Look like Focke-Wulfs!"

The formation pulled in a little tighter, and the German fighter planes made quick passes close by. By this time Clint had learned to accept the dangers of combat as well as any man ever did. So had all of them on the *Last Chance*. They all knew that every time they went into the air there was a chance that they would never make it back. Clint moved along the airplane, doing his job. He was praying, *Oh, God, be with me today and keep me from* . . .

"Navigator to crew, fighters at nine o'clock!"

"Hold it; it's our little friends! It's our escort!"

They crossed the edge of the enemy territory finally, then the P-47s dipped their wings and turned back to England.

"Why do they have to leave us just when we're about to bump up against Göring's crew?" Tom Smith, the copilot, grumbled as he saw a cloud of fighters coming.

Adam looked at his copilot. He never felt certain of Smith or of what he would do. The man, he knew, was terribly afraid, and since Adam never had that problem, he could not really grasp it. It, to him, was a tragic flaw, and he could not understand how a man could function with his mind filled with fear.

Looking out his window he hollered, "Pilot to crew, fighters at six o'clock. More fighters low and coming up!"

"Tail to crew, four fighters closing fast at six o'clock high!"

"Radio to crew, I think they're all gonna come in!"

Clint moved to his position in the top turret and could hardly believe what he saw. Four fighters were flying so close together that they looked like one enormous, four-engine aircraft. "Look at that!" he yelled. "We can't miss!"

Clint could not believe that they intended to attack that way. The greenest German pilot would have known better, but they kept coming. At six hundred yards, he saw the first flash of cannon fire, which was the signal for the formation gunners to let go. Every fifth round was a tracer, and soon all top turrets, some balls, and all tail guns were pouring a heavy barrage at those four fighters. The enormous mass of .50-caliber slugs was so devastating that there were four puffs of black smoke. The sky was filled, suddenly, with airplanes breaking apart.

There were no more fighter planes in sight, so Clint crawled down and moved to the cockpit. He was somewhat shaken by the experience. "Those fellas didn't know what they were doing—they must've been totally green."

"They're good Germans now," Adam said harshly. "I wish they'd all come at us like that and that we could kill 'em all with one burst!"

Smith turned his head jerkily and stared at him. "Don't you ever feel anything for those Germans?"

"I feel good when they die like that!" Adam said. His face was pale, and he kept his eyes on the skies for a moment. Then he turned around to find Clint behind him. "You got anything to say, Preacher?"

"No, Lieutenant, nothing—except I can't help but feel sorry for any man who dies, German or American."

"Well, you feel as you please, but we came out here to kill Germans, and I'm going to kill all I can!"

Clint saw the distaste in the copilot's eyes, but neither of them said a word. Both of them were aware that Adam Stuart was a man with an obsession to kill all the Germans he could. He was, they both recognized, an exceptional pilot, the best, perhaps, in the entire Eighth Air Force. They could not understand why he was kept on the Last Chance, but his skill at flying had kept them out of trouble so far, and as Clint moved away, back to check Cunningham's wound, he thought, *What a shame. Adam's not going to last like that. Hatred is going to kill him as sure as a bullet from a Messerschmitt.*

The trip to Chicago was exhilarating for Carol Stuart. She had lived in a small town all of her life and had never even been on a commercial airliner—or any other airplane, for that matter. She sat beside Harry Bledsoe, grasping the seat as the plane lifted in the air, expecting any moment for it to fall down. As the earth fell away, Harry said with a grin, "Open your eyes, Carol, and you can see what your hometown looks like." As they rose in the air, Carol looked over and exclaimed, "Why look, there's our house right over there! It looks so funny from up here—and the people, they look like dolls!"

Bledsoe was amused at his secretary. "Flying's fun, isn't it?"

"Well, it is so far."

The flight proved to be very successful. Carol did not get sick, as she had feared, and when they arrived at the airport in Chicago, she was stunned at the masses of people. "I've never seen so many people in one place in my entire life!"

"It's busy, all right. Come along; we'll get a cab and go to our hotel. You can rest up while I go out and get things ready."

Carol was apprehensive, as she had been since she had agreed to make the trip, but when they reached the Stevens Hotel, Harry left her at the desk, saying, "I've got a lot of work to do. You rest up, and we'll have breakfast together in the morning." She was tremendously relieved.

"All right, Harry," she said. "I'll be ready." She went to her room on the sixteenth floor and looked out at the skyscrapers of Chicago rising majestically in the sky. She was too excited to sleep and finally changed her clothes and daringly went on a shopping tour. She kept her eyes on the hotel, not daring to go more than a block away, but she did enjoy seeing the people and buying her meal in a restaurant all alone. More than once, she caught the eyes of men who were watching her, but she quickly glanced down and wondered if she were doing the right thing.

She went back to the hotel and spent a restful night. The phone rang at eight the next morning. It was Harry: "Are you ready for breakfast?"

"Yes, I'll be right down."

"I'm just down the hall. We'll meet and go down to the restaurant."

When she stepped outside her room, Carol saw that, indeed, Harry was only two doors down, for he was exiting even as she stepped out into the hall.

"Well, look at you! Been shopping, huh?" Harry took in the dress that Carol had bought and shook his head, his eyes alight with admiration. "You look good enough to be in the movies," he said. Taking her arm he said, "Come on; I'm starved."

They ate breakfast at a small table where a waiter with a white coat saw to their every need. Harry talked constantly about the business and said, "I'm going to work you pretty hard, Carol. Things are breaking quicker than I thought."

"Oh, it's so exciting, Harry; tell me all about it!"

She listened as he described the events and meetings that he had had for prospects and said, "I've got a friend who will let us use his office here. He's got a typewriter and everything we need."

And so the day began. All day long, Carol was buried with details of the work. It took all of her concentration to keep up with what was going on. Bledsoe came and went. He brought men in, introduced her from time to time, but mostly it was work—work—work.

For three days, Carol worked unstintingly. She had supper each night with Harry, and usually breakfast, although he was sometimes gone by the time she arose. She had been terribly apprehensive about his behavior, for he had flirted with her more than once, but here, he was another man. Business stimulated him, and he flitted around over the city, apparently, from place to place as if it were his natural habitat. Carol was pleased with her job, for she knew she had done it well, and flushed when he said, "Well, I picked the right secretary all right. No one could have picked this up quicker than you, Carol."

On the third day, they finished somewhat early, and Harry said, "Well, we're going out to celebrate tonight. You worked hard, and you deserve a break."

"Oh, I really shouldn't, Harry!"

"We'll just have dinner, maybe a few dances."

Carol was unsure about going out but said to herself, "This is just for supper; just a meal together won't hurt anything."

Harry took her to a place called the Pump Room. "This is the fanciest eating place in Chicago!"

Carol was helpless in the face of the menu. "What is beef *forestiere?*" she asked.

"I don't know," Harry said, "but if it's beef, it has to be pretty good." They had laughed a great deal, and Harry had ordered a bottle of wine.

"Oh, I don't think I should!" Carol protested.

"It's only wine!" Harry said, smiling. He filled her glass and his, then held his up for a toast. "Here's to the best secretary in the whole country!"

Carol could not refuse and finally drank the wine. Soon that bottle was gone, and Harry ordered another, and Carol began to feel rather sleepy and excited at the same time.

"This is such fun, Harry!" she said.

"Come on; let's dance."

"Oh, I can't."

"Of course you can!" Harry pulled her to her feet, and soon they were out on the dance floor, which was packed. He was holding her close, and Carol wanted to protest, but the wine had gone to her head. She was tired, also, after the hard three-days' work. The music was soft, and she had always liked to dance. They danced several times, then had their meal. Afterwards, there was more wine, more dancing.

Finally, Carol said, "I think I'd better go."

"Well, all right. It is getting late."

On the way to the hotel in the cab, Harry talked a little and held her hand, saying, "I'm a very lonesome man, and you made my trip here very successful."

Carol did not attempt to pull her hand back, and when they reached the hotel and got to their floor he said, "I forgot to tell you; we got the Donaldson contract. Come along and look at it. It's the best we've gotten so far."

Carol's head was reeling. She had taken more wine than

she had ever drunk in all of her life put together, and she protested, but he said, "Oh, it won't take but a minute."

She followed him to his room, and as they entered he said, "Sit down on the couch; I'll get the contract." Carol's head reeled, and he came back with a sheaf of papers in one hand, and a bottle in the other. "One more toast!" he said.

Carol protested, but he insisted. One toast turned into another, and finally her eyes would not focus on the fine print. She felt him pull the papers out of her hand; then he sat down beside her and put his arms around her.

"Please don't, Harry—"

"You're so sweet, Carol. You're the sweetest woman I've ever known."

Carol attempted to speak, but she could not respond, for he was kissing her. She knew deep inside that she should resist, but she was lonely and Harry had been so kind. Her head was swimming now; then after a time she knew that she had gone too far.

I shouldn't have come to this room, she thought. She tried to get free from his arms, but she felt weak. He was holding her tightly, and his hands were moving over her in a familiar way. "I love you, Carol," Harry whispered.

Carol Stuart had lost her sense of direction. The wine had made her dizzy, and she was about to faint. She tried to protest, but she could not, and at last she put her arms around him and said, "I'm so lonesome, Harry—"

Harry held her tighter, and his lips were on hers. Carol knew something was dreadfully wrong, but she could not think straight enough to do anything about it.

Outside the hotel, the traffic moved around, and overhead airplanes flew over the mighty city. But inside the hotel room, Carol Stuart was making the biggest mistake of her life.

"It's not as bad as you make it out, Honey."

Carol had spent the night in Harry's room and had awakened confused but filled with a sense of shame. Quickly she had dressed and gone to her own room. He'd come down and gotten her, and she faced him with concern in her eyes.

"I—I never thought I'd do such a thing," Carol whispered.

Harry spoke rapidly and earnestly. He was surprised to find that he did care for this young woman. Now he came over and tried to take her hand. She pulled it back, but he insisted. "Carol, I love you," he said. "I want us to get married."

"I'm already married."

"You can get a divorce. It won't be hard. I'll help you; then we can be happy together."

Carol Stuart thought of Clint's face, and shame swept over her. *I can never face him again, not after this—not ever! God will never forgive me for what I have done.* She listened as Harry began to make plans. There was a deadness in her such as she had never known. She knew that there would be no way that she could ever block this out of her memory, and the thought of going back and facing Clint was like death to her.

They left Chicago that afternoon and returned to Arkansas. Carol kept to herself, seeing as few people as possible, but by the end of the week she had made up her mind. *I can't live with Clint—not ever. He would know what I am with just one look at me.*

Harry was joyful when she agreed to get a divorce, but she could not enter into his joy. She tried to, but late that night when she went to bed, she wept, knowing that she had lost something irrevocably, something that could never come back again. The night closed in over the Ozarks—and it closed in over Carol Stuart as she lay in her bed weeping over what was gone forever.

Part Three

WINGS OVER ENGLAND

13

DEATH OVER GERMANY

C lint awoke early and waded through the mud during the murky hours of the morning toward the bathhouse, which was located some distance from the personnel huts. Stepping into the shower, he turned on the water, then flinched when the water hit his bare skin. He scrubbed for ten or fifteen minutes, resisting the desire to yell. He turned the water off and made a run back for the hut. All he could find was dirty underwear, so he put them on, feeling not much better than he had before the shower.

He sat down outside the hut and listened to the faint sound of air-raid sirens from the east, toward the coast. They made a spine-tingling wail, and he hoped they would fade away to the north or to the south. Sometimes at night the sirens would open up and nearby towns would come alive, for that was the sign that German bombers were coming toward them. There were no air-raid shelters at the base, and during the winter, many had chanced the bombs rather than sit out in the freezing water and the mud. Sometimes the dark shape of a bomber could be seen in the sky, silhouetted across a searchlight beam or the moon. But as Clint looked up he saw nothing in the skies but a few faint stars gleaming in an effort to light the darkness.

There was no mission that day, and the crew had been given four-day passes. When Clint had rejected all urgings to go into London, Cisco Marischal had said, "You got to be crazy missing a chance like this, buddy! Come on, we'll find you some female companionship!"

"I'm already married," Clint had said quietly.

Marischal had stared at him and shrugged his muscular shoulders. "So am I, but this is war, man! Anything goes!"

"I don't think so. Not for me anyway."

Marischal had scowled. "You're missing out on a lot of living, Clint!" He had turned and walked away, and on the way to London he complained to the rest of the crew while they all were crammed into a taxi, "You know, Clint's the best combat engineer in the wing, I guess—but he makes me nervous with all his religion."

"He means it though. He ain't no hypocrite." Frazier shoved his muscular shoulders against Cunningham and Columbo, making some room for himself. "Scoot over, you guys! You're taking up all the room!" He thought hard for a moment, then shook his head. "I seen lots of hypocrites in my time, but I got to say this: Old Clint, he ain't one of them. I ain't seen him take a drink or chase a woman since I've known him. That takes something in a guy out here in this kind of war."

Peabody agreed at once. "I almost got saved in a revival once back when I was a kid. The preacher preached on hell—scared the daylights out of me! I was ready to go up and get converted."

"Why didn't you?" The question came from Moon, who turned his steady brown eyes on Peabody.

"Ah, I was about ready to when I seen this little ole gal I'd been chasing for quite a while. She was looking at me all the way across in the brush arbor, and I forgot all about being scared or what would happen to me after I die."

"What's a brush arbor?" Moon inquired.

"You don't know what a brush arbor is? Why, you go out into the woods, cut down saplings, make a big framework, and put tree limbs on top of it, leaves and things. Then the preacher comes, and everybody from all around comes to the meeting—it's a camp meeting."

"I don't believe there's anything after we die, anyhow,"

Moon said moodily. "You die, and you're just like a dog—that's all there is to it!"

"Me, I don't believe that," Manny Columbo said with his intense black eyes on Moon. "All my folks got religion; we're all Catholics. Not that it's done me much good, but I know there's more to life than what we've got here."

The argument continued all the way into London, and when they piled out of the cab and paid the driver, Red Frazier said thoughtfully, "Well, either we're right or Clint's right. If he's right, we're all in bad shape if the *Last Chance* goes down."

"Shut up! It's bad luck to talk like that!" Asa Peabody snapped.

Moon laughed. "It's all a matter of luck. If we don't go down, the ship next to us might. If they don't, we might. Come on, let's go find some broads! . . ."

Clint ate a leisurely breakfast, enjoying the peace and quiet. He walked around the base watching the maintenance crews service and repair the battered B-17s, stopping by to go over the *Last Chance*. He had developed a particular relationship with this aircraft despite its bad reputation. He had kept it flying, along with help from the ground crews, despite numerous chunks taken out of it by cannon fire and machine gun bullets from the Luftwaffe. Clint had developed into a very fine combat engineer, mastering the thousands of technical adjustments that must be made constantly to keep a ship of this size and complexity in the air. He knew now why sailors called a ship "she," for he had learned that the men of this crew, himself most of all, had developed an almost husbandly affection for her—taking care of her needs, anticipating them, grieving when she was harmed.

Suddenly he thought of Carol, and he turned abruptly and walked away, his head down, his mind far away. He had been unable to elicit a letter from her since the one in which she had declared their marriage was over. He had even tried telephoning, but the number had been disconnected. His father,

Logan, had made several attempts to speak with her, but so far had been unsuccessful.

Of all the things that had happened to Clint Stuart, this had been the most difficult of all. Even though he faced death or dismemberment in the skies on a regular basis and had become inured to this, he could not ignore what was happening with this woman that he loved so dearly. As he walked along closing out the world about him, he seemed to see her face. He remembered the sweetness that was in her smile. He could almost feel the touch of her hands on his cheeks, for she had a way, when she kissed him, of putting each of her palms on the sides of his face lightly, gently, almost like a butterfly's touch. The memories were bittersweet, and as the hot July sun began to beat down on the fields and the base, he sought desperately to find some reason for what had happened.

After walking aimlessly around the base, he decided that he would go out to the stream, some four miles away, and spend the afternoon fishing. He had done this before, and although he had not made any great catches, the quietness and the setting had reminded him of home. Attempting to throw off thoughts of Carol, he collected his long pole and fishing gear and walked out of the base shortly after one o'clock. The sun was warm on his face, and he began to perspire very quickly. He watched the cows as he walked along. He was interested in anything that had to do with farming. He'd had many conversations with the farmers of the region, going to visit with them, taking in their methods. The farms were very small compared to those in the States, and the English farmers were intently interested in what it was like to be in America.

At last he reached the small river that wound in a serpentine fashion between green fields. Selecting a spot on the bank, he baited his hook, tossed it out, then sat down to wait. The river produced mostly a small fish that the English called roach. He had tried to eat his first catch, and although people did eat them, it was generally agreed that if you liked the taste of old cotton, you might like roach well enough. But the grass was soft, and the wind was stirring on his cheeks. Far off he saw a flight of Thunderbolts, P-47s, clinging close to the curvature of the earth, headed on some mission to aid the bombers, he supposed.

For two hours he sat there, catching three roach and releasing them. They were not a fighting fish, and it was not exciting fishing. Finally he decided to move downstream. He followed the curving bank for almost a mile, his quick eyes taking in the minnows that formed in silvery, darting schools up close to the bank. He was totally aware of his world out-of-doors, having spent most of his life in the fields and forest. The peace of the countryside was soaking into him, driving away the constant tension of waiting for a burst of flak to destroy him or the cannon fire from a Focke-Wulf to blow him to death.

The river bent around a stand of trees that leaned over it, and he moved toward the shade, for the sun was hot indeed. As he stepped inside the embracing arm of the grove, he was startled when a man turned to face him. It was Adam.

"Why, Lieutenant," Clint said at once. "I didn't know you were here."

Adam had put on his oldest uniform, stained with oil from the airplane and worn thin. A battered uniform cap was shoved back on his fair hair. "Hello, Clint. Come fishing?"

"Yes, Sir! Nothing doing though."

"Never mind the 'Sir.' When we're out here I guess we're just cousins." Adam shrugged. "I never did like the distinction between officers and enlisted men anyway."

"Has to be, Adam," Clint said, taking his cousin at his word. "Somebody has to be in command, and when the fighting starts there's no time to decide that. It all has to be decided ahead of time."

"That's right; it does." Adam was holding a fishing rod with a reel in his hand, and with an expert flick of his wrist, he sent the plug to the other side of the river. It landed within a foot of the bank, and he let it lie there for some five seconds, then gave it a twitch. Turning, he smiled and said, "I found out this is the way to catch fish. If you throw it out there and drag it in at once, nothing ever happens."

"You're right about that, Adam. I have caught many a bass back on Eleven Point River like that."

Clint took a seat on an old log and continued to speak. "I guess the fish are gonna see if it's edible or not, I don't know. Anyway, what do you catch on one of those fancy reels?"

"Not much of anything. They say this river's got pike in it up to ten pounds, but I've only caught two and neither of 'em much over a pound."

Adam cast the repulsive looking bait over and over again, retrieving it in short spurts. They talked of past missions, of the strategy of the war. Adam paid more attention to this and, as an officer, had more information.

He sent the plug across the river in a smooth arc. "The thing is, there's got to be an invasion of France. That's the only way we'll ever beat the Germans. We can pound their factories and rail yards, but sooner or later the ground troops are going to have to go in, infantry and tanks."

"When do you figure that will be?"

Adam gave the rod a twitch. "I figure next year, and it'll have to be launched from England. No other place to hit Germany except from this country. Probably land in France or somewhere, and those fellows that'll cross the Channel will be sitting ducks if we don't have air cover. Imagine being out there in a little boat with a Focke-Wulf coming at you with machine guns blazing and cannon fire bursting. They wouldn't have a chance!"

"You're right about that." Clint shrugged his shoulders and looked out to where the plug was resting quietly on the smooth surface of the water. "I guess that means they're going to expect the Air Corps to get command of the skies."

"That's right. We're knocking down too few of their planes, and we don't have enough bombers to knock out all their factories. I look for a big buildup any time now—more planes and crews—but until they get here, we're going to be sent out deeper and deeper into Germany."

"Well, that's what we came for, I guess."

"I guess!—" Suddenly the slender rod in his hand bent almost double, and the reel screamed. "Hey, I got one, Clint!" He began reeling in, but the fish was so large that it nearly ripped the line off of the reel. "I can't hold him!"

"Let him take it! Just hold your thumb on there and slow him down. He'll tire pretty soon." Clint's eyes glowed with excitement, and he leaped to his feet as he watched Adam struggle with the fish. "Careful now, that's a good one."

Adam played the fish until the line was almost exhausted on his reel, but finally the fish tired, and he began reeling it in slowly, hoping that the line wouldn't break. He caught a glimpse of a silvery, slender body, and gasped, "It's a monster, Clint!"

Clint said, "Don't try to lift him up. You get him close, and I'll pull him out so he won't break the line!"

"Okay!"

Clint took off his boots and waded out into the water, watching carefully as the fish thrashed the surface, moving closer as Adam reeled him in. Reaching down in a swift gesture, he grabbed the fish in the middle, and with one quick twist, threw it up on the bank. "Watch him; don't let him get back," he yelled as he clambered back up on the bank.

Adam threw the rod down and went to place his foot on the fish. His heart was beating faster than it did in combat, and he turned and glanced at Clint, who'd come to stand beside him. "I never caught a fish that big!"

"Me either! Mean looking sucker isn't he?" Clint answered, looking at the mouth full of teeth. "That's a pike, though. They're pretty good eating, I hear."

"It'll be enough for the whole crew," Adam said. Cautiously he reached down and pulled the fish up, saying, "Why, he must weigh fifteen pounds. Look at the size of him!"

Clint had been happy that Adam had thought of the crew.

"I'll clean him myself." And then he thought, *Oh, the crew's gone to London—won't be back until Tuesday.*

Adam was deflated. "Well, we'll share it with the rest of the fellows." He laughed shakily and said, "I go crazy every time I catch a fish."

"So do I," Clint grinned. The two men felt closer than they had since Adam had joined the group. They gathered their gear together and headed back toward the base, Clint carrying the fishing gear and Adam awkwardly carrying the huge pike as best he could. They laughed and relived the experience, then related other fishing tales.

When the camp came in view, Adam seemed to sober. "How come you didn't go into London with the rest of the crew?"

"Not much for me there."

Adam flashed a quick glance at his cousin and knew exactly what that meant. The rest of the crew, he understood, would be drinking and chasing women. He had developed a sincere admiration for Clint and knew that he was fortunate to have a combat engineer of his caliber. "How's Carol?" he asked, glad that he had managed to remember her name. When Clint did not answer at once, he glanced at him and saw with some surprise that there was no smile on his companion's face. "She's not sick, is she?"

"Not—not that I know of."

Instantly, Adam understood Clint's reticence. "She not writing to you?"

"I guess this is the worst thing that's ever happened to me, Adam."

"You want to talk about it?"

Strangely enough, Clint did want to talk about it. He had mentioned his problems to no one, but he saw Adam as family, and despite the fact that the lieutenant had been hard on the crew and had kept himself aloof, he felt the need to say something to someone. He began to speak awkwardly, stressing how Carol had depended on her father and that his death had been terrible for her. He defended her behavior, not once blaming her, and there was a sadness in his voice but no anger whatsoever.

Adam listened carefully and wondered if he could've handled the situation as well. He finally decided that he could not, and when it came time to separate he said, "I'm sorry to hear it, Clint. Don't let it get you down—you can make it right when you get home."

Adam did not feel this was the case, but it was all he could think of to say. After he left Clint to go to his own quarters, he shook his head and his lips tightened bitterly. "What kind of a woman would leave a man who's risking his life every day? Probably run off with some other man. Couldn't even wait until Clint got home," he muttered. He was unhappy and miserable in his own life, and somehow Clint's stability had been a help to him. A puzzled frown came to his face. *I don't see how he can be so calm about it. He's hurting inside, anybody can see that. He really loves that woman, but he didn't say one word against her—not one!* As he moved toward the kitchen to deposit the fish, he wondered if he ever would be that kind of man.

Red Frazier had steady nerves and was a tough individual. He had manifested no fear at all in the ring, and his reputation as a fighter had been that he could take anything that was thrown at him. But as the weeks passed, and Red saw more and more Forts going down to earth bearing his fellow airmen, a gloom settled over him. During the trip to London, he had gotten blind drunk, and he stayed that way as long as possible. But when he had come back, he had discovered on the very next mission that somehow he had lost something. He did not call it a loss of courage, for it was not exactly that. He performed his duties as radio operator and waist gunner as well as ever, but inside something was wrong with him, and he struggled to keep the crew from finding him out. To him a loss of courage was the most shameful thing that could happen to a man, and if anything, he became louder and more aggressive than ever.

Late one afternoon he was talking to Clint, whom he trusted more than any man in the crew—or any other man he had ever known, for that matter. Something about the quiet steadiness of the tall engineer drew him, and the two had had several long talks together. Red had even gone to services twice at Clint's insistence, although he laughed at himself for doing so.

As usual, the question of their odds for living through the war surfaced. Red actually brought it up, and he said, "You know, every time I fly another mission, my luck and chances for survival get a little bit less."

"How do you figure that?"

"Well, the more raids you go on, the more the odds catch up with you."

Clint had been through this before. He paid little attention himself to the twenty-five-mission goal and said, "You mean you think the odds on your twentieth mission will be twenty times more than on your first mission?"

"Sure. The odds stretch and stretch. That's why so many men go down on their last two or three missions."

Actually, Clint had noticed this, but he had tried to assuage Red's doubts. He could see that the tough-faced radio operator was struggling inside, and he had privately decided that it was a struggle against God. "The way I see it," he said easily, "the odds start all over every day on every mission."

"Naw, that ain't right. The more you fly, the closer you get to the breaking point—then *bang!* They just catch up with you!"

They argued for some time and finally Clint said, "Look, you take a pair of dice and you roll them, and the mathematical chance to get a seven or an eleven will repeat every time you throw those dice. It's the same thing for a mission, Red. What's already happened doesn't count."

"Oh, I think it does!"

"Look here. Every raid we learn something new. We get

smarter, and we learn how to dodge around. We got the best pilot, I think, in the whole Eighth Air Force. We're supposed to be a hard-luck crew, but look how we've made it when others who didn't have our reputation aren't with us anymore."

Red shrugged his burly shoulders and scratched his cheek. He had not shaved, and his fingernails made a raspy sound on his tough beard. "I understand what you're saying, but gamblers wouldn't agree with you. There's a law of chance somehow or other, doesn't make any difference whether it's cards or missions."

Red sat silent, thinking hard, and Clint did not attempt to rush him. Clint mentioned the sermons that they had heard from the chaplain, saying in an offhand fashion, "That was an unusually good sermon the parson preached last Sunday."

"I didn't understand it. I'm too dumb to understand things like that."

"You're not dumb, Red, but I found out that smartness doesn't have much to do with the way we find God."

"How do you figure that?"

"There's a verse in the Bible that says 'The natural man receiveth not the things of the Spirit of God.' That just means that there's some things that you can learn by going to school. For instance, you had to learn how to operate that radio just by study. Anybody with a little aptitude can do that, but you can't find God out that way because he's not like a radio."

"Well, how do you find him out then?"

"Different ways. The old preachers used to say we would never search for God if he hadn't searched for us first."

Red's eyes narrowed. "What does that mean, Clint?"

"I think it means that we've gotten so rotten that we're gonna go our own way if we're left alone. I know I probably would have. Most of us would, I think, so God comes looking for us."

"He hasn't never come lookin' for me!"

"I think he has, though you may not have noticed. Jesus said that he had come to seek and to save that which was lost." Clint spoke easily and pulled a New Testament out of his pocket. "Here!" He turned the pages and said, "There, you see where I've got it underlined?"

"'For the Son of man is come to seek and to save that which was lost.' I still don't get it."

"Red, it's a big thing—bigger than anything in the world. In the Old Testament, you read how man was created perfect, he lived in a perfect place, and yet, he didn't stay there. Something happened to him—he went sour. That's not the way the Bible describes it," he grinned, "but that's what it means. So, he's cut off from God. Now, how does he get back again?"

"I don't know. How does he?"

"Well, that's what the New Testament is all about. Here, over here it says that Christ died to save sinners."

Frazier listened intently as Clint moved from verse to verse, and finally he exclaimed, "Why, even I can see that, dumb as I am!"

"If you can see that you need God, then you're not dumb. Lots of people don't understand that," Clint said gently.

"A man would be a fool if he didn't know that he needs *something.*"

"You really need to get *converted,* as the Bible puts it."

"Yeah, I've heard that before, and that preacher last Sunday talked about being born again. I don't get that, Clint. A man can't be born but once."

"Physically that's true, but spiritually it's not. He can be born in his heart. These bodies are going to die. If we don't get killed on a raid, we may go home and get hit by a car. We're all going to die; it's just a matter of when. Inside, Red, our hearts can be changed, and we'll never die in our spirits. But only Jesus can do that for you."

"How can he do it, since he's dead? He lived two thousand years ago; the preacher said that."

"He came out of the tomb, and now he's alive." For some time the two men talked, and Clint urged Frazier to give his heart to Christ. For some time there was a struggle, for Frazier led a hard, sinful life. Finally, Clint saw a brokenness in him and said, "I don't have all the answers, Red, but I've found Christ myself. I know he can forgive us and make us new inside. Are you willing to let him do that for you?"

"I–I don't know what to do, Clint. I'll do anything I can so I can get rid of the kind of guy I've always been. I've never really liked myself."

The two men bowed their heads and prayed a simple prayer. When Frazier looked up, there was awe in his eyes as he said, "You know something, Clint? I feel *good*. I feel all—well, all kind of cleaned out."

"So do I, Red." Clint slapped the radio operator on the back. "We're both cleaned out now, and whatever happens, we belong to Jesus."

In July, after a three-week period of sodden weather, General Eaker stepped up the size and the frequency of the Eighth's attacks. It was called Blitz Week, an around-the-clock bombardment in cooperation with the Royal Air Force. On the twenty-fourth, Eaker sent 309 Forts to targets in Norway: a chemical factory, a smelting plant, and a submarine installation. On the next day the Eighth teamed up with the RAF's bomber command, and they hit Hamburg. The RAF sent out 791 heavy bombers. Two nights later a similar force struck again, causing a firestorm that reached twelve-hundred degrees centigrade, incinerating most of the old city. On the twenty-eighth, when the mission was scrambled, the men were tired and exhausted. The bombers had flown far beyond the range of P-47 escorts, and 88 Fortresses had been shot down.

"Where we going this time, Sir?" Clint asked as the two pilots met them after the briefing.

"We're going into Oscherleben."

"Where's that?"

"Only ninety miles southwest of Berlin. It'll be a rough raid."

This was an understatement, for the *Last Chance* was riddled with machine-gun fire even before they reached the target.

"Bombs away!" Moon Wilson cried. "Let's get out of here!" He leaped to his guns, for the Messerschmitts were coming at them, swarming like angry bees.

"Fighters at three o'clock! Fighters at three o'clock!"

"Watch out; they're on our tail! Watch out back there, Peabody!"

"I see 'em, Lieutenant!"

The plane rattled as the twin fifties fired at the fighter planes, and Clint followed the fleeing form of one until the tracers from his guns met, raking it from nose to tail. He watched as the plane burst into a fiery ball and exploded, and he muttered, "God have mercy on him."

"I'm hit! I'm hit!"

"Who is it? Report!"

"Frazier! They got me!"

Since the sky was free of enemy aircraft, Clint dropped out of the top turret and stepped into the waist of the plane. Manny Columbo was bent over Frazier, who manned the other waist gun. Columbo's eyes were stark with tragedy. "He's hit bad, Clint!"

Clint leaped at once to the fallen radio operator and asked, "Where'd they get you?"

"In the belly—"

Red was holding his hands against his stomach, but his flight jacket was already stained with bright crimson arterial blood. Frazier's face was drained pale, and he reached out a bloody hand. "I–I ain't going to make it, Clint!"

Clint took the bloody hand, and he knew that it was hopeless. The life was draining out of the man. He had been hit by several heavy machine-gun bullets in the body, and no one could survive that. Clint held the bloody hand and bent closer to catch what Frazier said.

"Good thing—we had that talk last week, ain't it—"

"You'll be with Jesus, Red. Wait for me there; I'll come someday."

For a moment, light gleamed in the eyes of the dying man. The pain racked him, and yet he managed a smile. He moved his other hand to take Clint's and whispered so faintly that Clint had to put his ear to Red's lips. The words he heard were, "I'll wait for you—Clint."

Clint felt the body slump, and he turned and put the bloody hands over the chest, then turned to face Manny. "He's gone, Manny."

Manny swallowed hard, "He–he was a good guy."

"He gave his heart to Jesus last week."

"Yeah, I know; he told me." Manny Columbo was a hard man, but tears came to his eyes. "I'm glad about that, Clint— you done right."

The B-17 plowed home through heavy cloud cover. Clint went about his duties, but when the plane landed, he helped move the body of his friend. Adam came to stand over him. He said nothing, but there was grief in his face. It pained him that he had not really made contact with his crew. He watched as the body was carried away and thought, *I wish I'd known him better; I wish I had*.

14

"I STILL LOVE YOU"

As the airliner circled Los Angeles, brilliant sunlight flooded through the window temporarily blinding Wendy Stuart. Shutting her eyes quickly, she turned away; then as the plane banked for what seemed to be the final approach, she looked out again, studying the city. California was a land of sunshine and lived up to its reputation on this first day of July, 1943. Far off she saw the mountains rising with the desert lying below them.

The wheels touched the runway with a definite *whump*, causing Wendy's head to jerk; then she was thrown forward slightly as the brakes took hold, slowing the plane. Wheeling around with the propellers swirling, the plane taxied off the main runway, and Wendy watched with interest as it approached the low terminal that lay stretched beside the long white runway. As soon as the plane stopped and the stewardess announced, "You may move around now," Wendy got up and retrieved her carry-on from the storage compartment overhead. Patiently she waited as the passengers gathered their luggage and filed off the airplane. As she moved down the steps, the sunlight again seemed to blind her, but she welcomed the warmth as the pale white sun soaked down into her bones. Moving across the cement, she entered the airport and looked around to find Mona approaching with a smile.

"Wendy, I'm so glad to see you!" Mona was wearing a white dress with a purple scarf around her neck, and two large jade earrings swung as she moved forward. She looked every inch a Miss America, which was what she had almost been, with her glorious blonde beauty and classic calendar features. Throwing her arms around Wendy, she hugged her, then stepped back with her eyes shining. "Your plane was late. I was beginning to get worried about you!"

"We got held up for a while in Nashville," Wendy said. She felt dowdy and colorless next to this glorious young woman, but then she always had. There was something about Mona that made other women look this way, or seemed to, but this did not trouble Wendy. She was resigned to the young woman's beauty, and as they walked along the baggage area, she listened as Mona spoke excitedly of what had been going on with the troupe.

"You're going to love the tour, Wendy!" Mona said, her enormous eyes flashing as she used her hands to make expressive gestures. A large, gold bracelet gleamed on her right wrist, and she wore several rings, all looking expensive and, to Wendy's taste, a little garish. "It's going to be the best troupe that's ever been sent to the Pacific. I just can't wait to leave—but of course, we've got to rehearse some first!"

Wendy allowed herself to be caught up in Mona's excitement. After they collected her larger bag, an attendant carried it outside of the terminal, where they got into a taxi. Wendy studied Los Angeles as they moved into the heart of the city and once interrupted Mona long enough to say, "Just think, I might look out and see Clark Gable."

Mona laughed and shook her head, making the jade earrings swing freely. "I doubt it! That's what everyone comes to Hollywood to see. They think movie stars walk up and down every street—but the truth is most of them don't."

"What is their native habitat? Where do they stay?"

"On the sets mostly. I've been to several of them, and you wouldn't believe how hard movie stars work. It's a dog's life really—getting up early, memorizing lines all day. They have to move from set to set, sometimes go on location."

Wendy teased Mona saying, "You wouldn't do it for any-thing, would you?"

Startled, Mona gave her cousin an incredulous glance, then seeing the smile on her lips laughed and said, "Well, you've got me there. I guess I would—it's exactly what I want to do, Wendy, and I think I've got a good gamble at it. I've got an agent now, you know. His name is Nick Chance. He's been teaching me all sorts of things, and I've got an acting coach now, too. Of course, I won't be taking any more lessons until we get back from the tour, but he says I've got as much talent as anybody in Hollywood."

Wendy listened indulgently as Mona spoke with enthu-siasm about the Hollywood life but was thinking to herself, *She's got the bug! I've never seen her so taken with anything—but then she always did like the limelight.* She thought of how Mona had been in countless plays in high school. Wendy was a little apprehensive about the whole thing. She knew a little about how hearts were broken every day—hearts of young women who came from all over the United States to Hollywood to become big stars only to discover that very few ever made it to the top. Most of them, Wendy was convinced, had unhappy, miserable lives and gave up normal living for the tinsel virtues that passed in Hollywood for a normal life.

The taxi drew up, and Mona saw to getting the baggage inside and tipped the taxi driver. She said, "This is the Bell-mont Hotel. It's a really nice place, and all the troupe is stay-ing here."

Wendy was somewhat apprehensive. "I didn't bring much money," she said. "I hope somebody is responsible for the hotel bill."

"Why, you silly thing, everything is paid for! All you'll need is a little spending money—and none of that once we get to the Pacific. Come along; I'll take you to your room." She led Wendy to the elevators, and when they arrived at the third floor, moved down the hall until she came to room

308. Unlocking the door, she stepped aside and said, "Your boudoir awaits, Madam!"

Wendy stepped inside, and her eyes opened wide. It was a luxurious suite—at least to her. The room contained a black-and-white striped couch in a modern style and a glass-topped cocktail table in an abstract shape. Chairs made out of black steel with orange-and-chartreuse cushions were scattered around the room. On the walls were abstract paintings that looked to Wendy like smears left where an artist cleaned his brush. "This is lovely," she said, and walked over to the window and looked out where she could see, stretching far off, the fall that led to the ocean. She followed Mona to the bedroom, which was fairly large with two double beds. The bathroom was tiled with apricot-colored tiles, and the towels were lime green with a red-gold embroidered coat of arms that consisted of a lion with one paw raised. "That bathtub's big enough to go swimming in," Wendy remarked, staring at the large pink tub with awe.

"Isn't it wonderful!" Mona exclaimed. "You're going to love it here—not that we have much time to spend in the hotel. We spend all day rehearsing. It's really hard work."

"When will we be leaving, Mona?"

"We have three days before we take off. You're the last one of the troupe to come. Did you bring your music with you?"

"Yes, but I'm a little bit worried. I'm not convinced that fighting marines will want to hear grand opera."

"From what I understand, they'll be glad to hear anything from a pretty woman. They must be starved for the sight of girls."

Wendy could tell this was exactly the kind of situation that Mona loved. She herself was less than excited about that aspect of it. It had taken a great deal of adjustment in her thinking to make this tour, and she had spent much time praying that God would give her an opportunity to witness for Jesus Christ. This might not be acceptable, she was aware, to the rest of the troupe, but she had made up her mind that that was the reason that God had placed her with the group, and she was determined to speak out as well as she could for the Lord.

"Why don't you shower and change clothes, and we'll get right over to the studio—if you're not too tired, that is?"

"Oh, yes, I'd like that."

"Good! I'll go down and give you thirty minutes; then you'll get your start as a USO girl."

"This is Monarch Studios, Wendy," Mona said, waving her hand at the low-lying buildings that made up the scene where the taxi let them out. "Aunt Lylah and Uncle Jesse donated one of the studios for us to rehearse in."

"Have you talked with them much?"

"Yes, we went out to dinner last night. They're anxious to see you."

"What do they say about Adam?"

Mona shook her golden hair in the sunshine and smiled at a couple of actors who walked by giving her a careful examination. "Oh, he's a pilot in the air force."

"They must be terribly worried about him."

"Yes, they are, but they said maybe the troupe would go over to Europe and we'd get to see him, but I don't think so. I think we'll stay in the Pacific. Come on now, let's go."

The young women entered the ugly boxlike building, and Wendy looked up to the high ceilings where steel and aluminum gridwork held enormous lights. On the floor were different sets, which looked odd to her, rooms with only three walls with cameras and lights banked outside the bare space. As she walked quickly to keep up with Mona, she saw that one set was half of an airplane. It had been apparently cut in two so that the cameras could move back and forth from the pilot's station down to the seating sections. They were not shooting at the moment, and technicians were moving over it.

"They'll never get that one to fly again," she remarked.

"Oh, it never flew. They build those things from scratch. It's wonderful what they do! Why, they build a whole house,

Wendy, and then just burn it up if that's what the script calls for. It's so exciting! As soon as we get back from the tour, I'm going to get to be in a movie. You just wait and see! If I have to I'll make Aunt Lylah let me play a part."

Wendy did not comment on this, for they had passed through a door into a large room with fifteen-foot ceilings. It was not as large as the other, and at one end a band was playing on a stage raised about two feet. The band members were not wearing dress jackets and looked rather scruffy, Wendy thought.

"Come on, I'll introduce you to everybody." Wendy felt herself propelled into the group that seemed to be drawn from different walks of show business. Besides the ten band members, she met Danny Brothers, whom she had seen in a movie in a bit part. He was a comedian, and Mona said, "This is my cousin, Wendy Stuart."

"Hi, Wendy," Brothers said. He was a small man with a fair complexion and an easy smile. "Glad to have you aboard. I'll need to be talking with you so I'll know what to tell the GI Joes about you."

"Come on, you can do that later," Mona said. Quickly Mona pulled Wendy across the room to where a man and a woman were juggling. They were standing about ten feet apart and throwing what looked like bowling pins toward each other. The pins sailed through the air, revolving rapidly, so quickly that they were just a blur. Wendy studied the man and the woman, noting that they seemed to be Latin, Spanish perhaps. "That's Carlos and Lolita; they're jugglers."

"I can see that. What's their last name?"

"Oh, I forget, but they're good, aren't they?"

"Yes, they are." Wendy waited until the man adeptly plucked the pins out of the air; then the jugglers turned to face the young women. As they were introduced, Wendy saw that Carlos was a handsome enough fellow, but Lolita was a really beautiful young woman—dark complected with liquid black eyes and a sensuous mouth.

"We're glad to have you with us," Carlos said with a Spanish accent. "My Lolita and I are honored to do this service for this great country, the United States. We are new citizens, you know."

"Well, congratulations. I know you are very happy."

"Oh, yes!" Lolita said. She ran her hand through her jet black hair and smiled languidly. "Now, we will go show the soldiers our appreciation."

"And what do you do, Miss Stuart?"

"Oh, I sing a little."

"Sing a little," Mona jeered. "She sings like no one you ever heard. You'll love her! Now, come on, there's Rob over there. I know you've seen him."

As Mona tugged her across the floor, Wendy recognized Robert Bradley instantly. He was a tall man with light hair and blue eyes. She had seen him in several movies. He was never the main character but always the friend of the main character or the boyfriend who lost out in the fight over the girl. Still, he was the first movie star she had ever seen and when she was introduced she said, "I've enjoyed your movies very much, Mr. Bradley. You have a fine voice."

"Well, not as good as yours, from what I hear." Rob Bradley cocked his head to one side and studied the young woman in front of him. There was an experience in his eyes that Wendy recognized at once. *He's known a great many women*, she thought. *As a movie star, I guess he would.* Still, he seemed nice enough, and she said, "I particularly liked the role you did in *Our Country*. That was a nice movie."

"You liked it, did you?"

"Oh, yes, and your singing was very good!"

"Well, maybe we'll get to do some duets together—not that I'm in your class, from what Mona tells me." He turned to Mona and put his arm around her in a familiar manner. Looking down at her he said, "She says you're better than Jeanette McDonald!"

"You shouldn't have said that, Mona," Wendy protested.

"Why not? It's the truth!" Mona was looking up at Rob with

something like adoration in her face. She did not seem to mind his familiarity. Indeed, she reached up and patted him on the cheek and said, "I can't sing, but Rob's working out a dance routine that we're going to do together. Isn't that super?"

"That's fine. I'll be anxious to see it."

"Have you introduced Wendy to everybody?"

"Oh, almost, except for Lori and Cathy. There they are over there! They're acrobats and dancers, too, very good."

Wendy was taken to where two small but well-formed women were doing a series of tumbling maneuvers on mats laid out for them. They wore brief costumes and their muscles were firm. Both of them had dark hair and were obviously identical twins.

As they left the two young women doing back flips, Mona said, "They're both crazy in love with Rob."

"I suppose that's natural enough. He's a handsome man and a movie star."

"He has real talent. He's not just a half-baked second banana."

Wendy smiled at Mona's show business slang and said, "You like him yourself, don't you?"

Quickly Mona turned to face her and said defensively, "Well, what if I do? He likes me. We've gone out together twice already."

"He seems very nice, but movie stars aren't exactly the most stable people in the world."

"Don't be so full of prejudice! You sound like Uncle Owen. He's against Hollywood down to his bones. There're good people here just like there are everywhere else."

"I'm sure of that, but be careful. You always were too easily impressed by men." Mona's mouth tightened, and she did not answer. Wendy realized that she had offended her and determined to say nothing else.

Mona was quick to forgive, and her mood changed almost instantly. With a roguish grin, she said, "Come on; you should meet our tour director. There he is over there."

Wendy followed Mona to one corner of the room where a man was standing with his back toward them. He was bent over a desk and was writing something.

"Well, here's the last of our troupe, Wendy Stuart, my cousin." As the man turned around she added, "You've met Alex, I think, haven't you, Wendy?" She laughed aloud and hugged Wendy, saying, "I wanted to surprise you. I've been wondering how you let him get away. Now—you've got him where he can't run!"

Wendy could not speak for a moment, the shock was so great. She had not expected to see Alex Grenville, since no one had mentioned his name, and when he saw her he smiled easily, saying, "Hello, Wendy, I guess you're surprised to see me here."

"Well—yes, I am. No one told me you'd be leading the tour."

"I wasn't supposed to, but Neil Carrothers got appendicitis, so they called me at the last minute."

"I'm glad they did," Mona said instantly, nodding firmly. "You're much better at the job than he was."

Wendy felt foolish and could not think of a thing to say. Finally, she said lamely, "I brought my music, Alex, but I'm not sure it's the thing that the soldiers will want to hear, arias from operas."

"I've got some ideas about that," Alex said quickly. "You're great at opera, but you can handle the popular stuff, too. I'm thinking maybe we can mix it up a little bit, a little serious stuff but with some light things, too."

"I don't know much about the new songs."

Alex shook his head. He was looking fit and tanned and very handsome. "You'll pick it up. You were always quick. I guess we'd better start right now. There's not much time."

"I'll leave you two alone. Don't forget," Mona said. "We're going to do our dance routine later on this afternoon, all right?"

"You talked it over with Rob?"

"Oh, yes, he's excited about it!"

"All right, I'll have the music ready." Mona left, and Alex turned back to Wendy. He was silent for a moment, and there was an awkwardness about him. "I feel strange, Wendy," he admitted. "I thought I had a little poise, and I knew you were coming—but somehow just seeing you brings back old memories."

"We don't need to talk about those."

Alex looked at her quickly. He saw that she was upset and did not wonder. Quietly he said, "I guess not, but we'll have to be working together, and we'll do the best we can. I know you'll do that."

"Of course, Alex; I want to do this for the men in service. I've had doubts about it, though."

"They'll love you. Well, what shall it be first, see to your costume or the music?"

"Oh, let's go over the music. I can wear anything."

"That's what you think." Grenville grinned suddenly. "We're going to give these guys something to look at. You'll be outfitted from head to foot courtesy of Monarch Studios. Your aunt and uncle have just been princely about this. They've put themselves out, of course. The fact they've got a son in service doesn't hurt any.

"They talk about him all the time. I can tell they're worried, and I guess they have reason to be. It's not easy going over Germany in those bombers day after day—after every mission some of them don't come back." He looked serious and then suddenly added, "I'm like you; I wanted to do something. Have you ever wondered why I'm not in the army?"

"Well—"

"Of course you have. Well, the truth is, I've got a little heart murmur. Nothing serious," he added quickly. "Just enough to keep me from passing a physical. I tried every service—army, navy, marines. Got turned down by all of them, so I thought this was something I could do."

"I'm glad you told me, Alex. It must be hard on you," she said suddenly.

"You know, I think it is. I want to stop people when I think I see them looking at me and wondering why I'm not in uniform—but I can't stop everybody I see and explain my physical condition, can I?"

"No."

"All right, let's talk about the music. Come sit down over here. We can have coffee, tea, or Coke." He glanced around and said, "I know you don't want anything stronger, but they'll be after you to take it."

"I wish they wouldn't."

Alex shrugged his shoulders. "It's just the way they are. They drink alcohol the way other people drink water. It's kind of an occupational hazard. They won't believe you when you say you don't drink."

"They will by the time we get back."

Alex laughed at the firmness in Wendy's lips and said, "I could tell them something about that! Well, you brought some music; let's see what it is."

By evening, Wendy was totally exhausted. The flight had been long, and the day had been difficult. Alex had been everywhere, directing the band, working with Rob and Mona on their routine, and between times the two of them had gone through all the music she had brought and worked on some sort of program for her.

At seven o'clock Alex finally said, "OK, that's it, everybody. Get a good night's sleep. I want you all here at six o'clock in the morning." Ignoring the groans, he turned to Wendy and said, "Come on; I'll take you out for supper. No argument now!" When she stared at him, he said, "I'm not the big, bad wolf with long, white teeth, but I think we might talk a bit more about how you're going to fit in. You're getting a late start."

"All right, Alex."

The two went to a small restaurant where there was quiet music and the lights were low. As she sat across from him, Wendy slumped down and said, "I'm tired. I can't imagine what it'll be like when we're flying around the Pacific. I don't know if I'm tough enough for it."

"I think you are." Alex smiled at her and gave the order to the waiter. Then the two sat there letting the frantic activities of the day seep out. "This is nice," Alex said finally. "Won't be any of this when we get in the Solomons."

"What will it be like? Will it be dangerous, Alex?"

"Oh, they'll route us around the hot areas, but from what I hear there's always the chance of a bomber flying over those islands. The Japanese are out to cause all the trouble they can, as you might imagine." He sipped the water in front of him and asked curiously, "Are you afraid?"

"I don't know. Not now." She looked around the restaurant. A few couples were talking, speaking quietly. Waiters were moving back and forth with food, and danger seemed far away. "Nothing to be afraid of here." She smiled at him wanly. "But if a bomb were falling, and the bullets started flying, I think I'd run like a rabbit."

"Me, too, but we'll hope that doesn't happen. Tell me about your folks; I've missed them."

She brought him up to date on her life, and then asked him about the symphony.

"I'm on a leave of absence, actually."

"Will you go back after the tour?"

"Probably. It's going well." He hesitated then said, "It'd be going better if you were there as soloist."

"Alex, let's not talk of that."

"All right. But one thing I better talk to you about is Mona."

Instantly Wendy knew what he was going to say. "She's falling in love with Rob Bradley, isn't she?"

"I wouldn't call it love. She's infatuated with him."

"That's the way she is. She's always been like that with men."

"I sort of thought that was her way. She's a beautiful young woman and sweet, too, but she's absolutely crazy over the movies. Rob Bradley's just exactly the wrong kind of man she needs to be around."

"What's wrong with him?"

"Oh, he's just Hollywood. They've got different standards out here. They don't think anything about divorces. Their morals aren't the highest—as you probably already know."

This was exactly the sort of thing that Wendy had feared. She waited as the waiter served their meal before returning to the subject. "I am worried about Mona. She's really very vulnerable. She's so beautiful, and men are drawn to her."

"I know. I haven't been here long, but I can see that this is the wrong atmosphere for her. You'd better try to talk to her about Bradley."

"It won't do any good," Wendy said slowly. She took a bite of the steak that was in front of her and chewed it thoughtfully. "She's never been one to take counsel—very headstrong."

"I think all Stuarts are headstrong. It must go with the breed."

Suddenly Wendy smiled and reached over and put her hand over his. "I think you're right about that. You might as well write us all off as a bunch of stubborn mules."

Alex looked down at her hand, and memories came back to him. He did not try to touch her, but when she removed her hand, he leaned back and said, "Well, we'll be thrown together a lot, and I'm looking forward to it. Being with you and being on this tour, it's the biggest thing I've ever tried to do. I hope I can cut it."

"You can, Alex; you can do anything you want to."

"Except one."

His words came with force, and his eyes were intent. Wendy knew exactly what the one thing was that he had not been able to accomplish—to win her love. She thought suddenly, *He already has my love, though he doesn't know it*, but she only smiled and said, "What's good for dessert here? We should call it a night early since we have to be back to rehearse at six."

15

DEATH FROM THE SKIES

After Guadalcanal, Will Stuart and the bloody remnant of the First Division left for what seemed to be a paradise. Will was so weak from fever he could not make the climb into the waiting boat. He fell into the water, pack, rifle, and all and had to be fished out. A baby-faced man named Bobby Carr, who had turned out to be one of the most ferocious combat marines Will had ever encountered, reached down and yanked him up.

"Hey, you can't drown now, Will," he cajoled, a cocky smile on his face. "We're gettin' out of this place!"

Coughing and choking the salt water out of his mouth and lungs, Will gasped, "Thanks, Bobby, I'll save your life the next time."

The marines finally got aboard the ship and Will and Bobby set out for the galley. The soldier who watched them as they drank hot coffee from thick white mugs said, "How was it?"

Will blinked with surprise, "You mean Guadalcanal?"

"Sure!"

Carr stared at him. "I didn't know that anybody ever heard of the place!"

"What are you talking about?" the soldier said. "Guadalcanal, the First Marines. Everybody's heard of it. You guys are famous—you're all heroes back home!"

Carr grinned broadly. "Well, what do you think of that,

227

Will; we're heroes! Maybe we'll get to meet Lana Turner when we get back."

They did not meet Lana Turner, but to their immense relief they did not go to another island. Instead the *President Wilson* took them to New Hebrides, and for three weeks they languished. Finally, they loaded again and went to Australia. There, the men who had won the battle at Guadalcanal went mostly in two directions. Some went to the hospital for the malaria that racked them and finally brought collapse. This was Will's fate. No sooner had they arrived than he began shaking so badly he could hardly walk. Carr took him to the barracks at once, and he was clapped into the hospital to recuperate.

The other destination for the marines was the fleshpots of Australia. They spent their nights in the bars, their days sleeping. Carr was one of these, for despite his cherubic features, he was worldly to the bone. He came to see Will almost every day—usually late in the afternoon after he had slept the mornings away.

They were sitting outside the hospital in the shade of some trees one afternoon when Will said, "I wonder where we'll go when we leave here."

"Not home," Carr said. "That's the scuttlebutt."

"I guess it will be another island. Did you read about what happened to the invasion at Tarawa?"

Carr made a face. He had heard, as everyone had, of the terrible casualties the marines had suffered in taking that little piece of rocky island. "It wasn't worth it," he scowled. "What good is it, anyhow? All these little islands, I wouldn't give one square mile of Michigan for the whole bunch of 'em!"

"I guess we've got to take 'em back from the Japs, though," Will said. "We're winning the war, but it's costing a lot of blood. Did you hear what happened in Russia last week?"

"No, what?"

"The biggest tank battle ever fought." Will nodded. "The Russians beat the soup out of the Germans. The Krauts had all their big new heavy-duty tanks, and they got zapped!"

"I'd hate to be in one of those things." Carr gave a slight shudder. "It'd drive me crazy being cooped up inside a tank, nowhere to run." This coming from a man who had crept through the jungle with bloodthirsty Japanese on all sides night after night was rather grimly humorous.

"I've got a brother in the tank corps," Will said. "I'm like you, though; I just don't see how they crawl into those little tin cans. One hit with a rocket or a fire bomb and they're gone."

The two men spoke mostly of home and when the war would be over, and finally Carr rose and said, "Well, I got to go see my sweetie pie. When you gettin' out of this place?"

"Two or three days, I guess. By that time I reckon we'll be leavin' here."

"Yep, they've always got another island for the First Division," Carr replied. He grinned, slapped Will on the back, and left.

Will was discharged three days later and discovered that their days in Melbourne were drawing to a close. He had no sooner gotten back to his outfit than they were marched from the huts down to the docks, onto the ships—and back to the war.

Crowds of women lined the dockside, and Carr jabbed his elbow into Will's ribs. "See that one there, the blonde one up front—the big one? That's Susie; ain't she something?" He waved enthusiastically, and the blonde woman waved back.

Curious, Will asked, "Was that the only one you knew here, Carr?"

"Nah, I think I had four pretty serious squeezes."

Will was silent for a while as the ship began to pull out. He asked, "Do you think you'll ever see her again?"

"Nah." Carr shook his head. "I'll miss her; she was a sweet kid, but in a war that's the way things are."

The liberty ship pulled slowly away from the dock, and the voyage began. Will ate on the deck where, in a strong wind, it was hard to keep the food on the mess kits. The ship plowed its way up the Australian coast, sailing inside the Great Barrier Reef. Will was amazed at the natural phenomena that flanked them to starboard and to port. The reef was a natural protective barrier, and there was no danger of submarines in such a labyrinth.

The days were long, and the ship was slow, and Will found that he had lost much of the tension that had built up in him at Guadalcanal. He had no idea where he was headed, nor did any of the other enlisted men. They only knew that it was somewhere back to the war. By this time the Japanese had been cleared from the Solomons and most of New Guinea, and the marines and other forces had launched the northward island-hopping progress across the watery waste of Oceania. The bloody losses at Tarawa were on their minds, but as veterans they could talk more and joke more about the place where they were going than of the hard days that were behind. Conjecture kept their tongues wagging. Every day a new rumor about their destination spread as they sat gossiping on the greasy canvas covering the hatches. Sometimes it would become a word game or a slogan-inventing contest.

"Keep cool, fool, it's Rabaul," Carr said, naming the impregnable Japanese fortress at New Britain.

Will grinned back at him, relatively sure that not even the officers in charge would have little enough sense to attack Rabaul.

"No, it's the Golden Gate in forty-eight."

"I hope not! That means we've got five years of this," Carr said.

A big marine sitting beside them, named Abe Mattell, said, "I heard one. 'Will you be on the roster when we get back from Gloucester?'" This was a gloomy reference to Cape Gloucester on the further end of New Britain, with the prospect of invading Korea.

Will studied the men, wondering how they would all take another battle. They were idle, immobile, and bored. This meant they were irritated rather easily. The food, which would have been manna back on Guadalcanal, was exasperating. It got to be irritating to assemble the mess gear, to arrive and get in line, then afterward to clean the mess gear to stow it away.

They sailed on the narrow seas fringed by green jungles crowded into steep banks. "That's New Guinea," Carr nodded confidently.

"How do you know that?"

"I was talking to one of the swab jockeys, and that's what he said." He pointed and said, "Look, there's a harbor!"

There was no more time for talk. Will, along with the rest of the marines, grabbed at their belongings and gear. The crew swung the landing craft free of their davits, and lowered them into the water. The marines were drawn up on deck and at a command clambered over the side, down the cargo nets, into the boats, and finally ashore.

This was no uninhabited island. There were a few buildings thrown together, and a harbormaster stood on the beach bellowing into his megaphone to direct the unloading, and there were lines of olive-green trucks waiting to carry the marines and their stores inland. But first the ships had to be unloaded. As this took place, Will looked out over the green wilderness that lay ahead and murmured, "I wonder how many Japs are up there?"

Bobby Carr grinned at him and cocked his head to one side. He looked no more than seventeen as the sunlight fell across his fair features and caught the reddish tinge of his hair. "Enough to go around, Buddy," he said cheerfully. "Enough to go around."

Wendy's head jolted forward as the tires of the C54 slammed down on the runway. She heard the screeching of the brakes and the rattling, shuttering sound of the engine shutting down, and she straightened up as the big plane slowed to a stop.

"Well, we made it!" Mona said cheerfully as she unstrapped her safety belt and stood up. She was wearing marine fatigues, the camouflage model, and her bright, golden hair cascaded down from under the marine fatigue cap, giving her an incongruous look. She had managed, however, to get the smallest size uniform available, which had taken some doing. Wendy had taken what was given her and was practically swallowed by the outfit. When she got up she laughed and said, "When I stand up, these fatigues are still sitting down."

The two women made their way off the airplane amid the hubbub of the other members of the troupe. They were helped down by two tall marines bearing submachine guns.

Mona gave the taller of the two a dazzling smile and said, "Is there likely to be action, Sergeant?"

The sergeant grinned broadly. "This is just to protect you, Honey. All these guys out here aren't safe. They haven't seen a woman in so long they've almost forgotten what one looks like."

The other marine helped Wendy down and asked in a soft southern accent, "Did y'all have a good flight, Miss?"

"Very nice, Sergeant, thank you." Wendy turned a winsome smile on him and saw him respond immediately. "Will you be at the performance tonight?"

"Yes, every man on the island that ain't pullin' guard duty will be there; you can bet on that! We've been lookin' forward to this show a long time."

"I hope you're not disappointed."

The tall southerner grinned. "That ain't possible, Ma'am! You wait and see; you'll get applause like you've never heard before."

Bradley stepped down out of the plane and came over and put his arm around Mona in an intimate gesture. "I guess I'd better be your protector. On the other hand, it looks like these fellows are armed to do the job. Where do we go, Alex?"

Alex Grenville had descended carrying a briefcase. "Beats me," he said, "but I guess somebody will be here to take care of us."

He had no sooner said this than a short major came up and saluted. "Well, we're glad to receive you here at the base," he said. "I'm Major Cox. If you folks will come with me, we'll help you get set up. Need any help with the gear and the instruments?"

"We could use some," Alex said quickly. "Our folks wear out so quickly moving equipment that they're too tired to toot their horns."

Major Cox took over at once, and the four men that had been assigned to move the sound equipment and the rest of the gear for the troupe had an easy time of it.

Major Cox said, "The performance will have to be outside, I'm afraid. We don't have anything big enough for an auditorium to put all the men in. It'll be right over there."

Wendy looked where the major was pointing and saw that a platform had been built, set up on poles made of palm tree trunks. The sun overhead was brilliant, and she blinked as she saw dark-skinned people mingling with the marines, who were eyeing the troupe avidly. "Are those the natives, Major Cox?"

"Yes, Ma'am, fierce lookin' bunch, ain't they? But they're peaceful now—at least those we let into the camp. I wouldn't be surprised," he mused, "if they hadn't cut off a head or two in their times. Maybe a little cannibalism on the side, but we've got 'em tamed down pretty well."

Danny Brothers had just stepped up beside them, and he gave a disgruntled look at the situation, but he brightened at once and said, "Well, what time will the show be, Major?"

"How long will it take you to get set up?"

Alex, who was the leader in matters like this said, "It'll take at least three or four hours, I'm afraid."

"Well, by that time you can all get rested up. It was a long flight, I guess."

"We touched down on two other islands during the past few days," Alex said. "One in Australia, so we're just now getting the troupe shaking together where it comes out all right."

Major Cox shook his head. "Whatever you do will be all right with my boys, Mr. Grenville. They're hungry for entertainment. I'll be sittin' in the front row myself when you put on your show."

Wendy and the others were escorted to two small Quonset huts that had been converted into dressing rooms. There were cots inside, too, but the heat was so stifling that neither one of the women could lie down. They did manage to take a bath of sorts in a shower that had been improvised out of an empty oil drum. Holes had been punched in the bottom and it was mounted up on a tree. The enterprising Major Cox had arranged a tall shelter of canvas to be thrown around it so that the women could pour water out of buckets into the oil drum, and it was better than nothing. When they had bathed and had put on dresses instead of the fatigues, Mona and Wendy left the others and, with a marine guard, took a quick look at the fortifications. Both young women were aware of the stares of the marines. "It seems like they've all found something to do just so they could take a look at us, doesn't it?" Mona giggled.

The stares were a little bit disconcerting to Wendy and she shook her head. "I feel sorry for all of them. They're so far from home and have a long war ahead of them. I know they miss their mothers and sisters."

"They're not thinking of mothers and sisters when they look at us," Mona said archly. "That's not what they've got in their eyes."

Wendy did not answer, but later on in the afternoon, she found herself talking to one of the guards attached to keep order during the performance. His name was Leonard Scott, and he came from Wichita, Kansas. He was also, Wendy discovered, one of the most homesick young men she had ever seen. He was bashful, which surprised her, for she did not know there were any bashful marines. Finally she got him talking about his home and found out that he was engaged but couldn't get married until he got a leave.

"That may be quite a while," he said. "We've got a lot of Japs to get rid of before we get to go home."

"What's your fiancée's name, Leonard?"

"Mary." He grinned at her, saying, "It's simple, isn't it? So many fancy names going around, but I like that name."

"So do I," Wendy said. "Will you be at the performance tonight?"

"Why, sure! I'll be on guard duty to keep these gyrenes from going for you folks. Why?"

"Well, sometime during the performance I'm going to sing a song, and it'll be just for you and Mary."

"Gee, that'll be something, Miss Stuart."

At five o'clock the performance began, and it went sensationally well. As Major Cox indicated, the troops were thrilled at anything in the way of entertainment. They applauded until their hands hurt, or so it seemed, when Rob Bradley and Mona did their specialty together. They sang romantic songs, or at least Rob did; then they danced, which was something to see. Until the tour, Wendy had not known what an accomplished dancer Mona was, but now as the two moved from fast jitterbugs to ballroom waltzes to fast South American sambas, she was amazed at the young woman's grace, and her beauty dominated the small stage.

After they finished, Danny Brothers came and had the marines in stitches with his jokes about the accommodations on the island. He was very good, Brothers was, at this kind of thing—as good as Bob Hope, in a way, although not as well known. Carlos and Lolita were warmly received as were Lori and Cathy DeMarco with their acrobatic dances.

Alex stood beside Wendy as she moved close to the band. Twice she came out and sang light opera numbers and some hits from Broadway plays—not that the marines knew them, but they were light and easily sung. When the performance was coming to an end she said, "Alex, could I change this last number a little?" It was the final number on the program, and she remembered her promise to Leonard Scott.

"Why, sure."

She turned to the band and said, "Fellows, do you know that old Cohan tune, 'Mary'?"

The drummer sent his stick up in a whirling spin, caught it adeptly, and grinned. "That's from the old days, but I know it. We can fake it. Do what you want to Wendy, and we'll be with you."

Wendy heard her name being called by Danny Brothers and went out to take her spot. She was wearing a simple white dress and did not have the spectacular beauty of the other women. She was well aware of this, but she was also well aware that young men at war were thinking of mothers, sisters, and sweethearts. She said, "This song is for one young man. He's right there." She pointed to Leonard, who blushed to the roots of his hair. "Leonard is going to marry a young woman when he gets home, and I know that some of the rest of you probably are thinking of your sweethearts. All of you are here to serve your country, and I can only speak now for myself, but I know that if the entire population were here from America, they would say what I have to say." She paused and all was quiet. "Thank you so much for making it possible for there to be a country like America. Without you, there would not be."

Wendy hesitated, then nodded at the band, and began singing, "For it was Mary, Mary, plain as any name could be." The melody was sweet, and her voice was strong and clear, and when she finished the song, she went over and gave Leonard a kiss on the cheek and said, "You tell Mary that that's from her, Leonard."

A wild yell went up, and there was loud applause, and she knew that Leonard Scott would never forget this moment.

"That was a good thing to do," Alex said as he stood next to her. The troops were still cheering and calling her name, "Wendy! Wendy, more!" "You'll have to do one more," he said. "Any choice?"

"Yes." She looked at the band and leaned over, saying loudly, "Follow me if you can."

Going back to the microphones she stood there and without a word began to sing, "Amazing grace—how sweet the sound—that saved a wretch like me! I once was lost but now am found, was blind but now I see."

Before she had gotten very far, the male voices joined her, and soon the whole crew of marines was singing the old song that they had learned, many of them, when they were boys in Sunday schools back in America.

When Wendy sang the last note, her throat was tight and tears were in her eyes. "God bless you and keep you, every-one!"

There was much applause as the performers moved away. Major Cox came to stand beside Wendy, and she was surprised to see that he had tears in his eyes. "I'm a Christian, Miss Stuart," he said. "Many of the boys are out there—and those that aren't, they heard something during this performance they won't soon forget. Thank you for your witness to the Lord Jesus."

Alex heard the major. He said nothing as he walked with Wendy, accompanying her through the ranks of marines that were still applauding and calling their names. Finally, he leaned over and said, "You'll never do better than that, Wendy."

Wendy looked at Alex with surprise. She saw that he was moved and said, "Why, thank you, Alex." There was no more said, but she knew that the moment meant something to Alex, more than he acknowledged, and she was glad that she had sung that last song.

Wendy stepped out of the C54 and was never more shocked in her life, for there in front of her stood her brother Will. He was wearing marine fatigues, like most of the rest, and the grin exposed his white teeth against his brown face. "Will!" she said, and broke away from the group to throw herself in his arms. Wolf whistles went up, and wolf howls, but Wendy did not hear them.

"I was hoping I'd see you!" she exclaimed, holding onto him, stepping back.

"I been hoping the same thing," Will nodded. "I got myself promoted to head of the guard detail to take care of all of you Hollywood actresses."

"Oh, I'm not one of those! Come on; I want you to meet the group."

Alex was surprised but pleased to see Will. He said, "This is some little sister you've got here. She could be singing in the Met for all I'm concerned, but she'd rather be out here with you fellas."

"I'm glad of that," Will said. He remembered his father talking about the romance that Wendy had had with Alex, but he did not mention it. Inwardly he was thinking, *I wonder what this all means? Have these two gotten back together again?*

"Come along; I've got a lot to tell you!" Wendy said after she had proudly introduced Will to all of the troupe.

Will said, "All right, but I want you to meet somebody first. This is Bobby Carr." He turned to Bobby, who also had been given status as a guard for the troupe. "He's pulled me out of more than one scrape on Guadalcanal, saved me from drowning once."

"I didn't get a medal for it, though," Bobby said. He jerked his hat off and bowed. "Hey, I didn't believe Will when he said he had a sister that was a star, but he wasn't lying to me!"

"You come along, and I'll introduce you to two of the prettiest girls you ever saw, Bobby." Wendy turned Carr over to the two vivacious young acrobatic dancers, Lori and Cathy, and when she left with Will, hanging onto his arm, Carr was already beginning to tell how he was the hero of Guadalcanal.

"Those women better watch out for themselves. Bobby's quite a ladies' man," Will cautioned.

"I think they're used to it. We've been touring for three weeks now, and at the last count I think those girls have had 726 offers of marriage—other offers, too, I imagine." Wendy looked up at this tall marine who was her brother, and her heart warmed. "I want to hear everything, all about Guadalcanal, if you don't mind talking about it."

"I don't mind, but first I want to hear about everybody at home."

The troupe had been scheduled to perform twice, but it

turned out that they performed four times. Every man on the island within walking distance came to one or other of the performances.

Will attended them all, of course, as a guard, and after the first one he asked, "Do you always sing a hymn at the end of the performance?"

"Yes, I just did it once because I wanted to do something like that, but the marines liked it so much that I did it again."

"Well, we try to be tough," he said, "but we're just like everybody else. We need to hear that kind of thing, about the Lord."

The two talked constantly, and finally Wendy admitted, "I'm afraid that Mona is getting too involved with Rob Bradley."

"He seems like a nice enough fella," Will observed.

"He is, but he's got the show business morality. I'm afraid for her, Will," Wendy said simply.

"I never knew Mona that well, but she's so beautiful. That must be a bit of a handicap for a young woman to have good looks like that."

"I think it is—it never bothered me," Wendy said, winking at him.

"I don't believe that for a moment." Will hesitated then asked, "What about you and Grenville?"

"Oh, I didn't even know he was going to be with the tour. He was a last-minute choice when someone else got sick."

"I've noticed him, Wendy, during the performances. He's always watching you. Even when you're not performing. You two have got some kind of chemistry."

"We're good friends, I suppose. I admire him tremendously, and he's a wonderful musician."

Will knew that there was more to it than that but said no more. This was the last night, and he did not want to spoil it by bringing up anything unpleasant. "Well," he said, "I wish you could stay longer. I'm looking forward to the last performance."

"Where's your friend Bobby; is he gone?"

"Oh, he's been here all right. He and that Cathy DeMarco have gotten thick as fleas. I think he's proposed to her, too, but so far she's turned him down. She likes him, but everybody likes Bobby."

"You think a great deal of him, don't you?"

"Well, he saved my life. You can't hate a guy like that." Then more seriously he said, "I wish he knew the Lord, but he won't listen to me. He's not ready yet." He looked over the island at the many marines that were milling around preparing for the last performance and shook his head. "It's hard for me to understand, Wendy, how men can face death and not know God. To know they might be thrown out into eternity to suffer forever. It seems like many of them have just locked that part of their minds and their hearts away. They've gotten hard, and it breaks my heart sometimes when guys who ought to be at home living normal lives just go out like that!" He snapped his fingers.

"It must be awful," Wendy whispered. "I'll pray for Bobby and for you, too, Will."

The performance began as usual. It went well, as it always did. Alex was standing in front of the band, leading, as they played a soft tune for one of Wendy's solos, when suddenly his keen ear picked up something. "What's that?" he said aloud.

No sooner had he spoken when a loudspeaker blared out, "Take cover! Take cover! Enemy aircraft approaching!"

Instantly, everything seemed to go to pieces. The marines, more accustomed to this sort of thing, dispersed at once, running for the slit trenches. Alex and the others stood watching in dismay, not knowing what to do. Alex saw Wendy standing in front of the microphone and heard the sound of the airplane getting closer. He at once went to her and said, "We'd better get down from here, Wendy." He pulled her arm and they descended and started walking across the open field. They had not gotten far when the roar of the airplane broke as a dark shape suddenly rose over the horizon, cresting the top of the trees. It did not seem more than a few feet over the treetops, and Alex and Wendy could do nothing but stare at it. From the aircraft, winks of light began to appear, and Alex thought, *They're shooting at us!*

He had no time to do more than think that one thought when suddenly something crashed into him. He grabbed at Wendy and the two of them hit the ground. "Keep down!" a voice shouted.

Wendy got one glimpse of Bobby Carr's face, who had thrown himself on top of them. She had uttered one frightened cry, and then the shatter of the guns drowned her out. She felt Carr's body stiffen and saw dust kick up over to her left. There was a crash as a bomb exploded and it seemed to deafen her.

The noise of the airplane diminished, and hands were pulling Wendy to her feet. Will had come over shouting, "Get up; he'll be coming back for another pass."

Wendy looked at the small form of Bobby Carr, and she cried out, "What about Bobby?"

Will leaned over and put his hand on the back of the young man. He drew it back bloody. He whispered, "Bobby—" and then he turned a tragic face to Wendy. "He's dead," he said grimly. "Come on; that plane will come back."

Alex Grenville had gotten to his feet. His hands were trembling, and he had difficulty thinking for a moment. He looked down at the bloody form of the marine, and it came to him suddenly. He thought with astonishment, *He died for me and for Wendy!*

Grenville had no time to think any more, for rough hands were pulling him away. He only saw Will Stuart lean over, pick his friend up in his arms, and run to cover.

The plane did not return as they expected, and Wendy knelt beside Will, who was holding the bloody form of his friend in his arms, staring at him with a terrible intensity.

"I'm so sorry, Will," she whispered. "He put himself in danger for us."

Will could not speak. Tears rolled down his cheeks, and he held the dead body of the young marine tightly as sobs racked his body.

16

A NEW MAN

He's going to marry me, Wendy!"

Wendy Stuart had been washing out her underthings in a steel basin furnished by the quartermaster. Looking up from the pale soapy water with a start of surprise, she saw that Mona's eyes were wide and her entire face was animated with happiness. Wendy did not speak at first, but she gently wrung out the nylon slip she had been soaking and then looked at the young woman who had come into the tent like a small whirlwind. "But he's already married, Mona."

Impatiently Mona shook her head. Her hair was tied back by a ribbon, and as usual, even though it was not time for the performance, she had spent a great deal of time on her makeup. Holding her hands out in an impatient gesture she said, "Well, of course, he's married—you knew that, Wendy! But he's going to get a divorce." She hesitated for one moment, then added quickly, almost defensively, "You don't have any idea what that woman's done to him! He's had a miserable life!"

Wendy wanted to ask, "Well, she's his third wife; did the other two give him a miserable life also?" However, she was too wise to put such a direct challenge before Mona. As she hung the slip on a cord that she had stretched out as a temporary wash line, she tried desperately to think of some way to reason with Mona. Ever since Rob and Mona had begun their steamy romance, Bradley had made it very obvious that he considered Mona legitimate property. It was impossible to keep the affair a secret, and Wendy had been heartbroken over Mona's total infatuation with the actor. Turning quickly, she said quietly, "You know this is wrong, what you're doing, Mona. I don't want to preach to you, but you've been brought up better."

A flush suffused Mona's smooth cheeks. The words touched a nerve, for she did indeed know better. Ever since she had become involved with Rob, she had stubbornly pushed all thoughts of speaking to her parents about her love for the movie star out of her mind. There was a wild streak in Mona Stuart—but at the same time, sound principles had been part of her life. She knew right from wrong. She had seen the steady, strong love and the steadfast commitment of her parents in their marriage. It would, perhaps, have been better if she had not been such a beautiful young woman, but ever since adolescence she had been subjected to a steady flood of admiration from boys—then later on from young men. It had given her a sense of false security, for she thought she knew how to handle all affairs of the heart. The attention of Rob Bradley, however, had been of a different nature, and now she had no other defense but to say angrily, "You just don't understand, Wendy! It's not easy being in show business. A handsome, successful star like Rob draws all kinds of women to him. He's made mistakes, but he's learned from them!"

"So, you're different, is that it?"

"Yes, that is it!" Stung by Wendy's simple statement, Mona added quickly, "I'm different because I really, *really* love him, and he knows it!" Mona was standing in front of Wendy, her back straight, and there was a tenseness in her features as she added, "I couldn't expect you to understand! You've always been so—" Mona could not finish the sentence. She had almost said "so good and straight," but if she said that, the words would condemn her own actions. Shaking her hair in an impetuous gesture, she snapped, "I don't want to talk about it anymore. I thought you would be more understanding, Wendy!" Turning, she walked out of the tent, her head held high, leaving Wendy staring after her.

Slowly Wendy turned back, washed out a few more things, then hung them up. She put on a simple outfit of khaki slacks and a light green blouse, looked into the small mirror that was hanging from the tent pole, and gave her hair a little attention. And as she did so, a voice outside called, "Wendy?"

Quickly she turned and moved to the tent flap. "Alex," she said. "Come on in. You'll have to excuse the place. I've made a Chinese laundry out of it."

Alex Grenville entered the tent, blinked at the lingerie that hung from the string, and said, "It's kind of a nylon jungle in here."

"I know. What do you do about your laundry?"

"The same as you do," he said with a grin. He had a Bible in his hand and remarked, "I've been reading some of the selections you gave me, and I have to say I've gotten in over my head."

"Here, sit down, Alex," Wendy said quickly. She took one of the two folding canvas chairs and motioned Alex to the other one. Ever since the attack, Alex had been a different man. She thought as she watched him sit down and open the Bible, *He's different from what he was when we began the tour—and even before that.*

He had come to her two days after their brush with death saying, "Wendy, this thing has–has shaken me up. Would you mind talking with me?" They had talked long about why they had been spared and why a fine young man had been killed, and finally Wendy had suggested almost offhandedly that Alex might like to have a Bible. He had accepted at once, and for the past week, in their off times he had come to her with passages as he had done now.

"What is it, Alex?" she asked quietly.

"Well, I never read the Bible before," he said slowly. "And there're so many things I don't know. Why, I hardly know how to *begin!*" He looked up at her, grinning crookedly. "I guess I'll have to take off a few years and go to seminary to find out about God."

"I don't think that would do at all," Wendy said, answering his smile. "You don't learn about God like you learn about engineering. It's two different kinds of learning."

"How do you mean?"

"Well, if you wanted to become an engineer, you would go to college and take courses in scientific things such as stresses and mechanical drawing. You'd learn how to do that with your mind. As a matter of fact, I think some people do go to seminary to try to find God that way." Wendy had thought of this a great deal and now took out her own Bible and opened it, saying, "That won't work." She began to read, "'But the natural man receiveth not the things of the Spirit of God: for they are foolishness unto him: neither can he know them.' God is not like one of the sciences. He's a spirit. When he speaks to us, he doesn't speak through the mind but through the spirit."

"Well, I've been reading in the Gospels as you advised, and the Gospel of John especially. And I must admit, whatever else happens, I've learned to admire Jesus Christ. There's nobody like him, is there?"

"No, there isn't. He's absolutely different from everyone else."

"I've been reading about his death." Alex grew sober and shook his head. He turned to a marked page and said, "The strangest thing about it is when they killed him, he didn't hate the ones who were doing it." Shaking his head in wonder, he said quietly, "I couldn't do that, Wendy."

Wendy hesitated. "But that's exactly what Christians are commanded to do. Jesus said to forgive your enemies and to pray for those who despitefully use you."

With a futile gesture, Alex ran his hand through his hair and then looked her in the eye, saying, "Could you do that?"

"I couldn't do it in the natural, because, as you say, it's the natural thing when someone strikes us to strike back. But the Lord Jesus did it. He forgave those who crucified him, while he was on the cross. The big secret of the Christian life isn't very well known. You see, when you become a Christian, Alex, you won't be alone anymore. Christ will be in you."

"How can that be?" Alex asked.

"It's difficult to understand, and I don't think anyone can ever explain it, but I know that when I called upon God when I was fourteen and asked Jesus to forgive me, he did, and he *did* come to live in me. I can't explain it, but I know he's there. He's never left me, and he wants to make me like himself. The apostle Paul said that Christ is formed in us. Somehow through Jesus' power, he makes us to be what God wants us to be."

The two talked on, Wendy going through the Scriptures, glad for the hours and years that she had spent reading them and memorizing verses, and finally she said, "Alex, there are two kinds of people for whom it's very hard to find God."

"You mean murderers and people like that?"

Wendy smiled and shook her head. "Those people usually get saved very easily once they make up their minds. They don't have to be convinced that they need forgiveness—they know it. And once you know you need God and need his forgiveness, that makes things much easier."

"Well—I know I need something. I can't go on like I've been going, Wendy." Alex shook his head and looked down at the Bible. "I haven't been sleeping well at night. I think about Bobby dying to protect us. I can't get him out of my mind. Somewhere," he said quietly, "he had a life before him and now he's gone, in a moment."

"He was one of the casualties of this terrible war. There are thousands of people dying all over the world, going out to meet God. We live in a wrecked, ruined world. Because we're wrecked and ruined, that's what Paul meant when he said, 'all have sinned, and come short of the glory of God.' And in Romans 6:23 he said, 'the wages of sin is death.' That's the world we're living in, Alex; it's flawed with death. But the last part of that verse says, 'but the gift of God is eternal life through Jesus Christ our Lord.'"

Alex quietly listened as Wendy spoke of her faith in Jesus.

He had been afraid that she would try to cram religion down his throat, but she had not. Quietly, and with obvious concern in her eyes and in her voice, she spoke of the love of God and how he could find it, too.

They were interrupted when the voice of Danny Brothers, the emcee for the troupe, rose stridently outside the tent: "All right, rehearsal time! Get out of those tents; let's get at it!"

"I guess we'll have to wait until later to talk about this—but I want to hear more," Alex said. He rose and suddenly put out his hand toward Wendy, and she automatically extended her own. He held it for a time and said nothing. There was a confusion in him, and yet when he looked at this woman, he recognized that the steadiness he saw in her was what he had always yearned for himself. "You said it's hard for two kinds of people to find God. What kinds are they?"

"People who try to find God with their minds, intellectuals who won't have faith in anything except what can be proven," Wendy said. "That's one kind."

"I don't think I'm like that."

"No, you're not. You're the other kind. You have an artistic, emotional approach to things, and sometimes people with that mind-set demand that their conversion be emotional."

Alex looked at her with surprise. "But I thought it was emotional!"

"Coming to Jesus is a decision of the will. You decide to do it, and then you obey his commandments. Some people have a great emotional experience, but some don't. My own experience was very quiet. But I knew that I had done what God said. I just went on, and as time passed God began to fill me with joy."

"I guess," Alex said slowly, "you're telling me that I've got to have faith."

"That's his only way of saving people—by their faith. It's his gift to people through faith, I suppose you might put it." She hesitated then said, "There's going to be a service for the men tomorrow morning. Why don't we go?"

"All right, I'd like that." As Alex left the tent, hope burned in Wendy as it never had before. She knew that she loved this man, but it had looked so hopeless. Now, in the midst of war and death, God was doing a miracle of grace in the heart of Alex Grenville, and Wendy breathed a prayer of thanksgiving and a petition that the gospel would find lodging in Alex's heart.

That night she lay awake waiting for Mona. Her cousin came in, but it was very late. Wendy did not know where Mona had been, but her heart was heavy because she recognized that, wherever it was, she had been with Rob Bradley. Wendy did not speak, for Mona would not be spoken to, but all through the night she slept fitfully, praying alternately for her cousin and for Alex to find God.

She rose the next morning, dressed quickly, and met Alex coming out of the tent he shared with some of the band members. "Good morning, Alex," she said. "Are you ready for breakfast?"

"I could eat a horse."

Wendy laughed. "That's what some of the marines say we're eating around here. They don't have very complimentary remarks about the food, do they?"

"You should hear what they call it when there are no ladies present." Alex made a grimace and took her arm. "Come on; I'll buy you the best breakfast on the whole island."

As they ate, they talked about the tour, but Wendy could tell that Alex was not thinking primarily of music or performing. He was preoccupied, and she hoped it was with the matter of his soul.

After breakfast, they gathered in a large, open space with several hundred marines dressed in fatigues and listened as the chaplain preached. The sun shone down brilliantly, and soon they were all soaked with perspiration. Looking around at the weary fighting men, Wendy whispered, "They all look so tired—but they must be hungry for God to come out in this heat and listen to a sermon."

Alex had been looking around, too, and said quietly, "I

know a little about how they feel. Of course, I'm not facing death like they are, but I didn't sleep a wink last night. I've got to do *something*, Wendy! I'll lose my mind if I don't."

There was desperation in Alex Grenville's voice, and as the chaplain continued, Wendy was very happy to hear him preaching a simple gospel sermon. He spoke for a while on Romans 3:23, "All have sinned, and come short of the glory of God." There was no condemnation in the chaplain, a tall, wiry man with very light blue eyes, who spoke in a pronounced southern accent. He simply pointed out that everyone everywhere had sinned. "We haven't all sinned alike—but we've all alike sinned," he insisted. He proved by the Scripture that sin was not always in its most horrible form, but it was unacceptable to God. Then he moved on to the sixth chapter of Romans and dwelt on the verse Wendy had quoted to Alex: "The wages of sin is death." Wendy was glad that he did not preach a loud, raving, hellfire-and-damnation sermon. Instead, the chaplain pointed out that death was separation from God. "It wouldn't make any difference if you were not in fire but in the most pleasant circumstances you can imagine. Even an eternity of that would be hell without God, for you were made for God to dwell in you. It is Jesus Christ in you that makes men and women what they ought to be."

"He seems to be echoing what you said yesterday," Alex whispered.

Wendy saw that his hands were trembling, and without thinking she reached over and put her hand over his. "The gospel's always the same," she said quietly.

The chaplain said, "Though we've all sinned, and although the wages of that sin is separation from God, yet, the Scripture says, 'The gift of God is eternal life.' Jesus Christ is his eternal gift, and he wants you to take that gift. You've all received gifts at Christmas. What did you do to earn them? Nothing! You just took them." The chaplain stressed that salvation is not a wage to be earned. He showed, through the Scripture, that by faith one is saved, not by works. A great quiet fell over the congregation. Birds were crying in a weird, unearthly voice somewhere out in the jungle, and that gave an exotic flavor to the service. The pale sun was rising overhead, pouring out its white-hot heat, but the minister ignored this. "It is time for you to make a decision," he said quietly. "Will you have Jesus Christ as your Lord, or will you refuse him?"

Alex Grenville had never felt quite as he did at that moment. He had slept little since his brush with death. The tour had brought him into contact with men that were facing death on a daily basis, and he realized the frailty of his own life, even though he was not a soldier. As he stood with the others at the chaplain's request, he was trembling. His knees were weak, and he found it difficult to swallow. The chaplain said, "I'm going to pray. You pray, too. Ask God to forgive your sins because Jesus Christ received the wages of sin that were your due when he died on the cross. He did that so that he could give you eternal life as his gift. Accept his gift." A shock ran across Alex as he felt Wendy grip his arm. He glanced at her quickly and saw that her head was bowed and that her lips were moving in prayer. Somehow that gave him hope. *She really cares!* he thought. *She really cares what happens to me!* It was a sign for him somehow, and resolutely he bowed his head and began to pray.

Wendy did not turn to look at him but felt the tenseness of his body. She felt that if he left this place without finding Christ, he might never be saved. She had prayed almost all night, and she prayed now. She glanced at him and, with a shock, saw tears running down his pale face. He was trembling.

Alex spoke, almost in agony, "Oh, God, have mercy on me in the name of Jesus." He continued to pray, and Wendy took his hand and he gripped it so hard that it hurt her fingers. He took a sudden deep breath and turned to look at her. "Well, I've done it, Wendy. I don't know where I go from here, but I know one thing. I'm going to follow Jesus, whatever else happens."

"Oh, Alex, I'm so happy!" Wendy wanted to throw her arms around him but was very conscious of the others who would be watching. She whispered, "It's going to be so wonderful, Alex; you'll see!"

"You'll have to help me, Wendy."

"I will, Alex."

Triumph swept through Wendy Stuart, for she realized that God had done the impossible. Salvation is always an impossible thing, a miracle—and now to see it in this man who had never loved God, who had fought against him all of his life, caused joy to fill her. She seemed to hear the Lord saying, "Well done, my daughter!" and this assurance from God gave her faith to face the future. The two stood under the blazing sun and saw others going to the front to be prayed for. Alex said, "Let's go, too. I've got to make this thing public. I can't be a Christian in secret."

This, for Wendy, was the final evidence that Alex Grenville was serious. She said eagerly, "I'll go with you, Alex."

That day on that small island soldiers and marines gave their hearts to God—but there was something different about it when the young man and the young woman dressed in civilian clothes came forward. Everyone watched as the chaplain prayed for them, and somehow that service remained fixed in the minds of those marines as no other during the war.

As the plane winged over the blue waters of the Pacific, Wendy saw that Mona and Rob were sitting together and that the actor had his arm around her shoulder. So far as she knew, he had made no public statement about an engagement. Mona had said it was because he had to wait until after the divorce was final—but this had not satisfied Wendy. Her heart was heavy because of this, and she knew that Mona's parents would be shocked and dismayed at what had occurred. There was nothing she could do except pray, and Wendy had prayed often for this wild cousin of hers.

A sudden touch on her arm turned her around, and she looked into Alex's eyes. He asked, "You're worried about Mona, aren't you?"

"Yes." She hesitated for one moment, but she had talked this matter over with Alex before. "She's making a great mistake, Alex."

"I agree, but she's very stubborn, isn't she?"

"It's beyond stubbornness, I think. All of us Stuarts are a little bit stubborn."

The plane dipped suddenly, dropping several hundred feet as it hit an air pocket.

"Wow, that always catches my attention!" Alex gasped. "I always think we're never going to come out of it!"

"So do I, but we did."

Alex said, "I'll never forget these last days. It's changed my whole life, Wendy. I don't know what I'll do now, what changes will be in my life."

"They'll be good, whatever they are. You're so different, Alex."

Alex took her strong hand in his. Suddenly he brought it to his lips and kissed it and said, "I'd planned to wait until we got back to take you out in that old Cord of mine to some romantic spot."

"Were you?"

"Yes, and you know what I was going to say?"

"What?"

"I was going to say, 'Wendy Stuart, I love you and I want to marry you and live with you the rest of my life.'" He looked into her eyes. "When I say that, what will you say?"

Wendy swallowed hard. Impulsively she reached up, touched his cheek, and whispered, "I'll say, 'Yes, I'll marry you and live with you the rest of my life!'"

Not caring who saw, Alex leaned forward and kissed Wendy lightly on the lips. It was a sign of love, a token of what was to come, and he heard a low whistle go up from the guitar player who sat across the aisle of the C54, but he did not care. Her lips were sweet under his, and he held the kiss for a moment, then turned and looked at the guitar player who was grinning broadly and returned the smile. Standing he declared, "I have an announcement to make!" When he had everybody's attention he said proudly, "I have the honor to announce that Miss Wendy Stuart has agreed to be my wife."

Wendy never forgot the exuberant congratulations that followed. Everyone stumbled to come to her. All of the women hugged her, and most of the men, too.

Finally, Mona came, and there was something odd in her expression. "I'm very happy for you, Wendy," she said haltingly.

Wendy took the kiss that Mona put on her cheek, then said quietly, "Thank you, Mona. We love each other very much, and God's leading us—so I know it's right."

Mona Stuart listened for a note of condemnation, but she heard none in Wendy's voice. Nevertheless, her own heart smoldered, and she turned around and went back, her shoulders stiff and her back upright.

The plane flew on toward America, and as Wendy sat down beside Alex, and they talked of the future, her eyes kept going to Mona, who seemed to be oblivious to whatever it was that Rob Bradley was saying to her. Once again she prayed for her cousin; then she turned her face toward her fiancé and said, "Oh, Alex, we're going to have such fun!"

"As they say in the movies," Alex added, "we're going to make beautiful music together!"

17

OVER THE EDGE

The target of Gilze-Rigen in Holland was not considered a tough target. The full-scale attack consisted of three squadrons, and they had fighter escort all the way.

As they began their bombing run, Adam Stuart broke his concentration long enough to look out and see the flak burst exploding around them. There was a strange beauty in the deadly black blossoms that seemed to appear magically in the space around the B-17s as they roared toward their target. When Adam had first encountered flak, he thought it was the ugliest thing he'd ever seen and had hated the very sight of it. Now, some transformation in his mind had made him able to ignore the deadly explosions. Off to his right, he saw a sudden cluster of the burst explode simultaneously in what looked like a fireworks display he had once seen over the skies in Los Angeles. True enough, those bursts had been red, yellow, green, and all the colors of the rainbow, and these were somber flowers in a funereal black. There was a morbid fascination as he considered them, knowing that out of any one of them one tiny shell fragment would be enough to kill him instantly if it hit the *Last Chance* at exactly the right angle and then passed through his skull or his heart.

Involuntarily, his hands tightened on the control yoke, and he put his eyes on the Forts in close formation around him.

"Bombardier to pilot!"

"Go ahead!"

"We're on the bomb run!"

As the Fortress continued straight as a ruler toward the target, a few fighters suddenly appeared, and instantly Adam said, "Pilot to crew, fighters at eleven o'clock high comin' in! Shoot 'em down! Shoot 'em down!"

The airplane shook with the rattle of the twin fifties from the turrets, and as more Focke-Wulfs appeared, Adam saw one fighter whiz by him so close that the pilot's bright red scarf could be plainly seen. Instantly, the thought passed through his mind, *The Red Baron flies again!* But he had no time to think more. The formation leader was shot down; then he saw two more Fortresses explode, hurtling toward the ground far below. Sixty seconds later he heard, "Bombs away, let's go home!" from Moon Wilson. He kicked the plane into a sharp bank, and even as he did, a twenty-millimeter cannon shell ripped through the cockpit's side window. It brushed him slightly on the back of the head and zoomed out through the other side without exploding.

Tex Smith had seen the glass shatter on both sides and the back of Adam's helmet rip. He stared and gasped, "Stuart! Are you all right?"

But Smith had no time to say more, for at that exact instant a machine gun bullet from one of the fighters struck him in the temple. His eyes rolled upward; then he slumped in his seat.

"Tex! Are you all right?" Adam had not seen the bullet strike, but when the copilot's body rolled over, he saw the black hole in the side of the helmet, and his heart seemed to stop.

Adam flew mechanically, gathering with the fragments of the formation, and as they went back toward England, all he could think of was how he had bawled Tex Smith out for a simple mistake before the mission had begun. Death, in all its finality, had struck, and now he was whispering, "If I could only tell him I didn't really mean it!"

But there was no telling the copilot anything. Clint Stuart stepped through the door, took one look at the dead man, and without a word unstrapped him and moved him out of the cockpit. He asked no permission for this and stole one quick glance at the pilot. Adam's face was stiff and pale, and though he handled the controls as adroitly as usual, there was a strange woodenness to his expression that Clint had not seen before.

"Are you all right, Sir?" he asked after he came back to stand behind the empty copilot seat.

"Yes, I'm all right."

Clint was not happy with the clipped tone of Adam's voice, but there was nothing he could do about it. Quietly he went about his duties, and after the plane landed and they went through interrogation, he saw that more than once the officer conducting the interrogation gave Adam a quizzical look, although he said nothing at the time. Afterward, however, he asked Clint to remain. The two had grown fairly well acquainted through many such meetings as this, and Captain Harrod said, "The lieutenant is shook up. Was he friends with Smith?"

"Not really, Sir."

"I thought he might be. It happens that way sometimes." Taking out a cigarette, he lit it with a Zippo lighter, then asked abruptly, "Have you got any comments to make about Lieutenant Stuart's performance, Sergeant?"

Clint hesitated. A series of thoughts flashed through his mind. Actually, Adam had not been flying as well. Technically, it would be hard to fault him. Still, his attitude toward the crew had become more and more one of isolation, and now not a single member on the airplane would speak to Adam Stuart unless it was necessary as a part of operating the aircraft. Adam had also withdrawn himself from Clint. At first the two had spoken of family matters briefly from time to time, but lately there seemed to be a wall built up that Clint could not cross. Noting then that Captain Harrod was watching him closely, he said quickly, "He's under a great deal of strain, Sir—but then we all are."

"So you don't find any fault with his flying? Don't think I'm just making conversation, Sergeant Stuart. I know that the lieutenant's your cousin, but I know, also, that this airplane has been a problem for a long time." Harrod ran his fingers along his jaw thoughtfully and studied the tall flight engineer. "I think you're the stabilizing influence on it. Things have gone much better since you came aboard." He grinned then adding, "You've become kind of a mother hen to these poor lost sheep on board the *Last Chance*, haven't you?"

"I try to do the best I can, of course, Captain. Actually, I think we've got a pretty good crew. Some of the men have problems, but they're getting them under control."

Harrod hesitated, then said, "Some of the men have been complaining that the lieutenant is cold as a block of ice. They don't like that; they like to trust the man they're flying with. It would be nice if they even liked him, although we can't arrange that. What's eating Lieutenant Stuart, Sergeant?"

"I really can't say, Captain—and I would tell you anything I knew. He's under more pressure, I think, than most of us. He's the pilot and has to make most of the decisions."

"That's true in every ship," Harrod consented, "but not all pilots turn to a block of ice. We try to spot trouble coming up. If he's going to break down, I'd rather he not do it on a mission over Berlin."

Clint hesitated, "I really can't be of much help, I'm afraid. I do all I can to support our lieutenant. He's a fine flyer."

"No doubt about that, probably one of the best." Harrod hesitated, started to say something, then seemed to change his mind. "Well, I'm going to have him go through some psychological tests. I'll have to camouflage it by having some others take it, so maybe one of the shrinks can find out what's eating at him. I hope so anyway. That's all, Sergeant."

Clint turned and went back to his quarters. He found everyone tense, and the conversation stopped as he entered, but Moon said, "I don't care if you are his relative, Clint. I wish we had another pilot!"

Beans Cunningham was sitting on his bunk but looked up with a protest in his dark brown eyes. "I think the same way. I don't know if we can go on strike, but I'd like to."

"They'll shoot you for that, you idiot!" Manny Columbo

said. He had stripped out of his flight uniform and was bare chested, the sleek muscles writhing beneath his olive skin as he slipped on another shirt. "We're stuck with him, and that's all there is to it!"

Clint said quickly, "There are worse pilots, guys. He gets us there and back."

"No question about his flying ability. We know he can do that, but does he have to be so hard-tailed about everything?" Asa Peabody was also dressing, putting on a clean uniform. The tow-headed hillbilly stared at Clint and said, "Well, it's not your fault. Let's go into town; we've all got leave!"

Clint did not really want to go. He had the impulse to stay, to try to find Adam and talk to him, but he thought, on the whole, it might be better if he let the matter rest for a while.

There was a scramble to get ready, for nobody in the outfit wanted to be left behind. As they piled into the trucks, Clint commented to Cisco Marischal, "I think they like to get us out of the camp after missions to kind of let off steam."

"Yes, it's the same way after a bullfight," Cisco agreed. "No one wants to stay around after it's over, thinking about it. You know you're going to have to go back in the ring, and you don't want to think about that either. So," he said cheerfully, "bullfighters go out and get drunk, and I guess that's what we'll do tonight."

"I'm not sure that's a good idea. As a matter of fact, it *isn't* a good idea."

"Maybe not for you. You've got God, but the rest of us don't have anything like that."

"You could have if you wanted to, Cisco."

"Don't start your preachin' now, Clint. Wait until we get back. I'll listen to you then. I'll have too much of a headache to run away from you. Come on now; let's go have a good time."

London was an exciting place to be in 1943. It was packed with throngs of men far from home. They were all seeking pleasures of various kinds, trying to find some escape from the stifling military confinement. As the crew walked along

the area called the Strand and around Trafalgar Square, Clint
stopped to look up at the two huge stone lions beside the
statue of Admiral Horatio Nelson. Moon Wilson said, "According to legend, the lions roar whenever a virgin passes by
here." He grinned then and dug his elbow into Clint's side.
"I don't think that happens very often, Clint."

Clint floated along with the rest of the crew. He knew some
of them would be unable to get back alone, and although he
himself did not drink, he took it all in. Downtown London
was crowded with men and women in every kind of uniform.
From the open doorway, you could hear snatches of lusty
songs from groups well along in their drinking. Although the
nightly blackout was strictly enforced, there was always the
flare of a cigarette lighter so some soldier could get a look at
a woman standing in a darkened doorway. Clint was aware
of the lingering odor of cheap perfume used to camouflage
the need for a bath. Soap and warm water were rare luxuries
in this country at this time.

By 10 P.M., the bars were crowded, the noise was deafening,
and the brawls were beginning to break out. The singing went
on until the singers grew tired, and finally Clint succeeded in
rounding up most of the crew, except for Moon, who seemed
to have disappeared completely. Clint was shepherding the
rest along, some of them protesting in a drunken mumble but
obeying docilely enough.

As he passed through the crowded pub where he had picked
up Cunningham and the new radio operator, he happened to
glance over at a table that was wedged into an angle. The room
was dark, but he recognized Adam Stuart instantly. Adam was
staring at him, and Clint knew at once that he was drunk. His
shirt was pulled open, his tie awry, and his light hair was down
over his forehead. He did not move for a moment, and then
deliberately he turned away, avoiding Clint's gaze.

All the way back to camp, the survivors of the night's revelry
were singing raucously off key, until they finally passed out.
Clint was worried about Adam. *I know he's been drinking some.*

He's the worst kind, a solitary drinker, he thought as the truck joggled and bounced over the rough, broken road that led back to the airstrip. *Maybe I should have tried to get him to leave, but I had to get these guys back*. A sense of helplessness swept over him, and he finally put all his efforts into getting the crew bedded down. Afterwards, he stepped outside and looked up at the sky, wondering if he should go back to London and try to find Adam. Still, he knew that was impossible. He slowly turned, went back, took off his clothes, and stretched out on his bunk. *I'll have to try to talk with him tomorrow. Maybe he'll listen*, he thought, just before going to sleep.

There was no opportunity for Clint to speak with Adam the next day, and the day after that they flew a mission. The men had brought back liquor from London and had pretty well anesthetized themselves the night before. It nearly brought on one of the greatest casualties of the *Last Chance*.

Clint was working over his gun in the upper turret when he felt someone pulling at his foot. Looking down, he saw an officer who said, "Sergeant, we've got an inspection today on the Sight you're carrying. How long will you be here?"

"Oh, about thirty minutes, Sir."

"Good, I'll have the Sight back by that time."

"Well, that's Sergeant Wilson there; he's in charge of the Sight." The word *Sight* was shorthand for the Norden Bombsight, the most closely guarded secret in the American air force. *Never* were these precious instruments allowed to get into any position that might give them away to the Germans.

Clint went back to work. He saw the technician leave the aircraft carrying the bombsight and paid no heed to it. Soon, a scream reached him, and he looked down to see Moon scrambling through the plane. "Clint! Where's the bombsight?"

Clint whirled around and followed Moon who was staring in utter disbelief at the gaping empty space in the nose where the Sight should have been.

At that point, Adam came in and said, "What's wrong here?"

He looked down, and then blinked with shock. "Where's the bombsight?"

"I don't know, Lieutenant!"

Adam turned to Moon, his face stiffened with anger. "Sergeant Wilson, where is the bombsight?" This was a stark tragedy, and for some time the meeting was conducted with shouts on Adam's part, who was losing it completely. "You've just succeeded," he screamed, "in losing the air force's top-secret device! You'll go to prison for this, Wilson!"

"Just a minute, Sir," Clint said. He had turned around, and said, "I think one of the inspection officers took it."

This did not satisfy Adam. He beat on his head, his lips pulled back in a snarl. "Why couldn't I get nine sane men like the other pilots do!"

"I–I only looked away for a few seconds!" Moon said.

Just then Asa Peabody, who had come up to witness the fiasco, said, "Hey, isn't that somebody carrying a bombsight?"

Instantly they all rushed to the door and fell out. "That's him! That's him, catch him! Don't let him get away!"

Everybody in the crew, including Adam, took off, with Moon leading the way determined to redeem himself. He was cursing, and if he had had a gun, Clint knew he would have shot it.

The technician was swarmed and the bombsight was ripped from his hands. He stared in utter incomprehension saying, "What's wrong?"

"Nothing," Clint said quickly. "We just got a little confused about the bombsight."

"The lieutenant told me to get it so it could be inspected."

"I know; it's not your fault," Clint said. "Moon, go along with him, and be sure that the bombsight gets back in place."

Adam was not going to let the bombardier get off so easily, however. He jerked him around, held his lapels, calling him incompetent, idiot, and other names, although he never actually used profanity. Moon's face grew pale, but he stood silent until Adam finally whirled and walked away.

"He didn't have to act like that," Moon whispered. Anger blazed in his eyes, and he shook off Clint, who tried to explain the situation.

It all would have been comical except for the fact that Adam had driven one more wedge between himself and the crew. As they took off on their mission for Romilly, Adam was aware that not a soul on the airplane said one word to him that was not actually required. His lips tightened and he thought, *Let them be soreheads; they're nothing but a bunch of clumsy cows anyway.* Viciously he swung the plane around, throwing the crew helplessly toward the bulkhead and taking satisfaction in it. The new copilot, a short, chunky lieutenant named Larry Felson, stared at him but said nothing. He had heard about the hard-tailed lieutenant of the *Last Chance* and was determined to keep in good standing with him as long as possible.

The next week was the worst for the entire Wing. Missions went out in fully operational groups and came back in tatters; planes were shot to pieces—those that managed to make it back at all. All of the men grew ragged and tense, most of them unable to keep food down just before a mission. Adam Stuart, although he did not reveal it, was worse off than most. He'd lost weight, for he could not keep food down, either. Keeping to himself, he was able to camouflage the nervousness that had come over him. Since he could not speak without the danger of his voice breaking, he spoke only in choppy, short, harsh, and guttural sounds, which gave him the impression of being an angry wolf.

Clint tried more than once to speak to him, but was turned away by the pilot's abrupt manner. Only once did he break through. That was when he encountered Adam coming out of his quarters. There was no avoiding Clint, so Adam grunted and Clint said, "A rough mission, wasn't it?"

"They're all rough."

Clint fell into stride with him and said, "I got a letter from your mother. It was a big help to me."

Adam turned and stared at Clint. "What did she say?"

Surprised at Adam's roughness, Clint said, "Nothing much. She asked how I was, said she was praying for me and Carol."

Adam stared at the taller man, and said, "I suppose you're praying for her, too."

"Why yes, Sir, I am."

"Even after she left you and went off with some civilian?"

Clint did not want to talk about Carol, at least not to Adam. He shook his head. "I love Carol, no matter what she's done."

Adam seemed to find this incredible. He stared at Clint, appeared to be thinking deeply. His face was thin, and there was an unusual nervous tick in his right eye. He did not want to continue the conversation, and said, "When you write back to my mother, tell her I'm doing all right."

"I couldn't do that, Adam." They were alone now, and Clint knew that he might not have another chance. "You're not all right. You're going to pieces on the inside."

"I do my job!"

"Yes, you do, but how much longer can you keep it up?"

Suddenly Adam looked at Clint with suspicion. "Did somebody put you up to talkin' to me? Captain Derry, maybe? He's always looking to label somebody a nut so he can bust 'em out, but I'm not nutty. There's nothing wrong with me!"

Clint saw that it was useless to try to reason with him. "Adam, you're only hurting yourself," he said quietly. "I won't try to say more, but your mother and your father have been praying for you all your life. God's not going to let those prayers fall to the ground." Seeing anger rise to Adam's eyes, he turned and walked away without another word.

Adam stared after him, but as he turned and walked unsteadily along the gravel pathway, he could not get away from the even look he had seen in Clint's eyes nor from what Clint had said about his parents. Finally, he gritted his teeth and said, "Kill Germans, that's what I'm here for! We'll kill 'em all, and then things will be all right again!"

18

THE *LAST CHANCE*

A wind blew from the southwest making the letter Clint held in his hand tremble slightly. It was a dank, rainy afternoon, and although the rain had stopped, it might start again at any moment. He was waiting outside headquarters to see if the mission would be scrubbed, and had picked up the v-mail letter just before he arrived. He opened it and saw his wife's carefully structured handwriting. The letters were all round and thick and heavy, made with a blunt pencil:

Dear Clint,

I am writing to tell you how sorry I am for what I have done to you. I do not expect you to forgive me; I cannot even forgive myself. I now must live with my sins and the consequences of those actions. I know that you will want a divorce when you return home. I am living at home again as I have left Harry for good. You can have your lawyer contact me there; I'm sure you will want to see me as little as possible. I do truly regret messing up the best thing in my life, my marriage to you. I wish you all the best and a safe return home.

Carol

Clint looked at the letter blankly and shoved it back into his shirt pocket. There was an unseeing look on his face, and for a moment the war and missions and possible death in the skies all seemed very far away. All he could think of was Carol's face, and to him it was as sweet as it had ever been. God had given him a great victory, for after the first rush of rage and anger that had come as a natural result of being abandoned and betrayed, he had fought a good fight, and now every day he breathed a prayer for Carol, that she would discover God's forgiveness.

"Hey, the word's out!" Clint looked up to see Moon Wilson coming by. "It's going to be Berlin."

"In this weather?"

"I guess so. Whoever knows why these idiots send us out in weather like this and let the pretty days go by. I guess we better get going."

The base began to swarm with activity, but things had changed in the Eighth Air Force. They had been worn down and were operating, almost, with a skeleton crew of ships. Help was on the way, or so the rumor went, but it had not arrived yet. Some of the men said bitterly that it would never arrive. "They're going to use us up, get us all killed, that's what they're going to do," one disgruntled bombardier had complained that morning at breakfast. "They won't give up as long as there's one of us left alive!"

Clint found himself too busy to think about such things. It was basically his skill that kept the *Last Chance* flying, for she had taken flak and bullets, everything except exploding cannon fire. "She's been a good ship," Clint said finally as the crew began to get on board for the mission. He patted the aluminum skin of the ship almost affectionately, much as he would have patted a hard-working horse back on the farm. He grinned at his own action, then looked up to see Adam and the copilot entering. Adam's face, he saw, was drawn tight, and he looked at Clint without a word.

Adam had deliberately looked past Clint Stuart, for he wanted no conversation with him. His nerves were drawn out as thin as a piece of wire, and he kept his mind only on the business of flying the ship. He moved the *Last Chance* around into position and then took off. He thought suddenly, as he almost always did, *I may get killed on this one.* A wry and rather bitter thought came to him: *I used to worry about flat tires and cavities in my teeth. Now, I don't think much about those things.* He glanced across at the copilot, Felson, whose blonde hair was covered by the flying helmet and thought, *I don't know this man. I don't want to get close to him—he may get killed, too, like Tex Smith.*

The *Last Chance* roared into the air, and the formation was made up quickly. Adam gave commands crisply as they flew. He was aware that Felson was a rather talkative young man. He had heard him at the mess talking to other pilots, but Felson never said one word to him. This brought a pang for a moment to Adam, but it was too late for him to change his ways.

Finally, the coast appeared underneath them, and tension began to creep over Adam. He was always afraid it would ruin his judgment, and desperately he sought to put everything out of his thoughts except flying the airplane. They were attacked twice on the way by small groups of fighter planes, but none of the Forts went down.

"There's Germany up ahead!" It was Felson who did speak this time, and Adam glanced ahead through the windshield and gave the command over the loudspeaker: "Pull the bomb fuse pins!"

"Yes, Sir!" the answer came at once.

The flak started blooming almost at once, and Adam thought how thin the Plexiglas and the aluminum skin were as the shells exploded.

"Bombardier to pilot!"

"Go ahead!"

"We're on the bomb run!"

Two fighters were reportedly flying low and to the left, and soon the cry came, "Radio to crew! Radio to crew! Fighters eleven o'clock high! Blast 'em!"

The action grew hot and heavy, and two Forts went down. The planes went straight through the exploding burst of flak, and once again Adam thought how there was a strange, deadly beauty in the black bursts. As they were approaching, almost ready to drop the bombs, Beans Cunningham yelled, "Four fighters coming in, trying to get that Fort that's limping!"

Adam looked to see a B-17 swarmed by the fighters. It was as if wasps were zipping in. He had read articles about wounded Fortresses holding off ten or fifteen fighters. Most of that, he knew, was purely imaginary; it did not happen against experienced fighters. He saw the Fort go down, and hated the sight of the German fighters as they wagged their wings in a token of victory. "I wish they were all dead!" he said aloud.

Startled by the sudden outburst, Felson said, "What did you say, Stuart?"

"I said, I wish they were all dead!"

Felson stared at him curiously. "Well, they're probably wishing the same thing about us."

They were suddenly jolted by the tail gunner's voice: "There's a lone 109 coming in fast!"

"What's he going to do?" Adam demanded.

"I don't know, but he's going around to our left."

Adam watched as the audacious fighter pilot pulled ahead of the formation, circled to eleven o'clock and, with guns blazing, came right at the entire formation.

"Look at that guy!" Ozzie Franklin, the new radio operator and waist gunner said. "He's got guts!"

Adam said, "Shoot! Shoot!" But for some strange reason, nobody in the entire formation fired back. "Why don't they shoot! Kill him! Knock him down!"

Felson watched as the plane passed through unharmed. "We could have got him," he said. "I guess there's a little chivalry left in us. The formation let him go right through. Well, it's hard to kill a man with that much courage."

Adam was shaking with fury. "That's just the kind that needs to be killed!" He had a sudden memory of an incident he had read in a history book, when a courageous Yankee had ridden on horseback in full sight of the Confederate troops.

The troops had let up a cheer, but Stonewall Jackson had said, "Kill him! Those with courage, those are the ones we want dead most."

"Bombs away!" The *Last Chance* lurched upward, and at once, freed from the rigid flight plan, Adam threw the plane around in a tight turn, hoping the wings wouldn't break off. "Let's get out of here," he muttered.

One glance below revealed Berlin, flames rising from where the bombs were dropping in rows. He wondered who was dying down there. It seemed so clean and safe up here in the airplane, but he knew that down where those black clouds were rising, men and women and maybe children were dying, bleeding to death. He had thought of this often before and, as always, closed his mind to it. He pushed the aircraft ahead at maximum speed, joining others who were fleeing.

But they did not get far, for fifteen minutes later they were attacked by the most massive array of German fighter planes that he had ever seen. The sky seemed to be black with them, and the *Last Chance* shuddered with the recoil of all guns blazing. Soon the ammunition was running low, and Adam said, "Save it! We've got a long way to go!"

He had no sooner spoken when suddenly the whole aircraft seemed to be tossed like a toy. They had been struck by a rocket from one of the planes, or perhaps more than one. Looking out, Adam grabbed the yoke and struggled to right the plane, which started to fall toward the earth.

"Can you pull it out?" Felson yelled.

"I don't know. Look at that wing!"

Felson looked out and saw that the right wing was broken off. "It'll never fly like that," he cried. He started to move from his seat, but five Focke-Wulfs suddenly converged on the *Last Chance*. Adam tried to turn, but it was all he could do to keep the plane in the air. He felt the plane shake as the bullets struck, and he heard Felson cry out.

"Felson!" he yelled, but the copilot had been struck by several bullets. Blood stained his flying suit, and he tried to speak, but his eyes glazed over and he slumped dead in the copilot seat.

Back in the airplane, things were bad. Clint had run out of ammunition at the top turret. From his position he could see the broken wing and did not think that the airplane could last long.

When he had no more ammunition at all, he jumped down and ran to the cockpit. "You can't fly it like this, Adam."

"No, have the men bail out! I'll hold it as long as I can. Tell 'em not to open their chutes right away. Those Germans might hit 'em as they go down!"

Clint ran through the airplane, and when he got to the waist he saw that Franklin, the new radio operator, was slumped on the floor. As he bent over him, Manny Columbo shook his head as he turned his gun. "He got it; he's dead."

"Bail out, Manny!" Clint ran down to the ball turret, yelling at Beans. "Come out of there; we got to get out of this thing, Beans!" He was aware that Moon Wilson, the bombardier, was approaching. "Adam's been hit in the leg, and he can't hold this plane level! It's going down!

"Bail out, Moon!"

"What about Asa, back in the tail?"

"I'll get him!"

Clint ran as the plane bucked and he swayed more than once, falling down. Finally, he got to the tail gun and said, "Asa, bail out! We're going down!"

Instantly Clint started making his way forward to the cockpit. He put on his own parachute, aware that the plane was rolling all over the sky. As he passed by the waist, he looked out and saw four parachutes. "At least the guys got away." But then he thought about Adam. Quickly he crawled his way to the cockpit. When he got there he saw Adam, his face white as a sheet, hanging on to the control yoke. Adam turned around and whispered, "Get out of here! Bail out, Clint!"

Clint took the situation in. Without a word, he reached out and yanked Adam out of the seat. Picking him up, he carried him to the door, and paused for only one moment. He saw that Adam had passed out. Without a second thought, he leaped out of the airplane in one motion, wrapping his arms and legs around the body of the unconscious man. When he had fallen clear of the airplane, he pulled the ripcord. When the chute opened, it almost tore Adam from his grip, but he held tightly with the full strength of arms and legs, and then they were floating downward.

Looking around, he could not see the other chutes and knew that the airplane had traveled miles since they had bailed out. Looking down, he saw Germany beneath, a rich green forest. Then his eyes turned to watch the *Last Chance* as it nosed down and headed straight for the earth. Clint's eyes followed it until it struck and blew up, sending black smoke and flames high in the air.

"She was a good ship," he whispered. He held tightly onto Adam and looked down as the earth seemed to rise to meet him. He well knew that nothing good awaited him and Adam—either death by German soldiers or civilians—or prison camp, which was little better.

Looking up at the inside of the white chute, he breathed a prayer: "God, you're in charge here. Look out for me and for Adam. It doesn't matter much about me, but Adam's got to find you before he dies, so please look out for us, Lord."

Part Four

ENEMY TERRITORY

19

SURVIVAL

The cold sky seemed to hold Clint in a vast fist as he plummeted toward the earth. With all his strength he held onto Adam, desperately trying to remember what he had been told about parachuting. He had never made a jump before, but he was well aware that what he was doing now would *not* have been covered. Vaguely he remembered that he was supposed to hit the ground, let his knees bend, and then roll to take the shock from the fall. As the ground rushed up at him, he knew he was falling at twice the rate of speed that he would have reached had he jumped alone.

The wind caught him and his burden, swinging them like a pendulum beneath the pure-white silk canopy above. Dizziness swept him, and he gave up all hope of making a safe landing, simply praying that he and Adam would survive. The wind whistled in his ears and his face was numb with the cold—then the two of them struck.

Clint's feet hit first, and then he crumpled, unable to do more than simply hang on. The shock of the landing ripped his hands from Adam, and the two separated, sprawling out. For one brief moment he felt gratitude—they had landed on what appeared to be an open field rather than in an icy river or in the tops of tall trees. For several minutes Clint was unable to do more than lie there, for his breath had been knocked out by the force of the landing. A silence lay over the field as he struggled to his feet, thinking of a bit of information that had been given to him at various briefings: *Surrender to a soldier*

273

if you can; the civilians are likely to kill you with pitchforks. They may have lost sons in the war. . . .

Struggling to his feet, Clint cast one quick look about the field. Darkness was falling rapidly, and he wondered if anyone had seen the parachute. No one appeared, however, and he saw no buildings of any kind. Quickly he moved over to kneel beside Adam, who was lying on his back.

"Are you okay, Adam?"

Adam's eyes were shut, and he did not appear to have heard. When Clint leaned forward, he saw that Adam's eyelids were moving and his chest was rising and falling. Quickly he freed himself from the parachute, then looked around, still half expecting to see farmers rushing across the fields with shotguns or pitchforks. The other instruction that came to him was hide the parachute, but he had no time for that. He unstrapped the harness and rolled the chute up into as small a bundle as he could, then stood confused for a minute, looking around.

The field they had landed in was surrounded by tall trees, evergreens of some kind, and Clint knew he had to get under cover. Without a clue as to which way to go, he leaned over and pulled Adam into a sitting position. With a grunt, he picked him up over his shoulder. Then straightening up he began trudging across the field. The edge of the tree line was only a hundred yards away, but he was breathing heavily by the time he got there. He had one quick thought—*I'm glad Adam's not as big as some of the Stuarts*—then he reached the tree line. Instead of going in, he turned and moved to his left, hoping to see some sort of shelter.

He had not gone more than two hundred yards before he felt a burning sensation on his cheek and, looking up toward the sky, blinked as tiny, icy fragments touched him.

"Snow!" he grumbled, and for one moment could not decide if that was in their favor or not. Finally he put it out of his mind except to mutter, "We've got to find shelter of some kind!"

By the time he had gone another hundred yards, he was gasping for breath and the snowflakes had grown larger, swirling across the field in diagonal lines. Another fifty feet and the tree line broke slightly. Glancing toward the thick forest, Clint had a moment's exultation when he saw a dark barn held in the depression that had been cut out of the woods. Taking a deep breath he muttered, "It's okay, Adam, we'll get some shelter and get you out of this cold."

Trudging across the broken ground, half stumbling on numbed feet, Clint finally reached the barn, and without putting Adam down, he pulled at one of the two double doors. It had obviously not been opened for some time and was difficult to move. He did manage to get it open enough to squeeze through, then stepped inside. For a moment he stood there unable to see, then his eyes became accustomed to the darkness. The interior, he saw, was filled with what seemed to be a jumble of old wagons and farm equipment. He could not make out more than this and could not hold Adam much longer. Moving around the equipment, he found at the back of the barn a pile of moldy hay, and with a grunt of relief, knelt gently as he eased Adam down. He said, "Adam, are you awake?" When he received no answer, he rose and left the barn. "Got to get that parachute," he said and moved as quickly as he could through the ever-thickening snowflakes, some as large as dimes now. Reaching the parachute, he bundled it up and made his way back to the barn as quickly as possible. He entered and wondered whether to close the door. There was a window in the loft above that let in some light, but night was falling fast and he knew that it would soon be pitch dark.

Making a quick decision, Clint moved back toward the double doors, opened them wide, and let the gray light flood the floor of the barn. The equipment, he saw quickly, included an old thresher and what appeared to be a pony cart, very old and with a broken tongue. Several bits of machinery, random parts, and some old furniture cluttered the floor. The barn was evidently storage for things that were not to be thrown away but were fairly worthless. *They probably built a new barn and use this one for worn-out stuff*, he thought to himself.

Clint's mind raced as he thought of what he had to have. A fire would be essential in freezing weather—but how to build a fire in a barn? He began to move among the various pieces and suddenly came upon a piece of sheet iron, some two-feet square. He had no idea what it had been used for, but at once he picked it up and carried it back to where Adam was lying on the hay. Clearing a spot out carefully, he put it down, and then returned to the equipment. After rummaging through the piles of junk, he found an old pot that would do for cooking and a rusty ax with a broken handle. Using this, he demolished an old, heavy wardrobe and breaking off several very small pieces, he began to build a fire on the sheet iron. He had, as part of his equipment, a box of matches in a waterproof case, and when he had splintered several pieces with the ax, he made even smaller pieces with his knife. He touched the curling pieces, and the dry wood caught at once. Slowly he fed the tiny flame, careful to keep the fire in the center of the piece of sheet iron. Soon, the fire began to crackle, and he fed it until it made a small but cheerful blaze that seemed to cut the gloom of the barn.

The temperature was dropping, and Clint was glad for their heavy fleece-lined flight uniforms, for he knew that the cold could get fierce in Germany in February. He turned to Adam and saw that his eyes were open. "Hey, you're awake!" he said.

"Where—are we?" Adam asked, his lips moving stiffly. His eyes were half shut as he looked around. "What is this place?"

"An old barn. We were lucky," Clint said. "How you feeling?"

"Leg hurts."

"Let me take a look at it."

Clint awkwardly maneuvered the wounded man's trousers from his hips and leaned forward to peer at the wound, which was in the fleshy part of his thigh. It was a nasty looking tear that was seeping blood, even now, and Clint was appalled at the seriousness of the wound. *A piece of flak must have torn right through there*, he thought. Aloud he said, "Got to get the bleeding stopped."

He ripped up part of the parachute into smaller fragments and then bandaged the leg. "I don't think it broke the bone," he said, "but I imagine it hurts pretty bad. I wish I'd thought to get the emergency kit when the plane was going down, but there wasn't time."

"How'd I get out of the airplane?"

Clint hesitated. "I dragged you out. We came down in the one chute," he said. He smiled and patted Adam's shoulders. "Here, let's get your pants up, or you'll freeze to death. I'm going to see if I can find some water around here—maybe something to eat."

Picking up the ax, he took a short journey around the barn and managed to find an old tree that had fallen. "That'd be enough firewood," he spoke aloud. He hewed off several of the larger branches and dragged one back to the barn where he broke it up into foot-long lengths, then moved inside and shut the door. "Nothing to eat," he said cheerfully, "but if it keeps on snowing, we can melt some of that for drinking water. I'll see what I can do to make this place more comfortable."

Clint made a canopy out of the parachute that would hold some of the heat in for the two of them, arranging it more or less like a tent. It at least kept some of the heat on Adam. Afterwards he fed the fire carefully, making certain it didn't spread. Most of the smoke floated up to the ceiling and Clint thought, *That's good—I don't think anybody can see it.* He settled back and was shocked to discover how weak he was. The mission, the jump, and the stress had drained him of all strength, and he went to sleep after one last look to see that Adam was resting comfortably.

The light struck Clint's eyes, and he blinked and rolled his head to one side. He smelled the moldy hay and knowledge came rushing through his senses. He sat up at once, and his first movement was to look toward Adam. He saw that the wounded man's face was pale and quickly moved to see if any blood had seeped through the bandage and the uniform.

With relief he saw no fresh blood. *I wish I could sew that up*, he thought. He saw Adam's eyes open and said, "You stay right here. I've got to go get something to drink." Taking the pot he had found, he moved outside. The snow was at least three inches deep. It had almost stopped falling, but there would be enough snow for water if he could not find a stream.

He did find a stream, however, a small one, less than a hundred yards from the barn. It curved around a clump of large trees in a serpentine fashion, standing out sharply as a dark line beside the white banks of snow. Gratefully he took a drink, then filled the pot and moved back. When he was inside, he helped Adam to a sitting position. "Have some of this."

"Thanks." Adam guzzled thirstily at the pot, drinking awkwardly, and when he lay back he whispered, "That was good."

"Well, we're alive, we've got water, and we're out of the weather," Clint said.

"We'll never get out of here, Clint." Adam's voice was raspy. He looked around at the barn and said, "We're right in the middle of Germany, and I'm wounded and can't walk." His eyes were feverish, and he hesitated for a moment then looked up. "Clint," he muttered urgently, "get out of here and save yourself! No good waiting around for me—I can't make it."

"Hey, that's no way for a Stuart to talk!" Clint admonished Adam. "We'll make it fine. God's kept us this far. He's going to keep us the rest of the way. Now, let's take a look at that leg."

Clint changed the bandage and kept the other, knowing that he would have to wash it out. He helped Adam dress again, then sat for a few minutes thinking hard. Doubt gnawed at him, for he knew enough geography to realize that their chances of escape were slim. Even if Adam were not wounded, they were hundreds of miles away from any border. Very few downed airmen had ever made their way out of the interior of Germany. Only those who had gone down close to the borders of Switzerland or other neutral territories had managed such a thing.

Lord, you're just going to have to do a miracle, I guess, Clint prayed. He sat there putting the doubts away and after praying steadily for some time, smiled. *You told me to cast all my cares on you—so I'm doing that right now. It's all yours, Lord!*

Peace came to Clint Stuart then. He got up and began searching through the jumble of worn-out equipment and managed to find a few items that might help. He knew that they would have to have food, and when Adam woke up, he said, "I'm going out foraging for food, Adam. You just stay quiet and keep warm." Clint struck Adam's shoulder lightly, saying, "Hang on."

He left the barn and made his way along the tree line, his eyes searching constantly for any sign of movement. It seemed to be a purely rural part of the country—no signs of a road anywhere. Finally he passed an open field where a thin gray horse lifted its head and looked at him.

"What are you doing out here in the snow, old fella?" Clint moved closer. When he stuck out his hand, the horse came to him, moving slowly. Clint patted its nose, saying, "You better get in out of this. It's going to get worse." He looked around and saw at the far end of the field what seemed to be a small barn. Quickly he stepped across the fence, and as he moved across the snow, the horse followed him. When he got to the shed, he saw that it was no more than a shelter for animals with some ancient harness hanging on the wall.

"Got to be *something* around here. They wouldn't leave you out like this," he muttered. He slapped the horse on the flank and then moved outside, searching for other signs of habitation.

Clint found it five minutes later when he stepped out of a grove of trees—then stepped quickly back inside the shelter again. Less than a hundred yards away sat a house with smoke ascending out of the chimney, scoring the gray sky. He stood inside the shelter of the evergreens searching for signs of life but saw no one moving outside. It was a large, two-storied house with several outbuildings. Uncertainly, he waited, then began to circle around following the tree line, which held the house as in the crook of an arm. One of the buildings, the largest of the barns, was close to the tree line, sixty or seventy yards from the house. Carefully keeping himself hidden from anyone who might be inside watching, Clint followed the tree line until he had put the barn between himself and the house. Then taking a deep breath, he stepped out and walked across the open space. His breath was coming shortly, for he expected to hear someone calling each moment, but there was nothing. He got to the barn and found that there was a small back door. Holding his breath, he opened it carefully, and peering inside, saw that no one seemed to be there. He stepped inside, shut the door, and at once heard the lowing of a cow, a most familiar sound. He peered into the gloom to see a cow in a stall who lifted her head to examine him. A calf stood close by.

Grinning suddenly, Clint said, "Well, good thing I'm a country boy. Adam and I'll have milk if nothin' else." He found a milk bucket and stool, and immediately sat down and leaned his forehead against the cow's withers. He heard the warm, frothy milk drilling against the bottom of the tin pail. When it was half full, he stopped, lifted it, and drank thirstily. Then he filled it again and rose, slapping the cow affectionately. "Thanks, old girl," he said. "I'll probably be coming back for more of the same."

He carefully stashed the bucket of milk and looked around the barn. Finding an old blanket and folding it up, he put it beside the milk.

He searched the barn but found nothing edible. Moving toward the front, which had two double doors, one of which stood slightly open, he peered out at the house. He still could see no sign of life, although it was ten o'clock in the morning, he guessed. Still, he was nervous, for someone might leave the house at any moment and come right to the barn.

A movement caught his eye and he heard a familiar sound. "Well, well, well!" he mused. "How about that!" Looking out, he saw several chickens pecking at the snow-covered ground, and his eyes lit up. He began to cluck as he had done a thousand times at home. "Chick, chick, chick," he called softly. *I don't know what* chicken *is in German, but I guess chickens understand that noise*, he thought. He proved to be right, for several of the chickens came curiously toward the door. Looking around, Clint found what he expected, a can close to the door with chicken feed in it. Taking out a handful, he moved toward the door, tossing several grains out. The chickens came close and began pecking at the snow.

"Come on, chick, chick, chick, chick," he crooned, and soon the chickens were stepping inside. Carefully throwing the feed closer to his feet, Clint waited until one of them, a fat white hen, came to his very feet and was pecking at the feed. "Welcome home," Clint whispered. Leaning over, he picked up the hen, and with one smooth motion, broke the neck of the fowl. It shuddered for a moment, but he held tightly, and the others did not even notice. Quickly he moved back, wrapped up the chicken in the blanket, then grasped the milk bucket with his free hand. *Have to be careful not to spill it*, he thought. He left the barn by the back door, made his way into the trees, and soon was out of sight of the house. He hurried as fast as he could, and when he came to the barn where he had left Adam, was glad to see no signs of footprints except his own. He did think for a moment, *If somebody comes by here, they'll see my prints—unless it snows again*.

Entering the barn, he made his way to Adam. Adam had braced himself up against the wall; his cheeks were red, and Clint knew that he had a fever. "Did you find anything?"

"Yup," Clint said, putting his burdens down. "Here, try some of this." He handed Adam the milk bucket, and Adam looked into it curiously, then lifted it to drink. When he put it down, he had a white mustache and said, "That's good, Clint. What's in the blanket?"

"Supper. Chicken soup for what ails you!" Clint said as he unfolded the blanket and pulled the limp body of the hen out. "Here, wrap up in this blanket while I fix supper."

"I'll have mine fried."

"No, you won't. You'll have it boiled—better for you that way."

Quickly Clint dressed the hen, and within thirty minutes the chicken was boiling in a pot that Clint had set over a make-shift tripod he'd fashioned from some pieces of machinery. Soon the smell of cooked meat began to permeate the barn, and from time to time Clint tested the bird with his knife.

Adam watched, saying little, but listened as Clint told him how he had found the farm and obtained the chicken. Finally he asked, "How far away was it?"

"Not more than a couple of miles." Clint looked over and added, "I don't think they'll be out much in this snow. I did see a horse in a field, so they'll have to feed him. But I don't think anyone comes to this place much."

"They'll have to come sometime." There was a despondency in Adam's voice, and his eyes were gloomy with doubt. "We can't make it, Clint."

"Sure we can. All we have to do is just keep on finding chickens—and believing in God. That's pretty good theology."

Adam studied his companion, who was poking his knife into the chicken. "You really believe that, don't you?"

"Sure I do."

"You really believe that God cares what happens to us? Here we are in the middle of Germany, me shot up, we don't know anybody, don't have a friend in the world—and you still think we're going to make it out of here?"

"Well, it might take a little miracle or two—but there are precedents." Clint looked over at the pot and waved the smoke from the fire aside. "Look at it this way. We didn't die when the *Last Chance* went down."

Adam dropped his head. He had forgotten in his misery about the crew members who hadn't made it. "I'm sorry about them," he said. "They were good guys."

"Yes, they were."

"You think the others will make it?"

"Probably wind up about like us, but they're not praying men, I'm afraid."

Adam sat quietly. His leg pained him every time he moved, but he said nothing of this. A gray cloud of doubt had settled about him, and he had no hope whatsoever. He was afraid that he'd be killed, or he would die of his wounds, or he'd go to a prison camp—and none of the three had any appeal for him. He'd felt himself beginning to shake and murmured, "I'm getting a fever, I think."

Clint looked up and saw the flush on Adam's cheekbones. "We'll get some soup down you and keep you warm. May have to sweat it out, but we'll make it."

Five minutes later he said, "Well, I think we're ready to have dinner." He cut a leg from the chicken with his knife, almost burning his fingers, and said, "Watch it, this is hot!" He passed it over to Adam, who took it and began to nibble at it cautiously. "This is good," Adam muttered. He ate the chicken and said, "Don't think I want any more."

"Try to get some sleep. If you get cold, holler, and I'll build the fire up. Wrap up in that blanket, pull it around you, and I'll take care of everything else."

"All right." Adam studied the face of his cousin, then nodded. "Thanks for the supper."

"My treat!"

Clint ate his own share of the chicken, keeping the rest of it boiling until it fell to pieces. He had done things like this as a hunter many times out in the woods of Arkansas, and his training stood him in good stead now. He savored the food but knew that he would have to make another trip.

"Never thought I'd turn out to be a chicken thief," he whispered, grinning into the fire. "We always ranked them pretty low back in Arkansas."

For some time he sat staring into the fire, keeping it going. When Adam began to toss around, he moved over and felt his forehead. *He's burning with fever! I'll bet there's some metal in that leg of his—but I don't know how to get it out.*

Adam woke three hours later asking for water. When he had drunk from the small pot that Clint had salvaged, he could only whisper, "If they find us, Clint, they'll kill us or we'll go to a prison camp. I'd rather be dead! Clear out of here!"

Clint shook his head. "God knows where we are, Adam. I believe we're going to see home again."

Adam stared out of hollow, sunken eyes. The fever had drained his strength. He felt sick and nauseated, and all hope was gone. "Get out, Clint, save yourself. I'm not worth saving anyhow."

Clint just shook his head and gave Adam another drink of water. That night darkness covered the barn, wrapped them up, and Clint slept fitfully. Time and again he waited for God to speak and prayed that there would be some way to show Adam Stuart that God had not forgotten them.

20

"THEY'RE THE ENEMY"

T he wedding of their daughter gave Owen Stuart and his wife, Allie, more pleasure than they had ever imagined. They had been alarmed when Wendy had come back from her tour with the USO with her announcement that she and Alex Grenville were to be married. But when Wendy had told them with shining eyes that Alex had been converted, they had been more open to the idea. Wendy had brought Alex for a prolonged visit, and Owen had been so pleased with his prospective son-in-law that he had said to Allie, "Well, Wife, God's heard our prayers. We're going to have a Christian son-in-law."

"Now don't try to make an evangelist out of him, Owen."

"Well, maybe he can be my song leader."

Allie had laughed at him, then hugged him, saying, "Oh, I'm so excited! And Wendy—I've never seen her look so radiant!"

The wedding had come, and the only drawback had been that Will and Woody could not be there. Two days after the young couple left for their honeymoon, Owen did get more serious news. He came in looking strained, and Allie said at once, "What is it? Is it Will or Woody?"

"No, it's Adam. I just got a call from Lylah. She got a telegram that said Adam's missing in action."

"Oh, Owen! He can't be dead! And isn't Clint with him?"

"Yes, Clint is with him, and it doesn't say *dead*," Owen said quickly, "just *missing*. Their plane went down, but a lot of the

285

crews made it out. We'll just hope that they made it down, and pray they will be safe. I'm going to call Lylah again later. I know she's going to take it bad."

"Is there any word from Mona?" Allie asked.

Owen shook his head. "Nothing good, I'm afraid. I talked to Pete over the phone. He said she hadn't said anything to him, but she's still tied up with that movie actor. I'm afraid she's making a bad mistake."

Allie took his arm. "Come on, we need to spend some time with God for our family. We can pray for Mona, Clint, and Adam at the same time."

Two of the objects of Allie's and Owen's prayers were deeply in need of those intercessions. Hunched over and wrapped up in a smelly old horse blanket, Adam Stuart was peering at the map of Germany that he had taken out of his flight jacket. Fever had drained him, and his leg was no better. He could see the rawness of the wound and knew that it should have been sewn up, but there was no way that could be done.

"How's the leg?" Clint asked. He had come in with water that he had obtained from the creek and squatted down saying, "I'm going to leave pretty soon and go get another one of those chickens. I'm hungry, and I know you are."

"No, I'm not hungry."

"You've got to eat," Clint insisted. He looked down at the map and said, "What do you think? Do you know where we are?"

"All I know is that sign you saw back on the road, about that little town. Lucky you saw that, because it's right here." Clint had daringly taken a trip on the road that passed by the farmhouse where he had gotten the chicken and made out the name of a small town called Lurtz.

"That little town's on the map?"

"Right here!" Adam said, as he pointed a trembling finger to the map that he held on his lap. Clint leaned over and looked at it as Adam muttered, "I know where we are—but it doesn't help us much."

Clint sat down and studied the map. Lurtz seemed to be so far inside the interior of Germany that there would be no hope of an easy escape. "Well," he said practically, "we'll have to get you healed up a little bit; then we'll walk out of here."

"I'll never make it, Clint," Adam said, shaking his head. "You know that."

Clint tried to be as cheerful as he could. Later on in the afternoon, he made his way back and, following the previous methods, snatched another chicken and obtained another supply of milk. He got a fright coming out, for even as he left the barn, he heard a voice and thought he was caught. As he turned quickly, he saw a man and a young boy leave the house, and they were calling to a neighbor who was coming down the road. Quickly Clint disappeared into the woods but was still shaken when he got back to the barn. He mentioned nothing of his narrow escape to Adam but said, "Another chicken and some fresh milk." He cleaned the chicken and made another chicken stew, but Adam could eat little of it. He went to sleep after a few bites, but it was a troubled sleep. He tossed and turned and more than once called out something that Clint could not understand.

Clint ate and sat down across from Adam. There was nothing for him to do but to keep the fire going and to read out of the New Testament that he always carried in the pocket of his flight jacket. The food had refreshed him, and he read all day, stopping only when Adam would awaken and need water. He kept trying to get him to eat more, but Adam could not.

Finally, late in the afternoon when the sun was dying, Adam did wake up, and he struggled into a sitting position.

"Your leg's hurting, isn't it?"

"A little bit." Adam pulled out the map and looked at it again. His eyes were hooded, and he kept his head down, but finally he looked up and said, "Look at this."

Clint leaned forward and saw with the flickering light of

the tiny fire the name "Schweivnitz." Clint said the name aloud, pronouncing it clumsily, and looked up at Adam. "What about it?"

"I know that place, Clint."

"You mean you've *been* there?"

"No, I've never been in Germany—but I know that town. I've studied it."

"Why would you study a little town in Germany called Schweivnitz? I never heard of it."

Adam was lightheaded and, weak. He was only half conscious, and his voice seemed to come from far off. He had been dreaming off and on, in his delirium, about Germany, about his father, about his ancestry. And now, sick and weak as he was, he did what he had never done before—he began to speak of his heritage.

"My father was from this place," he whispered, his voice thin and reedy. His eyes were bright with fever. "His name was Richthofen. He was a flyer—the most famous ace in the German Luftwaffe in the First War. . . ."

Clint listened with shock as Adam related the story of how his mother Lylah had met Richthofen, the famous flyer—and was even more shocked to find out that Adam was the fruit of their love. He said nothing, however, but listened, until finally he heard Adam say, "I hated the Germans because they killed my friend." Then he looked up and whispered, "But how can I hate them when they're my own people—my father's people—and they live right there in Schweivnitz."

"You mean they're still there?"

"Yes, I think so." Adam swayed back and forth and said, "I found out all I could about the family. It wasn't easy. Some of them are in the army now. One of them, Wulf Richthofen, is a leader in the Luftwaffe. I found out that much." He looked down at the map and said, "I even know what the place looks like. I've seen pictures of it. It's right here, this side of Schweivnitz, the Richthofen estate. It's a big house with three white spires and the name Richthofen on it." He went on to describe clearly what the Richthofen home looked like, and Clint did not ask him how he had found all this out.

Adam subsided into silence, and Clint spoke almost without thinking. "We've got to get to the Richthofens."

Adam opened his mouth to speak, then closed it and shook his head.

"We've got to go there! They're your family!"

"They're the *enemy*—I'm *their* enemy!" Adam whispered, and then he began to lean to one side, and Clint had to leap forward to keep him from falling over. Adam had started falling asleep into a delirium like this. His fever was very high, and Clint watched helplessly as the wounded man shook violently with the effects of it.

Clint had never known such a problem. Finally, he prayed until he could pray no more. Looking down at the flushed face of Adam Stuart, he knew that sooner or later death would come. *He's got an infection, and if he doesn't get medical attention, he'll die*, was his thought.

Getting up, Clint walked back and forth, trying vainly to think of a way to get medical help, but could think of nothing. Finally he looked up and between clenched teeth said, "God, I don't know what to do. All I know is, some of Adam's family is here. They're the enemy, I suppose, but that's all I know to do—try to get to them. Is that what you want me to do?"

No answer came, and Clint stood for a time struggling, and finally he said, "Well, Lord, I'm going until I get a red light." He began to think more calmly, and somehow the elements of a plan came together. Taking a quick look at Adam, he covered him up with a blanket, then left the barn. He moved quickly across the snow, noting that it seemed that more snow was likely to come. He kept watch carefully for any sign of life, but saw no one. When he got to the field where the horse was kept, he did not see him and his heart sank. "If the horse is gone, it's all off," he said aloud. However, when he went to the shed, he found the horse inside. Someone had been there and fed him. Clint let the horse finish eating while he selected a harness. Slipping a bridle on the animal, he said, "Come on, boy, I've got a job for you."

Leading the horse back across the field, he kicked the fence down hoping that the snow would come and cover up his tracks, and that the owners would assume that the horse had just broken through. When he got back to the barn, he tied the horse outside and went inside and examined the pony cart. It was a simple enough affair, and he dragged it outside and hitched it on to the waiting animal.

Going back, he stood over Adam and saw that he was totally unconscious. He filled the cart with straw, then carried Adam outside and put him in it. After this, he brought the remains of the parachute and covered Adam, then filled the cart up with straw.

Finally, he moved inside and saw that it was useless to try to disguise the signs of their stay in the barn. He gathered up such things as he thought he might use, loaded them in the cart, then moved around, took the harness, and said, "Come on, boy, we've got a way to go."

Clint found that the roads were empty and was glad to see the snow begin falling. He did pass one wagon, driven by a farmer who raised a hand briefly in greeting but did not speak. Clint, his heart in his throat, was thankful that the swirling snow apparently covered the sight of his flight jacket and the man did not notice. He had his hat pulled down over his eyes and had given scarcely a look.

His only hope, he knew, was in finding the Richthofen estate, and he knew from Adam's words that it was on a road about a mile before reaching Schweivnitz. He had no way to measure the distance, and he passed no other travelers. The snow fell harder, and it became difficult to see more than a few yards ahead. He plodded on thinking, *I'll probably have to go all the way into town, then turn around and come back. Thank God for weather like this! Most people will be inside to get out of it.*

He did not have to enter the town, however, for as they

plodded on he saw a narrow road open up to his right. Stopping the horse, he got out of the small cart and moved closer until he stood peering down the winding lane. He finally turned and, as he wheeled, saw a worn wooden sign nailed to a fir tree. Scraping the snow off with his forearm, Clint saw with a wild joy the word *Richthofen*. He could not read the rest of the German but exclaimed aloud, "This has *got* to be it!" Going back to the horse, he grabbed him by the cheek harness and said, "Come on, boy, we'll find something."

As the snow fell out of a leaden sky, Clint moved forward, leading the horse. The temperature was well below freezing now, and he was worried about Adam. He knew he had to find shelter.

He walked for what he thought was approximately an hour, until he saw, off to one side, a large manor house. He tied the horse to a fence that outlined the estate and went forward on foot. As soon as he got close enough, even through the driving snow, he could see it was no common farmhouse—and when he saw the three spires rising to the skies, he exclaimed, "That's it! That's what Adam said—three spires!" He stood there for a moment, only a moment, then whirled and ran back to the cart. His mind raced: *We can't go right in there. We better take shelter, and I'll try to find out more about this tomorrow or when the snow stops.*

Knowing that a large place like this would have many out-buildings, he led the horse down the road at an oblique angle to the large house. A side road broke off, and he took it, his eyes searching for anything that might do. Soon he passed one house with smoke coming out the stone chimney and began looking for a barn or a toolshed—anything to give shelter until the next day.

When he was almost ready to give up, he saw two large sheds, apparently deserted. Leading the horse forward, he stopped and looking inside saw they were empty. Evidently they had been used for chicken houses for the smell was still strong, even in the freezing weather. He went back and brushed the straw from Adam, picked him up, and carried him inside. He wrapped him up in the blanket and then moved back outside, thinking, *Got to get this cart out of sight—and the horse.* He drove the horse down the road, unhitched the animal, then dragged the cart, by force, off into the bushes. Stripping the harness off the horse, he gave him a fond slap on the flank. "Go on, boy—go find a warm place." The animal turned and ambled away, and Clint moved as quickly as he could back to the shed. He found Adam still unconscious and sat down beside him, praying and waiting for daylight. The night was cold and bitter, the temperature dropping. Clint stayed close to Adam, wrapping up with him in the blanket so that the heat from his own body would offer some protection. His own teeth chattered, and he knew that tomorrow he would have to do something.

Finally he dozed off and slept fitfully until a thin pale line of light appeared under the door of the shed. Stiffened with the cold, he arose and stepped outside the door, noting that the snow was starting to fall again. He half turned to go back inside when a voice came from his left, catching him off guard.

"Halt!"

The unexpectedness of the command hit Clint with a sudden force, and he whirled to see a young woman, wearing a fur jacket and a cap down over her ears, looking at him.

But it was not her dress that caught his attention so much as the two barrels of the shotgun that she pointed at him!

Despair hit Clint almost like a bullet, for he knew that he had failed. The eyes of the young woman were determined, and he knew that here the last chance had been taken and that he could do no more. Slowly he held his hands up and said numbly, "I surrender."

21

ANGEL IN BLACK

Clint noted at once the steadiness of the dark blue eyes of the woman. He straightened up and would not have been surprised if she had pulled the trigger of the shotgun. A silence fell over the scene, and he was vaguely aware of a blackbird making a harsh, guttural call somewhere close by. The moment ran on for what seemed like a long time as he stared at the steadiness of the woman's weapon. A line of light ran down the blue barrel, and the certainty of her grip was reflected in the fact that it did not waver. *She's got nerve!* Clint thought with a sudden flash of admiration and then asked, "Do you speak English?"

"Yes."

The brief monosyllable came curtly, and Clint studied the face of the woman carefully, knowing that perhaps his life and Adam's lay within her keeping. She was a tall woman dressed in a black skirt with a dark-colored fur jacket. A strand of ash-blonde hair curled out from beneath a rich-brown fur cap. Her face was oval, and the blue eyes were large, well-shaped, and steady as they observed him. There was a calmness about the woman that was almost unnerving, and Clint let his breath out slowly saying, "I'm glad you didn't shoot without asking questions."

The barrel of the shotgun suddenly lowered, but the woman still held it loosely, trained on him. "I suppose you were shot down over Berlin." It was not a question but a statement, and the calm tenor of her voice matched the cool expression on her face.

"Yes, and I have a friend inside—my lieutenant. He is wounded." Clint waited for the woman to reply, but she still said nothing. *I can't figure her out. If she was going to shoot me, she would have done it already.* Aloud he said, "I suppose you'll turn us over to the army?"

"Step inside. Let me look at your officer."

Surprised at the woman's curt command, Clint blinked, then shrugged and turned to move back inside the hut. When he got inside, he turned and saw that the woman followed him and said, "It's his leg. He took a piece of flak or maybe a bullet, I don't know. It's infected."

"Move back against the wall!" The woman watched carefully until Clint backed up into the angle of the wall, then stepped over to look down at Adam, who was staring up at her with fever-bright eyes. She said nothing but studied him carefully, holding the shotgun generally in Clint's direction.

Adam was in that condition of a severe fever patient when it was almost impossible for him to tell reality from the dreams that came and went like ghosts. He had awakened during the jolting trip and had been only vaguely aware of Clint moving him around when the pain of his injured leg ripped through him. He stared up at the woman, and in the darkness of the shed he seemed to see a pale, oval face of a woman dressed entirely in black. He was only mildly interested in the shotgun, for a thought came to him and with dry lips and a raspy voice he said, "Well—an angel—I never thought of an angel in black." He began to cough and cried out involuntarily as the convulsions made him jerk his wounded leg.

Somehow the statement seemed to affect the woman. Clint was watching her, and when Adam said "an angel in black" something flickered in her eyes that Clint could not understand. He said, "I haven't been able to do anything for him. He needs some sort of medicine to get to that infection or he'll lose the leg."

"And he may die." The woman made the statement calmly, but there was a difference in the tenor of her voice. She hesitated for one moment, then with what seemed to be a sudden decision, lowered the barrel of the shotgun and eased the triggers off. The twin clicks sounded very loud in the silence of the shed, and Clint felt himself heave a sigh of relief. He thought of telling her about Adam's identity but then decided that that was not his secret. "Let me show you the wound," he said. "Is it all right if I move?"

The woman had made her decision. She leaned the shotgun against the wall, and her lips made the very briefest of smiles. "It won't do you any good to shoot me," she said. "You'd be caught at once." She did not wait for him to move but knelt down and loosened Adam's belt. Pulling the trousers down, she studied the wounded leg and said quietly, "He's very close to blood poisoning."

"I know," Clint said. "He should've had attention before this."

"Why didn't you give yourself up to the authorities?"

Clint hesitated. "I don't know. I suppose all of us have some idea of escaping."

"You would never make it through Germany. The authorities are very conscious of pilots who bail out. Most of them are captured at once."

Clint said, "Can you help us? Not me, but I'm worried about my friend."

Again, there was a brief silence, and Clint saw that something was going on inside the woman's mind. Her eyes were so dark blue they seemed almost black in the gloom of the shed, and her face reflected the struggle that seemed to be going on. He waited until she finally conceded, "I can't do anything here. Can you carry him?"

"How far?"

"About three hundred meters."

"Yes, I can manage that."

"Pick him up then."

Clint said suddenly, "My name is Clint Stuart and this is my cousin, Adam Stuart."

"You are relatives serving together?"

"Yes, what's your name?"

"Maris Richthofen." She studied him to see if the name meant anything, but Clint kept his face passive despite the slight shock that ran through him. *This might be Adam's relative,* he thought. Aloud he said, "Miss Richthofen, I appreciate your kindness. I thank the Lord for it."

The woman named Maris turned to face him squarely. "You are a Christian then?"

"Yes!" Suddenly Clint's eyes narrowed, and he studied the young woman. "Are you a Christian, Ma'am?"

"Yes, I am." Just this single, blunt statement, but for some reason it gave Clint hope that he had not had before. "Pick up the lieutenant. My cottage is right over there."

Clint stooped and got Adam on his shoulder. He moved as easily as he could, but he felt Adam tense with the pain and then suddenly go limp. "He's passed out," he said.

"That will be best. Come quickly!"

Clint followed the young woman to a cottage that lay almost concealed within the circle of some tall evergreens. It was a small cabin, built of logs and stone, with a steep roof. Smoke was coming out of the chimney, and Clint glanced around, seeing no one close by. He was breathing hard by the time they reached the door. The young woman opened it and said, "Come inside." Clint stepped in and the woman said, "If you can get up the stairs, that would be the safest place for you to hide."

Clint suddenly turned. "You're going to hide us and help us?"

"Don't ask questions!" Maris Richthofen said. She appeared to be no more than twenty-one, but there was an authority in her bearing and in her voice that told Clint that she was accustomed to being obeyed. She motioned toward the stairs along one wall that went to a room upstairs. Clint made his way up, and when he got to the top she passed him and stepped to a door, then opened it. "In here," she said.

Clint stepped inside, and saw by the one large window at the end that it was furnished with a green rug, a large bed, a heavy dresser, and a desk. It did not seem to be in use, and as he moved toward the bed, Maris stripped the covers down and said, "Set him on the side of the bed."

"All right." Carefully Clint took Adam from his shoulder and kept him from slumping. The woman began removing the stained uniform and soon had stripped Adam down to his underwear. Carefully, she lifted his leg as Clint eased him into the bed, onto the pillow.

"I'll have to be gone for a few minutes. I have to go get something to stop that infection."

"Into the village?"

"No, we have some things at the house." She looked at the leg and shook her head. "It's not going to get better until that metal comes out of there."

Clint hesitated. "If you have to get a doctor, get one. It doesn't matter if we're captured. All I want is for Adam to live."

"There may be another way. Wait here!"

The woman left and Clint sat down, astonished to find that his hands were trembling. The shock of being apprehended caught up with him, and he sat on the chair beside the bed watching as Adam breathed roughly in a rather shallow fashion. His face was pale, except for two fever spots on his cheekbones, and Clint reached over and felt his forehead. "Fever coming back," he muttered and shook his head. He glanced toward the stairs, wondering who would come back up. *Maybe she's got a member of the family who's a doctor. But he may not be so quick to welcome enemy soldiers as she is.*

Adam suddenly spoke as he looked up at Clint, then cast his eyes around the room. "Where are we?" he whispered.

"A woman found us. Her name is Maris Richthofen. Did you ever hear of her?"

Adam was still struggling with the fever but was conscious enough to think slowly. "No, I haven't. Is this her house?"

"Not the big house where the family lives. Sort of a cabin,

maybe for servants, I don't know. She's gone to get something for your wound." Clint leaned over and touched Adam's shoulder with a gesture of reassurance. "I think it's going to be all right, Adam. She's gone to get some medicine and maybe somebody to take that iron out of you."

"A doctor? He'll turn us in."

"She didn't say so. Don't worry about it though. She's a Christian. She told me so."

Adam's eyes opened somewhat more widely, but he did not respond. He lay quietly drifting in and out of sleep. From time to time, Clint got up and looked out the window. He could see over the top of the trees the three turrets of the Richthofen lodge and, despite his assurances to Adam, felt somewhat nervous. Finally, he saw a dark figure outlined against the snow and was relieved that Maris Richthofen was coming alone. She had, he saw, a small dark bag of some sort in her hand, and he turned and moved back to Adam. "She's coming, and she's all alone. It's going to be OK!"

Adam did not answer, but the two men waited, and when the woman came in she had taken off her jacket. She wore a black wool sweater underneath it, and as she set the bag down, she stripped the sweater off over her head. Underneath she wore a white blouse with long sleeves, cut like a man's shirt. She rolled her sleeves up and came to stand over the wounded man. Her eyes were unfathomable, and Adam had time to note that she had a classic beauty that seemed to be found in many German women. Her hair was not dark, but an ash-blonde color such as he had not seen often. "I want to thank you for not turning us in," he said.

Ignoring his words, the woman reached out to touch Adam's forehead. Her hand was cool and firm and steady. "Your fever's high. It won't go away until we get that leg cleaned up and fill you with medicine."

"You didn't call a doctor?" Adam asked in alarm.

"No, he would at once report you to the authorities." She hesitated for a moment and said, "I have served with doctors many times as a nurse. I can try to take the metal from your leg, but I can make no promises. I'm not a surgeon. The choice is yours."

Adam did not even hesitate. "Take it out, Miss Richthofen."

"You're certain? I am not skilled, and it will be very painful."

"Do it!" Adam said, nodding firmly.

"Very well." Maris turned and said, "We will need some boiling water to sterilize the instruments."

"How do you happen to have medical instruments?" Clint asked curiously.

"My cousin was studying to be a doctor."

"What was his name?" Clint asked.

"Manfred."

A shock ran along Adam's nerves, and the woman saw him flinch. She thought it was pain, however, and said, "I'll go get the water to boiling."

As soon as she left the room, Clint said, "Aren't you going to tell her about your father?"

"No, it may not be best. She seems to be sympathetic, but we don't know how the rest of the family would be. As a matter of fact," he said slowly, "have you noticed that she hasn't offered to tell anyone else we're here?"

Clint nodded slowly. "I thought of that. She brought us here and is hiding us. I think she might be afraid that someone here might turn us in. Anyway, God's brought us this far."

Adam was not a great believer in the providence of God, but he said slowly, "It does seem like it, doesn't it? Out of all the places we could have gone down, we land just a few miles from the home of the Richthofens—and the one person that finds us, for all we know, is the only one who would help us." His eyes closed, and he whispered, "Maybe you're right—maybe God is looking after us."

Thirty minutes later, Maris came in bearing a basin of water. Steam was rising from it, and putting it down on the table beside the bed, she removed some instruments from the small bag and placed them in it. Then she removed a hypodermic needle from the bag and carefully filled it with a clear-looking fluid from a bottle. Approaching, she came and held it over Adam's arm. Looking down at his face she hesitated, "This may be deadly poison," she said, an odd look in her eyes. "Aren't you afraid?"

Adam had passed that stage. He smiled up at her, and despite the fever, he looked rather winsome as he said, "An angel wouldn't do that, Miss Richthofen."

"I'm no angel, but I will try to help you all I can." She plunged the needle into his arm carefully, pushed the plunger down, then withdrew it. "This will make you sleep," she said.

Clint watched as the medicine took effect almost at once. Within five minutes, Adam was breathing very shallowly, and Clint said, "That was powerful stuff."

"My father died a month ago. He had a tumor of the brain, and he was in much pain." The memories turned the face of the young woman still as if she held herself under firm control. "We kept him at the house, and I nursed him through his last illness. This was the medicine we used when the pain was very bad." She held her back straight, and there was a fragility about her, for all of her strength, Clint saw. She was looking down at Adam, and her face softened. "I could not help my father—perhaps I can help your lieutenant." Then her jaw tightened, and she moved over to pick some instruments out of the boiling water with a set of tongs. She sprinkled something over her hands and said, "I wish I had some rubber gloves, but I do not." Then she moved down to the leg and said, "Remove the bandage, Sergeant; then hold the leg as still as you can." A trace of anxiety showed in her fine eyes, and she showed one moment's hesitation. "I wish I did not have to do this, but there's no one else."

Clint removed the bandage and looked at her. "I don't believe you're an angel, Miss Richthofen, but I think you're the one God has sent to save Adam's life."

A flush came to the young woman's cheeks, and she studied the tall soldier before her. She had seen pictures, drawn by the Nazi propaganda movement, showing Americans as vicious thugs that one would expect to find in prisons, but there was a leanness about this man's face and a calmness in his eyes and a goodness that somehow reassured her. She allowed herself one moment's smile toward him, then turned and began to work on the wound.

Adam had been drifting in and out of sleep for what seemed like years. Time had ceased to become a factor for him, and once he thought, *Why, the Pyramids could be built while I'm in some of these deep sleeps!* At other times, time seemed to race by. He was aware of Clint and had learned to recognize the roughness of his hands as he changed the bandages, as he had learned to recognize the gentleness of the woman's touch. More than once he had awakened in a sweat to see the face of the woman who called herself Maris over him. Now, as he came out of the sleep, he was aware that there was a coolness on his face and on his neck and chest. He opened his eyes to see, by the sunlight that filtered through the window and lay in pale, yellow bars across the room, that it was morning. He was aware that the young woman was bending over him bathing his face with a cool cloth.

"Ah, you're awake," she said. "That's good!" She sat down, put the cloth back in the basin, and then looked at him. "How do you feel?"

Adam licked his lips and was surprised that he felt so well. "Much better," he said, and found that his voice was not as raspy as it had been. He reached up and touched his forehead, and exclaimed, "I think my fever's gone!"

"Yes, you had a hard time of it."

"What day is it? How long have I been here?"

Maris studied him as she answered, "Three days. I thought you were going to die at one point, but as your sergeant says, God has his hand on you."

Adam smiled suddenly. "He always says things like that. He believes it, too!"

"Don't you believe it, Lieutenant?"

Adam was surprised at the question and said slowly, "I suppose I do now. Only a miracle could have saved us this far. I really expected to be shot down or slapped into a prison camp somewhere."

"I must change the bandage on your leg."

Adam watched as she removed the bandage and studied the smooth curve of her cheek and the unusual color of her ash-blonde hair. "Why are you doing this for me?" he asked curiously. "After all, we're the enemy."

Maris did not answer but continued to change the dressing. She did observe, as she was tying on a fresh bandage, "I took two pieces of metal out of your leg, both rather small, and the infection is almost gone now. I did some stitches, but you'll have a bad scar."

Adam shrugged as she came back and sat down on the chair beside his bed. Then as if nothing had happened, she answered his earlier question. "Why do I do this for you?" Hesitating for what seemed like a long moment, she shrugged her shoulders. The light blue blouse that she wore revealed her womanly figure, and she seemed to struggle to find an answer. "It is all very complicated, Lieutenant."

"Look, you might as well call me Adam. We don't have to be so formal."

"Very well, and I will be Maris to you."

"Maris? I've never known anyone named Maris. Is that a German name?"

"No, it's Latin. It comes from the phrase *stella maris*—that means star of the sea."

Adam lifted his eyebrows. "That's very pretty," he said. "Star of the sea."

"It has another reference to the Virgin Mary," Maris said. "My father was a Latin scholar, and he chose it because he thought it was pretty. My mother wanted to name me Brunhilda."

Adam chuckled. "I'll bet you were glad she didn't." Then he said suddenly, "I'm sorry, I didn't mean to make fun."

"I realize our German names sound a little harsh to American ears."

The slight interchange had lightened the mood, and Adam said, "I haven't really thanked you properly, but I'm sure Clint has." She only nodded her head slightly and he prodded, "If a German parachuted down in America, I'm not sure he'd get such good treatment. Your name is Richthofen, so I'm sure your family is pro-German." He studied her carefully, and wondered if it was time to reveal his identity. He hesitated, and finally said, "Really, Maris, why have you helped us?"

Maris Richthofen drew a deep breath and shrugged her shoulders. The movement expressed a grace that lay in her, and she clasped her hands together and began to speak. "My father is Heinrich von Richthofen. My family has a long tradition in the military. My father's cousin—you've heard of him no doubt—Manfred von Richthofen."

Adam took a deep breath and thought, *This is my cousin then, at least a distant one.* "Yes," he said carefully, "I have heard of Manfred von Richthofen. The Red Baron we call him in America."

"He's well known in America?"

"Oh, yes, very well known! What about your father?"

"He was a distant cousin of Manfred's. As a matter of fact, he was on his first patrol the day Manfred died. He finished the First War with eight kills to his credit, and he went on to study engineering." Pain came to the dark blue eyes of the young woman and she suddenly clenched her hands. "I wish he'd gone on and become an engineer."

"What did he do?"

"He joined the Luftwaffe and fought in the war in Spain. Afterwards, he was given command of the Luftwaffe's Eighth Flying Corps. He was in charge of the dive bombers and the fighters that overran Poland. Later he was sent to Russia. He was an unhappy man. Sometimes I think he was not sorry to die."

"Why do you say that?" Adam inquired gently.

"He was not in sympathy with Hitler." She looked at him suddenly and said, "You Americans can never understand that. Many in our country hated everything Hitler stood for. Many stood against him and were executed. I have thought it would have been better if my father had done that, but he did not." She straightened her shoulders and looked straight into Adam's eyes. "He always said he fought for Germany and that some day Hitler would die, and then Germany could be purified."

Adam had no answer for that and said, "What about the rest of your family?"

"There is the countess, of course; she's seventy-two. That's Manfred's mother. She had two other children who were killed in 1925 in a flying accident. The other brother is Karl Bolko. He's still alive. As a matter of fact, he's at the house now. He stays quite often with his mother."

"There was a sister, wasn't there—Ilse?"

"How did you know that?" Maris stared at him with surprise, then shrugged. "I must have mentioned her. Yes, she comes here often, too. I'm very close to my cousins. Manfred, my cousin, is in flight training to become a fighter pilot. Ann is eighteen and engaged. Nicol is sixteen and dying to get into the war, and we're determined to keep him out of it. Wolf, the son of Lothar, is an army engineer. He hates what he does—which is designing sub pens."

"He does a good job of it," Adam said wryly. "We've dropped a million pounds of explosives on them and still haven't knocked them out."

"You're a bomber pilot then? I never asked."

Adam thought of the bombs that had fallen on Berlin and studied the woman for signs of anger or bitterness. When she did not speak he said quietly, "You must hate us very much."

"Why, no!" Maris looked surprised. "Did I not tell you I am a Christian?"

"Yes, you did say that, or Clint told me."

"Jesus Christ forbids his disciples to hate."

Adam stared at her with an incredulous look in his eye. "We have many Christians among our people, and I have seen hatred for the Germans."

"I am not responsible for them. It is the same with my people, of course. I'm not their judge, but for me, I cannot hate. Jesus has shown us that we should forgive our enemies."

A sudden thought came to Adam. "Is that why you have taken me in and helped me?"

"Of course!" Surprise washed over Maris's face. "I do it in the name of Jesus. Why else would I help an enemy?"

Adam shrugged his shoulders. "I can't think very clearly." He hesitated, then put his hand out. "Let me thank you, though. If every Christian were like you, I'd become one myself." His hand closed on hers. It was soft but firm and held his own hand tightly. He squeezed it and said, "From the bottom of my heart I thank you for what you've done for me and for my cousin."

Maris flushed. He was holding her hand tightly, and something passed between them during that brief handshake. She removed her hand, her voice unsteady as she said, "I did hate you and your people once."

"When was that?"

"I was in love once with a young man. His name was Franz."

Tragedy worked around the edges of the tone of the young woman's voice. It showed itself in her eyes and Adam said intuitively, "He was killed in the war, I suppose?"

"You're very quick! Yes. He was a medical student, and I was a nurse. We were very much in love. We planned to go as missionaries to preach the gospel of Jesus in Africa, but he was forced to join the navy."

"How did he die?"

"His sub went down in the North Atlantic." She hesitated; then tears came to her eyes. She dashed them away at once and said, "I've not wept in a long time—but then I haven't talked to anyone else about it." She found a handkerchief, wiped her eyes, and looked at him strangely. "Odd that I should be telling all this to you. I buried it in my heart long ago—but I still think of Franz, and I still think of Africa and the lost dreams that are gone forever."

Adam sat in the bed, his hand still tingling from the woman's handshake. He saw something in her he had rarely seen in a woman—strength and gentleness combined. "I don't see how you keep from hating me and others like me," he said.

Maris Richthofen said, "If it were in my own strength, it would be impossible. I did hate, but then the Lord came to me and said, 'I did not hate those who crucified me, and you must not hate those who harm you. We must love them.'"

"You mean," Adam blinked with surprise, "you actually saw Jesus?"

"Oh, it was a dream." Maris smiled and her face cleared. "But it was so clear to me! So I like to think that it was the time Jesus came to me when I needed him most. If I had allowed hate to come into my heart, I would have become bitter. Hatred destroys the one who has it, don't you agree?"

Adam dropped his head. He himself had been filled with bitterness for so long that he had not allowed himself time to think. He looked up and said slowly, "I'm afraid I've let bitterness come into my own heart. I wish I could be like you."

Maris leaned over, her lips soft and almost maternal. They were full, well-shaped lips, and as she spoke he saw the compassion there and in her eyes. "Jesus will give you himself, Adam Stuart. When you break down the wall and let him come in, he brings his love, and he dwells within you. Then it will be not you but he who will let love override the hatred that's there."

Adam was fascinated. He had heard the gospel before but never from such a source as Maris Richthofen! "I don't know if I can do it," he said. "I've heard the gospel all my life. My mother and my father are fine Christians, but I've been a rebel."

"We were all rebels. Jesus came to hunt rebels down and to bring peace to them."

Adam dropped his eyes again. "Well," he said, "I need peace—that's certain enough."

Maris reached over and put her hand on his. "He will help you, Adam. I will pray for you as your friend prays for you. He has told me."

"Clint? Yes, he always has. He's a real Christian; I know that." Adam was very conscious of her warm hand on his and did not move. Finally he looked up and said, "My mother would be glad to know that someone was praying for me. She's prayed for me for years."

"Then our prayers will join together, your mother's and mine, and you will see God do something in you, Adam Stuart."

"It doesn't seem possible we've been here a week." Adam was standing beside the bed testing his leg. He held onto the cane that Maris had found for him and looked over at Clint. "Why, look, I've got this thing licked, Clint!" He walked the floor, leaning heavily on the cane, and grinned broadly. "I'll be running the high hurdles in a week!"

"Well," Clint nodded with approval, "maybe not that, but you're certainly better. That young woman's some doctor."

Adam turned and made his way across the room. "You're right about that. I've never known anybody like her! I've got the feeling the rest of the family wouldn't be so keen on helping a pair of American fliers."

"I don't think so." Clint watched as Adam made his way back and forth across the room. "You better take it easy on that leg. I know Maris said to exercise, but you've probably done enough."

"I want to go downstairs."

"Might be too much for you."

"I'm sick of this room! Come along. You go first and if I fall I can fall on you."

Clint laughed. He was glad to see Adam doing so well, but he was even happier to find out that Maris's witness about Jesus was having a great effect on his friend. As he went down the stairs slowly he asked, "What do you think of Maris? She's sort of a relative of yours, isn't she?"

"A very distant cousin as far as I can figure it out." Adam said no more until he reached the first floor and took a deep breath. "She's like no woman I've ever known—except my mother. She has a sweetness in her that's very rare. I think she's risking a lot to help us."

"Come on into the kitchen. I can make us some coffee."

The two men moved into the kitchen and Clint, who had mastered the art of doing the cooking, stirred around and soon had coffee ready to pour into the thick mugs. He poured two cups, set one before Adam, and then sat down across from him. The two men sat there talking for some time, and then Clint lifted his head. "I hear her coming. It's a good thing she had this cabin away from the big house."

Both men turned to the door, and Clint said, "Hello—" But he broke off suddenly, for it was not Maris.

A short, stocky man wearing a black overcoat stood staring at them. He had pale blue eyes and blonde hair. For one instant he stood staring at the two men, then at once stepped back outside and slammed the door.

Adam hobbled to the window and watched him run toward the house. "Now, we're in for it! I think the vacation's over."

He was right about that. Five minutes later a car pulled up and a man got out, accompanied by another man, much younger. Both men had pistols, and they came straight for the house.

"We'd better not resist. They look as if they'd like to shoot us!" Clint said. He turned around and as the door burst open, both men put their hands up saying, "Don't shoot! We surrender!"

The short, older man moved into the room, covering the two with a Luger. "What are you doing in this house—but I see you are both downed fliers."

"Yes," Adam said quickly. "I was wounded, and—"

The younger man, a tall individual with the same blonde

hair and blue eyes as the other said, "How long have you been in this house?"

Adam had some idea of saving Maris from discovery and said, "Not very long."

"We must take them into town and turn them over to the authorities," the older man snapped. "What are your names?" When he received them he said, "You'll be turned over to the authorities and carried to a prison camp." He would have said more, but the door opened and Maris walked in. She took in the situation in one swift glance and said, "Don't shoot them, Karl."

"Why, of course not!" This, Adam knew, was Karl Bolko, his real father's brother. Bolko shook his head in surprise. "Why would you think such a thing? But you have done wrong to shelter them."

The younger man asked suddenly, "Why did you do it, Maris?"

"He was wounded, and I thought he was going to die."

Adam had figured out that the younger man must be Wolf, the son of Lothar. He had studied many pictures of his uncle, and the young man was a dead ringer for him with his handsome, chiseled jaw and light blonde hair. "But I might have expected it of you," the young German nodded.

"Come, we will go to the house," Karl said. "I will call the authorities from the telephone there."

Adam was helped into the car by Clint, who whispered, "Don't give up; it's not over yet."

"I think it is," Adam said. "They don't have any choice."

They all got into the car, which was driven by Wolf. Karl Bolko kept his pistol trained on the two men, turning backward over the seat. When they got to the large house, they all got out and Bolko said, "Come," and waved with the Luger.

As Adam entered the big house he felt very strange. He knew this had been his father's home, and he had read many descriptions of it. He limped, leaning heavily on the cane, into the large room and suddenly stopped short when a woman arose and came toward them. He knew at once that this was Countess Kunigunde von Richthofen, his grandmother. She was tall and strongly built. Her silver hair was arranged neatly, and she had the same direct, light blue eyes as the other members of the Richthofen family.

"What is this, Karl?"

"Two downed pilots—Americans, I think."

"Where were they?"

Bolko hesitated, and it was Maris who said, "They were in the cottage. The lieutenant was wounded. He had infection and a dangerous fever and I wanted to help him."

"That was foolish, Maris!"

"No, it was not foolish."

The countess gave her a look of compassion, saying, "Your father's death is still with you, but these two men are our enemies."

Maris said, "The war is lost. What good would it do to send these young men to a prison camp? We know what the camps are like. They may die there!"

Karl Bolko said, "We have no other choice. It is our duty!"

"We have a duty to God," Maris said, "and that is to show love where we can. These men are not dangerous."

"If we turn them loose," Wolf said, "they'll be dropping bombs on Berlin again."

The argument went on for some time, and Adam and Clint stood silently. Adam was studying the face of the woman he knew to be his grandmother. He knew she had been the strength of the Richthofen family for years, even before her husband had died, and now he could not help but admire her.

Finally, the countess said, "I'm sorry, Maris, but we really have no choice. Karl is right. We must turn them in."

As soon as she said this and nodded to Bolko, who started toward the phone, Adam spoke up. "Countess—" he hesitated. Bolko had turned, stopping as he made his way to the phone. They all were looking at him, and Adam wondered if he were doing the right thing.

"Look at me very carefully, Countess."

The countess stared at him steadily. "Very well, I am looking."

"Do I resemble anyone to you?"

The countess blinked with surprise. She had not expected this question, and her eyes flickered toward Clint then back to the speaker. "What do you mean?" she asked. She spoke English fairly well, although with a thick accent.

"I think if you will look at me closer, you will see that I resemble someone very dear to you." Adam saw the eyes of the old woman narrow and then he said, "My father was Manfred von Richthofen."

A gasp escaped the countess's lips, and although Adam did not take his eyes off her, he was aware of the exclamations of surprise that came from the others. The countess grew pale and whispered, "That is impossible!"

"If Helen Ulric is alive, she will remember my mother. I think you may remember her yourself, Countess. Her name is Lylah Stuart, and you will remember that she was a guest in this house during the First War."

Karl Bolko broke in, "Mother, what is he talking about?"

Countess von Richthofen began to move forward. She came until she was standing no more than three feet away from Adam. Her eyes went over his face carefully, and she turned to her son. "Karl, look at him."

Karl Bolko came to stand beside his mother. He, too, studied Adam's face, and finally expelled a breath of air. "He is very much like Manfred, but Manfred's son—?"

Slowly the countess said, "I remember the young woman who came here with Helen—though I had forgotten her name."

"That is my mother. She was very much in love with your son, but he was killed before I was born. For years I did not know who my father was. Only a few years ago she told me. She loved him very much."

Countess von Richthofen studied the young man. Everything in her told her what he was saying had to be a lie—still there was the face of her son Manfred, as he had been at that age. Somehow the discovery took all the strength from her, and she refused to believe it or refused to admit it. "We will send for Helen Ulric," she said, "but I cannot believe you are Manfred's son." She turned to Karl and said, "Send for Helen, Karl. In the meanwhile we will wait."

Maris came over to stand in front of Adam. The others were all watching. She reached up and put her hand on his cheek. "So, Cousin, now we know why God brought you to this place. Do you believe now?"

Adam looked at his grandmother, his uncle, then back to Maris. He said quietly, "I'm beginning to believe that God can do anything!"

22

A MATTER OF FAMILY

A s Karl Bolko entered the high-ceilinged room, he glanced around at the photographs on the wall. He was already familiar with them, of course, having grown up with them from childhood. His eyes fell on the picture of his father, Albrecht, Baron von Richthofen. For a moment he stood studying the stern face of the man that had so molded at least two of his sons in the military traditions. Karl had always felt himself in the shadow of Manfred and Lothar, who were almost mythological in their heroism—at least Manfred could be so described.

Karl shifted his eyes to the picture to the right of his father's and studied the face of Lothar, the second brother, and felt a moment's remorse, for he had always been very fond of Lothar. He had been saddened after the war when Lothar had been killed in a flying accident, but now in Lothar's son, Wolf, he had hope. *If only this war would end,* he thought almost desperately. *Wolf wouldn't have to face a useless death.*

The thought disturbed him now, and he moved over to look at the portrait of Manfred von Richthofen. The portrait was one of Manfred in his billed cap, his jacket collar open and lapels laid back to show the Blue Max, the Pour le Merite, the most coveted decoration that Germany offered her sons. The large, steady eyes seemed to look back at him, almost as if the picture were alive. The mouth was straight but full, and the nose was straight. It was a strong face and most disturbing to Karl Bolko, for the resemblance of the young American to the portrait was almost frightening.

313

"Put a bill cap on him, a collar like that, and it would be hard to tell the difference," Bolko spoke under his breath.

"I have thought the same thing, Karl."

Karl Bolko whirled to find that his mother had entered the room. Even at the age of seventy-two, there was no sign of frailty in her. She was strong-bodied, as she had always been, and her eyes were clear, though now filled with trouble as she came to stand beside her son. "It's uncanny, isn't it?" she murmured, staring at the picture.

"Very like–very like, indeed, Mother." The two stood there quietly, studying the portrait, and Bolko turned to her, saying, "But there's no proof at all."

"If Helen were alive she might have helped."

Helen Ulric had been sought by Karl, but he had discovered that she had died a year earlier in a Berlin air raid. "I'm not sure she would have helped, even if she were alive," Bolko said quietly.

"She was very close to the young man's mother," the countess answered. She turned and walked over to the window and stared out. The snow had not melted, and its whiteness reflected the sun. It hurt her eyes and she turned away and moved to sit down in a brown leather chair beside a heavy oak table. "I've thought of nothing else since he came," she said simply.

"Nor have I." Karl went over and laid his hand on her shoulder. It was an unusual thing for him to do, for he was not demonstrative. When his mother looked up with surprise he smiled. "It's like something out of a very bad novel, isn't it?"

The countess reached up and put her hand over his. "I don't know how to think anymore. Few things ever disturbed me this much." She kept her hand on his but closed her eyes and leaned her head back against the chair. Her age was more evident now with her brilliant eyes closed, and Bolko saw the fine lines etched across her brow and in her cheeks. "I don't think a day has passed," she murmured so quietly that he could barely catch her words, "that I haven't thought of Manfred. Not since he died."

"He was always your favorite."

The countess opened her eyes quickly. "I don't know that that's true."

"I don't know that it is either. It just always seemed so to me." When she removed her hand, he took a seat opposite her and folded his own hands across his legs. "What about the family? What do they think? Have you talked to them?"

"Oh, yes, we've talked of little else. Ilse doesn't believe for a minute that this man is Manfred's son."

"Why would he come up with such a story, and why does he look so much like Manfred? How does she answer that?"

"You know Ilse. She gets an idea in her head and will not let go of it. She just simply decided the man was an impostor, and she's busy convincing Ann and Nicol that he is."

"I suppose Ilse has to be contrary. She was always that way." He spoke of his sister affectionately, though his words sounded harsh. "I think she's bitter and refuses to accept what we see before us because he's an enemy. She's always been stronger than the rest of us for this war."

The countess did not answer. She herself was sick and tired of the war. The First War robbed her of one son, and for all practical purposes, of Lothar as well. Now, she was afraid for her grandson Nicol, who at sixteen was terrified lest the war should end before he would have a chance to fight. "I'm worried about Nicol. He might run away and join the army."

"And be sent to Russia and get killed. What good would that do? This war is lost."

"He can't see that, though." The countess clasped her hands and stared down at them. "I don't know what to say, Karl. What if he is Manfred's son—what would that mean?"

"It would mean God has played a funny trick on all of us."

"Maris doesn't think so. She thinks God sent him here to be saved so that the line will go on."

"His children won't be Richthofens. They'll be Stuarts."

"I know, but Maris says that no matter what the name is, Manfred will still live in his son and grandchildren."

Karl Bolko rose and showed nervousness as he paced back and forth. He'd thought much about this and worried about how it would affect his mother more than anything else. Finally he came and resumed his seat. "Well, we would never see them. He's an American. He'll go home when the war is over, when he gets out of prison camp. Certainly he'll never come back here nor name his sons Richthofen."

Suddenly the countess asked, "What do you think of him—as a man I mean?"

"Why, I've been surprised. He's not like I thought Americans would be—quieter for one thing, and that sergeant of his, he's a very steady chap—a cousin, of course. The Stuarts must be very fine people. I've talked to him quite a bit, Mother, and if they weren't the enemy I'd say I admire them tremendously. I say it anyway."

"I've talked a lot with Adam Stuart. You know he has one of Manfred's ways. I don't know if you remember."

"What was that?"

"Manfred always had a way of closing one eye slightly, the right eye, when he would ask a question. Adam Stuart does the same thing," she said, and touched her cheek with one hand as she added, "The first time I noticed it, it brought back everything about my son. He did it when he was just a child." She turned to Bolko and said, "Karl, I think he is Manfred's son—but I don't know what that means for us, for the family."

Karl Bolko crossed his legs. "It presents a practical problem. What we will do with him? Turn him over to the authorities? He'd go to a prison camp, of course, he and his cousin."

"Is that what you want to do?"

The question disturbed Karl Bolko and he shook his head jerkily. "I'm not ready to say. I think it's your decision."

"He's your nephew if he is Manfred's son."

"But he's *your* grandson."

Countess von Richthofen rose and walked again to the window. She stared out and said quietly, "I can't decide. If he is Manfred's son, how can I send him to a prison camp? On the other hand, what else is there to do?"

"The war will be over soon. Germany can't last long—we all know that now. Even Hitler and the others must know it. It's all over."

"We can't keep him here. It might go on for six months."

"I doubt it, but you're right." Karl thought hard for a moment and said, "You'll decide what you want to do; then I'll decide how I can help."

"All right, Karl." She came to him, took his hand, squeezing it. Managing a smile she said, "You were always the steady one, Karl—the baby, but you were always the steady one."

"Well," Karl Bolko said wryly, "that's something, isn't it?"

February came to an end, and Adam and Clint were in a strange state. Ilse was ready to turn them over to the authorities. Karl Bolko, her brother, was not, and as for the countess, she kept aloof.

"It's almost as if she were afraid to talk to you, Adam," Clint said. The two were sitting in the room that had been given them, waiting on the evening meal. Adam was walking up and down and testing his leg, which was healing admirably. He looked up and said, "That's true, she's very cold."

"I expect she's afraid."

"Afraid? Afraid of what?"

"Afraid that you *are* her grandson." Clint leaned back in the chair and locked his fingers behind his head. "If you are, that presents a real problem. What will they do with you?"

Adam put his weight on his injured leg and made only a slight grimace. "Well," he said, "if I had to I could make a run for it."

"I don't think we'd get far. Neither of us speaks German, and we're a long way from the borders. We'd probably be captured in twenty-four hours."

"I guess you're right." Adam moved over and sat down on the window seat. He held the cane in his hand, running his hand along the polished length of it, and thought furrowed his brow. "I guess we'll have to wait until they make up their minds what to do with us."

"If they listen to Maris, we know what they'll do," Clint said at once.

Adam gave him a quick glance. He had not mentioned Maris much, but Clint had noticed that the two had spent considerable time together. They had begun taking walks outside as soon as Adam was able, and once when Clint had come upon them they were speaking of poetry, of all things. He said to Adam now, "That young woman's brought quite a change in your life."

"Yes, she has," Adam said briefly. He did not want to talk about it, so he asked, "How about you, Clint, are you all right?"

"All right?" Clint was surprised. "Why, yes, what makes you ask that?"

"Don't you think a lot about Carol?"

Clint dropped his eyes for a moment, then lifted them. "Yes, I do, but I guess I'd go crazy if I thought about it all the time. There's nothing I can do about it right now, but there's a verse in the Bible that says we're to cast our cares on God, and that's what I've done."

The two men talked quietly, and finally there was a knock on the door.

Clint walked over and opened it and found Maris there. She was wearing her coat and she said, "The countess wants to have tea with you, Sergeant."

"Tea, with me?"

"Yes, go on down; she's waiting in the small parlor."

Clint gave Adam a quizzical look and said, "All right. I feel like I'm being sent to the principal's office for some reason or other." He left at once, and as soon as he was gone, Maris said, "Come I want to show you something."

Adam took the heavy fur coat that Maris handed him. "This is a fine coat," he said, slipping it on.

"It belonged to your father."

A shock ran over Adam, and he looked at her quickly, blinking with surprise. "My father? This was his?"

"Yes, the countess gave it to me. She said she wanted you to wear it."

Adam felt odd. Somehow, putting on the coat that his father had worn made a difference. He ran his hand along the thick fur and murmured, "I feel so strange, Maris."

"I suppose you do. It would have to be." She stood watching him and then said gently, "Come along; let's go out to the pond."

Ten minutes later the two were walking alongside a pond that bordered the Richthofen estate. It was a small body of water in an L shape, the banks bordered by small trees. As they moved along silently for a while, Adam studied the young woman beside him. She had clean running physical lines, and her face was a mirror that changed often. He had seen laughter in her eyes, and pride, but something touched these things like a cloud. She had a self-sufficiency and was always on guard, but he had already discovered she was a beautiful and robust woman, with a woman's soft depth and a woman's spirit and a woman's fire.

As they moved along, he said, "Things have been so strange, Maris. I guess putting on this coat brings my father to me more than anything else. It is the first thing I've ever touched that actually belonged to him."

"I expect he and your mother walked around this very pond when she was here," Maris said. "It's the sort of thing lovers would do."

Her words struck Adam hard, and he stopped and turned to look at her. She was looking at him silently, and a woman's silence means many things. He was not sure what it meant in her, but it pulled at him like a mystery.

She drew away her curtain of reserve then, and a provocative challenge came to her eyes. "God brought you here," she said firmly. "There's no other explanation!"

Adam ran his hand over the sleeve of the coat, noting again

the thick fur. He looked around the pond and said, "That gives me a strange feeling. My mother was in love with him. She told me. She said what they did was wrong—their affair."

"I wager she's not sorry though."

He looked at her quickly. "What makes you say that?"

Surprise came to Maris. "Why, because she has you! How could she be sorry to have a fine son like you? As a Christian, I know she is sorry about the sin, but not about you."

Her words warmed him, and he reached out and took her hand. "Believe it or not, that's exactly what she said. How did you know that?"

"Why, I'm a woman!"

Impulsively Adam grinned. "I noticed that."

His words brought Maris's eyes to him, her lips parted slightly as she studied him. She was a woman with a great degree of vitality and imagination, but these things were held under careful restraint. The hint of her will was revealed in the corners of her lips and the steadiness of her gaze, and as she looked at him, Maris was shocked to find that she had grown very fond of him. After the death of her fiancé, she had locked herself away behind a cold reserve. Life in Germany was so uncertain, especially for the young. Almost everyone that she had grown up with of her generation was either dead or wounded or fighting the last deadly battles in which many would die. Now, however, as she looked at him her face suddenly flushed, and she could not answer him.

"What's wrong?" Adam asked quickly. He was sensitive to her moods, and now her long, composed lips held back some hidden knowledge. "Have I offended you?"

"Oh, no, Adam!" she said and impulsively put a hand on his chest and held it there. Before she could move he put his own hand over hers. He held it there, and the two stood silently, caught up in a moment that neither of them had imagined. Adam admired the picture of a full woman and felt the strange things that a man feels when he looks upon beauty and fears that it will never be for him. There was fire in this woman that made her lovely, although she kept it hidden behind the cool reserve of her expression. He suddenly felt the urges that a lone man always knows, and it moved him like a needle in a compass toward Maris. She caught his glance and held it as directly as his own. She was attracted to him, and she knew she was a picture framed before his glance. Her assurance said as much as she watched him.

Suddenly, without thought, but on some urgings that rose deep within him, he reached out and put his arms around her, letting the cane fall to the snow. She came to him then and her body was soft and yielding, yet firm against him. He bent his head and kissed her, and there was a softness and firmness and sweetness there that he had never known.

Maris knew something was wrong with letting this man kiss her. She had not kissed a man since her fiancé had died, and now the strong lips of this man who had come out of the sky, plunging into her life and disturbing it, moved her deeply. She felt his arms around her, pulling her closer, and despite herself responded to his caress. A loneliness that had built up in her seemed to drive her to him. She put her hands to his neck and pulled him closer, and there was a moment when she felt complete and utter surrender—and then with a gasp she pulled back.

"I shouldn't have done that," Adam said slowly, "but I can't be sorry for it. You're such a lovely woman, and you've been so kind to me."

Maris could not answer. The kiss had stirred, had broken something loose inside that she had thought securely locked away, and she said, "You shouldn't have done it, Adam!"

Adam gave her a keen glance. Her response had been passionate, and she was not a woman to give herself cheaply to a man. His coming had changed something for her, and he knew that from this moment on they could never be the same again. "This changes things, Maris," he said.

"No, it changes nothing!"

He took her arm unconsciously and held her. "You feel something for me, and I feel something for you."

Maris was breathing rather shallowly. The experience had frightened her, and she shook her head and forced herself to be calm. "It was just a kiss, Adam."

"It was more than that."

"No, that's all it was!" she insisted. She pulled her arm back and said, "Come, let's go back to the house."

"Wait a minute! Why are you so upset if it was just a kiss?"

"I don't want to talk about it, Adam!" Her voice was nervous, and she knew that she would not sleep well for days, so violent her reaction had been. Such things had been buried and dead to her, and he had disturbed emotions that she had safely put away for the rest of her life, or so she had thought.

Slowly she turned to him and the two stopped. "We would make poor sweethearts, Adam. Everything is against us. Even if we did fall in love, nothing could come of it."

Adam was listening, but her nearness sharpened the long-felt hungers that had been stirred within him. The sight of her struck him—the things he saw and the warm things he felt in her. There was a frankness and a softness in her expression, a sweetness that trouble had not destroyed, and it gave her a fragrance and a desirability. No other woman had ever stirred him as this one. It was an inward beauty and an outward grace. He knew that he would not forget her, and now said quietly, "I don't know much about love, but I don't think you can turn it on and off with a switch."

"You don't love me, Adam. You're just lonely and a long way from home."

"No!" He shook his head. "It's not that, nothing like that. There's something in you that I have never seen in another woman, and I think you see something in me."

His accurate remark frightened Maris, and she turned and said, "Come, we mustn't speak of this again, and you must not kiss me, not ever again!"

"I can't promise that," Adam said quietly. He allowed her to pull him along in the snow and from time to time saw that her expression was disturbed, and he knew that this was not the end of the thing.

23

"I'LL BE BACK"

Adam walked slowly through the snow, his eyes on the distant line of mountains. A huge, orange sun touched the crest as he moved along the edge of the woods, then seemed to melt and began dropping rapidly out of sight. It never ceased to amaze him how quickly the sun disappeared. He could see the movement of it as it slid behind the rugged curvature of the earth, and he found a strange satisfaction in it. However, he wanted to get back to the house before dark and moved along more rapidly. Snow had fallen again the night before and left a two-inch crust on top of the older crust. There was a satisfying crunching sound as he moved along, and the thought passed through his mind, *I bet the skiing would be wonderful here*, but the twinge in his leg reminded him that he would not be doing any skiing for a while.

Reaching the side of the chateau, he entered and encountered Hilda, the servant, who said, "The countess wishes to see you."

"Where is she, Hilda?"

"In the big room."

This, Adam understood, meant the large living area with the vaulted ceiling, and he moved quickly, ignoring the twinge in his leg. He had discarded the cane the day before and now considered that he might have been too hasty. Maris had warned him against it, but Adam was so anxious to begin to get back his strength that he wanted to test himself. As he limped into the large, spacious area, he saw the countess standing by the fireplace. She turned to greet him, and he moved forward until he stood before her. "You wanted to see me?"

"Yes." The countess studied him carefully for a long moment, then said, "You have thrown away your cane?"

"May have to take it back," Adam said ruefully. "Maris warned me against it, but I guess I'm a little too anxious to get back my full strength." He waited, expecting her to speak, but for some reason she seemed reluctant to do so.

Finally she said, "Come, I want to show you something." Adam limped after her as she moved to the east side of the room where a rectangular dark-walnut table rested beneath a window. Pulling a chair out, the countess nodded at it, then seated herself. When Adam had seated himself she said, "I want you to see these things—Adam."

Adam noticed the slight hesitation as she used his given name. It was the first time she had done so. Always before she had called him "Lieutenant." He watched as she opened one of a series of what appeared to be photograph albums bound in rich cordovan leather. She turned several pages over and stopped at one, saying, "This is the first picture of Manfred."

Adam leaned forward and peered down intently at the page. It was a portrait of the countess herself with her husband standing by the chair she sat in. The child she held was no more than two or three months old. He peered at it intently, then asked, "How old was he?"

"Only three months. He was a fine baby, very quiet, not like Lothar. Lothar cried constantly, sometimes for attention, sometimes just to be crying, but Manfred—never." Turning the page, she said, "Look, here he is at one year."

"A sturdy, fine-looking baby." The child that was his father was wearing a rather feminine looking outfit, but the look out of his eyes was the same as that of the adult pictures that Adam had seen. He sat as the countess turned over the pages, and once he stopped and said, "Who is this?" He pointed to a picture of two children in a goat cart.

"That is Ilse. I don't remember how old they were there. I think Manfred must have been perhaps five."

"Ilse doesn't believe what I've told you."

"No; no she doesn't."

Adam waited for her to comment on her own belief, but the countess continued to turn the pages. She stopped at a picture of a young boy wearing knee-length pants, dark stockings and shoes, and what appeared to be a sailor's top with a neckerchief. "This is when Manfred was seven. I remember it was four years before the Wright brothers flew in your country for the first time. Manfred told me that once when we were looking at this together. He was always good at dates and knew the history of aviation very well."

He saw many pictures of the whole family, and Adam, of course, was fascinated by them. When they got to the later pictures, he noticed a portrait of Albrecht von Richthofen with Lothar and Manfred.

"This was just outside the airfield. Their father had gone to visit them. They were so proud of their life as soldiers."

"I can understand that. They were very fine pilots, both of them."

Quietly the countess turned her eyes upon him. She looked with a strange, haunted expression and seemed less assured than usual. "You have read much about our family?"

"Everything I could find," Adam said, "which wasn't too much."

The countess thought that over, then continued to turn the pages. Finally she showed him a picture of Manfred with his head bandaged. He was standing beside a nurse, and the countess said, "This is after his crash. He was never the same after that, Adam. There were complications with the surgery to his head; then he had tremendous headaches." Below, there was a picture of him in front of his famous red Focker Tri-Wing fighter plane. A huge dog was reared up on him and Manfred was laughing. It was one of a few pictures where there was a smile on his face.

"He seems very happy. He loved the dog?"

"Very much; he took him when he was just a tiny puppy and he grew into the large animal you see there."

Adam studied the picture carefully and said, "He seems very happy."

"I do not think he was. This was after the time that he was here with your mother."

"Did he ever talk about her?"

"Yes, twice, but he did not say much."

"I would appreciate anything you could tell me. I know she would like to hear it."

The countess related the two brief conversations, which were not at all satisfactory to Adam. The countess said, "I think, perhaps, it was my fault. He knew I was not sympathetic with his attachment with your mother. She was, after all, an American, and there was no hope of any life for them. I had no idea they were so close."

"He never said anything about her, about how he felt?"

The countess dropped her head and seemed to be deep in thought. Finally, she lifted her eyes and her lips moved carefully as she said slowly, "I remember one more time. It was just before he went back—just before this picture was taken. He was getting ready to leave. I was helping him pack. I remember we had not talked about the possibility of his death. He thought it was bad luck, and so did I, but he did mention your mother."

"What did he say?" Adam demanded eagerly.

"He was putting his shirts into his kit, and he turned to me and asked what I thought of your mother. I said, 'She is a very beautiful young woman.' I declined to say more because I was afraid of an attachment between them." She hesitated, then said, "I remember what he said, although I had not until we began talking. He said, 'She is the most gentle woman I have ever known, Mother. I wish you knew her better. I think you would like her very much.'"

When the countess faltered, Adam asked, "What did you say?"

"I said something such as, 'I do not think she will be returning, do you, Manfred?' And he said no more. I could see he was hurt by my attitude."

For a moment, the only sounds in the large room were the crackling of the fire and the ticking of the large clock that hung on the wall. And then the countess said, "I wish now that I had talked with him more, but he was a very private person, you understand. You may tell your mother that is what he said of her—and you may tell her that I regret that I did not know her better."

Adam then asked directly, "Do you think that I am your grandson?"

"My eyes tell me that you are, and there are other things." The countess began to say, "You are like him in many ways. You keep things to yourself as he did. You move like he did, Adam." She hesitated, then added, "There's no doubt in my own mind that you are my grandson."

Adam felt very strange. He looked at this aged woman, still strong and growing old, and realized how difficult it was for her to say this. He impulsively held out his hand, and when she took it with surprise, he held it gently. "I am sorry that I did not get to know you while I was growing up."

To Adam's surprise, tears came into the eyes of the countess. She let them run down her cheeks and struggled for control. When she regained it, she squeezed his hand and said, "You are very like your father. I do not know what will happen in this war, but I want you to know what he was like. I will tell you everything, and you must tell me about yourself. . . ."

"Adam is spending a lot of time with his grandmother, isn't he, Maris?"

Maris looked over at Clint Stuart, who was watching her as she was preparing supper. "Yes, he is. It is good that she sees the truth of the thing."

"Are you so sure yourself? After all, there's no proof."

"The countess says he is, and she knew Manfred better than anyone. Better than his father, I understand, and you can see the resemblance."

Clint studied the young woman, and as they talked about the strangeness of the past days that the two fliers had spent there, he was surprised when she turned and asked him, "Are you married, Clint?"

"Yes, and my wife's name is Carol."

"What is she like?"

Afterward Clint never knew exactly how it happened. He simply began to talk about Carol, and before long he surprised himself by telling Maris about Carol's problems.

Maris listened quietly; then she turned to him and said, "But you still love her, even though she left you for another man?"

"Of course!"

"Not, of course! Most men would not think so." Maris came to stand beside him and put her hand on his arm. "I thank you, and I must pray for your wife. I will join you."

Clint Stuart smiled at the young woman. "I need all the prayers I can get, and I'd appreciate it very much if you'd pray for Carol."

Clint did not tell Adam about that conversation. He watched the young man carefully, for not only was Adam spending a great deal of time with his grandmother, he was also spending a great deal of time, Clint noticed, with Maris. Between the two women, they kept him occupied.

Adam was experiencing strange things. As his grandmother told him more and more about his father, he came to see the man that had sired him as a human being—not just as a famous ace, the idol of the entire German nation. He saw him as a young boy, sometimes insecure, and as the countess told him tale after tale of his boyhood, Adam felt very close to his roots. Once he said to his grandmother, "If he had lived, what do you think would have happened?"

"I have thought of that often," the countess said softly. "His life was with airplanes, as yours is now, but when Germany lost the war many lost heart, such as my son Lothar, but I wish Manfred had lived."

"I don't know what he would have thought about me fighting for the Americans."

"I think he would have understood."

"Do you really, Grandmother?"

At the use of the name "Grandmother," the countess started slightly. It was the first time Adam had called her that. She smiled then, tremulously, and said, "It is good to be called that. It reminds me that Manfred is still alive in you and will be in your son. You are not married?"

"No, I'm not."

"Are you engaged?"

"No, not that either."

There was an ancient wisdom in the countess. She had seen the eyes of this young grandson of hers follow Maris almost incessantly. A thought came to her, but she knew better than to speak it aloud. A purpose came into her heart to speak to Maris later, but she only said, "I'm glad you came to this place. It is good to know that the blood of the family will continue—even though it is in a different country. Manfred, in a way, is alive as long as you are."

For several days Adam spent his time either speaking with his grandmother or with Maris. He and Maris had become very close. There had been no more talk of love, and he had not attempted to kiss her again. Nevertheless, he knew that something had come into his life that he could not walk away from easily.

What happened next he could never explain. He had been reading the Bible at the direction of Maris, who seemed to find such joy in it that he himself was caught up in it. They had talked endlessly about doctrine, although she talked more simply about the Lord Jesus Christ than about doctrine. Al-

most every night as Adam went to bed, he read a passage
that she had recommended, and one evening she had recommended the story in the Gospel of John of the woman at the
well. He had read it before, of course, but she had spoken with
shining eyes of what a wonderful thing it was for this woman,
who had never known anything but unhappiness from men,
to find peace from a stranger sitting by a well. Adam had read
the story again and again, just before he went to sleep.

The next morning he rose early and went out before breakfast, moving cautiously to avoid waking Clint. As he stepped
outside and moved along the walkways, his feet leaving im-
prints in the snow, he was still thinking of the Bible passage.
He found out that he had almost memorized it, and when he
was some distance from the house in the midst of a copse of
trees, he stood thinking for a long time of how strange it was
that Jesus would speak so to such a woman.

The air was quiet and as he stood there his mind went back
to the many times that his mother had spoken to him of God.
He regretted that he had been so adamant and had given her
such pain, and he resolved to make it up. He began walking
again, slowly, thinking of the encounter, and suddenly the
words of the Scripture came to him. He seemed to see the
eleventh verse almost as clearly as if he were looking at a
printed page. "The woman sayeth unto him, Sir, thou hast
nothing to draw with, and the well is deep: from whence then
hast thou that living water."

The words seemed to echo within him, and he remembered
that Maris had said, "That's what most people do, Adam; they
don't think Jesus is able. The woman said, 'You don't have
anything to draw with.' She didn't really believe that he was
able to help her. Most people feel that way about Jesus. They
really don't think he can save them as he says he can."

Adam slowly continued his walk, thinking about his own
spiritual condition. "I guess," he murmured aloud, "I've done
exactly what Maris said. I've said to God, you don't have
anything to draw with—which is foolish." He thought of the

consistent Christian lives of his mother and stepfather and of others that he had known, and he thought of the faithfulness that seemed to shine out of Maris's eyes—and a great hunger suddenly came upon him. It was something that he had never experienced before. *If I could be like them*, he thought, *I'd become a Christian.*

The search began in Adam Stuart's heart. For two days he kept to himself more than usual. Maris seemed to know what was happening and she mentioned it to Clint. "God is after him, and we must pray much," she said to the tall sergeant.

Strangely enough, Adam found Christ not through the direct help of either Clint or Maris but simply sitting in his room alone. Clint had gone outside for something, and all of the Scripture passages and all of the pressure that had been building up in Adam came suddenly like a rushing flood, and he looked down at the Bible he was reading—the same chapter that he had been seemingly trapped in: "Whosoever drinketh of this water shall thirst again; but whosoever drinketh of the water that I shall give him shall never thirst; but the water that I shall give him shall be in him a well of water springing up into everlasting life." He closed his eyes and the next verse seemed to leap into place: *The woman saith unto him, Sir, give me this water, that I thirst not.*

The hunger for peace that had been in Adam seemed suddenly insatiable. Quietly he said, "Lord, you know what I am. You know what I've been. I haven't prayed, and I've been guilty of every sin that a man could commit, but I'm thirsty now for something better than this. Just like this woman wanted water that would give her life, I want that, too. So I'm asking you to forgive my sins and to save me from them, and I ask it in the name of Jesus."

The room was still, and Adam sat there. He experienced no great emotional upheaval, but a quietness had come into his spirit. He sat motionless until the door opened, and when Clint came in Adam said, "Clint, I've just asked God to come into my life."

Clint stared at him, speechless; then a smile came to him and tears came to his eyes. He moved quickly across the room and gave the smaller man a hug. "I'm glad, Adam," he said huskily, "and life will never be the same for you again."

"I've got to tell Maris," Adam said.

"Yes, she's been praying for you."

Adam left the room at once. He found that Maris had gone to the cottage. He moved quickly with scarcely a limp, until he reached the cottage. When he entered, he found her dressed in working clothes, cleaning. She looked up, startled, and said, "Adam, what is it? Is something wrong?"

"No," Adam said. He came over and smiled, saying simply, "Something has happened to me, Maris. I've heard about it all my life, and it's not like I thought it would be."

Instantly Maris took a deep breath. "You have found the Lord Jesus?"

"Well, I've asked him to forgive me and save me. I don't feel much different, but I know that I am. I–I don't know if I can live like a Christian."

Maris took his hands, "He will teach you. The Holy Spirit will be your teacher, and I will help, and Clint will help. Oh, Adam, I am so happy for you!"

Adam saw the tears in her eyes and felt his own eyes sting. "Well," he said awkwardly, "I need all the prayers I can get. I've got a long way to go."

For three days after Adam's quiet prayer, he seemed to live in a different world. Outwardly very little had changed. The two fliers were still conscious that they were in enemy territory, and one word from a servant could throw them into a prison camp. But a peace had come over Adam that revealed itself in his countenance. He spent much time with Maris and Clint, and as the three studied the Bible together, it was amazing how his ideas had changed.

He spoke of this on a Thursday afternoon when he and Maris were walking beside the pond, as had become a daily habit with them. It was midafternoon, and the sky was gray overhead. A line of waterfowl made a ragged V, and the two watched them until they disappeared. They walked around the pond, talking quietly about small things, but finally Adam said, "One of the walls that was between us has broken down."

Instantly Maris knew that he was speaking of the two of them. "There's still too much between us," she said quietly. "Don't think of it, Adam."

She saw a peace in him that he did not have when he came. "The war is almost over, and you will go back to America. You must marry a young woman there—one of your own people."

Adam did not speak for a long time, but finally he said, "I don't know much about God or how he works, but one thing seems clear to me, Maris. He brought me here for a reason, and I think you're part of that reason."

"We could never marry. I am German; you are American."

Adam reached forward and took her by the arms. "You know, I can't help thinking that my father stood here once with my mother, probably. I wonder if he told her that he loved her? I don't know whether he did or not, but I know one thing. I love you, Maris. Germany and America have nothing to do with that." He pulled her forward and kissed her, and there was a gentleness in him that Maris sensed, and she clung to him for a moment. When she drew back she said, "I wish it could be so."

"Do you love me, Maris?"

"It doesn't matter."

"Of course it matters! If people love each other, that's what matters most. I've never needed anybody," Adam said, "but now I know that I need you. I never understood that about a man's and a woman's love before. It's you I need, not just your body, but you, yourself. Somehow you're inside me, and I can't just walk away from here and forget it."

"You must, Adam. It would be a tragedy. Germany will lose and I must stay here and help try to pick up the pieces. My family will be fragmented. This place—I think we will lose it. What would happen to the countess? I must help."

The two stood there speaking quietly, Adam pleading and Maris adamantly refusing to listen. Finally she reached up and touched his cheek. "I wish life were always nice, and ended like the romances in the books, but we must be wise."

Adam took her hand and held it for a moment, then kissed it. "I love you, Maris, and that's all there is to it."

But Maris shook her head. "No, you must not say this again." She turned and walked away, her back straight, and Adam followed her, a determination rising in his heart.

Karl stared at his mother, saying, "I knew you would ask this of me." He had been summoned from his office to the estate, and as soon as he entered, his mother had said, "Karl, we must help my grandson and his friend escape. I could not bear the thought of their going to a prison camp."

When Karl answered, he suddenly smiled. "I knew you would ask it of me, and I have already been making plans."

"You've thought of something?"

"Yes. I think it can be done with a little money and a little luck. Let me go get them, and we will have a counsel of war."

Thirty minutes later, Adam and Clint were in the large room. Karl Bolko had summoned them, and now he looked over at his mother and Maris, who were watching carefully. "I think I have found," he said slowly, "a way to get you out of Germany."

"How?" Adam asked. "I understand everyone is looking for escaped fliers."

"That is true, but there is a way. We can get to the North Sea, and there are boats that go from there to Holland. Once you get there, it will be fairly simple to get away on a ship to England."

Strangely enough, Adam's first thought was not freedom and England. His first thought was, *But I will have to leave Maris*. He looked across the room and met her eyes and knew that she read his thoughts. She shook her head slightly and turned away. The countess did not miss this, her sharp, old eyes catching every movement, but she did not speak.

Karl spoke for some time about the plan, and finally he said, "But we must leave at once. My connections say that the ship will leave the day after tomorrow. We will have to find a way to get you on board without speaking, but I will think of something."

Clint said, "This is more than we expected, Sir. You are putting yourself in jeopardy helping escaped prisoners."

Bolko winked at Clint and said, "It's all in the family, Sergeant. Besides, my mother tells me it must be done, so there you have it!"

"Well, I think we're ready," Karl said. He looked with a critical eye at the two young men who were dressed in civilian clothes. "Now remember, let me do all the talking. With luck we won't meet anyone you will have to speak with."

The plan was simple. Karl would take Adam and Clint to the ship, where he had obtained three passages. He had somehow obtained passports, although Adam and Clint never understood how, and the three of them would get on the ship bound for Holland. They would make the trip, disembark, and he would help them to find a ship bound for England. He himself would return to Germany. "It's a little bit risky," he admitted, "but not as much as some other things that are happening around us now."

Adam straightened the hat on his head and looked at Clint. "You don't look as German as I do," he said.

"Maybe not, but I'm going anyway," Clint answered.

Bolko said, "Come, the car is waiting."

They moved out of the bedroom, and when they got to the foyer of the house, the countess and Maris were waiting. The countess came forward, reached up, and pulled Adam's head down. She kissed him and said, "Good-bye, Grandson. God keep you."

"Good-bye, Grandmother," Adam said hastily, "but this isn't the last good-bye. You will see me again."

"As God wills."

Maris held her hand out first to Clint, who took it and said, "Maris, you've been a lifesaver. Thank you for all you have done for us."

"I will be praying for you and your wife, Clint," Maris said. She turned to Adam, and her lips seemed to grow tight. "Good-bye, Adam; may God give you a safe journey."

Adam took her hand and held it. He raised it to his lips and said quietly, "I'll be back." Then he turned and walked outside, stepping into the car, followed by Karl and Clint.

As the car moved away, the countess came over to stand beside Maris. "You love him very much, don't you, my dear?"

"Yes, I do."

The two women stood quietly watching the car disappear into the distance. Both of them were thinking of the words of Adam Stuart. "I'll be back." Finally the car was gone, and Maris turned and looked at the older woman. "He's a fine man, that grandson of yours."

"Yes, his father would have been proud of him," the countess replied. She turned and moved away, her thoughts filled with two men—one who had died long ago, and the other who was now on a dangerous mission.

Maris went outside and walked around the pond thinking of the time she had spent here; she looked up at the sky and for a while stood silently. Finally, she moved back to the house, and still the words of Adam Stuart came to her: *I'll be back*.

24

Homecoming

The old C54 lumbered in for a landing, striking the runway with a jar that shook the teeth of the two men who sat side by side.

"Wow," Clint said, "that fellow needs to have a lesson or two!"

"I guess he does!" Adam Stuart looked out the window and said, "Well, there it is, the good old U.S. of A. You know, there were times I wasn't sure we'd ever see it again, Clint."

Clint looked around and said, "I guess I'd better call you *Major* Stuart from now on."

Adam shrugged. "I suppose so." He looked with affection at the tall man beside him and said, "Did you ever think we'd make the twenty-five missions?"

Clint Stuart sat quietly for a moment, thinking over the past months. The two of them had made their escape from Germany, almost miraculously, with no problem whatsoever. They had rejoined their Wing and had begun flying at once in a new aircraft. The other members of the *Last Chance* were in prison camps, which saddened the two men. Their new airplane called the *Cincinnati Belle* was a good ship, and the crew had done well also. Clint had finished his twenty-five missions before Adam, but he had flown Adam's three last missions so that the two of them could come back to the States together. Adam had been promoted soon after his return, and Clint had risen as high as a noncom could go in the Air Force. Clint now said sensibly, "That last one, I was a little bit worried. I thought about how many fellows we knew that made twenty-four but never came back from the twenty-fifth. It was almost like it was, well, a matter of faith or something."

The plane's engines were shut off and they left the airplane. Their military ranks prevented them now from the familiarity that they had become used to, but they soon found their way into a cab, and on the way to the hotel where they were staying Clint said, "You know, the worst part of coming home is thinking about Woody." Woody Stuart had been seriously wounded in the Battle of the Bulge, and the entire Stuart clan had been concerned and much in prayer for the young man.

Adam gave him a quick look and said, "He's going to be all right—and Mona is, too." Both men had been disturbed when they'd gotten the word that Mona had been more or less dumped by Rob Bradley. "It might be the best thing for her in the long run. Hollywood marriages aren't the most stable things in the world."

"I think Mona can come out of it. She had a bad bump when that actor let her down, but she's young; she'll get over it. At least that's what your mother said in her last letter to me. Are you flying out to California right away?"

"Yep, and I bet you'll be headed for Arkansas. Have you heard from Carol?" he asked abruptly.

"No, but I'll find her."

"I know you will, Clint, and I'll be praying that you will."

"Have you heard any more from the countess or from Maris?"

"Not in the last month." Adam was rather abrupt, but he made himself smile. "I'll never forget those days there. I guess a fellow never forgets the time he finds the Lord."

"That wasn't all you found there," Clint said. Adam stared at him briefly, but by that time the taxi had pulled up to the hotel. They took a room and slept hard after their transoceanic flight. They got up early the next day, had breakfast, and Clint saw Adam off on his plane to Los Angeles. They shook hands, then oblivious to the fact that several in the airport were watching them, they embraced briefly. Then Adam stepped back and said, "I'm coming to the Ozarks. Remember, you're going to show me how to catch the biggest bass in those hills."

"And I'm coming to California. You're going to introduce me to John Wayne." They smiled at each other; then Adam turned and left for his plane. Clint watched the plane take off, then went to inquire about his flight times. The ticket agent looked at him, "Fort Smith? Where is that, in Missouri?"

"No, it's in Arkansas. You can find it. It's part of these United States." As he waited, he thought about the hills and all the things that he had missed—but mostly he thought about Carol.

Lylah was on her hands and knees in the garden jabbing a small trowel into the earth. She wore a pair of faded overalls with patches sewn on the knees, and the sun beat down on her back.

"Well, is this the kind of welcome a returning hero gets?"

Lylah leaped to her feet, and when she saw Adam, who had entered from the house and was walking across the garden, she dropped the trowel with a cry and ran to him, throwing herself at him.

"Now, that's a little bit more like it." Adam grinned. "You're looking fine, Mother."

"Adam, why didn't you tell us you were coming?"

"I wanted to surprise you. Are you surprised?"

"Well," Lylah said quickly, "we knew you'd be here, but we didn't know when. Come on, let's go call your father." She pulled him into the house, and after calling Jesse, who was at the studio, she drew him down and said, "Now, tell me everything."

"I'll just have to tell it again when Dad gets here."

"That's all right; I want to hear it twice." Lylah held his hand, and could not stop smiling from time to time. She was thinking how fit he looked, tanned and sure of himself, and she listened avidly as he described his experiences in Germany.

Jesse got there thirty minutes later, just as Adam was re-
counting the details of his conversion. Jesse suggested, "Let's
go out to celebrate!"

"No, I'm going to cook tonight," said Lylah. "We can go out
any other time, but now we're going to have steak and baked
potatoes, and I'll make a cherry pie, Adam's favorite."

"I guess I can stand that." Adam grinned. "Come on, Dad,
I picked up a few pointers in pool. I intend to take you for
all you're worth."

They had a fine, quiet supper, all of them laughing loudly,
as though they were almost out of control. Then later, after
supper, they talked far into the night. Lylah listened avidly
as Adam told of his experiences in the Richthofen house. At
first Adam was afraid that Jesse might be offended, but then
he was quickly reassured when his stepfather seemed to be
as interested as Lylah herself.

Finally, Adam said slowly, "I got to know my father while
I was there. His mother showed me every picture he ever
had taken."

"Did–did she mention me?" Lylah asked falteringly.

"Yes, she did." Adam related what the countess had said
and then said gently, "She said she wished that she had gotten to know you better."

"It wasn't to be," Lylah said gently. "She was different in
those days. I suppose the loss of two of her sons has broken
her."

"It bent her a little bit, but she's not broken. She said she'd
like to see you again, Mother."

"Maybe we can go after the war is over."

"What about this woman, Maris," Jesse said. "Tell us some
more about her."

His words opened the gate, and for the next hour Adam
spoke of Maris. When the party finally broke up and Jesse
and Lylah were in their bedroom, Lylah said, "He's in love
with that woman."

"It's pretty obvious, isn't it?" Jesse said, buttoning his pajamas. He got into bed and pulled the covers up and shook his head. "It presents kind of a problem, doesn't it?"

"You mean because she's German?"

"Yes, of course, she's halfway around the world now, and things will be difficult."

"Things were difficult for us, if you remember. The first time I ever saw you I broke a pot over your head." She saw his smile and slipped into bed beside him, turning the light out. The two lay holding each other, talking quietly, and Jesse said, "That's a pretty stubborn son we've got there. I wouldn't be surprised if he didn't go back to see that young woman."

"I'd like to meet her myself." She held Jesse tightly, kissed him, and said, "God is good to bring our son back."

"And to bring him back knowing the Lord—that's a miracle! Thank God for it, and for that young woman, and for Clint. Those two really prayed him through, I think."

"Yes, and now we've got to keep on praying."

Carol locked the door of the library, turned, and walked along the sidewalk toward the street. She got into her car, started it, then pulled out and drove slowly along under the huge elms that lined the street. Her day had been long, for Mrs. McCracken, the librarian, was away on vacation and Carol had manned the desk constantly. Her mind was on the multitude of details that went with keeping even a small library going, but she managed to remember that she was almost out of gas. Stopping at Ed Hathcock's Gulf Station, she waited until the burly owner came to her window saying, "Fill 'er up, Carol?"

"No, Ed. I don't have enough coupons. Just five gallons."

"Sure. Be good when this blasted rationing is over. I get tired of dribbling gas out with an eyedropper. Check that oil?"

"Yes, you'd better."

Carol sat quietly as Hathcock serviced the Hudson, thinking idly of what she had at home to fix for supper. *Guess I better stop by and see if Safeway has any good steaks. . . .* She calculated the number of ration stamps she had, for this had become a way of life during the war. It was almost impossible to imagine going into a store and buying all the butter and meat you wanted without having to add up the government stamps in the small books everyone was issued. *Someday the war will be over*, she thought, *and things will be for sale again.*

Then she blinked and shook her head imperceptibly, for every time she thought of the war, she thought of Clint—and that was what she had tried to keep away from her mind. But thoughts can't be restrained, and Carol sat on the worn seat unable to stop the flow of memories that came with a rush. She thought of how miserable she'd been with Harry from the first—and of the nights she'd awakened him crying until he'd grown edgy and had shouted and raged at her. She thought of how she'd read the newspapers fearfully, dreading the constant flow of statistics that meant death for so many American fighting men. The news from the bombing raids over Germany had been the most difficult, for she'd lived in an agony of fear that Clint might be one of those who never came back.

"Quart low, Carol."

Startled, Carol blinked and turned to see Ed Hathcock's face framed in the window. "Oh—please put in some, Ed."

"This old heap ain't gonna make many more miles. Better let me look around for a trade."

"Yes, I think you might do that, please."

Carol watched as the proprietor added the oil, then slammed the hood down. She paid for the gas and oil, and Hathcock said, "Looks like the war's goin' good. All the boys will be coming home soon."

Instantly Carol glanced at the burly man's face, for she was sensitive about what people thought. But then she remembered that Ed Hathcock was new in town—that he could not possibly remember that she'd left her husband. *Not unless someone told him!* The thought came quickly to her mind, but she saw nothing in Hathcock's expression other than friendly interest.

Shifting into gear, she nodded, saying, "That will be good, Ed."

A pale sun was setting as Carol drove slowly down the street, but she could not get Hathcock's words out of her head. *All the boys will be coming home soon.*

For some time, shortly after she had left Harry and returned to her home, Carol had experienced a vivid dream that she and Clint were still married. But when she had awakened, she had wept—for she had no real hope of any such thing.

Letters had come from Clint, but Carol had been so ashamed that she had never answered them. She still kept them, however, and as the months had worn on, she came to the grim realization that no happiness lay in her future. Several men had tried to take her out, but she had curtly refused, so that finally such offers had ceased. She had gotten her old job back at the library, and her life consisted in her work and keeping her house. Her father had left her the house free of debt, in addition to a moderate sum from his life insurance, so that she did not have to worry about money. When she'd come home from Chicago, she'd become a recluse for a time, but slowly had forced herself to face the world. Her church had been receptive, so that she had been able to attend services, though she was still too ashamed of her behavior to take an active part.

As she pulled up into the carport and shut the engine off, Carol felt the usual relief that came each day at this time. *Home—and now I don't have to wear a fake smile.* She entered the house and went at once to her bedroom, undressed, and took a long shower. Afterward she put on shorts and a light top, then went into the kitchen to fix supper. But she was not hungry and decided to make only a salad.

She listened to the local radio station as she cut up carrots and shredded lettuce. Bing Crosby and the Andrews Sisters were soon singing "Don't Fence Me In," followed by the Ink Spots with "Till Then." She hummed along as Judy Garland belted out "The Trolley Song," thinking of the new record player she was planning to buy.

As she set out the iced tea and crackers and sat down at the large dining room table, a plaintive song came over the station—Frank Sinatra singing "I'll Be Seeing You." As the baritone sang the words, which were simply a reflection of a lover who was saying that one day he and his sweetheart would meet again, Carol's throat grew thick and tears came to her eyes.

"I'll–I'll never be seeing you, Clint!" she whispered. Dashing the tears away, she rose and changed the station, then walked shakily back to the table. She could not eat, for memories came flooding through her again, and rising abruptly, she left the dining room and went into the living room where she lay down on the couch.

For a long time Carol lay in the silence of the room, nerves crying out in despair like a fever. This had happened many times. As the tears ran unheeded down her face, she was overwhelmed by grief. Finally she turned her face to the back of the couch and buried it against the rough upholstery.

Sleep came and the welcome fading away of memories. She fell into a fitful state, almost waking at times, but then forcing herself back into the comalike doze. She jerked violently as the doorbell rang. Sitting upright, dazed and confused, Carol stared around the room, then rose to her feet. She had few callers, mostly salesmen or bill collectors, and decided not to answer the door. Going back into the kitchen, she sat down and stared at the salad, now limp, and the glass of tea, which had only a few slivers of ice.

But the doorbell rang and rang—and finally with a gesture of impatience, Carol rose and left the kitchen. *Probably someone selling waterless cookware*, she thought, for several salesmen of this product had come to her door recently. She brushed her hair back, thinking of how awful she must look, but then shrugged. *What does it matter what I look like? The salesman won't care.*

Opening the door, Carol blinked with confusion for the sun was behind the tall man who stood there, shadowing his face. All she could see was an outline, dark and tall, so she said, "I'm sorry—I don't need anything."

"Hello, Carol."

The voice ran like an electric current through her! She clutched at the door frame for support. The kind of weakness ran through her that one feels after narrowly escaping a serious automobile crash. Her lips were numb so that she could not speak, and a strange light-headedness caused her to sway.

"C–Clint! . . ." She managed to speak that one word, then could not have pronounced another syllable if her life had depended on it. Time seemed to stop for her, and without volition she stepped back—as if she would turn and flee.

"Can I come in?"

Carol mutely nodded; then as he stepped inside, she heard herself saying, "Yes, come in, Clint." It was as if another person had spoken, and she had the strange sensation of being a spectator watching herself from a distance. The numbness that had frozen her lips spread to her mind, for she could not think properly.

He looks older. This thought came to her, and she saw lines in his face that had not been there before. The ridiculous thought came, *My hair—it's all messed up—and my makeup is smeared.* Ineffectually she touched her hair and shook her head in a slight gesture of futility. Then she realized that he was looking at her with an expression she could not define.

I wish he hadn't come. The thought came dully, and Carol could not bear to look at him nor to see him look at her. "I didn't know you were home," she said, her voice tense and tight with strain. She turned and walked stiffly away, adding, "Come into the living room."

Clint nodded and followed her; then when she turned to face him, he said quietly, "I'm glad to see you, Carol." He waited for her to respond; when she remained silent, her eyes fixed on his, he added, "You're looking fine."

"You, too. Are you all right?"

"You mean was I wounded?" Clint smiled almost grimly. "No, I'm fine. Lots of good men got hit, but somehow I made it through without anything serious."

"I–I'm glad."

Clint had pictured this moment for a long time, but now that it had come, he found himself feeling awkward and tense. Carol had lost weight, and the set of her back and the way she held her mouth in a tense line told him that she felt as awkward and tense as he. But he had not come this far to be put off and said quietly, "Let's sit down." He moved to the couch and noted that she kept herself facing him—almost as if he were her deadly enemy. Her fists were clenched and there was a pathetic weakness in the manner in which she held her head high. She had been crying; he could see that, for tear stains marked her smooth cheeks.

Taking a deep breath, Clint said, "I wasn't always sure I'd make it home, but I always promised myself one thing—" he hesitated, then shook his head slightly, "and that was, if I *did* make it home, the first thing I'd do was find you, Carol."

Carol flinched as if he'd struck her. "You shouldn't have come, Clint!"

"Why not? It's the one thing I wanted to do."

Tears leaped to Carol's eyes and she let them run down her cheeks, making no attempt to reach for a handkerchief. Clint's eyes were gentle, and she could not bear that. For months she had struggled with her guilt, and the thought of how she had betrayed this man cut her like a razor. Turning from him, she whispered, "I can't go back to what we were!"

Carol's voice was no more than a thick sob, and she tried to rise, unable to continue. But Clint reached over suddenly and pulled her into his arms. Her face was buried against his chest, and the touch of his arm around her broke the resistance in her completely. She began to weep, great ropy sobs wracking her body. Clint held her tightly, his face pressed against her hair, his hand caressing her back gently. She seemed very small, and the helplessness of her surrender made him fiercely protective.

Finally Carol's weeping grew mild, and Clint pulled back and looked down into her face. Placing his palm on her cheek, he said, "I love you, Carol. I always will."

And then Carol knew what she had to do. Taking a deep breath, she said, "I've got to tell you what I did, Clint."

"I don't need to hear it."

"But *I* need to *say* it." Her eyes were filled with grief, but she knew that guilt must be confessed—and that this was the moment for saying all the tormenting things that she had kept in her heart. She began to speak, and for what seemed like an interminable time, she related the entire episode of her sin. From time to time, she had to stop, to struggle for control—but always she kept her eyes fixed on Clint's.

Finally her voice grew still, and she looked up to see his face. She expected to see disgust—even hatred—for that was what most men would have felt. But it was not so. Clint's expression was gentle and he took out a handkerchief and gently wiped her tears.

"I'm glad you told me this," he said, putting his handkerchief away. "Not for my sake, but for yours, Sweetheart. We have to say these things. Sometimes to someone else—and always to God. Have you asked him to forgive you?"

"Yes—but what I did was so awful!"

Clint shook his head almost abruptly. "I've found out that we can never keep God from loving us. He knows our whole life, past, present, and future. We can grieve him, but he never turns away from us when we come to him with all our wrongs. . . ."

Carol listened with wonder as Clint spoke quietly about how God forgives. Then he spoke of how bitterness against her had threatened him. "I was crazy with anger—but I knew feelings like that would kill me quicker than an enemy fighter! So I put it before God—all my anger and bitterness—and he took it all away."

"But, Clint—how can you ever forget?"

"I think God helps with things like that." Clint lifted his hand and held it up. "See that scar? I cut that hand wide open when I was fifteen. It hurt like nothing ever had—but it doesn't hurt now. I don't even think about it." Clint's arms tightened as he said, "God has forgiven us—and we have to forgive one another." He saw her doubts reflected in her eyes and said quietly, "Carol, I may let you down sometime in the future. Will you hate me if I do? Or would you forgive me?"

"Oh, Clint—I'd forgive!"

"Well, I forgive you—and that's the end of it." Clint pulled her close, and she came to him at once. Her body was soft against him, and her lips trembled—but her arms went around his neck in a gesture of abandon. Fiercely she clung to him, savoring the strength of his arms and the firm pressure of his lips.

Finally when they parted, she whispered, "Oh, Clint—I've always loved you!"

The two sat there quietly, speaking softly, and finally Clint said, "I've come home to a wife—and now we can begin living."

Carol's heart seemed to swell, and she nodded, her eyes bright as she said, "Yes, Clint—let's begin all over again! . . ."

EPILOGUE

President Franklin Roosevelt did not live to see the end of the Second World War—did not live to share in the world's horror over the full extent of Nazi atrocities. He died on April 12, 1945, and Vice President Harry S. Truman became the President of the United States.

American fighting men won the battles in the Pacific and in Germany. The end came on August 6, when the atomic bomb destroyed Hiroshima. On September 2, Japan signed a formal surrender on the *USS Missouri.*

The most devastating war in the history of planet Earth was over.

Now the healing could begin.

Countess Kunigunde von Richthofen opened the door and stood speechless for one brief moment—then she cried, "Adam!" and reached out her hand.

Adam Stuart ignored the hand, stepped inside, and pulled his grandmother into an embrace. He kissed her cheek, then said, "You'll have to forgive us rude Americans, Grandmother. We don't have fine European manners, but I'm so glad to see you again."

The countess flushed at the sudden gesture of familiarity, but then she laughed. "You are a fool! But I like it! What are you doing here?"

"I went to Schweivnitz, but the Russians have taken it over."

"Yes, after the war ended, the Russians took that sector. We moved to West Berlin to keep out of their clutches." She looked at the young man who was wearing a suit instead of a uniform and said, "You are no longer in the army?"

"I was just discharged a week ago. I've been in the States teaching in a flying school." He paused and said, "You're looking fine." He looked around and said, "This is a nice place. I had some trouble finding you. I finally located Karl, and he told me he'd found this house for you and Maris."

"Yes, it does very well." There was a sadness in her voice and she shrugged. "I miss my home, of course. The war has cost me that, but it has cost others more. Come in; sit down."

"Is Maris here?"

The countess smiled. "I thought you might be asking that, but I thought it might be later."

"I've come all the way across the ocean to find her, Countess." He looked at the old woman and said, "I guess you knew I'd be back."

"I always did. Maris is not as sure as I, but then I am older than she. She is in the garden, out through that door. We raise some of the vegetables we eat, you know."

Adam took her hands and held them, saying, "We'll have lots of time to talk. I want to tell you about myself, and I want you to know who I am." He hesitated and then said, "I want you to be proud of me as my father's son."

The old face glowed, and suddenly the countess leaned forward and kissed his cheek. "I will be that—I already am," she said. "Now, go to her. She will argue with you, but your father was a firm man. Don't listen to her excuses. You love her, and I know she loves you."

Maris had been working in the garden, but she had stopped, and she was sitting on a bench watching the sun go down. She had heard a car pull up in front of the house but had thought that it was Karl. She expected to hear his voice, for he usually came to see her, but when she heard "Maris" spoken behind her, she leaped to her feet and turned around. "Adam!" she whispered, her throat suddenly going dry. She watched as he came toward her, wearing a charcoal-gray suit and a wine-colored tie. He looked different from when he had been in uniform, but he was the same Adam. He took her hands and kissed them, then put his arms around her. "Don't tell me I shouldn't do this because I'm an American and you're a German," he said, his eyes dancing. "I've crossed the Atlantic Ocean to kiss you, and I'm going to do it!"

Maris stared at him, then said, "Why don't you do it then instead of talking about it?" She reached up, pulled his head down, and kissed him firmly. She held to him tightly, and even during that moment of embrace she knew that all of her excuses were false. She had told herself over and over again that he would never come back—but even if he did, they could never be happy together. Now she knew that she had been deceiving herself, and she clung to him as if she were drowning.

Adam savored the firmness of her body against his and held her tightly, noting that she was meeting him as he had not dreamed she would. When the kiss ended, he whispered, "I thought I'd have to tie you up and carry you away and make you marry me, but I won't, will I?"

Maris managed a smile. "No, you will not have to do that. I do not know how we will live or what we will do, but I know that God has put us together. All this time I have thought about you, Adam. I think I loved you from the first time I saw you."

"Well, I look a little better now than I did then, I hope!" Adam kissed her again, then put his arm around her and drew her down to the bench. "We've got a lot to do." He held her hand, looked at it, and saw that it was calloused. "You've been working hard."

She saw that he was trim and fit and asked, "How is Clint?"

"He and his wife are back together again, and they are expecting their first child. God's been good to them." He hesitated then said, "My mother and father financed this trip over here. I might as well tell you I don't have a job, I don't have a profession, but I'm going to take you back to America with me. I'll marry you here or there, but it'll have to be one or the other."

"Would you mind if it were here, Adam?"

"No, not at all." He held her tightly, and the two spoke for some time. Finally, he rose and pulled her to her feet. "We've got a long way to go. Let's go tell Grandmother our plans."

"I think she already knows them," Maris smiled. Her self-sufficiency was returning, and he saw again the soft depth in the woman's spirit and the fire that had first drawn him. She was tall and shapely and a fully mature woman. He said quietly, "The war's over, but things won't always be smooth." Then he added, "As long as I have you, Maris—you and the Lord—nothing can frighten me."

Maris Richthofen reached up and took his face between her palms. She whispered quietly, "You will never lose me, Adam. I love you now and I always will."

They kissed again, then turned and stepped out of the garden, leaving it to the large, white cat that had been watching them incuriously from his position on the wall. He rose, arched his back, yawned hugely, then leaped off the wall and ambled toward the door to follow them.